RAAJNEETI

The film & beyond

Compiled & Edited by

Pooja Varma

To my parents,

Who let me be me

Prakash Jha

Published by:
Prakash Jha Productions
201-A&B, Abhishek, Off New Link Road
Andheri (West), Mumbai - 400 053, INDIA
Tel: + 91 22 66781862 Fax: +91 22 66781863
E-mail: info@prakashjhaproductions.com
www.prakashjhaproductions.com

First Edition 2011
ISBN : 978-81-7991-674-2
(4422)

Compiled & Edited by:
Pooja Varma

Design:
Mayur Varma

Page Layouts:
Studio Link Pvt. Ltd.

Distributed by:
Popular Prakashan Pvt. Ltd.
301, Mahalaxmi Chambers
22, Bhulabhai Desai Road
Mumbai - 400 026
www.popularprakashan.com

Processed & Printed by:
Dynamic Printers, Mumbai

CONTENTS

FOREWORD

One of the things that you marvel at when you see an intricate, grand and beautifully woven Persian carpet or an exquisitely crafted French tapestry of the 15th Century is how well it has been realised. The normal instinct of a connoisseur of carpets and tapestries is to turn it over to look at the back to see how it has been put together; the finesse, technique and character of the weave. Similarly when you see a film that is both impressive and satisfying, you come away with a sense of curiosity as to how it was conceived, designed and made. Like with carpets, films too require the myriad talents, creative craftsmanship and dedicated labour of a large number of people. The time between conception and completion of a film is a period of great creative ferment that manifests itself in a combination and mix of innumerable specialisations and inspired work.

The book **Raajneeti - The Film and Beyond** is an attempt to deconstruct the whole process of how the idea of the film Raajneeti germinated in the mind of the director Prakash Jha, and how it took root and was nurtured and conceptualised by the writer and collaborator Anjum Rajabali, taking us through the various stages of planning, designing and drafting the structure of the narrative, working out the logic of the characters, their characterisation and their motivations that would serve as engines in driving the story forward and fleshing it out in terms of space and time. Next is the gathering of talent: production designer, cameraman, costume designer, casting director and all other technicians and crafts people, and the careful choice of actors and locations all requiring precise decision making. This will set the tone for the making of the film. And then to the different aspects of production: the physical geography in which the action will take place and the atmosphere required in terms of the time of day or night for the scenes to be played out. Until one comes to that stage, mind-boggling logistics have to be taken into consideration along with the economics and the practicability of what is intended to be realised; all these problems and more have to be tackled before the enterprise is brought to a successful conclusion, while all the time hoping that what has passionately engaged the conceptualiser, who in this case is the director, will translate itself into a film that will find favour with a mass audience and hold them in thrall.

The story of making Raajneeti is an exciting one for many reasons. The subject itself deals with the ruthless pursuit of power, the desire for which is irresistible. Everything else pales before the desire for power. The greatest story ever written that deals with the pursuit of power is the *Mahabharata*. Each character in this greatest of all epics, is an archetype. Every person who strides across the pages of this monumental poem is someone who we can recognise. Indeed each one of us can be recognised and identified in the *Mahabharata*. The personality of every person you see, hear or will ever meet is present in the *Mahabharata*. This book of life with its 100,000 couplets offers an incredible goldmine of plots, stories and characters that you can quarry to tell your own tales.

Prakash Jha who has experienced politics and particularly, electoral politics first hand, recognises that the largest number of people who are engaged in politics are motivated by an overwhelming desire for power. And those who are powerful, desire even more power. For them, power is all.

Mahabharata ends with a war that is not just a disaster but a holocaust and the end of a cosmic epoch. Prakash Jha's film points to that in his contemporary tribute to the *Mahabharata* – a cautionary tale about the manner in which politics is being conducted today.

Shyam Benegal
February 3, 2011

ACKNOWLEDGEMENTS

Ironically, in making *Raajneeti,* some people rose above all kinds of politics and gave it their all. Without their honest passion, *Raajneeti* could not have been what it is and I want to thank them with all my heart. First and foremost is Anjum Rajabali, with whom there is now a relationship of co-creativity. He argued and fought with me all the way, and I thank him for it. My long time friend Manmohan Shetty, the first producer I worked with. He has been an enormous encouragement and a sound critic since *Hip Hip Hurray* and *Damul.* Ronnie Screwvala for his fiercely compassionate approach – if he believes in it, he puts every inch of muscle behind it. Siddharth Roy Kapur, Shikha Kapur and the entire UTV team for their enthusiasm. Simon and Prasad from Pixion for the special effects, the Paddas for the exciting trailers, Studio Link for the promotional material and Digit 9 for their marketing innovation and support.

I want to express my gratitude to Zulfikar Ali who opened up Bhopal for us, and thank all the people of the beautiful city who welcomed us and our equipments into their homes and let us shoot! And each of the thousands of theatre artistes who worked tirelessly through the cold, the heat, through early mornings, late nights, through days of festivals... I am also grateful to the government of Madhya Pradesh for extending their complete support.

I also want to thank the pillars of my team – who are always there to bear the brunt of my anxieties. Sudhirbhai Mishra, the Production Controller on *Raajneeti,* who has been by my side for many long years. Alankrita Shrivastava, who was really the chief architect of this ambitious project and who skilfully carried the entire weight of it on her slender shoulders. She saw, read and understood what I wanted. And got it done. K.L. Chhabra and his entire team, for making such a smooth administration out of the circus! Sachin Krishn my D.O.P – for his classic creativity and for the selfless compassion he showed by sometimes restraining it. Wayne Sharpe, Aadesh Srivastava, Pritam Chakraborty and Shantanu Moitra for giving me their beautiful melodies. Priyanka Mundada who worked very hard and dressed so many thousands of people every day! Jayant Deshmukh who nodded in understanding even when all I told him was 'something' is not right. Santosh Mandal who kept a vigil on the shoot, studiously reminded me to take cutaways and sometimes got told off for it! I was glad at the editing table! And of course, the scores and scores of assistants, who when they were needed, appeared from nowhere like genies!

In today's age, any publicity is good publicity, so I'm thankful that the media for some reason kept alive the baseless issue of the resemblance between Katrina's character and Mrs. Sonia Gandhi. It led to an unprecedented pre-censor viewing by a panel of Congress representatives and finally the film was cleared by the tribunal appellate. That was some experience!

Raajneeti has given me a much, much wider platform nationally as well as internationally. It is immensely encouraging that this kind of cinema is now being patronised by viewers across nations. And, for that, I would like to thank the audiences all over the world.

Prakash Jha
November 11, 2011

CHAPTER 1

THE POWER OF POWER

Without doubt all kings, O son, must once see hell
- Dharma to Yudhishthir, The Book of Ascent to Heaven

"I want to make a film on politics. It's called Raajneeti." Trademark Prakash Jha - deceptively simple. Going back to the early days of Raajneeti, he would deliberate over the larger meaning of politics. That which goes beyond the realm of parliamentary fights and election campaigns. "I realised we play politics at various other levels," says Jha. "There is personal politics, professional politics, familial politics and social politics. In every relationship, at all times, we are playing politics." Why? He asked himself. And found the answer chilling in its starkness. For power. Vidura says in the *Mahabharata*, power is the biggest high. And even the quest to understand why, took director Prakash Jha on a high of his own, leading him to make one of the most dramatic, one of the most successful films of the year. That is the power of power.

My question is, victory at what cost?
Prakash Jha

It is a vicarious pleasure to see someone rise to power. And more so to then see them fall.

Jha has always been keenly interested in the changes that occur in society. "One of the most important changes in Indian history is democracy. We as a nation took a decision to be a democracy. We were in some sense, many nations within a nation. So it was an interesting development that took place when we became independent. And what is even more interesting is the way we have practiced democracy since. How we have created our leaders, how we have created our governments. All kinds of things are happening," he smiles. "And several characters that are operating in this democracy are astoundingly fascinating. Their thirst and quest for power at any cost, their manipulation...their own personal ideologies, beliefs or behaviour. . .going to the extent of becoming ridiculous!" So, in no way was he ever worried about making a film on politics and alienating a large section of audience because they might not be interested.

According to him, everyone is interested in politics, even if in varying degrees. It is a vicarious pleasure to see someone rise to power. And more so to then see them fall.

The fight for governance, officially termed politics, is perhaps the simplest, most naked form of it. "Winning is the only thing," Jha believes. "There is no second or third. Either you're up there, or you're not. You might win by a single vote, but you win. What matters is victory. But my question is, victory at what cost?" What better way to ask this question but by throwing together characters who would play, who would *have* to play politics with each other? Politics of every kind, at every stage. A family of politicians torn apart by differing ambitions, just before the elections. As personal as it gets. As political as it gets.

Now that the film is made, it seems the most natural thing that the saga of a family of warring young and old politicians be inspired by The *Mahabharata*. However it wasn't so decided from the very start. "We started with a family splitting into two rival units. As we developed it further, we realised that the characters were veering towards those from the great epic. And eventually we decided, why not?" Jha reveals. For him, finding the dramatic similes from the epic in his own story became very enjoyable. Once the decision to adapt was made, it became a question of creating The *Mahabharata* as it would happen today. The rivalry between the Kauravas and Pandavas mirrored the clashing ambitions of Virendra Pratap and Prithvi Pratap. Draupadi the divided victim found her counterpart in the thwarted heiress Indumati. Karna the abandoned became Sooraj the underdog. And so the blocks that were carved out from the epic, nicely and snugly fit into the crevices of the modern political saga.

This grand marriage of epic and politics very apparently gave a spiritual lift to the premise of the film. The question - power but at what cost, acquired a whole new meaning. The emptiness of victory yawned deeper. The power he got in the end, actually left Samar a smaller person. The king who must now see hell.

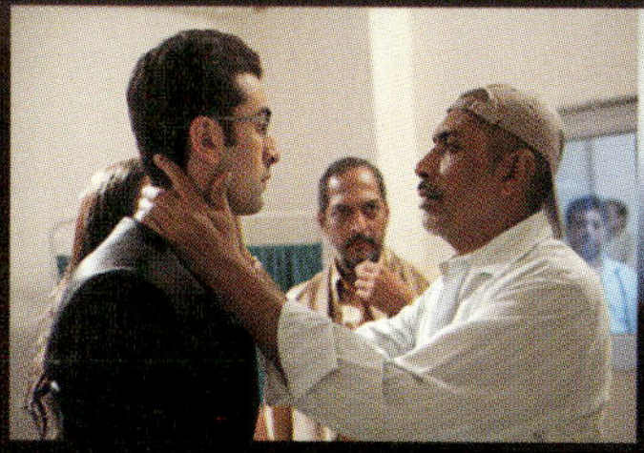

With the decision to adapt the *Mahabharata*, the film also acquired grandeur. At the very outset, Jha knew this was a big film. But with the epic entering the picture, it became a huge project. There would be many important characters, many stories; a humongous crowd. And he started preparing for it early on. As the film was being scripted, he made numerous trips to Bhopal with his crew. About eight thousand people were trained to play the crowds in the film. Details were discussed and revisited and then revisited again. Not even the colour of a junior artiste's kurta was left to chance. Meticulous planning and pre-production progressed through all of 2008. Producing a film himself gives any director a creative edge, and Prakash Jha was not going to lose that edge.

And sure enough, the edge stayed razor sharp through the shoot, cutting through every minor and major crisis. The schedule was stuck to, accounts were tallied daily, and actors arrived on time. There was always an advance crew working on the next day's shoot, readying the set. Juggling the dates of eight actors - all stars in their own right and playing major parts - and those of several veteran actors playing minor but important parts, managing a crowd of eight thousand people and commanding a crew of five hundred, Prakash Jha practically led his own army to battle every day in Bhopal. Raajneeti was scheduled to be shot in 103 days. It was shot in 102.

Prakash Jha practically led his own army to battle every day in Bhopal.

Raajneeti was scheduled to be shot in 103 days.

It was shot in 102.

So through the long process of making Raajneeti, one of his dream projects, what could possibly have been his 'aha' moment? "It is one thing to imagine such a huge film, quite another to pull it off," says Jha. "Through the year of preproduction, I would take my team and visit Bhopal, almost every month. We would hang around the locations, discuss the scenes. Obviously, they could not get into my head and see it the way I was seeing it. They could only interpret what I was explaining to them. In so many of the shots, several lines of people were required. There were crowds, there were policemen and there were party workers. There were cycles and motorcycles, there were bands being played, people on this side of the street, people on that side of the street, there were banners, there were garlands to be thrown… everything happening at the same time. So there would be fifty people probably doing fifty things at fifty different points and the camera would be moving. Every time a shot happened, I would feel, wow, they did it!"

While shooting, the most important thing for Jha is to enjoy his work. "If you are immersed in your work and really enjoying it, then everybody around you enjoys theirs. And they are there with you, all the way."

And so after years of being immersed in his work and enjoying it, Raajneeti was made. With no effort to send out a 'message'. The film is about some characters thrown in a situation where they get a taste of power and how they react to it. It is an observation of human psychology. A journey into the dark regions of the human mind. A reckoning that the demon exists in the best of us. As Jha says, "It does not even say whether *raajneeti* is good or bad. Raajneeti is about *raajneeti*."

It went unnoticed, but vodka played a very crucial role in Raajneeti. Screenwriter Anjum Rajabali had been consultant on Prakash Jha's Gangaajal and Apaharan. The two had struck the right notes and developed a rather satisfying working relationship. In January 2004, when Jha decided that he would make Raajneeti, he had a nascent idea and was determined to involve Rajabali in writing the film. Rajabali was not sure if his limited knowledge of electoral politics made him the most suitable person for the job. Jha was insistent and very sure that Rajabali's grip of the narrative form would result in a solidly anchored script. However, Rajabali was not sure enough to commit. So they decided to talk about the story, see where it went. Since Rajabali was working during the day, they decided to meet at seven thirty in the evening over the next seven days, to kick the idea around, hold it to sunlight. Almost a sign, their first meeting was on 26th of January. At seven thirty sharp, Jha landed at Rajabali's office. Vodka was called upon for company, and for the next three hours, the three of them (Jha, Rajabali and the vodka) talked. This became their routine for all the next seven days. Every evening from seven thirty to ten thirty, the two men would plunge into the world of drama, relationships, power equations, politics and emotions. Always with vodka.

CHAPTER 2

OF VODKA AND VISION

Whatever is here, is found elsewhere.
But what is not here, is nowhere else.
- The Book of Beginning

A passionate saga of betrayal began to emerge from their intense discussions. On the second or the third day, Rajabali pointed out that the sketchy storyline of the family and the rival characters fighting for power, held a resonance with the *Mahabharata*. Jha admitted he felt the same way. They debated an adaptation of the mother of all family dramas, against the backdrop of some gut-wrenching politics. The prospect sounded unbelievably thrilling. Yes, they would adapt, rather, reinterpret the *Mahabharata*. This unleashed the story and from then on, it almost told itself. In those seven days, in just about twenty one hours, they had a fifteen page storyline. They could see the characters, hear them talking, feel their terrible dilemmas and cringe at their fatal decisions. The excitement was now electrifying. Apprehensions were washed down (again, with vodka) and the decision was made. To tell the most gripping story of how much bad, good people can do. To experiment with the darkness which the human heart contains. At the end of those seven days, in that small office, a huge vision was born. And who was the sole witness, perhaps even one of the perpetrators of the birth of that vision? Yes, it was good ol' Alcazar vodka.

For Rajabali, the tempting thing about writing Raajneeti was the juxtaposition. "Taking people who are unsuited to politics and throwing them into it… the kernel of the idea drew me in," he says. The juxtaposition also brought with it the opportunity to explore what he calls 'a certain typicality to the concept'. The film talks about politicians being corrupt and dishonest, if that is not stereotypical, then what is?

But for Rajabali, the challenge was to break this stereotype, to pull out individuals and say yes, the pattern of corruption and violence is the same, when politicians start vying for power. But how do they deal with that as individuals, as people, as members of a family?

However, the clincher undoubtedly, was a chance to reinterpret the greatest epic. With a smile, he asks, "Who doesn't want to work on the *Mahabharata?* To draw the archetypes, to draw a certain understanding of some universal responses. And then to particularisae them into present day characters… The DNA of the story was just too rich, just too compelling."

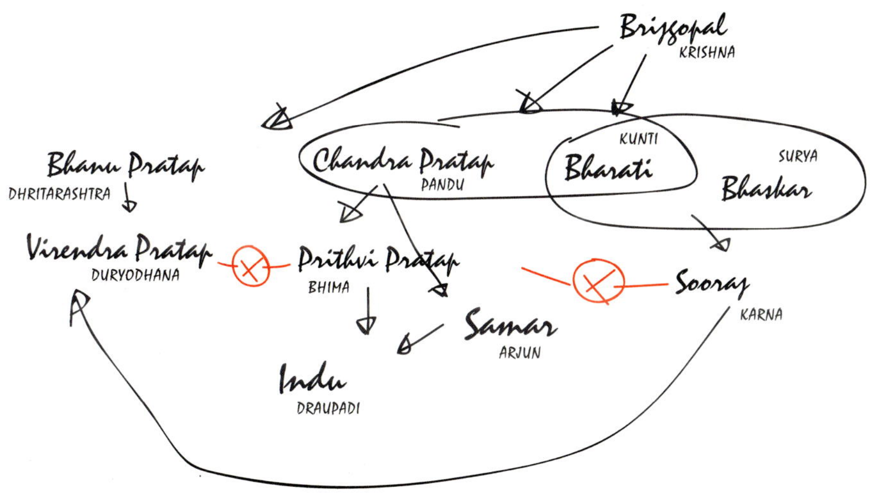

It's all very well to talk about Arjuna as the warrior and justify his actions ...

What if at some point he had actually reveled in what he was doing?

Similarly for Jha, who co-wrote the screenplay with Rajabali, it was an experience unlike any other. "In all my films, before I think of the story I have the content that I want to communicate, the issue I want to talk about," he says. "Everything stems from incidents I may have heard, seen or experienced. And then I find a thread and create a story. In Raajneeti I had a story first. A story of warring political families. Raajneeti doesn't deal with any issues, it deals with characters. Characters inspired from an epic. So to create their modern worlds, their modern particularities and finding their similes back in mythology, was the fun part."

Right from the scripting stage, Raajneeti was a fiercely ambitious venture. And it went through its own tribulations. After those seven evenings of Raajneeti spiked with vodka, Rajabali wrote a detailed draft over the next few months. And then, Raajneeti was forced into a three year exile. Jha was involved in numerous other things and was compelled to invest his attention elsewhere. He released a film, produced some others, fought two elections and worked for the Kosi flood victims. In January 2008, more than three years later, Jha called Rajabali. They had a detailed discussion and Jha decided to write the second draft of the script. Finally, the exile was over.

However, the real struggle had just begun. Draft after draft was written. Both the writers worked very hard, never shying away from a revision. It was a bittersweet ecstasy. The rich vastness of the text at once made the writing the easiest and the most difficult. It is said of the *Mahabharata*, that if a story is not in it, it isn't there. Rajabali believes while that might be a slight hyperbole, in its spirit it is true. The *Mahabharata* contains all the dilemmas of the human condition. A sprawling epic with scores and scores of enthralling tales; how do you choose? Rajabali had to remain accountable to the format of the film. "If I were asked to write a sprawling novel of my interpretation of the *Mahabharata* in modern times against the backdrop of electoral politics, I could happily produce a 550 page tome," says the writer. But the aim was to make a 150 minute film, which means a 120 page script, at the most. The first draft was about 265 pages. "Despite all the discipline that you can command while writing, there is just too much, very attractive material," he exclaims. "Which is why, a spine was imperative."

When adapting an epic like the *Mahabharata*, one can either adapt it in terms of its drama, or choose a character and tell the story from that point of view, or expand it on the thematic and philosophical level. For Rajabali and Jha, it started on the thematic level. The thought, that if a seemingly good person is thrown into a field that demands dishonesty, then he cannot fulfill his purpose without employing some amount of

Who doesn't want to work on the *Mahabharata*?
Anjum Rajabali

dishonesty and corruption himself. If he opens the floodgates, he will be drawn into the vortex. He will have to compromise virtually every shred of decency that he possesses. So then how will he deal with the step by step descent into immorality? This was the philosophy that fascinated the writers and it got personified in Samar Pratap, that is, Arjuna.

To reinterpret Arjuna's heroism was a delicious writing experience for Rajabali. "Prakash and I debated about following Karna's journey or Arjuna's," he says. "Karna was definitely more colourful as against Arjuna's goodness. Karna has many more dramatically interesting dimensions. However, I felt it should be Arjuna's story. But how would we make Arjuna more active, more interesting? We decided to look at Arjuna as a person who eventually begins to collude with all the actions he's being made to take in the Kurukshetra war. He did do some very questionable things. It's all very well to talk about Arjuna as the warrior and justify his actions by saying that Krishna took away all the guilt. But that doesn't really happen in life.

An individual has to own up to what he's doing. He has to somewhere negotiate with his actions. What if at some point he had actually revelled in what he was doing?"

This dimension to Arjuna's character came into a lot of criticism by purists and mythologists, who protested that Arjuna cannot be shown turning into such a dark character, it takes away from the sanctity of the text. "I don't know, we can debate about that," says Rajabali. "My take is that sometimes you have to fight evil with evil. And that evil then begins to get into you. You cannot remain insulated and untouched. And the text lends itself to this interpretation. That is the sophistication of the *Mahabharata*."

During the course of the scripting, after a point, the resonances found each other. The 'modernisation' happened very organically since the *Mahabharata* also had a backdrop that was political. It was decided that the kind of political sensibility that was being showcased would be best suited to a Hindi heartland setting. The basic nucleus was then confirmed. Two people in a family vying for the throne, fighting to rule. With the core configuration in place, characters then began emerging from the fabric of the setting. Both similarities and differences with the epic, developed as the story grew. For example, the Karna story was replicated in the script by changing the chariot to a car. Karna (Sooraj) was still the love child of the Sun god (Bhaskar) and Kunti (Bharati). However, Kunti's experiment with her boon in the film became the rebellion of Comrade Bharati. On the other hand, Draupadi (Indumati) being divided among brothers would not only be unacceptable in today's context, it didn't quite appeal to the two writers either. A mother instructing her sons to share a woman, and the sons bowing their heads and following, just would not fit in a modern story. So it was configured with Indumati's (Draupadi's) love being unreturned by Samar (Arjuna) and her having to eventually marry Prithvi (Bhima), who was understandably uncomfortable. But the ultimate humiliation of Draupadi in the game of dice, perhaps the most dramatic scene of the entire epic, could not quite belong in this story and was therefore not taken. The basic triggers of the plot were set up according to the driving premise - the greed for power. "One doesn't consciously decide to pick this scene or that," says Rajabali about the process of adaptation. "You allow your own individual story to develop and see which situations get drawn in. The stone of the original story rolled, gathering the moss off the *Mahabharata*. Or as if from the field of the *Mahabharata*, iron filings kept leaping out and attaching themselves to the magnet that was the story of Raajneeti."

Another somewhat bold decision while writing the screenplay was to divide the sympathy of the audience. They chose to go grey with practically every character in the film; with no 'right' side. "There was no doubt in our minds that we supported Samar and his family and that's we wanted the audience to do," says Rajabali. "And yet, we stretched it as much as we could.

The stone of the original story rolled, gathering the moss off the *Mahabharata*.

The good guys turned bad to the extent that it was difficult to distinguish between the two. Emotionally you will support them but morally you will not be able to choose." It might have been a risk from a commercial point of view, but it had to be done if the theme of the film was to be fully realised.

Rajabali's gripping drama was complemented by Jha's wonderfully textured dialogue. "That is his forte, he has a felicity with the language, he understands how political workers talk. His dialogue is idiomatically very colourful," says Rajabali. And so it was decided that once the screenplay was confirmed by both, Jha would do the dialogue in Hindi.

Rajabali observes that co-writing with a director can be tricky. It is important that in the early stages, they both look at the story as writers. "The later the director's persona kicks in, the better it is," he says. "If it comes in early, it disturbs the relationship. The other person is not able to fully realise his potential as a writer. Credit to Prakash, he resisted that." The two worked in a back and forth pattern. After Jha's draft, the two again discussed changes and revisions and then Rajabali took it away for the third draft. And so it went on. A draft, discussion, another draft, more discussion. A few months before the shoot, they decided to sit together in Jha's office and go over each sentence of the script jointly. It was an interesting time; these discussions would often turn into what can politely be called arguments. "Prakash is very stubborn and so am I. He is very tenacious, and so am I. He doesn't give in, and neither do I! When we would step out after an argument, there would be a tense silence in the entire office. His people obviously believed that we were having a war of our own! Prakash's office became our battle ground," recalls Rajabali with a grin.

These differences led to a film with so many wonderful moments that it is difficult for even the creators to choose a common favourite. "My favourite scene is the one where Indumati addresses the public for the first time," smiles Jha. "I really enjoyed writing that speech. Taking symbols of her weakness and protection – *aansoo, mehendi* – and turning them into her strength, her weapons." *Humaare aansoo sookhe nahi hain ab tak, aur unhe sookhne denge bhi nahi hum* (My tears haven't dried yet, and I won't allow them dry up).

Rajabali's favourite scenes are the ones where Indumati and Sarah respectively confront Samar. He believes in times like these, it is the women who show the mirror. "It is a blow when Indumati, the spirited girl who loved him so deeply that she gambles away her life simply because she trusted him, looks at him and wonders who this man is. And then Sarah, the woman who is carrying his child in her womb, wants to go away from him. These scenes come at a time when we see Samar's skyrocketing success, his rise to power. But he has to pay for it, and pay for it with his soul."

And that is really the heart of Raajneeti – power, but at what cost? And once the price has been paid with your soul, what do you do with the leftover shreds of your morality? It is Samar, the reluctant one, who did not want to be involved, who in his effort to restore order finally becomes the destroyer even of his own self. The other survivors all have some equilibrium, albeit unstable. Brijgopal does everything with conscious awareness. He knows exactly what he's aiming for. He will take care of his sister and try to redeem

Is there any redemption possible for Samar? Was it possible for Arjuna? Was it possible for any of the Pandavas?

himself. Indumati was blameless, really. She will continue to struggle with her inadequacies and rule, but morally she does not have any guilt, she is just a victim. Who was the perpetrator? Samar. Is there any redemption possible for him? "Was it possible for Arjuna? Was it possible for any of the Pandavas?" asks Rajabali. "Effectively, no. On the way to heaven, each of the Pandavas, barring Yudhishthira, fell by the way side because each one had a flaw that was unforgivable." As does Samar. He has hurt the very people who loved and trusted him. He has taken measured steps into this living, moral hell and is trapped there by the shards of his own shattered conscience. "So how is he going to live with it?" asks Rajabali. "This isn't where it ends. This is where, after the film is over, the story really begins."

I really enjoyed writing that (Indu's) speech. Taking symbols of her weakness and protection – *aansoo, mehendi* – and turning them into her strength, her weapons.

Prakash Jha

CHARACTERS

CHAPTER 3

A CLOSET FULL OF KINGS

For he who is drunk with power
Does not come to his senses before he falls
- The Book of Effort

Look closely and you will find that there is only one character in Raajneeti. And that character has been divided into many characters, like a coconut smashed into many pieces. Some are big, some small, some just tiny bits. Some are tough on the outside and soft inside. Some are just soft, all heart. Some are merely pieces of the shell, hard and unyielding. But they are parts of the same whole. They have a common core, a common characteristic – their thirst for power. Each and every one of them, from the top to the bottom, yearns to be in control. From Virendra Pratap who believes power is his birthright *(Iss baar hum chalne nahin denge)* to Beena Kumari who is ready to pay any price for it *(Yahaan* ticket *zaroor milega)*, every one wants to be king of their world. In varying degrees, the drive to rule exists in all of them. In fact, it exists in all of us. And instinctively so. In a classroom full of ten year olds, when the teacher asks who wants to be monitor, don't all the children raise their hands? Some shy ones might not, but do they want to? Most definitely. It is human nature. Some of us become the real kings. But each and every one of us is a closet king. And Raajneeti? Well, that's an entire closet full of kings!

It is the characters, primary and secondary, that make Raajneeti the film it is. With a combination of method and intuition, the characters were allowed to develop organically, even though they were taken from timeless archetypes. "They carry certain elements from the original characters of the *Mahabharata*, and yet there are certain dimensions that are added on," says Rajabali. Without this addition of elements, audience's identification with the characters would have perhaps been compromised. "The idea was to create believable characters, from today" says Jha. "Their ideologies, their personal relationships, their ambitions though rooted in the epic, had to find a resonance with the current times, the current audience."

And in a film with so many important characters, it must have been easy to fall prey to favouritism. "In every draft there was one favourite character for me, who then received a lot of attention, fascination," says Rajabali. "And then in the next draft it was important to encourage somebody else because otherwise it was getting lopsided." Not surprising, since the original text is a gold mine of richly textured, enthralling characters. There is an entire film in each character's life, be it Kunti, Dhritharashtra, Gandhari, Sanjay or in fact almost any character of the *Mahabharata*.

And yet, the temptation had to be resisted. In any well written story, each character is there to fulfill a purpose in the plot, not to decorate the frame. And the reason why even the secondary characters in Raajneeti are so fascinating is that they each had a fitting motive. They each had a definition, an emotionality. Characters that might have hardly five minutes of screen time were sketched out in detail. "If a character is in the frame, he's important," says Rajabali. "He has to take the story forward or else he shouldn't be there." And for this, Rajabali worked out character sketches for even secondary characters like Babulal and S.P Sharma. He wanted to be prepared if an actor playing a secondary part came to him and asked who he was.

This focussed attention to characterisation was matched by some very striking casting decisions made by Jha. Ranbir Kapoor had never done anything like Raajneeti before. All his other performances are in stark contrast. Arjun Rampal with his somewhat 'urban personality' portrayed the brutish Prithvi. The idea of Katrina Kaif in a deglamourised avatar, was like that of a star from the sky come down on earth! Shruti Seth, the proverbial sweetheart of Indian television was perhaps the most shocking choice for Beena Kumari. He obviously saw something which no one else did. "It's the presence of the actor in totality," says Jha. "The persona, the body language, the appearance. I take time to cast. It's a long, ongoing process for me."

But definitely one that works. The film is full of sterling performances. The veteran actors, no matter the length of the role, have delivered superlatively and the new talents have matched their standards with diligent hard work. "Every actor has given it their very best," says Jha. "We wrote it, but the actors have made us feel the characters' pain and joys, their fears and anxieties. They have made the film come alive."

SAMAR PRATAP SINGH
The Reluctant Arjuna

Moments before the great war of Kurukshetra was about to begin, Arjuna, the undefeatable archer who had spent years in preparation, attaining the most powerful weapons from the gods, suddenly faltered. He looked at the enemy – and saw faces of loved ones. He questioned the point of violence, of competition, of the empty victory after destruction of love and humanity. Arjuna was reluctant to fight.

It is at this stage of reluctance, that we find Samar Pratap Singh, who was the heir to a political dynasty, and was wanting none of it. He has acquired a doctorate at the Harvard University and plans to become a lecturer. Almost painfully aware of the moral degeneration that politics brings about in a human being, he has deliberately and firmly decided to stay away. Because somewhere, he knows there lies within him a deep darkness. "There is a certain touch of complexity in Samar's character which eventually comes into sharp relief when the war begins," says Rajabali. "But you notice the germs of darkness much earlier." The subject of his PhD is sub textual emotional violence in 19th century Victorian poetry. Even though the first time we see him, he is lovingly gifting an expensive watch to his chauffeur, we sense a strange coldness about him. He often helps his mother in the kitchen - peeling vegetables, wheeling around tea trolleys. He greets his brother warmly, indulges in friendly banter with him. He so obviously cherishes a quiet moment with his father. He seems to love his family, and yet he seems detached. He knows that if he comes down to it, he is capable of more destruction than everyone else put together. So he carefully holds himself back. However, as fate would have it, while he is on a holiday to India, his father is killed and he has to step in to avenge his death, to help his brother. He finds himself giving in to fate. He enters the vortex.

He knows that if he comes down to it, he is capable of more destruction than everyone else put together.

He now fights evil with evil. Because his goodness is ill equipped.

Anjum Rajabali

"He now fights evil with evil," says Rajabali. "Because his goodness is ill equipped to deal with what he's fighting against. He resorts to questionable means. And yet he is not devoid of a dilemma. Ironically, when he is at the cusp of victory, his conscience suddenly begins to play games with his mind." In the final battle, when he can finish the war by just moving his finger, he hesitates. *Nihattha hai Mamaji.* His original decency shoots up and throws him into turmoil. Brijgopal firmly urges him on, reminding him of his purpose. And so, Samar kills an unarmed man who is trying to help an injured one. It is the final betrayal. Of himself, of who he was.

Moral decline is therefore inevitable. No matter if Arjuna fought because he had to 'set the order right'. No matter if Samar too is pitted against the bad guys. They both hurt the people who love them. Arjuna's love for Bheeshma is beautifully mirrored in the brief moments that Samar shares with his uncle. Yet that love cannot redeem him. No amount of remorse can make Bhanu Pratap hold Samar's hand.

The sequence in which Samar deals with Babulal... That was when Samar dealt his first card, committed his first crime.

That was when Samar became a man.

Ranbir Kapoor

Like Arjuna, Samar was fated for this moral hell. "He has to do it," says Ranbir. "He's cringing inside. It's killing him, but he just has to do it. That is the tragedy of Samar Pratap." A tragedy that ends in him not being able to forgive himself. Because in the middle of 'doing what he has to', he let the headiness of power take over his mind, he let the evil enter his heart, for a brief moment. A very, very brief moment. And that is why Samar decides to punish himself into exile, knowing that it won't take away the pain he inflicted on his family, on Indumati, on Sarah, on so many others. Now that pain is his, for life.

As Samar does what he has to, Ranbir did what he had to. "I had to play Samar," he smiles. "It's the kind of character that comes very rarely in an actor's life."

Before Ranbir heard the script, he knew it was a multi starrer, based on the *Mahabharata* and little else. He wasn't sure if it was the right kind of film for him so early in his career, and he had actually decided even before meeting Jha, that he was not going to do it. Immediately after the narration, he promised Jha he was going to do the film, he didn't care who else was doing it or when they would be shooting. "Prakashji just had me gripped with the mind blowing story!" exclaims the young actor. Jha remembers that after the narration, Ranbir had told him he would love to do it, but was Prakashji sure he wanted him for Samar's character? Jha assured him he was. "I had seen Saawariya (a film by Sanjay Leela Bhansali) which is so different, but there was something about him that I knew was right," recalls the director.

"I've discovered qualities in me I didn't know I had," says Ranbir about playing Samar. "It was my first 'man film'. I'm not a boy in Raajneeti, I'm a man with a dark, dark side to him. And I can remember the exact moment that made me feel that way. The sequence - my favourite even on paper - in which Samar deals with Babulal, and then has him murdered. That was when Samar dealt his first card, committed his first crime. That was when Samar became a man."

No amount of remorse can make Bhanu Pratap hold Samar's hand.

There is nothing else for him... He wants to be Chief Minister and that's it!

VIRENDRA PRATAP SINGH

The Stubborn Duryodhana

Duryodhana had been abducted by the king of Gandharva and rescued by the Pandavas, while they were on exile! Out of humiliation, Duryodhana decided to kill himself. In a trance, the *daityas* and *danavas* told him he was born as a result of their *tapasya* and his mission was to destroy the purpose of the *devas* and Krishna. Duryodhana, which means 'difficult to conquer', stood for the forces that had disrupted the order which Krishna had come to set right. Duryodhana was the personification of all evil on earth.

And Virendra Pratap too is the clear voice, the personification of the evil that exists all around him, in every heart. He is the manifestation of the greed that everyone else feels. Because he steps forward and says it. *Party ka command humko apne haath mein lena hoga.* His father is the president of the most powerful political party in the state and he, as an only son, has grown up believing himself to be the obvious and deserving heir. But at the moment of opportunity, his cousin 'usurps' his rightful place, driving Virendra into a state of jealous frenzy and frustration.

Virendra's frustration is fuelled by the single mindedness with which he craves for power. "There is nothing else for him," says Rajabali. "No personal life, no love, nothing. He does not even look at a divine beauty like Indumati and think why not? He wants to be Chief Minister and that's it!"

However, in the modern context when everything and everyone seems twisted, manipulative and underhanded, the openness of his greed is perhaps some kind of redemption? Actor Manoj Bajpai certainly seems to think so. "He's almost childlike," he says. "He alternately sulks and pleads with his father for his 'right'. And in his mind, he has all the justifications, the logic worked out. He truly believes he is worthy of the position because he has roughed it out in the field, worked hard. And unlike Prithvi, he does not misuse his position to violate women! His lust for power is his only and blinding vice!"

This strange blend of pure evil and childlike innocence appealed to Manoj. "Duryodhana has always been portrayed in black. When I heard the script, I saw the grey areas I could slip into."

These shades of grey are beautifully explored. Manoj has somehow managed to get the audiences to hate Virendra and sympathise with him, all at the same time. He is impossible to ignore with his always, always immaculate clothes, not a hair out of place, sporting flashy gold accessories. Manoj worked very hard on his body language. Costume designer Priyanka Mundada observed how dot on 'Action', each of Manoj's eyebrows would curl into a taut S shape! "Yes, I had to always look tense, always be standing straight, turn sharply, always tower over the other characters," he says. "Even in the pre climax scene when he watches himself lose the elections on television, he's drunk and defeated and yet his slouch is tense! Because defeat is not easy for him to accept. Virendra does not know defeat."

That is who Virendra is. He will go down alone, but not compromise on pride. Like Duryodhana, he will break, he will not bend.

Duryodhana has always been portrayed in black. When I heard the script, I saw the grey areas I could slip into.
Manoj Bajpayee

The one and only thing she ever wants is Samar's love... And that decides the course of her life.

INDUMATI SAKSERIA

The Victimised Draupadi

The story goes that in her previous birth, Draupadi prayed to Lord Shiva and asked for a husband who would be wiser than wisdom, stronger than a thousand elephants, the greatest warrior, handsome as can be and a gentle lover. A perplexed Lord Shiva exclaimed it would be impossible to find one man with so many qualities. Draupadi shrugged the argument off as his problem and said she had already asked for what she wanted. Lord Shiva resignedly granted her wish. And it so happened, that Draupadi was married to the Pandava brothers who each had one of the five qualities she had demanded.

However, Indumati makes no such demands. Samar is everything for her - her world, the reason for her existence. The one and only thing she ever wants is Samar's love. And that decides the course of her life.

Indu starts to look for happiness instead of expecting it like a birthright.

She is the pampered daughter of a conglomerate, used to always getting what she wants. She drives around in a swanky red car, jokingly claims that she's going to be the youngest woman Chief Minister and will travel in a *laal batti wali gaadi*. She confidently assumes that Samar is going to marry her. She does not know what it feels like to not get something that she wants. When Samar clearly tells her he doesn't reciprocate her feelings, she throws a tantrum and storms out. And then comes running back like a little girl, to meet him at the airport, pleading for him to love her back, still not believing he won't.

No matter how unprepared she is for what fate has planned, she has to deal with it. Her own father treats her like a commodity, passing her around from one man to another, considering passing her to a third, all because he wants to be directly related to the Chief Minister. And Samar, the love of her life, who has agreed to marry her and has momentarily put her in heaven, the man who she believes is responsible for her honour, offers her to his brother. He assures her this is the right thing for her. Blinded by her love and trust and now anger for him, she agrees to gamble away her life. As the *mangalsutra* is being tied around her neck, her eyes tell him that she will love him for the rest of her life and hate herself for it.

Her life becomes a daily torture. A husband who sleeps on the sofa and a 'brother-in-law' who will not turn to look at her, no matter how much she wills him to. Her insides are in turmoil – she is torn between her love and her duty. And then Sarah arrives from New York. Indumati slowly and painfully realises that he had agreed to marry her despite being in a relationship with Sarah. He never made any 'sacrifice' by then giving up the privilege for his brother. He never truly wanted to be with her. This is perhaps her first real step to maturity. She grows up. And takes a step towards Prithvi, accepts him for who he is. Indu starts to look for happiness instead of expecting it like a birthright.

Just when she begins to pick up the pieces of her life and start again, it is all taken away from her. She was betrayed then, now she is widowed. This is when she truly becomes a woman. She does not break. She steps on to the *kurukshetra*, to fight her own battles. Led by Samar and Brijgopal, she hardens herself into a politician, cashing in on the tragedy of her life, using it to gain public sympathy. There is silence in her eyes, calmness about her person. Calmness that comes from accepting one's fate, one's limitations, one's wrongdoings. She has now fought many battles. She has won some, lost some and compromised in others. She has come out battered, but strengthened.

Yet, when Samar is about to leave, we see a brief glimpse of the old Indu, whose defining characteristic is her love for him. She pleads - *jaana zaroori hai kya?* But she now does not expect him to stay. She does not even need him to stay. She has made her peace with what he has done to her. Armed with her bruises, she now looks forward to becoming a mother, the only remaining hope in a life victimised by fate.

She has come out battered, but strengthened.

He's like a caged tiger, constantly restless, constantly moving.

Arjun Rampal

PRITHVI PRATAP SINGH

The Golden Hearted Bhima

During the *agyaatvaasa*, the Pandavas and Draupadi disguised themselves as servants in King Viraat's court. Draupadi would dress as a mere *daasi* but could not hide her splendid beauty. She attracted the attention of the queen's brother Keechaka who made untoward advances and insulted her in court. Draupadi later confronted Bhima, hurt that not one of her husbands came forward to protect her honour. Bhima had been held back by Yudhishthir then, but now lost control over his anger. He attacked Keechaka like a bull and beat him into a pulp of flesh. Keechaka was a strong contender and not just any one could have done this to him. Rumours blazed through the kingdom, increasing the chances of the Pandavas getting exposed and then having to go into exile for another twelve years. But looking at Draupadi's tears, Bhima had not cared about any of that. He was prepared to bear another long exile, but he was not ready to let Draupadi suffer. Bhima was the one Pandava who truly, deeply, reverently loved Draupadi.

And Prithvi was the one who truly loved Indumati. Despite his huge frame and crass exterior, he was a soft hearted man. "He's a brutish character, not overtly intelligent, not a tactician, one who believes in raw brute force," says Rajabali. "But he is loyal to the people he loves." He is not a man who thinks with his mind. He is all about passion. Arjun Rampal who broke away from his 'urban image' with a very convincing portrayal of Prithvi, opines that the character was a complete extremist. "He's like a caged tiger," says the actor. "He is constantly restless, constantly moving. You don't know when he will pounce on you!"

Prithvi is first seen as the corrupt politician who misuses his position to get his way with women. And then his relationships come to the fore. He greets his brother with so much warmth, he loses his mind when his father is shot, he is ready to avenge his brother's humiliation with his life. His loyalty for those he loves or cares for is unshakeable, no matter what else time changes. And so, when Indumati's father suggests she marry him instead of Samar, it is Prithvi who protests the loudest.

A character that takes advantage of women and commits murders and yet is liked by the audience is far from stereotypical.

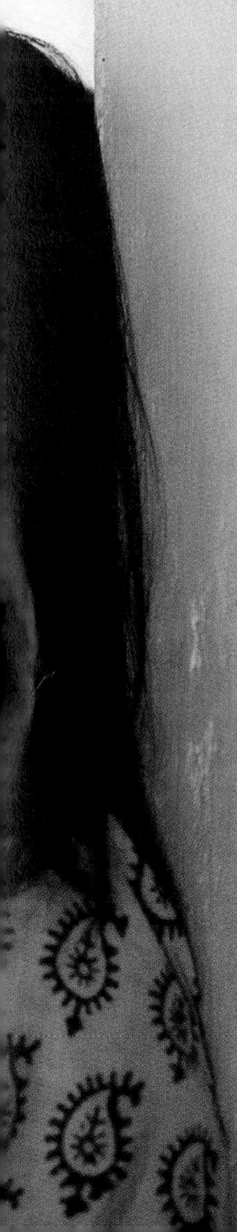

"He has always looked at her as his brother's sweetheart," says Rajabali. "And he is extremely uncomfortable sending a marriage proposal in his name, no matter what the exigencies of the situation." And this is what truly brings out the purity, the innocence of his heart. Even after the wedding, he continues to be hesitant and guilty, keeping his distance from Indumati, sleeping on the sofa and allowing her space and time. "He will violate a female party worker," says Jha. "But he won't do that to Indu."

This brings to light his multidimensional personality. He hangs out with the boys at the grass root level and is also capable of holding a conversation with someone like Sarah. He is brutish and yet seems to be like a child, the easiest to hurt. Says Arjun, "The beauty of Prithvi's character is that every emotion of his, whether anger or love, comes out so purely that he seems almost vulnerable."

A character that takes advantage of women and commits murders and yet is liked by the audience is far from stereotypical. The violence could not have come easy. And could have very easily gone overboard. "You can either play it to the galleries or you can internalise it and bring a certain level of realism," says Arjun. "That was the biggest challenge. If he kills someone it should be believable. When he sleeps he should look innocent." He adds that it does begin to happen when one gets into the clothes, does one's hair, the body language changes. In preparation, one thinks a lot about it, talks a lot about it. And in the process some traits do seep into your behaviour at times. He had this 'crazy hairstyle', he needed 'a bit of madness in the eyes'. "I'm just glad we shot the whole thing in Bhopal," laughs the actor. "The few times I came home, everyone was really glad when I was going back!"

But then again, that was the very reason he took up the challenge of playing Prithvi. "The guy scared me," he says. "And I have realised that the characters that you are scared to play are the ones which become worthwhile in the end." After the film, Arjun's inbox was flooded with compliments for his performance in the scene in which he murders the police officer and Beena Kumari. For his impromptu *akhiyaan milaaoon kabhi akhiyaan churaayoon*... But his favourite is the one in which Indumati comes to him and hugs him for the first time. "He is confused. For the first time, he doesn't know what to do. There's no dialogue, but in that one single shot, his entire character comes together. In that single moment of vulnerability, you understand Prithvi."

And perhaps it is this innocent child like vulnerability that makes this man with a heart of gold so utterly fearless. When his father is shot, he cannot think of anything else. He walks right ahead, mindless of the gun pointing into his head. Or when he realises that the car standing in the driveway is bombed and jumps right in to save Sarah and the others. His priority is his family, his loved ones. And this selfless fearlessness leads him into his death, into his last and lasting redemption.

SOORAJ
The Cursed Karna

Karna, known for his unmatched generosity was still the cursed one. Every one knew that after his morning prayers to the Sun God, the first person to ask anything of Karna was never refused. No matter what he asked for. Just before the war, Arjuna's father, Lord Indra disguised himself as a beggar, approached Karna and asked for his *kavacha* and *kundala*, the protective armour he was born with. Without hesitation, Karna tore off the armour and the earrings and offered them to Indra. And thus, the most endearing, redeeming quality of Karna the Kind became his curse.

Sooraj too was born cursed. He was the love child of Bhaskar Sanyal the great communist and Bharati Rai, daughter of a political king of his time. Abandoned in a basket entrusted into the river Ganges, Sooraj was found by chauffeur Ramcharittar. He brought him home to his childless wife who raised him more lovingly than she could have her own child. Sooraj grew up with a heart of a Dalit while in his veins rushed the upper caste blood. In the end, like Karna, Sooraj's blood becomes his curse.

But perhaps it was this very blood which never let him be like his foster father. He is the underdog, the *sutputra*, the Dalit. But he is not subservient or docile. Fiercely ambitious, he walks as if he owns the world. And you know that one day, he will. Karna was always eager to learn the art of warfare, he always yearned to be the greatest archer in the world. "Sooraj wants to be a leader of the Dalits, he really believes he's born to be a ruler," says Rajabali. "Maybe because somewhere the DNA is that of a 'ruler'. Now one might not believe in these genetic arguments, but nevertheless it plays at the back of one's mind that he belongs to the *kshatriya*, the political class."

Which is why, he rebels like a true blood when refused a party ticket. He is not disappointed, he is angered. After all, he is only asking for his right. Soon after he gets into the party, he becomes indispensable to Virendra. The latter might have been the face of destruction, but Sooraj is the mastermind. He is the true politician, matched by Samar on the other side. "They were both the quiet ones, but the 'real' politicians," says Jha. "Virendra and Prithvi were the mouthpieces, carrying out their plans. The actual fight is between Samar and Sooraj. Between Karna and Arjuna."

Despite the cunning and ruthlessness with which he plans the destruction of Chandra Pratap's family, he has an unshakeable sense of loyalty for his 'own' people. Despite knowing the truth about his birth, when his biological mother begs him to join her son's side, he refuses

The blood running through his veins - his mother's blood, becomes his nemesis.

He might not have promised her in so many words, but he cannot kill his mother's son.

without hesitation. Virendra stood by him when he needed someone the most, he is not about to abandon his friend. *Meri nishtha par sirf unka haq banta hai, marte dam tak unka saath doonga.* He convinces Bharati that he doesn't care about being her son.

But he does care, for such is the dilemma of his life. He is forced to challenge his own blood, his own brother. And he falters. When the moment comes to pull the trigger, his hand trembles. He might not have promised her in so many words, but he cannot kill his mother's son.

And he pays a heavy price for his compassion. Just like Karna had paid a heavy price for his kindness. He finds himself in the final battle, facing his arch enemy, his blood brother, armed with nothing but loyalty for the dying man in his arms. The blood running through his veins - his mother's blood, becomes his nemesis. Samar pulls the trigger that Sooraj did not. And Karna meets his cursed fate.

BRIJGOPAL **The Knowing Krishna**

The Pandavas and the Kauravas were both preparing for the great war of Kurukshetra. Representatives from each side toured the kingdoms of the country, soliciting support. By a stroke of fate, both Arjuna and Duryodhana reached Krishna's palace on the same day, within a few minutes of each other. Duryodhana reached first and entered Krishna's chambers. Finding him asleep, he settled down in the chair near Krishna's head and waited for him to wake up. A little later, Arjuna entered and stopped short at seeing his enemy in the same room. Recovering himself, he chose a seat near Krishna's feet. Shortly, Krishna opened his eyes. And saw Arjuna. Smiling at his dear cousin and friend, he asked him what he wanted. Duryodhana noisily made his presence felt and claimed that he should be allowed to ask first since he had come earlier. Krishna replied that he had seen Arjuna first. He offered Arjuna

a choice between him and his huge, invincible Narayani Sena, the greatest force in the country. He also informed both of them that he would not be picking up any weapons in the war. Without hesitation, Arjuna chose Krishna. Unable to believe his luck, Duryodhana grabbed the Narayani Sena - who needed a non fighting, trophy aristocrat? Krishna smiled. And at that moment, the outcome of the war was ordained. Krishna was making it all happen - the coincidence, the decisions, the war. Krishna didn't need a weapon.

Neither did Brijgopal. He is the puppeteer, the perpetrator, who maneuvers the course of events from the beginning to the end. As Bharati's foster brother, Brijgopal convinces her to give up her first born, her love child Sooraj. Because he knows that if word gets out, the political future of Ramnath Rai and his party would be over. The controversy would be just too huge. He then goes on to propose Bharati's marriage to Chandra Pratap, as he knows what this alliance could do for the two parties. He is the one who helps Bhanu Pratap make the critical decision of appointing Prithvi Pratap as the leader of the party. He is the one who frees Samar from the grips of the ranting police officer and leads him into the operation theatre. If Samar had not witnessed the death of his father from such a horrifyingly close distance, he would never have stepped on to the battlefield and taken command. All through his journey, Brijgopal is by his side, nudging him along to the fatal end. He is the only one who knows Samar's plans, possibly even plants them in his head. And then when Samar falters before killing an unarmed opponent, it is Brijgopal who urges him to carry his fight to its logical end or else prepare to lose all.

He's there, but not really there, he's a kingmaker.
Nana Patekar

Brijgopal, the *nishachar*, the one who never sleeps, is the true politician whose eyes are always on the goal. And he is the one who sometimes urges, sometimes commands and sometimes manipulates his wards' attention on that goal. "He keeps urging his nephews to focus, to not stray away from the target," says Rajabali. "There is a certain survival instinct that Brijgopal keeps bringing in."

And yet, there is no personal political ambition that Brijgopal displays. He is possibly the only one who does not have even a hint of aspiration. He is like the warrior who never fights for glory, and is therefore, the most dangerous. He has no interest in power because, in spirit he already has it. There is a godlike detachment about him. "He's there, but not really there," says actor Nana Patekar. "He's a kingmaker."

**He is the essence of politics.
The abstraction of politics personified.
He is the Krishna in all of us.**

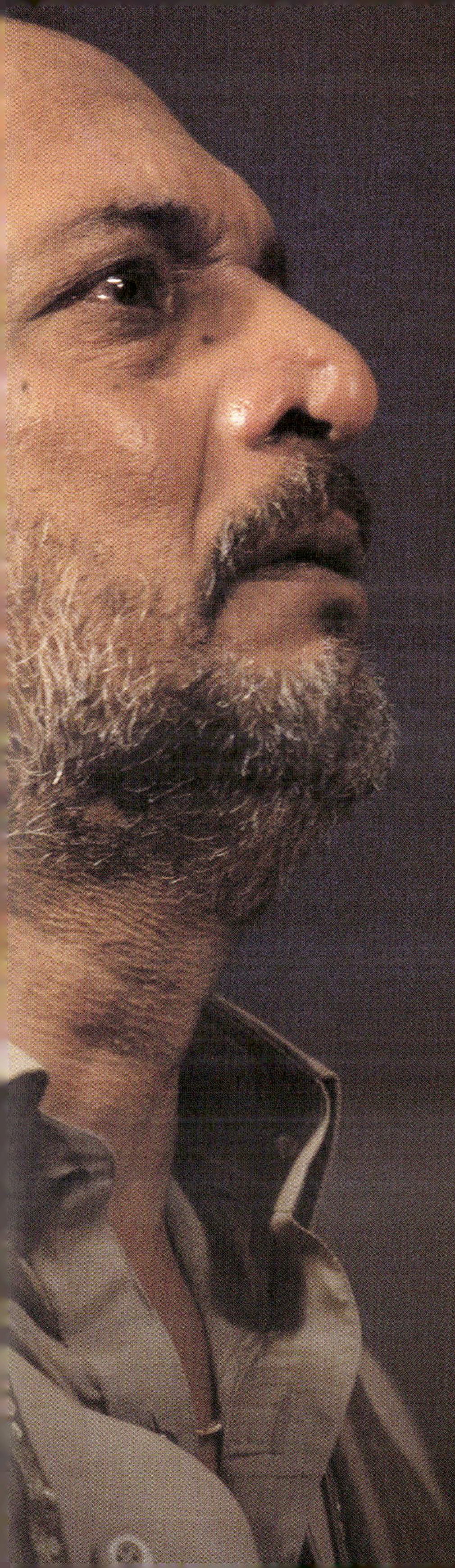

So if he's not really there, what *is* he doing there? What drives him to be so actively involved when there is really nothing in it for him? He's not even really related to the two brothers whom he so lovingly guides. He is Bharati's foster brother. And neither is his purpose to 'set the order right' like Krishna. That cannot be the case in the context of contemporary Indian politics. So what is his motivation? "In my mind, Brijgopal is an abstraction," says Rajabali. "He is a force which resides in every one of us, which constantly reminds us to stay focused on our goal." And that is why Rajabali concludes that Brijgopal's character did not require a material motive. Or even any real material attachments. In a film where characters with five minutes of screen time seem to have a history, a background, there is not a single mention of Brijgopal's family. We have no idea whether he's married, does he have children, any brothers or sisters? What does he like, what does he dislike? He is never shown appreciating anything material – we don't know what he likes to eat, what music he listens to, what does he read. "There is no material connection at all," says Rajabali. "Brijgopal as well might not have been there. Every other person has a definition, has a relation, a family, some connection in the worldly platform. Except him. He is the essence of politics. The abstraction of politics personified. He is the Krishna in all of us."

The most aptly cast actor of the film initially had his reservations. "I was reluctant, I wasn't sure if there was really much for me to do," says Nana. "I told Prakash anybody could do it, why me? And Prakash insisted that only I could. But now I am glad I did it. As we progressed I realised it was an amazing role. There are times when I'm there, and I have nothing to say, no dialogues, and yet I have to convey so much. Without using a word. That's a real challenge for an artist."

A challenge that Nana lived up to. One of the most memorable scenes in Raajneeti is the one at the party office when Sooraj asks for a ticket. Sitting apart from every one else, Brijgopal observes the fiasco, wordlessly. And then simply closes the session. Without a dialogue, Nana's presence was resonating even after he had left.

And so Brijgopal carries the action forward. And in the end tries to find redemption in taking care of his sister. Because the detached god has inflicted a few blows on his own conscience too. He has abandoned a helpless baby. He has allowed innocent women to be hurt. He has ordered the killing of an unarmed man. And he has then turned away from that murder, unable to look into the dying man's eyes, unable to see the final destruction of conscience. Now he must rebuild that conscience. He must again find, and become, 'the Krishna in all of us'.

SARAH JEAN COLLINS

The Innocent Conscience

In every war ever fought in history, the innocent pay the heaviest price. Be it the horrific war of Kurukshetra or the appalling political battle between brothers in Raajneeti, it is the innocent who lose their lives. And so does Sarah Jean Collins, Samar's girlfriend. She pays the price of falling in love with a man like Samar.

Basking in the love of a quiet, intelligent and sensitive man, Sarah is planning a happy, normal future. Her Indian boyfriend goes home for a holiday and doesn't come back. He's a different person, who has no time for her, no regard for her feelings. She packs her bags and lands at his house, determined to take them back into their comfortable life. She does not realise she has just stepped into quicksand.

She soon comes face to face with the other side of Samar. A side she does not know, a side she is scared of. But she recognises it. She has seen it before. In another time, in another country. She has seen the ugly face of death from close quarters at the tender age of six. "Her father and brother were shot in front of her eyes," reveals Rajabali. "She has suffered the trauma of the Irish political war."

Yet, she is untouched and innocent, vehemently against 'dirty politics'. "The idea of Samar being involved in political violence strikes a nerve and brings her right back to the moment she saw her father killed," says actress Sarah Thompson Kane. And so she protests Samar's actions, confronts him. The thread between them comes dangerously close to snapping. And she practically declares to him that she will not allow her child to come into a world where his father is responsible for destruction and death.

"The remarkable thing about Sarah is that she has not become bitter because of her traumatic childhood," says Sarah. "In fact she has become more open and idealistic and full of light." And this light comes so close to flooding the darkness in Samar's heart. He promises he will give it all up right after the elections. Sarah decides to go back, carrying the hope of a better tomorrow in her womb. And that's when the blast happens. Sarah dies. And with her dies hope. Hope for Samar's return. The impact of the blast makes him fall, and not just literally.

Even though it never appears in the film, an entire back story was worked out."We worked out how Samar and Sarah met, what their courtship was like, the first time they made love, the first meal they cooked together and so on," says Rajabali. It helped Sarah internalise the emotions because that is her general method – to create a history of the character she is playing. This brought together the scene where Sarah confronts Samar. "It required me to feel so many different emotions – anger, pain, regret, love, disbelief," says Sarah. "I had to find the right mix of strength and vulnerability. I also had to create a history with Ranbir. And the day we were doing that scene, I had met him the first time!"

Even though in some sense, Sarah is the Subhadra that Arjuna loved more than Draupadi, Sarah's character was a new addition to the reinterpretation of the *Mahabharata*. She seems to be an extension of Samar's suppressed goodness. She personifies the values that Samar started out with. She is really, Samar's conscience. The conscience that dies in that car blast.

She is really, Samar's conscience.
The conscience that dies in that car blast.

BHASKAR SANYAL
The Guilty God

Young Kunti was blessed by a sage with a special boon. She could call upon any God to beget a son. Curious and excited, Kunti called upon the Sun God. When he promptly appeared, she was frightened. She explained she was merely testing her boon and requested him to return. The Sun God could not return without fulfilling the boon. He assured the young princess that her virginity would be intact. And he promised he would watch over his son.

Bhaskar Sanyal, the compassionate political worker, does not even know he has a son. A staunch communist, his whole life is dedicated to the cause. He lives in a dilapidated house and cooks *khichdi* in the verandah, when he is not leading his followers into hijacking high profile rallies. One of these young, firebrand followers is Bharati, the daughter of the political giant Ramnath Rai. Bhaskar's idealism and heroic confidence in the face of obstacles posed by powerful adversaries, has her hero-worshipping and idolising him. He stands against people who are much, much more influential than him. He attacks them like a bull. She secretly feels much more than respect for him. And one rainy afternoon, alone with Bhaskar in his house, her feelings find expression. Bhaskar hesitates, but the storm of Bharati's feelings is too powerful. Later, even more powerful is the force of his guilt. He feels he has taken advantage of Bharati who was almost like a disciple. And he walks away into oblivion. To punish himself, to atone.

It is tragic that Bhaskar Sanyal, a man of such strong principles, gives up everything he has built, everything he is fighting for. There is something painfully idealistic about him. Perhaps that is what leads to the ultimate escapism. His only flaw is that one weakness. He cannot stay and face the consequences of what he has done. As a result his son grows up not knowing that he is the son of the great communist Bhaskar Sanyal.

Like all truly great people, his presence lingers long after he has gone. It is sometimes in Bharati's empty eyes. And sometimes in Sooraj's fearless voice. We think of Bhaskar Sanyal often. At times hope he will come back. We see Sooraj paying for the one mistake his father made. He struggles to find his own place, when he could have been the heir to a political legacy. What if Bhaskar had stayed back and faced his responsibilities? What if Bharati would not have had to give up Sooraj? What would the story have been then? But we will never know, because he does leave, the guilty God.

There is something painfully idealistic about him. Perhaps that is what leads to the ultimate escapism.

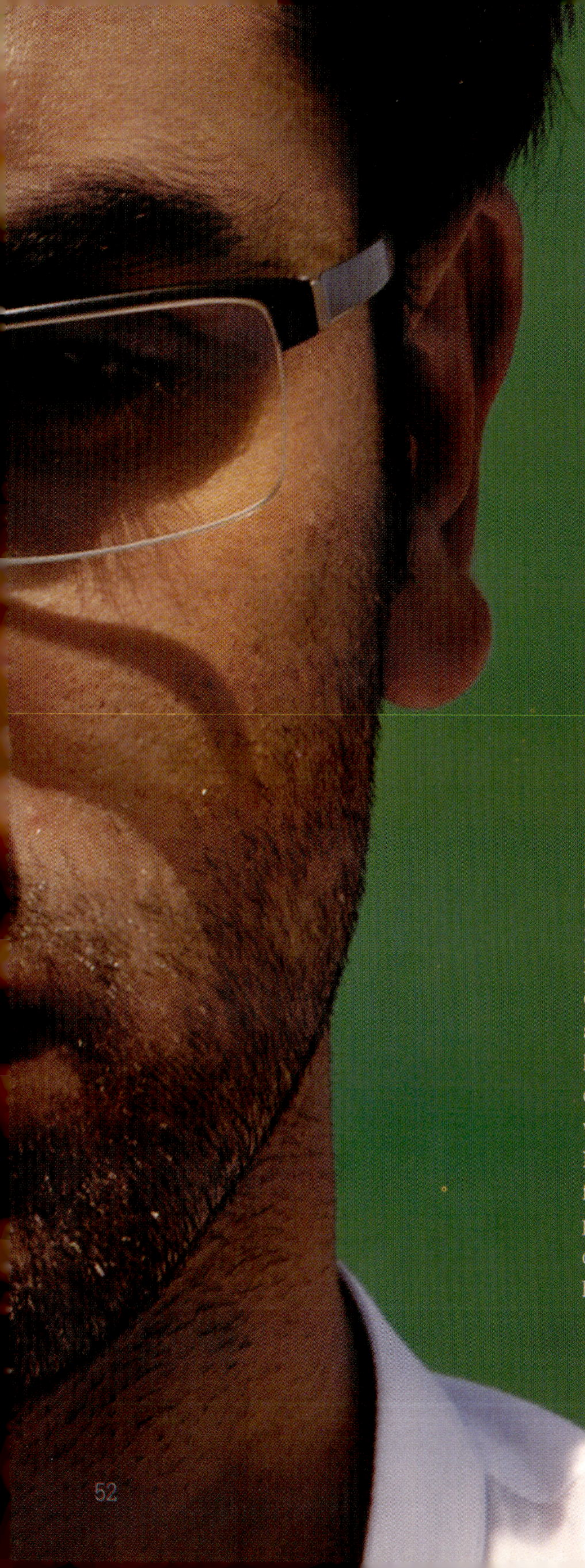

BHARATI PRATAP

The Torn Kunti

After the war was over, Kunti stepped into the field of death and looked at face after dead face, searching for Karna. She finally found him, the resplendent warrior now lying abandoned. She put his head in her lap and wept the love she could not shower on him when he was alive.

Bharati too pays a price for her lack of courage. Daughter of political emperor Ramnath Rai, she rebels against his ideologies, his politics and his control. She joins the revolutionary communist leader Bhaskar Sanyal whom she is helplessly infatuated with. But her idol falls from the revered position, when after one impulsive night of lovemaking, he leaves. She is left behind disillusioned and pregnant. Her reputation and her father's illustrious career both at stake, she agrees to give away the baby. She is not even allowed to see the face of her first born. But that's only the beginning of her punishment. With the child, she sacrifices her political and philosophical beliefs into the river Ganges. She settles down into the life of a quiet homemaker wife to high profile politician Chandra Pratap. Comrade Bharati is silenced forever. And yet it is not over, the punishment. Her sons' hated enemy turns out to be none other than their brother, her son.

For Nikhila Trikha, the most challenging part about playing the role of Bharati was the age shift. "Playing a young girl and then being transformed into a 60 year old, the idea was exciting," says Nikhila. "I had to keep her experiences in mind, understand them. She has been through a lot, she has accepted the sorrow in her life. So her body language changes, the look in her eyes changes."

Jha paid close attention to Nikhila's performance and look. Before the shoot, she would spend time at Jha's office, have lunch, chat with him. And he would casually check her posture, her body language. "He saw every kurta that I was going to wear, and he personally walked me to a salon to get my hair coloured. His detailing was inspiring."

Which is why even though Bharati doesn't speak much, remains in the shadows, her pain leaps out at us. Her silence screams. Almost as if like Bhaskar, she too finds herself deserving of life's punishment. The only time she tries to lessen her guilt and gives in to motherly love is when she pleads with her abandoned son to change sides. But deep inside, she knows he will not. Bharati will have to continue to pay price after heavy price. She will have to continue to live in the darkness of her guilt, because Sooraj will not come back into her life.

CHANDRA PRATAP
The Devoted Pandu

By convention Dhritarashtra should have been the king of Hastinapur, being the eldest heir. But due to his blindness, the decision makers thought it would be better to make his younger brother Pandu the ruler of the kingdom. And so Pandu became king and ruled Hastinapur until he was cursed, after which he retired to the forest with his wives.

Chandra Pratap, the Pandu in Raajneeti, was a king too, but behind the scenes. Chandra Pratap's overriding characteristic is his undying devotion for his brother. "He is like Bhanu Pratap's shadow," says Chetan Pandit. "Bhanu Pratap is the face of the party and Chandra Pratap the hands." He is indeed a keen observer and a shrewd planner. He is always in control, never loses his temper and thinks on his feet. He is the mastermind behind the party's agendas, while Bhanu Pratap is the charismatic, lovable spokesperson. The two brothers are a great team together who have scaled heights, come a long way and built an empire. All because of their solidarity. "If Bhanu Pratap would have said that Virendra and not Prithvi should get the seat of power, Chandra Pratap would have facilitated that without hesitation," says Rajabali.

Chandra Pratap is also a very loving and sensitive father. When Samar is about to leave, Chandra Pratap insists he will come to the airport despite having had a long day, and having so much on his mind. In the car, he tries very hard to have a conversation with his quiet son. "In that scene, the father and son roles were almost reversed," smiles Chetan. "Chandra Pratap was trying hard to make amends and Samar was trying to show him that it was fine. He also feels a little embarrassed when he does not understand the subject of his son's PhD. It was a wonderfully touching and enjoyable scene to do." For this scene, the camera was mounted in the car. Chetan and Ranbir were operating it themselves - bending over to switch it on and off and clicking their fingers for a clap!

Chetan who has worked with Jha before, had a wonderful time working on Raajneeti. "The temptation to try and make my mark in the limited number of scenes was there, but the realistic feel could not be compromised," he says. "And above all, Prakashji has always threatened us – acting *ki toh paise kaat loonga!*"

Despite the limited scenes, it is the death of Chandra Pratap which sparks off the downfall of the entire family. He is almost like the mind, the eyes of his elder brother. With Chandra Pratap's death, his brother loses the ability to think, to see. It is then that Bhanu Pratap becomes blind.

BHANU PRATAP

The Blind Dhritarashtra

After his sons died in the war, Dhritarashtra was consumed by anger for the Pandavas, especially for Bhima who killed his most beloved Duryodhana. When they came to meet him, Krishna insisted that instead of Bhima, his iron statue be offered to Dhritarashtra to embrace. Dhritarashtra, blind and mad with grief, crushed the statue, thinking he was killing the strongest son of Pandu.

Such was the blind love that the king had for his son Duryodhana. He was in many ways responsible for Duryodhana's questionable actions, because he never corrected them. Bhanu Pratap too loves his son to death. But he also loves Samar very deeply. He shares with his nephew, a special, private bond which only the two of them seem to fully understand. He is not entirely blind to his son's faults. Along with his brother, who is very dear to him, he has built a legacy. And he realises that Virendra's ambitions and high handed ways can destroy the fabric he has built with his brother. And he does his best to reign in Virendra's destructive intentions. However, by a stroke of fate, he suffers a massive heart attack that leaves him paralysed and out of action. It is this immobility which over time symbolically turns him blind to what is good for the party. He fights the temptation to give in to the love he feels for his son. He tries to do the 'right thing' by declaring Prithvi a successor. He isn't completely blind yet. He has the experience which Virendra is unwilling to use. Lying in that hospital bed, unable to even drink a glass of water himself, he categorically states that expelling Prithvi from the party will ensure he gets public sympathy. But Virendra is in no mood to listen. The turn of events and Virendra's insistence breaks his strength. He reluctantly gives in, with a sense of foreboding. Knowing somewhere that this is the beginning of the end, he has no choice but to support his son.

Yet, he expects greater things from Samar who surpasses every one else in the ugly race to moral degeneration. When Virendra dies, probably all of Bhanu Pratap's relationships die with him. He cannot understand Samar, he cannot see why he did what he did. He forgets the deaths of his brother, of Prithvi. With Virendra dead, none of it seems to matter. He cannot forgive Samar, so consumed is he with *putramoh*.

Bhanu Pratap is the face of the party and Chandra Pratap the hands.

BEENA KUMARI
The Ambitious Pawn

In political battles, many pawns are used and thrown away. Used as baits, as means to get to an end. Some of them are aware that they are being used and get the best deal they can. While others are truly led to believe promises that are never meant to be kept.

Beena Kumari, a female party worker in the Rashtrawadi Party, is that pawn who, blinded by her ambition and her lust for power, ends up being used and thrown away like a tissue paper. As is the fate of pawns in a battle that is much, much larger than they can fathom.

She is a young girl from Sitapur, who has strong political aspirations. Having been president in college, she has had a slight taste of power. And now wants a bigger share. In order to get where she wants to, she is ready to pay any price. She goes to the extent of granting sexual favours to Prithvi in the hope that she will get a ticket to contest elections in the Sitapur constituency, her hometown.

However, as actor Shruti Seth puts it, she's not a whore. She's a regular girl from a small town. Except for the time she goes to meet Prithvi, she dresses simply and conservatively. No sultry looks or padded blouses. "She's someone you might sit next to in a bus and never guess the truth about," says Shruti. "Every character in the film is using something or someone as a means to an end. She uses herself."

And yet, there is something sadly simple in her methods. Because she isn't the truly devious one. As she lures Prithvi in the hope of a ticket, she somewhere hopes to get him to marry her. She dreams of becoming the daughter-in-law of the most influential family in the state. Not only would that ensure a sterling political career but she would also get a famous, good looking husband. She really believes she can pull this off and that's what makes her almost pitiable. Because she is eventually tossed aside. And so, when she crosses over to the other side it is partly because she believes her political aspirations will finally be realised there and partly because she is the scorned woman, out for revenge. "She just goes after whoever she thinks will give her what she wants," says Shruti. So she's not really the strategic planner she thinks herself to be. Thinking she is using others to get successful, she's the one who actually lands up with a raw deal, a brutal death.

"I wanted a good looking girl for this character," says Jha. "Someone who people wouldn't imagine in this kind of a role." And nobody but nobody did. Despite being the last person anyone would have thought of for playing Beena Kumari, Shruti astounded one and all. Says Rajabali of her performance, "It could have so easily become the role of a floozy, but she became a livewire!"

Shruti had her reservations about playing such a grey character. But the temptation was too strong. And she couldn't be happier with her choice. She says with a laugh, "A lot of people are shocked by what I have done. But the most amazing thing is, some of them are hesitant to appreciate it even though they want to. They worry that if they compliment my work in Raajneeti, I might get offended!"

Every character... is using something or someone as a means to an end. She uses herself.

S.P. SHARMA
The Egoistic Officer

In the dirty fight for power, there are several contenders. The taste of power whether it is for a moment or a lifetime, is irresistible. The police officer, who is 'assigned' to look into the assassination of Chandra Pratap, reaches the hospital and immediately gets into an altercation with Prithvi. He knows the sands of power are now changing. And now Prithvi, in all his brutish splendour, will not be able to harm him. And so, S.P. Sharma wields the power of his position, arrests the leader of the most powerful political party, savouring the momentary feeling of being ruler of the world.

"But he's not stupid," says Rajabali. "He knows very well that if the tide turns again, he is going to be in deep trouble." Which is why his tune changes as the situation takes an unexpected turn. He exclaims worriedly that if Prithvi is released he is going to kill him. Sharma is like the child who gets a thrill out of teasing the chained tiger from a distance. Which is why, though he arrests Prithvi, it is the apparently smaller fish Samar that he dares to slap. Whereas all Samar is doing is pleading with him to let Prithvi go.

"Villains don't carry tags any more, they don't laugh strangely," says Kiran Karmarkar. "I just had to remember that!" Recalling the shoot as a very pleasant experience, he says he did manage to give the Bhopal airport authorities a scare on his way back. The 'blood' they had covered him with on the previous day for his death scene, refused to come off with any amount of scrubbing!

BABULAL
The Opportunistic Peddler

Politics is full of opportunistic entrepreneurs who slip in between cracks. Babulal is one such aspirant, who always tries to maximise his own gains. A small time political event manager, he starts off by doing odd jobs for various parties. He is a 'party worker' for all parties. When he was younger, he would drive around on his motorcycle, carrying the flags of several parties. He would change the flags depending on who he was with!

"He is astute, a keen observer. But his loyalties can be purchased," says Rajabali. In some ways, Babulal's character was fashioned with Narad as an inspiration. He observes the turn of the tide and decides his course accordingly. "He does not have any ethics," says Vinay Apte. "He will work for whoever will pay him."

And for someone with such lightweight loyalties, a secret like the one Babulal has, is an Achilles heel of the worst kind. And eventually, he pays for not having a conscience. His homosexuality, his biggest, most shameful secret is used to blackmail him. And as if that is not enough, Samar and Brijgopal push him up against the wall. He changes sides again, to save his life. But his time is up. He will not be forgiven for being a part of such a heinous crime. What he has done to Chandra Pratap is not the same thing as small time cheating to earn a quick buck.

"I like the fact that his homosexuality was revealed at a later stage," says Vinay, "Or else the character would be expected to behave differently. The challenge was to pack it all in together – the sexual orientation, the lack of conscience, the fear of life."

In the scene with Samar one almost sees regret in Babulal's eyes. The copious tears rolling down his face signal towards his impending doom. He clutches Samar's feet in desperation, wishing he had done things differently. But it is too late. He has never done anything without a price. And now it's his turn to pay.

RAMCHARITTAR
The Loyal Adhirath

Adhirath, the charioteer to blind king Dhritarashtra always tried to convince his foster son Karna to become a charioteer but Karna was interested in the art of warfare. Adhirath would worry about what his son will do in life.

Ramcharittar too feels the same worry for his ambitious and rebellious son. Having been chauffeur to Chandra Pratap and his family for so many years, he cannot understand Sooraj's negative attitude. He is extremely irked when Sooraj talks badly about them. He insists that his employers are kind to him because they care.

As his name suggests, Ramcharittar has a character like that of Lord Rama. He is the good man, the honest man. There is a heartbreaking simplicity in his character. He cannot dream of being disloyal to his employers. He feels a genuine affection for Samar and is overjoyed when he realises that Samar thought of him and brought a watch for him when he came back. He refuses to accept Sooraj's cynical argument. "He will give his life for his master," says Dayashankar Pandey. "His loyalty is his identity." He is one of the downtrodden lot, the simple man who never thinks of himself. The only time he does something for himself is when he picks up the baby from the *ghaats* of the river. And he guiltily looks around for giving shelter to an abandoned child!

Playing father to a man of his own age, Dayashankar worked on his body language, the look in his eyes. He was overwhelmed by the character that he was playing. "It's not a spicy role or something for the masses," he says. "But it felt so good."

In some sense, Ramcharittar represents the remaining shreds of humanity and heart, when he turns up to take Samar to the airport. Samar, the murderer of his beloved son is taken aback to see Ramcharittar. Smiling through his tears, tired and hurt, and yet strong enough to be good, he nods. His eyes ask – if not me then who else?

Ramcharittar represents the remaining shreds of humanity and heart

CHAPTER 4

THE SUN IS THE BIGGEST STAR

CINEMATOGRAPHY

O child, if you wish to see the battle, I will give you the ability

- Ved Vyaas to Dhritarashtra, The Book of Bheeshma

"The first word that came to mind was scale," says cinematographer Sachin Krishn, recalling the time Jha shared the idea of Raajneeti with him. "Prakashji said this film is his dream project and he wanted it to be huge. When someone like Prakashji says huge, you better start rethinking your concept of scale and canvas."

The script demanded a very particular tonality to the film. The colour palette had to be at once earthy and stylish. It was an intense story of a family against the backdrop of politics in the Hindi heartland. Inspired by the *Mahabharata*, it tells the story of many diverse characters – a foreign educated young man, his politically ambitious brother, his obsessed-with-power cousin, the proud but poor prince, the omnipresent godlike uncle, the spirited besotted young heiress, the 'white' girlfriend, the many me-too pawns and the herd like masses. Myriad textures and colours were brought together by the various sensibilities which the film embraced. And yet, the richness of this mesh had to be, more than anything else, real.

When someone like Prakashji says huge, you better start rethinking your concept of scale and canvas

Katrina would come up to him after a shot and ask him, "Will I look beautiful?" And Sachin would say,

"You will look real."

Reality can look bland.
Sachin Krishn

"Reality can look bland," says Krishn. "So the challenge is to depict reality in a way that is cinematically interesting. The story was divided between two eras, the eighties and present day. And both had to be depicted authentically and interestingly."

Having decided that realism would be the constant in all scenes, Sachin set about doing some research. He does not like to watch other, similar films while preparing for a shoot. So he scoured the internet for old photographs of Indira Gandhi's rallies, observed how they were shot, picked out elements that would make his frames more real. He also studied pictures of political photographers like Raghu Rai, to see how they had treated the subjects. Most of his research was for the rally and political sequences. After the preliminary research, Krishn took off for Bhopal for a recce and came back thrilled. The architecture, the mixed flavour of old and new in the city were just perfect. They could not have found a better location.

Like everything else that Jha does, even the nature of cinematography was understated and yet powerfully dramatic. The lighting would be set up as the logic and logistics of the scene dictated. If there was a scene in a bedroom, late at night, it would be dark, it would be dim. If it was taking place in an old factory, it would not be brightly lit up to make it more aesthetically appealing. Whether Sachin found this difficult to deal with or not, one person who did, is Katrina Kaif! Not used to being shot in anything less than dazzlingly glamourous frames, it took a little getting used to. "It's not shot with a lot of lights," laughs the beautiful actress. "Many times I would go and check the monitor and scream at Sachin – where is the light on my face?! And he would simply look at me and say - it's not that kind of film." Sachin too recalls with a smile, that she would sometimes get worried. She would come up to him after a shot and ask him, "Will I look beautiful?" And Sachin would say, "You will look real."

"I cannot light up different actors differently in one scene," says the cinematographer. The energy of the scene decides the lighting. And the actors – stars and juniors all included, are properties in the frame.

At the same time, cinematography was subtly used to accentuate the unique particularities of the characters. "The time of day in a scene was decided according to which character's scene it was and what time would his prowess be at its peak. I like to give particular dimensions to a character, by making slight camera movements," says Jha. Krishn elaborates on the camera movements and framing styles they used to highlight emotionality. "For instance, in almost all scenes of Virendra Pratap aka Duryodhana, the camera is constantly moving," he says. "For his close shots, the camera is kind of floating, conveying his state of mind - always disturbed and perturbed. On the other hand, someone like Ajay is stable and calm and controlled. And so is the camera with him."

In the hospital scene after Chandra Pratap has been shot, an altercation happens between Prithvi, Samar, Brijgopal and the police officer, the entire scene is one single 360 degree shot. It was shot with the camera moving in circles, the assistants running with it. In every rehearsal take, someone from the huge crew would get caught in the frame! "That was a huge lighting setup and a heavily lit scene," recalls Krishn. "It was very difficult but it wouldn't have worked any other way because the scene had immense energy and angst."

The fact that Raajneeti was inspired by the *Mahabharata* gave Krishn the opportunity to embellish his frames with rich motifs and symbols. The film is loaded with many visual cues that point towards the epic. There is a frame in which Brijgopal (Krishna) is standing on a raised platform with Ramcharittar aka Adhirath looking up at him with folded hands. It is a striking picture of God and disciple. "When discussing the scene in which Brijgopal reveals to Bharati that Sooraj is her firstborn, we knew the sun had to be an element in this frame. So, we shot that scene with the sun in the background." This one decision, seemingly trivial, lifted the scene by several notches, lending it a heartbreaking, tragic quality.

You pan to the left there are 8,000 people standing. You pan to the right, there are eight huge stars. Shooting this film was quite a killer because the frames were always full.

The shoot required meticulous planning, serious hard work and resourceful production. They set up multi camera setups, lighting up two to three axes. Krishn's assistants worked on autopilot. They just had to be told what to do and it would be done. The production would cater to most of their demands, even last minute ones. For a lot of the night shots, a crane was borrowed from the local municipal corporation. Rostrums don't go beyond 60 feet and take seven to eight hours to set up. One cannot set up and shoot the same night. But this wonderful piece of equipment which is used to repair the street lamps of Bhopal - a hydraulic machine with a platform, which goes up to almost a 100 feet in ten seconds, solved many problems. So all they had to do was fix the lights on it and the scene would be lit up immediately.

From the outset, Krishn knew the film would be a tall order. He fondly recalls the shoot as 'nightmarish'. "You pan to the left there are 8,000 people standing. You pan to the right, there are eight huge stars," he exclaims. "Shooting this film was quite a killer because the frames were always full. If you're shooting a romantic film or a children's fable, you have one or two characters, you have a beautiful valley and you have all the time in the world. But here, you had to worry that if you didn't can all the shots today, you might not get common dates of so many stars again for a long time. And the whole time you're thinking, I'm shooting in natural daylight. What if the sun shifts? And frustratingly, many times it would! And I had to run after it. Because the sun doesn't wait for anyone. The sun is the biggest star!"

Now I realise that if you want to make a good piece of cinema, the making of it can't necessarily be a dream. But it's absolutely every penny worth it.
Sachin Krishn

Many discouraged Krishn from doing this film, maybe because he's used to working in a certain way which was perhaps different from Jha's. So he started the film with some apprehension. But it took him and Jha just about five or six days to synchronise with each other. After the first few days, most times they did not even discuss the scene, the understanding was there. Sometimes, Jha would himself operate the camera. "I'm very thankful to Sachin for allowing me to do that," he says. "I feel absolutely frustrated and bored sitting with my arms folded. I CAN'T sit when the shot is happening! Plus when you're looking through the camera, at the same time you are aware of the set, you are aware of the light, you are aware of the sound, you are aware of the trolley movement, everything. All your antennas are working. Anything goes wrong, I've seen it there." Krishn, who grew up on Jha's films in the institute says the director's vision was amazingly detailed and precise in terms of art, costumes, cinematography, everything. And the clarity of Jha's thought made Krishn adapt to his vision and add his own style and finesse to it. "In many of my previous films, I had interpreted the script in my own way," adds Krishn. "But Prakashji knew exactly what he wanted and how he wanted it. So the biggest challenge for me in this film was to execute somebody else's vision."

The apprehensions, the hard work, the frustrations, the crises all culminated in some glorious images on screen. The nightmare proved to be pleasant after all. "The journey of Raajneeti has brought out a different person from within me, it has made me push my boundaries," says Krishn. "It has been a process of catharsis. Now I realise that if you want to make a good piece of cinema, the making of it can't necessarily be a dream. But it's absolutely every penny worth it."

CHAPTER 5

KILLING YOUR BEST BABIES

There is nothing lost or wasted in this life.
- The Bhagwad Gita

"While reading the script of Raajneeti, I had already started cutting in my head," says editor Santosh Mandal. It was a simple chronological structure telling a gripping tale. He was excited.

As preparation, he read and reread the script to make sure he had a good grip over the thrust of the story. He wanted to internalise the theme so that he could carry forward the energy of the script into the edit.

Mandal has worked with Jha for years and like many others, fondly refers to him as Bhaiji. He always accompanies the director on shoots. Parking himself in one corner, he keenly observes the shots being taken. And every once in a while, he gets up, goes to Jha and whispers in his ear, "*Bhaiji, iska ek close le lijiye.*(Bhaiji, take one close up of this shot.)" The soft spoken editor makes sure he has his angle variations and cutaways!

So as always Mandal was present through the shoot of Raajneeti. And still, when he came back and watched the rushes, he was left biting his nails. It was such a huge film. There was so much to say. How on earth would he be able to do it? 'One shot at a time,' he told himself. 'One shot at a time.'

Every film to a certain extent is rewritten on the editing table. As Jha says, "When you are writing, you are not always accurately aware of how much information will come from which scene." Perhaps while shooting, some good cinematography, or some good art direction or in most cases some good performances convey a lot more than one had expected while writing. "The purpose of every scene, every dialogue, every frame, is to convey new information," says Jha. "If it's not telling me something new, I will not keep a close up, no matter how beautiful, I will not keep a dialogue, no matter how well written and performed."

The primary objective of any film and therefore of any edit, is to keep the viewer engaged. Once you lose the interest of the viewer, it's very difficult to get it back. "If the audience is lost, I'm finished," says Jha. "We have to keep them guessing what's going to happen next. And we have to keep them guessing right. There is gratification in that. But at the same time, they must be proved right with an element of surprise." He goes on to give the example of the sequence in which the marriage of Indumati and Prithvi is fixed. The events progress in a certain direction, giving us cues and yet not

letting us believe our thoughts. Samar is speaking with Sarah on the phone and she complains about not being a priority for him anymore and sure enough right then, his priority walks in. Here is Indumati whose father has the money that Samar needs, and that is his priority. He agrees to marry her. Yet, there is an uneasy feeling in our stomach because we know about Sarah

and we know that Indumati doesn't. So we are expecting the marriage won't take place. We're right. And yet, we are surprised at how it happens. In fact we are shocked when Indumati's father suggests she marry Prithvi instead. Our hearts revolt, that's not going to happen, we say. Immediately after, Prithvi is seen fuming at the idea when Samar quietly asks why not? Samar has been shown to be capable of what he has just said. "The twists and turns should necessarily be in the realm of possibilities," says Jha. "That's when they are credible and enjoyable."

The twists and turns should necessarily be in the realm of possibilities. That's when they are credible and enjoyable.

Prakash Jha

How can there be no *karaara jawaab* in Raajneeti? The scene was back in the film. By popular demand! And sure enough, it drew the maximum whistles in the theatres - even more than Katrina Kaif's entry!

Santosh also points out that editing is also the greatest fix-it! A lot of glitches can be fixed at the editing table. Good scenes that are rendered unusable can be salvaged in post production. Sometimes, shooting with time constraints and other difficulties leads to certain undoable mistakes. Although not too much of fixing happened in Raajneeti, there is one shot where there was an axis jump and there was no other option but to use it. Mandal did something he does very rarely; he flipped the shot. When asked which shot he's talking about, he smiles and says, "Try to find it!"

After several weeks of editing, the first cut was ready but no one was rejoicing just yet. It stood at over four hours. "The length was a concern," says Jha. "But I felt very positive. I felt my story was moving. The story of characters, their dimensions, the shades they acquire in the political arena were all clear. It looked grand and the actors had performed well. It was working."

But it would have to work in a shorter duration. "We loved it," says Mandal emotionally. "But we started chopping again. The most difficult part was, the four hours were packed with so many beautiful scenes!"

But that is the ugly truth of writing and also editing films. No matter how beautiful the scene, sometimes you just have to take it out. Sometimes, you just have to kill your best babies.

After so long, Mandal still looks like he's going to burst into tears when talking about a scene in which Sooraj goes campaigning in a village, is encouraged to go independent and refuses. "It was a beautiful scene, spoke volumes about Sooraj's loyalty to Virendra," says Mandal. "But it was slowing the film down. I tried to somehow put it in but it just wasn't fitting in anywhere. Till today I wish I could have somehow put it in."

Due to the runaway length, several versions were experimented with, to shorten the film. In one of the versions, writer Rajabali suggested the reaction of Virendra to the death of Babulal, be omitted. Mandal gasped at the thought of removing the scene where Bajpai had delivered one of his most powerful monologues. With a heavy heart, he removed the scene, but could not sleep that night. Over the next few days the scene remained out. How can there be no *karaara jawaab* in Raajneeti? Santosh Mandal slipped into depression at the thought. Another few days and he started discussing the scene with other people in the office. And everyone reacted the same way - the scene was so dramatic, how could it be taken out? decided he had to get it back in.

He had a discussion with Jha and told him that if he were to see the film as an audience, the *karaara jawaab* would be one of the reasons he would come back to see it a second time. He told Jha that a lot of people felt it was an important moment in the film. "I was really connecting to the emotion in that line," says Mandal. The scene was back in the film. By popular demand! And sure enough, it drew the maximum whistles in the theatres - even more than Katrina Kaif's entry!

And this is really Mandal's methodology. Not formally trained, he relies on his instincts more than anything else. While reading the script he instinctively knew which scene would eventually face the axe. For example, he was sure that the scene where Sarah and Prithvi are introduced to each other will be out. And it is now in the Deleted Scenes section of the DVD. "When I'm cutting, I become the audience of the film and decide what will work for me and what won't," he says. And that's how he puts it all together. Of course, one shot at a time!

When I'm cutting, I become the audience of the film and decide what will work for me and what won't.

Santosh Mandal

CHAPTER 6

THERE IS A FOURTH WALL

Build a palace, it must be unique
- Krishna to Maya, The Book of Assembly Hall

"Politics, what a dry subject!" was art director Jayant Deshmukh's first thought, when Jha told him about Raajneeti. "All my other films have been love stories, family dramas and so on. But politics... I thought, now what can I do in this film? There will be some staid party offices, and some simple homes." He couldn't be more wrong. Because the challenge that Jha presented before Deshmukh, was to make this 'dry' subject come alive on screen. Deshmukh realised the potential of the challenge with Jha's detailed briefs. "He knew what he wanted. From pin to airplane," he says.

"Filmmaking is a complete process," says Jha. "When I'm writing, the characters are there, they're acting, the scene is happening in front of me. The sets are there, the props are there, the colours are there. It comes in flashes. So I've seen everything in it and I can draw it all out for my art director."

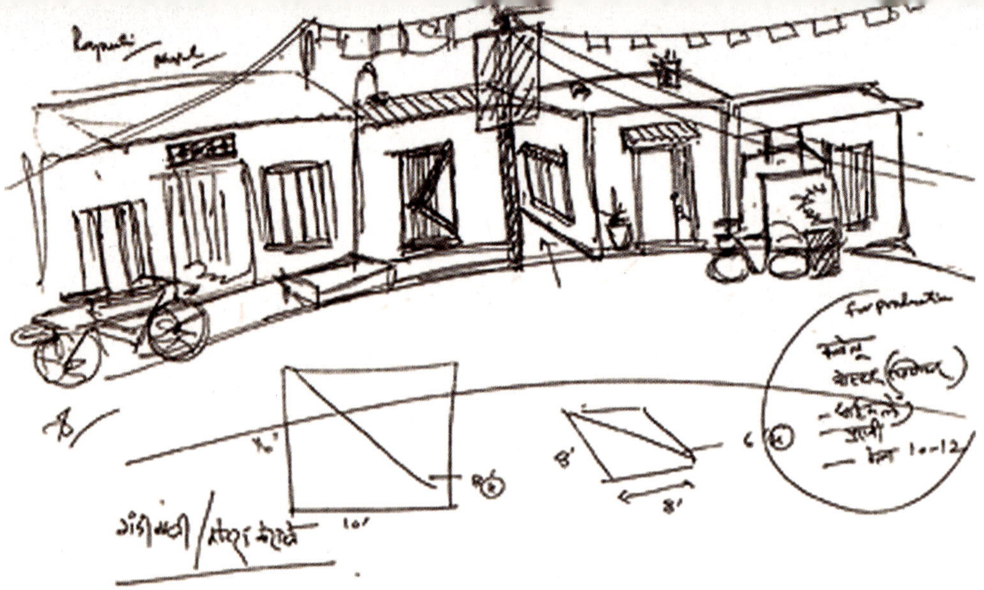

To 'treat the dry subject differently', Deshmukh relied on the best kind of research - observation. He went into Dharavi, the largest slum area in Mumbai, to get ideas for the set of the *basti* in which Sooraj lives. He gathered the logos and other paraphernalia of various political parties of India for reference. He browsed through the internet and dug up references of rallies in 1980's.

The script required Deshmukh to set up a variety of spaces. There were the two houses of Bhanu Pratap and Chandra Pratap, the *basti* in which Sooraj lives; there were two party offices - one of the Rashtrawadi Party and the other new office of the Janshakti Party, and there were the outdoor spaces in which the rallies took place. Some of the locations were real and others were sets. Some were a combination of both. For Chandra Pratap's house interiors, a farmhouse in the outskirts of Bhopal was chosen. The hall was converted into the kitchen. A set was built extending from the house, which became the huge living room. For the Rashtrawadi Party Headquarters, the old abandoned building of the former Vidhan Sabha of Madhya Pradesh was taken. It already had all the characteristics of an old political party office with high ceilings, huge doors and arches. All they had to do was paint the walls and rearrange the furniture. The *basti* on the other hand, was built from scratch. The location chosen for it was a slum area in Bhopal. The actual slums were in a circular arrangement with a huge *maidan* or field, in the centre. It was in this *maidan* that the set of the *basti* was built leaving out a section of the *maidan* to remain that way (where Sooraj plays the *kabaddi* match). The slums on the periphery were replicated on the outer edge of the *maidan*. A *basti* was created inside a *basti*. This inventive idea was appreciated by all the technicians and members of the crew. Assistant director Karan Talwar says, "We had the ease of shooting, we had our own space for lighting and setting up shots. Yet, whenever we wanted, we could do a wide shot and get the depth of an expansive, huge slum area."

A house in the slums is about six feet by six feet. But when replicating it in a film, one has to take into account the fact it will have to be lit up and shot. There has to be space for lighting equipment, cranes, trolleys and people! So the measurement changes. But, on the screen it must appear six feet by six feet! "I have to be prepared to give my director and cinematographer the freedom to do what they want," says Deshmukh. "If they ask me whether they can put a light here or place the camera there, I should be able to say yes. I should have calculated and accordingly devised the measurements. That is the mathematics of cinema."

Because time was of essence, Deshmukh decided to take his team of carpenters and workers to Bhopal. He employed local labour only for peripheral work. All material was bought locally, except planks of wood for the main structure of the sets. Those he carried from Mumbai. Work was initiated simultaneously on all the sets. The most challenging set was of the slum area. It took Deshmukh and his team a month to construct the *basti*.

Art direction is perhaps one of the strongest supports a story can get. The possibilities of enhancing the mood and emotionality through art direction are limitless. What would otherwise have to be said through lengthy, verbose dialogues can be said simply by placing an object in the frame. For example, we immediately understand the particularities of a certain character by the way his room is done up. And so, each of the spaces spoke volumes about the people who were supposed to own them. The new office that Samar sets up, reflects his way of working. It is full of gadgets, there is a huge screen flashing charts and statistics. Printers and fax machines are constantly working. Yet in the middle of all this, Samar's own cabin is clean and calm. His desk has nothing but a laptop and a pen stand. Just like in the middle of all the chaos and corruption, his heart remains untouched. Though not seen, on the bookshelf is a copy of The Bhagvadgita, The Art of War, a book on Shri Vivekananda's philosophy, some Shakespeare and lots of Victorian poetry. The flooring of his office and his living room is a chequered black and white and brown and beige respectively. And many times, he is shown playing chess and one slowly begins to feel the quiet boy is the most cunning strategist of them all.

Samar's house, especially the kitchen exudes warmth. Jha insisted on the huge table in the kitchen, where most of the family discussions take place. It created the feeling of the family being closely knit, having informal discussions and supporting each other. On the other hand there is coldness in the house of Virendra Pratap. He lives in a flashy, elaborately done up house with a bar, a pool table and a huge television (which belonged to the owner of the house - a lucky accident). Given that Virendra was an egotist, pictures of him were put up all over the house.

Bhaskar Sanyal's house was done up like a typical leftist's house. There were lots of books; it was slightly messy and dusty. There was a little courtyard, and the kitchen was in the verandah. His casual approach to the material things in life is very obvious in the way he lives. There are no dialogues required for that, because Jha had discussed the last detail with Deshmukh, right down to what the gas cylinder would look like. The *karchi* and the blackened old *pateela* were bought from an old utensils' shop in Bhopal.

Another challenging 'space' was the rallies. There was a rally set in the eighties and those in the present day. A huge amount of detailing went into making the rally scenes look authentic. There were posters, flags, mikes, cutouts – the list of properties was endless!

First the party symbols were designed. The symbol of Rashtrawadi Party was a handshake, that of the Janshakti Party was a rising sun and that of the Prajatantrik Party was a bird. For the communist party, a variation of the hammer and sickle was designed. Posters meant to be used for 1980's rallies were hand painted. The present day posters were printed on flex. There were mikes on stands in the former rally with *chungas* or loudspeakers put up all over the field. For the present day rally, there were cordless microphones and the sound was blaring through huge speakers.

The flags used in the rallies had been ordered much in advance. But the printer failed to deliver. Two days before the scenes were to be shot, there were no flags. A manufacturing unit was set up in the Bhopal production office and Karan Talwar, an asst. director, supervised it. The cloth was arranged. Five tailors were stationed there. All the screen printers of Bhopal were called and put to work. As the shoot kept happening, Karan kept ordering more flags. They printed over 12,000 flags! The communist party's flags were printed on regular cotton like the others. But Jha refused to shoot with them. He insisted that they had to be of a very cheap material and be shabbily printed. After some hunting, the correct material was found at a little Gandhian store. The flags were printed with the cheapest technology. And then, they were aged! Yes, the flags were aged. And 'just anyhow' put on sticks. For Jha, there doesn't seem to be anything extraordinary about this attention to detail. "How else could the communist flags look?" he asks.

Life size cutouts of the actors were also made out of sunboard. Some cutouts were even bigger. At the end of the shoot, some of the cutouts went missing. The crowd had taken them home as souvenirs. With a grin, Karan reveals that only Katrina's cutouts were missing!

Posters of party election campaigns were collected for reference. The format was followed and posters were designed. For authenticity, posters of other fictitious parties were also designed and put up. To maintain the continuity, the posters were plastered all over the *basti* according to the rally that had taken place on that day in the film. "We were telling a story of 20 years ago and shooting current times the next day," says Deshmukh. "So we had to plan what to put up first, what to keep, what to change."

Another very important property was the horde of cars that were used in the film. There was an assistant director responsible only for the cars and cavalcades. Each cavalcade was arranged after careful planning. The size of the cavalcade would depend on where the character was coming from or going. Earlier in the film, when Sooraj has not yet risen very high, his car would be accompanied by just another car. Later, he becomes a leader and has six cars travelling with him. If the character was coming from a rally, the cars would be decorated with flags. The cars in the cavalcade for a character remained constant, with the same fictitious number plates. And a car used as part of one character's cavalcade, could not be used for another character's.

However, not as many cars are as easily available on hire in Bhopal as they are in Mumbai. So apart from all the cars that were hired, many private cars were borrowed and begged for from the people of Bhopal. A lot of people were put in drivers' uniforms and made to drive their own cars in the shoot. "The prize would be that they drove in the same car as a star like Arjun Rampal or Manoj Bajpai!" smiles Karan. This prize ensured that a lot of people came even when they were not needed. So on any given day, there were at least five extra cars at the shoot!

A lot of the action sequences too, required support from the art department. Some scenes required dummies. The glass had to crack in a certain way; the scratch had to look real.

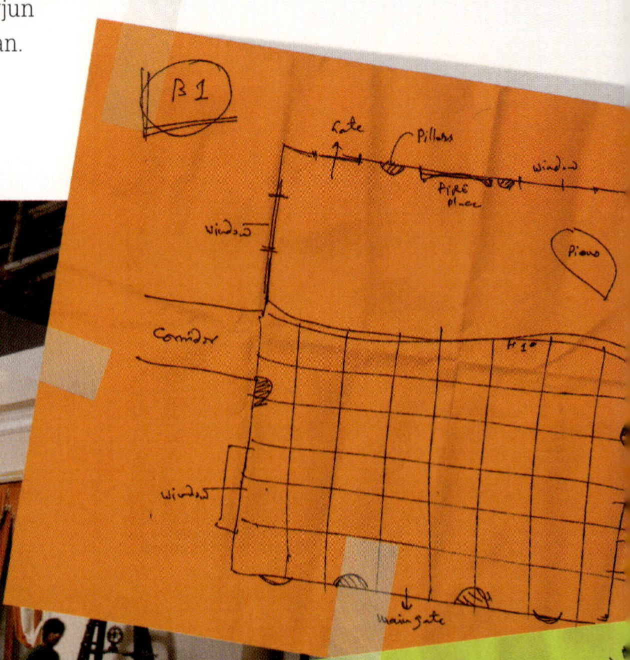

Pain is a constant
in our profession, but it all vanishes miraculously when you see your work on screen.
Jayant Deshmukh

Detailing was applied in all the scenes, all the shots. And if you decide to do painstaking detailing, you have to be prepared for the pain! Unforeseen circumstances sometimes made things very difficult. Once they had to shift location at the last minute. And they had just about two hours to set up an entire hospital! Sometimes, there was miscommunication and the entire shoot would stall because of one single property. Like when they were shooting the final fight sequence, Samar's headset was sent off to another set by accident. Sometimes, the wrong properties were brought in. Sometimes, they could not be taken care of. The thousands of flags printed with so much trouble would be strewn all across the field at the end of the day, and the assistants had to gather them all up. Sometimes nature showed them who's boss. An entire set broke down. The set of Samar's drawing room was to be constructed under an outer structure. This outer structure was built by the local labourers who put up tents in weddings. The set was constructed under it. It was complete and ready to shoot. Even the chandelier had been placed. After all that, a storm struck and the set came crashing down. The water had to be cleaned, many properties were destroyed beyond repair and they had to reconstruct the entire structure.

But Deshmukh shrugs these incidents as part of the job. "Pain is a constant in our profession," he smiles. "But it all vanishes miraculously when you see your work on screen. The most painful thing is when your work does not make it to the screen. So many times, I have done work which I am proud of but which no one else even knows I did. I'm happy that most of my work in Raajneeti can be seen on screen. But it's not always the case. So many times, the audience can see the three walls of a room in a scene. No one knows about it, no one can see it, but I remember I made it. I know there is a fourth wall."

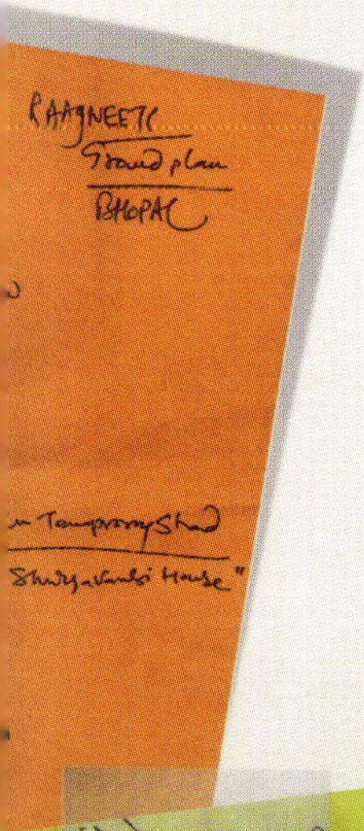

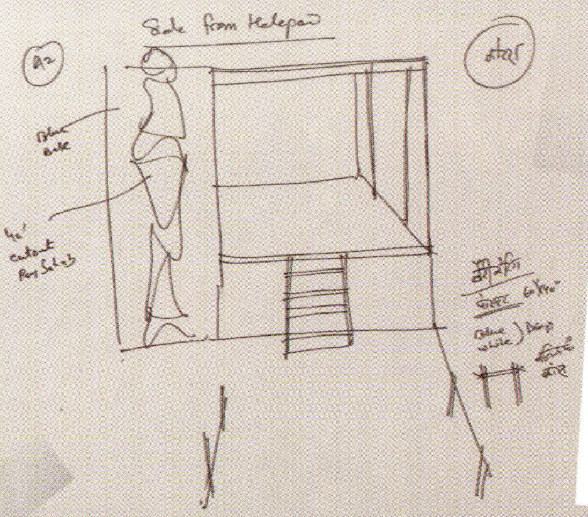

COSTUME

CHAPTER 7

40,000 METRES OF COTTON

Hundreds upon hundreds of robes of many hues
Came off Draupadi's person
- The Book of Assembly Hall

Raajneeti is like a Come-As-You-Are party, as far as costumes are concerned. None of the characters look like they're wearing a 'costume'. For costume designer Priyanka Mundada, the test of her creativity was to restrain and channelise it into the pool of realism. "Prakashji's insistence on realism formed the backbone of the film and we supported it with our efforts," says the young designer.

The script, the characters and the setting demanded that there be a conventional approach to putting together the costumes. "My efforts as a designer had to be inconspicuous," says Priyanka. "They're politicians, how much experimentation can you do with a *kurta pajama?* Fabric was the only thing we could play around with. So I sourced many different kinds of fabric from nooks and corners of Kolkata, Mumbai and Bhopal. There were so many major characters and each had at least 50 changes in the film. Then there were other secondary characters with several changes. And then there was the humongous crowd of 8,000 people to be dressed. I bought over 40,000 metres of cotton alone!"

The biggest hurdle in designing realistic costumes for so many different characters was the fear of repetition. "It could have easily looked like we were just changing colours," says Priyanka. "And even that would have been repetitive because the colour palette was within a certain range. We had to have distinct looks for each of the characters."

So Priyanka did some research on the way politicians dress in our country. She drew up some 'typical' references and some 'stylish' ones. Many politicians in the younger lot do try to create a style of their own, perhaps to add to their 'brand'. And this observation found a resonance in her work. As a result, though there are so many young politicians in the film, no two of them have similar styles. A lot of thought, discussion and planning went into each character's style. It wasn't only about what would look good on them but also what their character would be likely to wear, taking into account the way they thought, felt and behaved in situations. Moreover, elements were included in the styling so that the characters would remind the audience of their counterparts in the *Mahabharata*, on a subconscious level. These visual cues always work better than a verbal piece of information, they invoke the desired emotion in the audience.

My efforts as a designer had to be inconspicuous

Priyanka Mundada

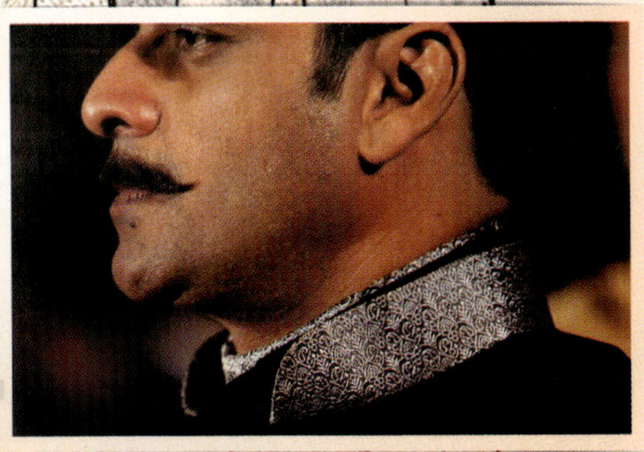

For Samar's look, Priyanka included a lot of contemporary clothes since he had just returned from New York. He wore denims with tweed jackets and sweatshirts in the earlier scenes. Later as his character gets more involved in politics, he sometimes wears white *malmal kurtas* with denims. It was ensured that Samar never ever really looks like a politician, because despite pulling all the strings, a part of him remains outside the chaos. So even in a scene where he addresses a huge crowd, he is still dressed in a linen jacket and trousers. Interestingly, because Samar was Arjuna from the *Mahabharata*, Priyanka has included a lot of whites in Ranbir's wardrobe. White was Arjuna's colour. In the last scene of the 'shootout' sequence, which is the battle of the *Mahabharata*, when Samar (Arjuna) kills Sooraj (Karna), Ranbir is wearing a white shirt. It was decided very early on, that he would wear white in that scene. It is ironical that he wears more whites as the film progresses, and he becomes more grey.

Samar's brother Prithvi, on the other hand was rooted in his heritage and politically ambitious. For him, Priyanka created a very stylish ethnic line – *kurtas* on trousers with *bundis* or crushed stoles. Keeping the lines simple, Priyanka's only indulgence for Arjun's costumes was the use of some lovely cotton fabrics. To keep it realistic, she gave him sneakers with *kurta-churidaar* for the rally sequences. So Prithvi's style reflected his main characteristic – simplicity.

Virendra on the other hand, was the modern day Duryodhana. His style, like everything else about him, stood out. His ego, his obsession with himself reflected in his ostentatious dressing style, so his fabrics had sheen. Priyanka used a lot of satin and crepe. She also used brocade waistcoats and *bundis*. His colours were bright and eye catching. His clothes were all stitched in clean, very sharp cuts and accessorised with gold bracelets, flashy watches and shiny shoes. Virendra never appears with even a hair out of place. "Virendra's style is my favourite in the film," smiles Priyanka.

Sooraj was dressed in fairly simple cuts in keeping with his background and upbringing. He was neither flashy like Virendra nor stylish like Prithvi. His style was more functional. His materials were also chosen for comfort. Priyanka made his costumes in linens and cotton. He was more casual in the beginning of the film and became slightly more elegant and classic, with *bundis* and stoles towards the second half, when he rises and becomes a politician. As his character was inspired by Karna, Jha decided Ajay should wear earrings like Karna's *kundals*. The *kundals* gave Priyanka sleepless nights because Ajay's ears were not pierced and no one in Mumbai was able to make the press-on variety the way they wanted. Finally, a jeweler in Udaipur was called and an order was placed. The earrings arrived just a day before the shoot.

Indumati was a bit of challenge for Priyanka because she goes through three different phases in the course of the film. She is a young, rich girl who gets married, and is then widowed. So in the earlier scenes she's wearing long *kurtas* with denims, even some dresses. After her wedding, Priyanka gave her *salwar kameezes* with embroidery and a lot of bangles, *bindis* and other accessories to make her look like a new bride. The third phase was the one Priyanka really looked forward to because Katrina had never been seen in this look. Indumati, now widowed, would get into politics and wear silk sarees. "The sarees required a bit of convincing," Priyanka smiles. "I hated those!" exclaims Katrina. "They were so thick and I felt like a box wearing them. I would tell Prakashji that and he would say that's how I'm supposed to look. He was of course right. It does work for the character because at that time, she's not really thinking about her figure."

For Brijgopal or Krishna, Priyanka decided to use rich textures because he has an aristocratic air, as if he rules the world. Silk *dhotis* with ornate borders were especially called for, from Kolkata. These were teamed with some classic *bundis* and *khes*. Because his character was inspired from Krishna's, Brijgopal wore a lot of creams and beiges – muted shades of yellow.

Bhaskar Sanyal the communist, was not someone who cared about how he looked. He was given *khaadi kurtas* that were first aged. Priyanka bought *jholas* for him and a functional looking shawl. He was made to grow a beard and tousle his hair. The careless look was carefully brought about.

A lot of attention was also given to the secondary characters' costumes. There were always these constant groups of politicians around the major characters. They were all given particular looks. Some wore *bandhgalas*, some wore *dhotis* and others wore *churidaars*. A lot of minute detailing was done. All the parties had different colour schemes. *Khes* and badges were made accordingly for these. For the short scene in which Sooraj is introduced, *kabaddi* uniforms were made with the party logo on them. Authenticity was the driving thought.

After buying all that fabric, Priyanka thought all she had to do was hand it to the tailors. But when the costumes came after being stitched, Jha looked at them and shook his head. These were not costumes of party workers and crowds. These were new clothes that you wore when you went to a shoot! And so, the new clothes were aged. Thousands of costumes were soaked overnight in good old *chai ka paani* and then scrubbed. Priyanka recalls, "Prakashji was very particular about the ageing of the clothes. Especially outfits for Bhaskar Sanyal. We aged them here in Mumbai. And then again in Bhopal."

After being stitched, the clothes were packed into about 200 trunks and carried all the way to Bhopal for the shoot. Priyanka and her team did a trial run with 2,000 people. The clothes were sorted, labeled and placed on separate racks. So all they had to do was pull them out before the actual shoot. The crowds were divided into groups. "We would wake up at 4.30 every morning and start dressing the crowd because they had to be ready by 7," says Priyanka. "Batches of 500 people were dressed at a time. A round the clock laundry was set up and the thousands of clothes were washed every day after the shoot." The dress department consisted of about 50 dressmen, 10 tailors, and many assistants. And still, they always seemed to be short of people. So everyone who could pitch in, did. From drivers to spot boys to caterers' assistants. While this largely helped, it also created some goof-ups! Sometimes, a new costume that hadn't been aged yet, would be handed out, sometimes the wrong sarees were worn and sometimes the clothes would simply get lost because people would 'forget' to return them.

"In the first schedule, we had shot with the crowd for four days and half our trunks were empty! So then, every day after packup, we would get into the buses that took the crowds home and get our costumes and accessories back with a vengeance!" laughs Priyanka.

Priyanka played police not only to the crowds but also to the stars. Arjun, Katrina, Ranbir and others took to playing cricket in between shots. "Arjun would be wearing whites or Katrina would be wearing a neatly pressed saree and they would be playing cricket! I would tell them not to, but they never listened," she laughs. "So I would just watch them from a corner and hyperventilate!"

It was a challenging job, especially for someone so young. The film was huge, and so was the dress department. But Priyanka worked hard and did a great job, even though she sometimes still dreams about being trapped in a maze of fabric! She exclaims with a grin, "I used to feel like Dushassana pulling yard after yard of Draupadi's saree!"

Thousands of costumes were soaked overnight in good old *chai ka paani*

LOCATION

CHAPTER 8

THE CONSTRUCTED SET OF BHOPAL

Those that will perish here in battle will attain heaven

- Lord Indra to Kuru, on Kurukshetra

Raajneeti could not be shot in Mumbai. While his assistants surfed the internet for pictures of a suitable location in North India, Jha decided to do some traveling. He landed in Bhopal and fell in love. It seemed "just right". When the department heads visited Bhopal, they unanimously seconded his choice.

Bhopal, the capital of Madhya Pradesh is located in the heart of the country. The 'City of Lakes', as it is called, is a quiet, beautiful town with two lovely lakes and some small hills. It has some exquisite architecture of the yesteryears that adds to the splendour of the city, making it a delight for any visitor.

Sachin Krishn was one of the most excited to shoot in Bhopal. The architecture of the city did it for the cinematographer. "The old and new architecture of Bhopal come together in a fantastic way," he says. "And the film required that. It starts in the eighties in *havelis* and narrow *gullies*. And it reaches the present day in computerised offices and farmhouses. One location after the other fell into place. We wanted an imposing-looking structure for the party headquarters, we found the old Vidhan Sabha, in ruins. We needed a modern looking road that goes to the airport, there was the VIP Road. Whatever was written in the script, I could see it happening in those locations. Even though it wasn't the case, it felt as if the script had been written around the city. Or as if the entire city was like a set constructed for the film. Bhopal just opened up itself for Raajneeti."

Rajabali too was delighted about how beautifully it all fit. "The setting of the story was the Hindi heartland," says the writer. "In Bhopal, in its architecture, you see reflected, the various stages of the history of India. The human topography of Bhopal is also very indicative of the people and sensibilities we were projecting. Bhopal was a serendipitous discovery. It looks and feels like an Indian city."

All locations were rapidly locked on the first visit itself. The gigantic Kotra Maidan was chosen to shoot the massive rally sequences. Prithvi Pratap's speech after being thrown out of the party was to be shot in the historic and very beautiful Iqbal Maidan. Indumati's speech, her plea for justice just had to be shot against the lyrical backdrop of the Taj-ul-Masajid. The slum, in which Sooraj lives, would be constructed inside Naya Basera, an actual slum area in Bhopal. Ironically, it is also called Gandi Basti.

The prospect was at once challenging and exciting for art director Jayant Deshmukh. He has lived in Bhopal for ten years, and worked as an actor and technician in many theatre productions there. He knows the city like the back of his hand. "I knew where to get my props and material. I was happy!" he says.

Another important reason for shooting in Bhopal was the thriving theatre scene of Madhya Pradesh. Scores of local theatre groups and *mandlis* house some serious talent and are silently doing brilliant work. It would be foolish to shoot in Bhopal and not make use of this talent. So these local theatre artists from all over the state were mobilised with the help of Bunty, a local co-ordinator for theatre groups. Bhopal became the base for artists from Indore, Ujjain and many other small towns and villages of Madhya Pradesh.

Bhopal also became the base for the 500 member team of Raajneeti. Fifteen hotels were booked for the cast and crew. The actors were all put up in the grand Noor-us-Subah with its beautifully done up rooms that have large terraces overlooking the lake. The director and the senior crew members stayed at the Jehanumah. An office was set up in a bungalow in Shyamala Hill, the central part of the city. Raajneeti had arrived in Bhopal.

Little did the Bhopalis know that Raajneeti had not just arrived, it would soon take over the entire city! The crew began setting up locations, requesting permissions, hiring cars, buying props. They were everywhere! And the Bhopalis welcomed them with open arms and tremendous excitement. Generally, the sleepy town opens shop only around eleven in the morning, indulges in a long siesta and shuts down at five. Not anywhere close to the home-delivery-at-midnight culture of Mumbai which the crew was used to. And so, very often, one would find a shopkeeper being roused from slumber to open his shop and sell his goods! No one ever complained. They were too excited to be providing things for the shoot of a film! One would imagine that this would be a fantastic chance for them to make some extra profit. But they would instead give discounts to the crew members, hoping that they might get to see the shoot!

PARTY
POLICE
MP03CA9931

There are only two major shopping centres in Bhopal – New Market and Maharana Pratap Nagar. This is where most of the shopping of properties was done. The shopkeepers became used to seeing walkie-talkie wielding, cargo clad assistants running around like headless chickens, hunting for properties. Karan once went to Mrignaini, one of the largest shops in New Market, to buy the red cloth which Brijgopal would wrap around baby Sooraj. It was so crowded that no one paid Karan any heed for a long time. When it was finally understood that Karan wanted that piece of cloth which the whole country would see on screen in a few months, the owner of the shop practically shooed all his other customers out and personally selected the shade of red for Karan!

Rajesh Chaubey, a printer in Bhopal, was responsible for printing the flex posters for the rallies. He was so charged to be working on the film, he stopped all his other work for two full months and focused all his energies on Raajneeti. Everyone wanted to be a part of the film in whichever way they could. People offered their homes, their cars and themselves for the shoot! Every day, thousands of people would turn up to watch. They would hang around outside the gates and wait all day, in the hoping to catch a glimpse of a star.

कार्यालय नगर निगम सदर मंज़िल

The entire city was enveloped in palpable excitement. Normal functioning had come to a halt in Bhopal, as if it was festival time. The people started recognising the crew and would jump in to help them – to shop, to eat, to find places. The Bhopalis even started using film jargon like 'cut' and 'action'! There was a general feeling of celebration in the air, with the enthusiastic hope of meeting the actors. Once, a shopkeeper confidently told a member of the crew that he had caught a glimpse of Katrina Kaif in the bazaar the day before, she had disguised herself very well but he was sure it was her! The assistant did not have the heart to take away what will be a story for his grandchildren.

The help and co-operation that the actors and crew members unanimously associate with Bhopalis, came from all quarters including the official bodies. Permissions were granted without any hassle. All cooperation that was possible, was extended to the guests from Mumbai. When the assistant director responsible for the cavalcades went to the DGP of Madhya Pradesh with a request to borrow some riot control and other police vehicles, the officer exclaimed that his list included all the vehicles the department had! He could not part with them without compromising on security. So instead of the cars, the DGP offered the police headquarter premises for a shoot. The place was converted to look like a court and a scene was shot there.

A happy discovery was one Zulfikar Ali, alias Pappu Bhai, a ghazal singer by profession, who was very well connected with all the officials. He facilitated all logistical support and became everyone's man-friday.

The scenic beauty of Bhopal was a surprise for the actors and crew members. Katrina says she had not expected such a picturesque

and peaceful town. Her hotel room overlooked the lake and she clearly recalls it was a 'stunning visual when the sun set in the evening'. But Jha would never shoot in a place just because it is breathtakingly beautiful. The energy of the city lent itself to the film, it shows in the earthiness of every image on screen. It was felt by everyone. "It kept everyone together, in the same frame of mind, and in character!" says Katrina. Ranbir feels the same way. "We didn't go to shoot in Bhopal because it was a new place to shoot in," he says. "We went because Bhopal seems to tell the story of Raajneeti and is a character in the film."

Jha has also shot his next film, Aarakshan in Bhopal. "The city is beautiful, yes. The lake, the architecture, Old Bhopal, New Bhopal... it's all very beautiful. But the most beautiful are the people of Bhopal. Every time I think of it, I am touched by the enthusiasm and large heartedness with which we were welcomed. Every one from the Chief Minister to the common man on the road, went out of their way to help us. And Raajneeti is dedicated to them. It could not have been shot anywhere else."

February 4, 2009. 4 am, Bhopal. Pitch dark. Freezing cold. Karan Talwar shivers in his jacket. And not because of the cold. In front of him, in the huge Kotra Maidan, are 8,000 people. Eight thousand actors who will all give a shot in less than four hours. They are not yet in their costumes, they still have to be fed breakfast. It's dark, they are bumping into each other, no one seems to know where to go, what to do, the microphones are not working and every minute, they get closer to daylight. Another shiver. *How the hell is this going to happen?*

Things don't seem so bleak to associate director Alankrita Shrivastava. She is just happy to see that the crowd came! "The entire lot of them arrived on time, so early in the morning!" she grins.

CHAPTER 9

CROWDING GLORY

I have an army of one million soldiers
Known as the Narayanas,
All equal to me in battle
- Krishna

CROWD MANAGEMENT

Everyone knew that Raajneeti required a huge crowd in many scenes. And like everything else, Jha wanted the crowd to be of real people. "Obviously, the crowd was not going to be arranged in a week or even a month," says Alankrita. "Not the kind of crowd we wanted. They would have to be a trained crowd, who knew what to do, how to react. Because at the time of the shoot, we would not have the time to explain details to them."

Jha has a method of working with crowds, and training them. He has done it before with about thousand to fifteen hundred people in Satara, where he shot Mrityudand and Gangaajal. But Raajneeti was on a much, much larger scale. The crowd training for this film became a revolutionary venture, and was insanely ambitious. Not something that has been done very often or will be done very often. But it was ingenious, and beautiful in its simplicity. This was the plan: They would first select about 200 core team leaders from all over the state of Madhya Pradesh. They would do workshops with them, tell them what the film was about, what they were expected to do and how it would all pan out. These core team leaders would then go to their respective towns and villages and choose another team of ten people each. And cascade what they had learnt to these teams. These ten would then each train another fifty and so on. All the training would be supervised by assistant directors. They would be working down the line with the last man.

In May 2008, Alankrita took off for Bhopal to meet representatives of local theatre groups. The basic story of the film and the plan of the training process were shared with them. Some actors from Jabalpur, Ujjain, Rewa, Indore and other parts of the state came to meet them. And then a tour of the entire state was organised.

A route chart was prepared and the team travelled to remote towns and villages of Madhya Pradesh. They met with a number of talented actors and thriving theatre groups. At that point, Alankrita and her team were testing waters really, to see if the artists were interested. The response was very encouraging even though they were not yet fully aware of the magnitude of what was about to happen.

In July 2008, a two day workshop for the core team leaders was organised in Bhopal. Jha personally conducted the workshop. He took them through a video of what the film would look like, what the making of the film would be like. The artists got a taste of the experience of working with Jha and the excitement escalated threefold. The artists began to realise they were about to launch into an experience of a lifetime.

The core team leaders went back to their native places, charged and excited. They had to build an army of 8,000 people. The word was spread. Everyone came. Not just theatre artists but people who do *nautanki*, puppeteers, standup comedians, *bandwallahs* who play in weddings, mimicry artists, dancers, even *kushti pehelwaans!* Hundreds of students enthusiastically got involved. Housewives with hidden acting aspirations showed up. Anyone who was interested in any kind of performing art was welcome.

Alankrita and her team closely supervised the training. They parked themselves in Bhopal for an entire year and prepared their army for combat. They personally met each member of every team. Their details were recorded, their photographs were documented. Everyone was told about the working conditions, pay structure and other such details. Hundreds of questions were asked and answered. The assistants devoted about two days to each village or town. They wanted to be absolutely sure that every one who was involved, wanted to be.

After the numbers were gathered, intensive theatre workshops and training programmes were initiated. They were showed how to react, how to emote. A number of scenes were simulated. They were shown how to shout slogans in a rally scene. They were taught how to behave in a riot like situation.

Each of the artists was then made to perform various roles. If you were a police constable or officer, you would have to behave in a bossy manner. If you were a party worker, you had to exhibit fervour. They were thrown in random fictional situations. In one exercise an actor was playing a police officer and in another, he was playing a goon. The idea was to prepare them in every way because at the shoot, if a casting decision was changed, there would be no time to teach thousands of people how they were going to behave in front of the camera.

Most of the actors had never faced a camera. They did not even know how a film is made. They were taught how to follow instructions while a shoot was going on. Every one learnt that if you were not in the frame , you turned into a statue as soon as the word 'action' was called out. And could breathe again when the director called 'cut'. With a few reference videos, they understood what it meant to be 'in the frame'. Continuity became a part of their daily conversation. They realised that if they were waving with the right hand, they would have to keep waving with the right hand, no matter if it took a month for the scene to be completed. No matter if their right hand fell off!

And so, after months and months of rigorous workshops, training sessions, lectures and discussions, it was time for the real thing.

Continuity became a part of their daily conversation. They realised that if they were waving with the right hand, they would have to keep waving with the right hand, no matter if it took a month for the scene to be completed.

No matter if their right hand fell off!

Just before the shoot, a dry run with a few thousand actors was conducted. Some casting was also done. People were divided on the basis of suitability for the roles of political workers, policemen, commandos and so on. The costumes were also tried. The dry run with the team leaders and their assistants went off smoothly. But this was just a rehearsal. Their hard work of so many months would have to show on the actual shoot. The direction team was thrilled to bits seeing what they had done. And yet, they were as nervous as first time parents. But the crowd seemed to feel no nervousness. They just couldn't wait! The moment finally arrived when, in that dark morning, 8,000 people came together to create magic.

There was some amount of disorientation and confusion in the first few hours. Perhaps the crowd was amazed at their own size! As if Ghatotkach had suddenly grown in size and then accidentally passed a mirror! But the production and direction teams were prepared for a few teething problems. Soon everything sorted itself out. By 8 am, the crowd was in costume, had had their tea and were ready to give their first shot.

Whatever remnants of fear or doubt were left in anyone's mind, were all dispelled as soon as Jha came on the set. He brought with him a fresh wave of confidence and faith. His relaxed demeanour put every one from cast to spot boy at ease. The show was about to begin.

With the first call of 'action' everything and everyone became automated. The crowds reacted beautifully. An astounding energy had enveloped them. They followed instructions perfectly. When asked to appear cheerful, their enthusiasm was infectious. When asked to move three steps, the entire lot, all 8,000 of them, would take three steps without confusion. When asked to move back three steps, they would do that without a glitch too. The months of training showed. Not a single person looked into the camera. They were all pros. And leading them from the front was their hero. That's what Jha had become in the short span of few hours. Every morning when he appeared on set, the crowd would actually cheer by way of greeting! An exclusive relationship rapidly formed between him and the crowd. He handled them so sensitively that they were like little kids, eating out of his hands, eager to do anything they could to please him. Even when he was strict with them, they could feel the warmth in his voice. He would make them laugh, he even sang for them! "From the first day, they just loved him!" exclaims Alankrita. "He was making them all feel like a very important part of the team. I cannot think of any other director who could have directed thousands of people for so many days together. He was very clear about what he wanted and yet he allowed the artists space for their kind of expression and performance. They were truly inspired by him."

He (Jha) handled them so sensitively that they were like little kids, eager to do anything they could to please him... he would make them laugh, he even sang for them!

This inspiration worked wonders on the passion that the artists possess in abundance. Yes, they were being paid and yes, it was just a temporary job. But it was obvious to everyone, that it meant much, much more to them. This was a landmark experience in most of their lives. They treated the film like they had a stake in it. They worked with single minded dedication. They came from faraway places and made Bhopal their base. They reached on time, patiently waited hours for a shot, never complained and always gave their very best. They brought to the film a grassroot flavour which would not have been possible with a group of jaded junior artists. This crowd was real. Their tears came from their hearts. Their smiles reached their eyes. Their screams truly made them hoarse. The shoot was in some sense, a culmination of their love for their respective art forms. They brought their love, their passion into the field. And it made all the difference. Jha effortlessly channelised their enthusiasm into the film. His leadership and their passion led to an explosive combination. One that makes you wonder what would have happened, had Krishna and his Narayani Sena been on the same side.

ACTION

CHAPTER 10

THE SILENT AND THE VIOLENT

**Once war has been undertaken,
no peace is made by pretending there is no war**
- The Book of the Effort

Tyres screech. Dust flies. Heads turn. Door opens. People watch with bated breath. A foot comes out. It belongs to Action Director Sham Kaushal. That is how he made his entry at the sets! Every morning. And as soon as he stepped out of his car, his assistants would run to him and touch his feet. And then the day's work would begin. As members of the crew recall fondly, the action director always came with a bang!

However, this spirit of high drama was kept on a tight leash in Raajneeti. There could not be any fancy stunts or choreographed boxing matches. "The action should never hijack the story," says Kaushal. "And this was a real story - people in a family fighting for political power. The audience had to be able to identify with it."

The film has several principal characters. And each of these characters possessed their own unique temperaments. Samar is calm and collected. He hardly ever raises his voice. Prithvi is volatile and aggressive. Sooraj is practical and down to earth. Virendra is severely impulsive. How they behaved and reacted in action scenes would be determined by these characteristics. The individuality of the characters had to be maintained. "If the audience feels that this person is behaving differently all of a sudden, it won't work," says Kaushal. And the interesting thing for him was, there were a number of different characters involved in a number of action scenes. In this adaptation of the *Mahabharata*, there was no dearth of prototypes. He says with a smile, "We had the silent and the violent!"

He followed the minds of the characters and made the actors react accordingly. So that the story could be helped along. Sooraj is introduced in a *kabaddi* match, sporting defiant body language. Just before the blast, despite knowing there is a bomb, the emotional Prithvi dives headlong into his death. In the pre climax scene where the shootout happens, Samar does not behave like a seasoned sharp shooter. He is confident but does not display any 'hero' like style. He is calm and collected. Virendra on the other hand, impulsively jumps out of the car and gets shot. Brijgopal despite being in the thick of things seems outside of it.

In this adaptation of the *Mahabharata*, there was no dearth of prototypes.

Action, action *na lage*

Sham Kaushal

Kaushal choreographed the sequences with his assistants so that there would be no time wasted on the sets. They were prepared with the moves, the list of properties they would need and so on. Kaushal headed a second unit and canned the long and wide shots of a few major sequences while the actors were busy with the other scenes.

One of the most elaborate action sequences was the chase towards the end. After Virendra is shot, Sooraj drives off to take him to a hospital. Samar's men are stationed at every hospital in town. Sooraj rushes from one hospital to another as Virendra fights with death. Brijgopal states it would be stupid to get into a gunfight in the middle of the city, they should drive the duo to the outskirts. And Samar with his army, chases Sooraj.

Most of the city had been captured while shooting the rally sequences. So Kaushal carefully planned the chase to make it stand apart. He marked out a route which would include a few important landmarks. A lot of helicopter shots were taken. It was a racy, exciting chase which would lead to the scene at the bridge, when the final altercation takes place. Kaushal was very pleased. Sadly, the chase had to be cut out because of the length of the film.

Another important scene was the car blast in which Sarah and Prithvi die. "They were principal characters who died," says Kaushal. "The story takes a turn in this scene, right after their death. It's what really sparks off the revenge. Samar and Indumati both break down. The blast scene had to have an impact."

Kaushal wouldn't dream of blasting the car at the incredibly beautiful house they were shooting in. The blast was shot against black separately, for the visual effects department. An exact replica of the porch and pillars, in the same dimensions, was built in black. The car was placed in position. Camera angles were recorded. The shots of Prithvi and Sarah and the others would be taken from these exact angles later, at the house. The explosives used in these kind of 'shoot blasts' are very mild. They're more about fire and dust than impact. The door and windows were pried out of the car and attached to wires. They were then placed back on the car. When the blast happened, the wires were pulled manually, yanking off the door. It appeared in the shot as if the door had flown away because of the impact of the blast.

At the house, the camera was placed in the exact position. Shots of Prithvi diving and the two of them being blown away by the blast were taken there. The burnt car was placed on the porch and small flames were created on its surface. Everything was covered with soot. But not before protective sheets were placed on the floor and cloth was wrapped around the pillars, so as to not deface the lovely porch.

With attention to detail, Kaushal attempted to blend into the earthiness of the film. He put thought in every punch and worked hard to stand out by becoming as inconspicuous as he could. For the experienced action director, the most challenging aspect of Raajneeti was just that - trying not to be there! "Action, action *na lage*."

CHAPTER 11

THE EPIC SOUND

The sound of the many conchs... the very heavens resounded with the terrible reverberation
- The Book of Bheeshma

A Prakash Jha film about hard core politics, set in the heart of India. And the man, who is to create the music of the film, does not understand a word of Hindi! Such an unusual combination can either be a crashing failure or a roaring success. What it was, is no secret.

New York based music director Wayne Sharpe has done the background score for Jha's Gangaajal and Apaharan and even won a Filmfare Award for Best Background Score, for the former. Their association goes back a long way, and even seems a tad bit surprising. Why would Jha do that, one is tempted to ask. Why would he bring in a 'foreigner' to make music for films that are so intrinsically Indian? "Music has no language," exclaims Jha. "And the background in our Indian films sometimes has too much music. It's cluttered. I want to use background music as an ambience. And Wayne with his sensibilities and training can create that ambience. But when the need is big, he can create the 'big sound' as well. Sometimes it is good to work with someone who does not understand the language and culture. He brings in a different sensibility. I find it very easy to work with Wayne. He catches on really fast!"

Sharpe was truly tuned in on the correct frequency. When he heard the story, he knew what Raajneeti would be like. "It felt big. It was an epic film." says the music director. "It would need an epic sound."

The most striking aspect of Sharpe's music for Raajneeti is the seamless blending of Indian and international elements. Years ago, before Gangaajal, Sharpe had studied Indian music. To blend Indian classical elements with Western, he had to know what the Indian instruments sounded like, how they were used. He learnt about the *ragas* and their emotional definition. "I did my research," Sharpe says. "But I had to be careful to not be too heavily influenced. After all, the reason for having me come in was to get a Western blend. Prakash did not want a 'Hindi' sound, but a fresh approach."

Sharpe decided to bring about the blend by creating Western melodies and then recording them with Indian instruments. Western instrumentation executed with Indian sounds. "It took some studying of the various instruments," says Sharpe. "I know how a string set like the piano would sound, the emotions it would bring out. On the other hand an instrument like *sarangi*, one of my favourites now, sounds beautiful but essentially sad. So I could not use it in happy situations. It took some time to learn things like that."

A wide palette of sounds was used for scoring the background which therefore sounds 'international yet Indian'. Sharpe describes his approach to the film as 'very Hollywood'. A vast orchestra with large strings and horns was used. For the chase sequences, a lot of Indian and Japanese big drums were mixed with intense orchestral sounds. On the other hand, the piano was used for a lot of the emotional sequences to bring about an ambient texture.

Before he starts scoring the background, Sharpe goes through a process that he calls 'plotting the film'. He makes Jha take him through the film, scene by scene. Each scene is discussed in detail - the dramatic movement and the emotional tone of the scene, character development in each scene and so on. This detailed discussion gets Sharpe comfortable with the entire film. And then the music director launches into the score - armed with synopses, scripts and of course, a subtitled copy of the film!

For Raajneeti, Sharpe created a set of themes. Apart from the main theme of Raajneeti, separate themes were created for each major character. These were then woven into the film through a pattern. They were used to create tension or throw relief into the narrative.

The melodies were designed in Sharpe's studio in New York. The orchestra was recorded in Prague, Czechoslovakia. The Indian instruments were recorded in Mumbai and then slapped on top of the programmes. So the best of all worlds was taken. "The orchestra in Prague is very accessible music," says Sharpe. "They're wonderful with intense strings and horns. And there are some musicians in India who are, frankly, just incredible. Their live music took the compositions up by several notches."

This cross continental collaboration, third time in a row, proved mutually very satisfying. Sharpe says it gets easier with every film, to work around the distance. Because they now understand each other's approaches and have developed an understanding. Perhaps this growing understanding made Jha confident enough to entrust Sharpe with another very significant piece. The theme song of Raajneeti. A re-interpretation of *Vande Mataram.* A bold step amongst so many others that Jha took while making this film. Sharpe had never, ever made a Hindi song. In fact, Sharpe had never even heard *Vande Mataram!*

He smiles as he recalls the first time he heard the national song of India. "We were in my studio when suddenly, Prakash started singing *Vande Mataram.* That was the first time I heard it." This song, which would accompany the closing credits of the film, would have to bring together, the cohesive theme of politics, relationships and patriotism. It would have to bring together the film.

Sharpe began by sourcing and listening to various renditions of the song. He experimented and came up with many 'western sounding' themes of *Vande Mataram.* He was aware that Indian songs are structurally more lyric based and that his composition would have to accommodate that. He designed the score with large drumming and large percussions. "This was the song of Raajneeti, it would have to have big sounds." And it did! *Dhan Dhan Dharti Re* is a unique rendition. It is a contemporary, independent score and yet an interpretation of the classic song of *Vande Mataram.* The sparkling new melodies are haunted by the timeless notes of the old song. As if inside a grand, untouched and unlived European mansion skips around the ghost of a beautiful Indian princess, her anklets making music.

The ethereal music was lifted even higher by the heartbreakingly beautiful lyrics that Gulzar penned. Jha's brief was simple. It should sum up the film. He asked Gulzar to imagine that in the *Mahabharata*, after the war was over, how Sanjay the charioteer, described to

Dhritarashtra, the complete destruction of humanity? Looking at the thousands of dead bodies, the rivers of blood, the bereft relationships, what did Sanjay say? He said: *Boodha aasman, dharti dekhe re, dhan hai dharti re. Dhan dhan, dharti re...*

An important thread of the story was the inexplicable relationship between Samar and Indumati. It encompassed the warring emotions of deep love, tender caring, shocking betrayal and aching remorse. 'Their' song would have to carry strains of intense love and intense pain. For this song, Jha decided to approach music director Aadesh Srivastava. After a long narration, Srivastava went back to think. He already had a song which he had been working on and was toying with the idea of putting it in an independent album. But when he thought of Indumati's unrequited love, he realised the song was meant for her. He went back to Jha and made him hear the song. Jha liked the melody as well as Sameer's soulful lyrics. The song which is in *raag darbaari* was given a lounge treatment with acoustic and electric guitars, live strings and so on. Srivastava decided to sing it himself. Mora Piya Moh Se Bolat Nahi was used often in the film like a theme. It stayed on top of the charts for a long time and became the most popular song of the film.

And in stark contrast to this was *Ishq Barse Boondan Boondan*. Music director Shanatanu Moitra says it is not like anything he's done before. Jha nudged him out of his comfort zone for this composition. The music director despises the term 'item number', his melodies are more classical based than anything else. And he was sure he would not, *could* not create a run of the mill item song. In one of his meetings with Jha, he talked about a pub he had been to in Amsterdam, where they used sprinklers to create a beautifully misty atmosphere. The song was inspired from that description. It was composed in *raag meghmalhar.* The lyrics came about as a result of Jha and lyricist Swanand Kirkire randomly throwing words at each other. From that tennis match of words the pattern of the lyrics emerged. *'Boondan boondan', 'champayi champayi', 'chun chun', 'resham resham, 'madham madham'* – the word repetitions gave the song energy of its own. The classical parts are sung by Pronob Biswas who works at the ITC Sangeet Academy in New York. He was in India for a holiday when Moitra caught hold of him to record the *alaaps.* There wasn't even a track ready yet, so he made Biswas just sing on a tempo! And then he worked backwards. The rest of the song was sung by Hamsika Iyer, who has also not sung anything like this before. So everything and everyone unlikely came together for this 'item number'. But it turned out beautifully as it was raining talent, *boondan boondan!*

The happy and romantic song of the film is *Bheegi Si Bhaagi Si* by Pritam Chakravarty. When you hear the beautifully composed song, you can almost feel the morning breeze gently tickling you. It goes up and it comes down, all very gently. It is much like the butterflies-in-stomach feeling of first love. Irshad Kamil's lyrics are delightful visual poetry. The thought of a *gulaabi subah* bringing you love messages immediately carries you to another world where there is always a winter sun and a green spring. The simplicity of the love song beautifully describes the innocence of Indumati's love for Samar, playing ironically somewhere at the back of your mind, when he betrays her.

And so the music of Raajneeti was compiled, like flowers in a bouquet. As Sharpe points out, the music has to enhance the emotional content of the film. And each composition serves this purpose wonderfully. The scores of Raajneeti are few and diverse. They set the balance of the film right, reinforcing the fact that film is about emotions and relationships. But all this without overpowering the story, without eating up undue attention. And still remaining memorable, still being hummed.

PRODUCTION

CHAPTER 12

IT'S GOING TO BE WAR

It is your duty to fight
- The Bhagwad Gita

The one thing production controller Sudhirbhai Mishra is prepared for after ten years with Jha, is tall orders. And yet, when he heard about Raajneeti, he knew this wasn't a regular tall one. Once the script was discussed, Mishra galvanised his assistants and vendors into action. Everyone was briefed in thorough detail. Quotations and estimates started flying around office, serious bargaining was carried out on the phone and new schedules and working systems were devised every few hours. "Preproduction and planning would be vital," says Mishra, "We might not have understood the magnitude of what we were launching into, but we knew one thing - it's going to be war."

One of the first and most important aspects that the production team had to look into was the management of the mammoth crowd that was going to be part of the shoot. Jha had insisted on 'real people' and their training had already been initiated by the direction team. They would come to Bhopal for the shoot, all 8,000 of them, from all over Madhya Pradesh. So the first thing they would need is a place to stay. Accommodation was required for 8,000 actors.

Mishra went on a recce to Bhopal to look into the lodging options. Some hotels could accommodate 150, some 200, some 400. Almost all the hotels, lodges, guest houses and marriage halls in the city were booked by Prakash Jha Productions. Mishra selected the hotels and lodges with great care, paying attention to the minutest detail. In some hotels, the capacity was 200, but there were only two bathrooms. If the crowd was expected to report on location at 6am, it would be unfair to expect them to be ready with only two bathrooms available. So in hotels and lodges where there weren't enough bathrooms, Mishra decided to get some extra ones constructed! The authorities happily agreed to adjust the costs in their bills. "This much we had to do," says Mishra with a smile. "The basic needs of a junior artiste are the same as a star!"

Almost all the hotels, lodges, guest houses and marriage halls in the city were booked.

Accommodation arranged, now they had to arrange for these thousands of people to be taken to location in the wee hours of the morning, every day. Thirty five buses were hired. Because they would have to make multiple trips, the buses would be stationed outside the hotels at 4.30 am every morning. The group leaders would ensure that all their actors reached the location in time for makeup and breakfast. Three transport managers were assigned to ensure the smooth transfer of the actors to location and back. A separate transport manager was allotted to the crew.

Then there were the 'food discussions'! Many suggested that breakfast, lunch and dinner for the junior artistes should be ordered from the local suppliers and caterers. It would save the production team some major hassle. But Mishra wasn't sure if this was a great idea. For one, no one single caterer would be able to meet the entire requirement. Which meant the food might arrive at different times. But there could be only one lunch break or else the schedule would go for a toss. They could not afford to over shoot by even a day, because that would mean a significant rise in the budget. They were spending over Rupees 60 lakh per day, for the crowds' sequences. Another concern was that the food might differ in quality. Mishra decided to go with collective opinion, but instinctively felt it wasn't the best solution. So he took caterers and their equipment from Mumbai, 'just in case'.

On the very first day, some people complained the dinner had gone bad. Mishra personally apologised to as many of them as he could. From the next day, his caterers from Mumbai were put into action. Thereon, breakfast, lunch and dinner were all cooked on location. Scores of cooks and assistants would work like parts of one huge automated machine. Fifteen women sat rolling *rotis* after *rotis*. The mounds of cooked rice would touch the ceiling of the tent kitchen! It was jokingly called the 'Himalaya'. The serving system was simple and fool proof. Meal coupons were distributed to the crowd, so there would be no confusion or misuse. As soon as lunch break was called, fifteen counters were thrown open with six people on each counter, working at lightning speed. Within an hour, 8,000 people would be served, fed and back in frame!

The kitchen area and eating area were set up under a huge tent. Those who were not in frame could come in for tea and water or just to rest. A tent was also set up for the costumes and makeup department. Since the situation was a rally sequence, the tents blended in with the entire set and seemed part of the action in long shots where it appeared. These tents had to be set up at various locations, which meant one would have to open up the tents after shoot was over, carry it to the next location and set it up there. This would eat into the shooting time. The production team hired two sets of tents. While the shoot happened at one location, another tent was being set up at the next day's location. Once the shoot on the first location was over, the tent would be opened up and set up at the third location while shoot was still happening at the second location. So when the actors and technicians arrived on location at 6 am every day, everything was ready for them. Basic presence of mind saved the production team a lot of time and anxiety.

Another task was to arrange for the many, many cars required in the film. In rally sequences there were a minimum of 25 cars in the shots. Each major character in the film had a cavalcade of his own. Hundreds of cars were hired. A Mercedes and an Outlander were bought! Mishra shrugs. "What about continuity if a hired or a borrowed Mercedes wasn't available halfway through the schedule? It would have cost much more to shoot again!" The man is all about common sense.

The mounds of cooked rice would touch the ceiling of the tent kitchen!

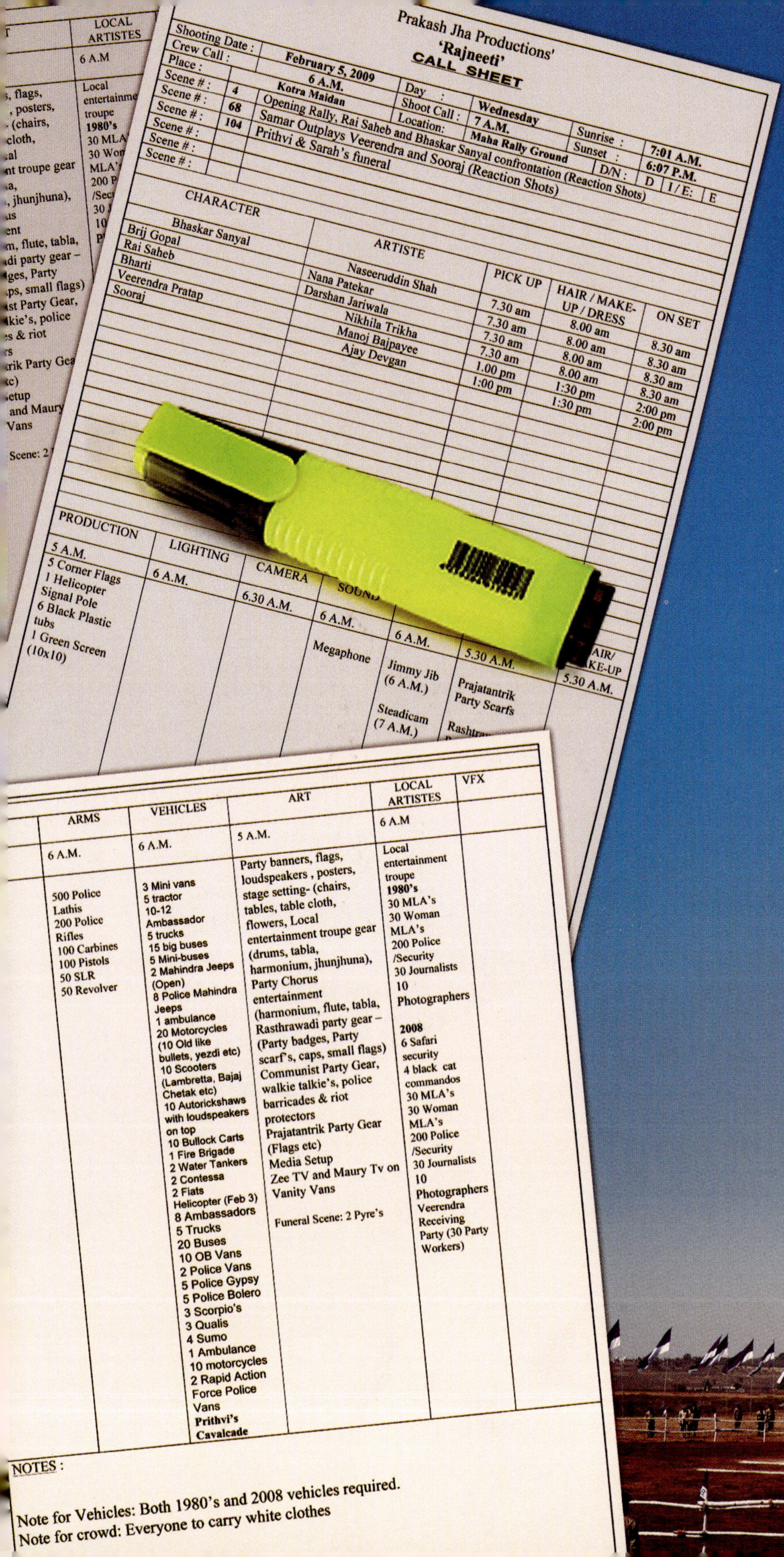

Prakash Jha Productions'
'Rajneeti'
CALL SHEET

Shooting Date : February 5, 2009 | Day : Wednesday | Sunrise : 7:01 A.M.
Crew Call : 6 A.M. | Shoot Call : 7 A.M. | Sunset : 6:07 P.M.
Place : Kotra Maidan | Location: Maha Rally Ground | D/N : D | I/E : E

Scene # : 4 Opening Rally, Rai Saheb and Bhaskar Sanyal confrontation (Reaction Shots)
Scene # : 68 Samar Outplays Veerendra and Sooraj (Reaction Shots)
Scene # : 104 Prithvi & Sarah's funeral

CHARACTER	ARTISTE	PICK UP	HAIR / MAKE-UP / DRESS	ON SET
Bhaskar Sanyal	Naseeruddin Shah	7.30 am	8.00 am	8.30 am
Brij Gopal	Nana Patekar	7.30 am	8.00 am	8.30 am
Rai Saheb	Darshan Jariwala	7.30 am	8.00 am	8.30 am
Bharti	Nikhila Trikha	7.30 am	8.00 am	8.30 am
Veerendra Pratap	Manoj Bajpayee	1.00 pm	1:30 pm	2:00 pm
Sooraj	Ajay Devgan	1:00 pm	1:30 pm	2:00 pm

PRODUCTION 5 A.M.: 5 Corner Flags, 1 Helicopter, Signal Pole, 6 Black Plastic tubs, 1 Green Screen (10x10)
SOUND 6 A.M.: Megaphone
6 A.M.: Jimmy Jib (6 A.M.), Steadicam (7 A.M.)
5.30 A.M.: Prajatantrik Party Scarfs

ARMS	VEHICLES	ART	LOCAL ARTISTES	VFX
6 A.M.	6 A.M.	5 A.M.	6 A.M	
500 Police Lathis, 200 Police Rifles, 100 Carbines, 100 Pistols, 50 SLR, 50 Revolver	3 Mini vans, 5 tractor, 10-12 Ambassador, 5 trucks, 15 big buses, 5 Mini-buses, 2 Mahindra Jeeps (Open), 8 Police Mahindra Jeeps, 1 ambulance, 20 Motorcycles (10 Old like bullets, yezdi etc), 10 Scooters (Lambretta, Bajaj Chetak etc), 10 Autorickshaws with loudspeakers on top, 10 Bullock Carts, 1 Fire Brigade, 2 Water Tankers, 2 Contessa, 2 Fiats, Helicopter (Feb 3), 8 Ambassadors, 5 Trucks, 20 Buses, 10 OB Vans, 2 Police Vans, 5 Police Gypsy, 5 Police Bolero, 3 Scorpio's, 3 Qualis, 4 Sumo, 1 Ambulance, 10 motorcycles, 2 Rapid Action Force Police Vans, Prithvi's Cavalcade	Party banners, flags, loudspeakers, posters, stage setting- (chairs, tables, table cloth, flowers, Local entertainment troupe gear (drums, tabla, harmonium, jhunjhuna), Party Chorus entertainment (harmonium, flute, tabla, Rasthrawadi party gear – (Party badges, Party scarf's, caps, small flags) Communist Party Gear, walkie talkie's, police barricades & riot protectors, Prajatantrik Party Gear (Flags etc), Media Setup, Zee TV and Maury Tv on Vanity Vans. Funeral Scene: 2 Pyre's	Local entertainment troupe. 1980's: 30 MLA's, 30 Woman MLA's, 200 Police /Security, 30 Journalists, 10 Photographers. 2008: 6 Safari security, 4 black cat commandos, 30 MLA's, 30 Woman MLA's, 200 Police /Security, 30 Journalists, 10 Photographers, Veerendra Receiving Party (30 Party Workers)	

NOTES :
Note for Vehicles: Both 1980's and 2008 vehicles required.
Note for crowd: Everyone to carry white clothes

But just hiring and buying did not end the car problems. Where on earth, or rather, where in Bhopal were they going to park so many cars? There were at least 25 cars required in the shots. Then there were 35 buses for the crowds, four generators vans, eight makeup vans, two cars each for the stars and their staff, eight cars carrying equipment and lights, another 45 cars of the senior technicians and unit members and a few extra cars. Apart from the rally sequences where they had the whole *maidan*, they were mostly shooting in houses and bungalows. They could not block the roads or cause inconvenience. The parking of cars had to be planned.

The night before the shoot, production assistants would go on location and plan how the cars would be parked. The generator vans had to be parked the closest. The stars' cars were parked right after that so they weren't mobbed. Behind them the senior technicians' cars were parked and so on, according to 'priority'. Mishra's team would consult the assistant directors to make sure they parked out of frame.

An ambulance with a doctor and nurse was always present at the shoot. A fire brigade and a water tank were also kept on standby. Mobile toilets were hired so the crowd and crew would be comfortable. The production assistants were always seen running around barking instructions or rolling up their sleeves and getting on with it. About 50 walkie talkies were hired to make sure there was no miscommunication or wastage of time. The production team left nothing to chance. Every detail, no matter how minute, was discussed. All contingencies were taken into account. Their planning was so thorough that they handled crises like last minute location shifts, important properties reaching wrong locations and cars disappearing in the middle of the shoot with perfect ease, always managing to come out on top of things. Mishra attributes this meticulous planning to Jha's precise instructions. "Bhaiji is so clear and explains everything on such a basic level, that we know exactly what to do if something goes against the plan," he says. "For example, if some costumes are damaged, we can find replacements without dragging the costume assistants away from the sets. If the art director falls ill, we can put up the set."

Similar organization was displayed in managing the budget. K.L. Chhabra, general manager - productions, was in charge of keeping the books in order. Once the script was ready, he sat with Jha and chalked out the major areas of expenditure. Since it was going to be a massive venture, it would be very easy to slip up and send the film spiraling out of budget. Chhabra and his team had to keep a very tight leash on the film and yet make allowances for creativity. As is the case with everything Jha does, the accounts were handled in a systematic manner. An office had already been set up in Bhopal and a team of accountants worked there. The one golden rule was to tally the accounts daily. It was never missed or postponed. Every night, after the shoot was over, the accountants would tally the accounts. And every morning, while the first shot was being set up, Chhabra would hand over to Jha, the tallied accounts of the previous day with details of all expenditure. "This way I could easily keep track of how much money was being spent," says Jha. "If we would have looked at the accounts two months later, I wouldn't be able to recall how many cars had been used on a particular day or how many junior artistes had been given the day off on another."

The payments were also made in the most organised and transparent manner. After the shoot, the team leaders and production assistants together took attendance of the crowd. The wages were handed out after taking the signatures of each of those 8,000 people. The suppliers' bills, the hotel bills, the transport bills and so on were all cleared on a weekly basis. They did not want to wait till the end of the schedule to make payments. "We wanted to make sure that every one was paid on time, and paid well," says Chhabra. "We wanted them to want to work with us again."

As a result of this attitude and some very meticulous planning, the budget comfortably stood at the estimated Rupees 53 crore, possibly over shooting by just a few lakh rupees, which too had been worked in under unforeseen expenses. And the day the shoot was over, the entire team was ready to leave Bhopal, all their dues cleared. Now the production team looks back and marvels at how easy it was for things to have gone out of control. "While working, it seemed like just another film," says Mishra. "Bigger, no doubt, but another film. It is only now, when we see the film, do we realise what we have achieved." But Jha knew before they did, that they could. "I have the best production team in the industry," smiles the director. "And when they do painstaking detailing, it is difficult for things to go wrong."

The basic needs of a junior artiste are the same as a star!

Every single person who worked on Raajneeti is amazed even today, at how smoothly things functioned while making the film. How everything just fell into place and clicked. There were no serious glitches, no schedule upheavals, no major interdepartmental miscommunications, no mishaps, nothing. Everyone knew their job and everyone did it, without being pushed or goaded. And for a film of this magnitude to not overshoot its budget or schedule is something of a miracle. The crew was a set of very busy but happy people. No one worried about how things would get done. Because they were getting done. Katrina exclaims, "The shooting went by with so much ease, there was no untoward event or anything like that. It was almost like, hey, where's the drama?"

Perhaps it was the confidence of a director who believed in the story he was telling, that spread the faith amongst his team members, all 500 of them. Perhaps there was something in the universal emotions that the film was expressing, that formed a sense of solidarity, a feeling of ownership in the crew members. It brought them together like a unified force. It wasn't just about making a good film for their own sakes, their own careers. Telling that story became important.

And so, on many occasions, the many departments merged. Besides their own defined jobs, all the members of the team stretched themselves to contribute as much as they could. They did jobs they didn't have to, stayed on set later than they had to. The drivers became dressmen in their free time, the spot boys became crowd controllers. One assistant director became an art assistant. Another assistant director in charge of cars was suddenly assigned the additional job of continuity. The actors' makeup assistants volunteered to take care of continuity for the respective actors themselves. Besides scriptwriting, writer Rajabali also contributed to the subtitling of the film, scripted the trailer, wrote some of the publicity material and even did a couple of edits! Director Jha was often seen helping with the props or picking up a hammer and driving nails into wooden planks. His get-on-with-it attitude was infectious on the set. "Beyond a point, it was not 'your work' or 'my work', it was work," says Mishra.

This camaraderie extended to the actors as well. They would support and encourage each others' performances. Almost each of them had to deliver speeches in front of a huge crowd and they were all anxious. They cheered each other on and shared the anxieties of the complex performances required of them. The day Katrina was to deliver her long speech in front of over ten thousand people, Arjun landed up on set even though he was not required, just to cheer her on. Before the shoot, Ranbir and Arjun spent an entire day chatting so there would be some chemistry when they played brothers. In a couple of days, they were backslapping buddies. Nana would cook new delicacies every day for the whole team. He had requested the hotel chef for permission to cook in his kitchen. To put it mildly, the chef was overjoyed. It was as if every one was aware that something special was being done, something special was being made in the sleepy town of Bhopal. The actors were pampered on set and yet there were no tantrums. Everyone arrived on time and the shots were canned every day with easy speed. Each of the actors talk about how Jha was so clear about the emotionality he wanted and yet they did not feel overworked or deprived of creative freedom.

The teamwork and dedication, the proactive enthusiasm which every one displayed, translated into a rivetting, heart wrenching tale of love, betrayal and moral downfall. There were those who loved it, there were those who didn't. But no one was able to ignore it. Raajneeti took the Indian film industry by storm. A film on politics. Inspired by the *Mahabharata*. A serious subject, no comic relief. Multiple starcast. The leading lady and leading man not getting together. And no songs! At best, it was going to be a film for the 'intellectual types'. No one, but no one was prepared for its astounding box office performance. Within a week of release it recovered almost the entire budget and went on to do a business of over 90 crores in the following weeks. As this book goes into press, Raajneeti stands as the fifth highest grosser in the history of the Indian film industry.

This success is supremely encouraging. But the real high is in the individual reactions to the story and the film that Jha receives. His inbox is still flooded with heartfelt appreciation and constructive criticism. Which means, that people sat up and took notice. He smilingly reveals that the people of Bhopal took band *bajaas* to the cinema halls when the film released. Director Mahesh Bhatt sent him a message after seeing the film saying - 'you have brought India back to India.' It is things like these that make him feel truly appreciated, blessed. "I am still not able to fathom the reaction of the people," says the director. "But it encourages my intentions. Raajneeti is only the first step to discovering the democracy of our country."

The director of one of the biggest films made in India says he was never ever worried or anxious. He never wondered for a moment how he was going to pull it off. As Ranbir says, he's a 'passion man'. He's just so passionate that all he worries about is what is going in and coming out of his film. "All the energy must come from within the frame," he says gravely. That's where the drama is!

> **Raajneeti stands as the fifth highest grosser in the history of the Indian film industry.**

CHAPTER 13

WHERE'S THE DRAMA?

Your right is only to the work. As for the fruits of the work, you have no right over them.

- The Bhagwad Gita

RAAJNEETI

THE SCRIPT

ANJUM RAJABALI
PRAKASH JHA

EXT. GHAT, BENARAS - DAY

It is the Ghat at Benaras. It is still early. The sun is not yet up on the horizon, but a crowd of beggars has been gathering since midnight. Several men have been unloading cartons of food, blankets and articles as the beggars patiently queue up on the side. Near the bottom of the steps, Brij Gopal watches the great river slowly wake up.

A Mercedes arrives at the top of the Ghat. Brij Gopal turns to watch as Bharati, who looks majestic in her early fifties, steps out. The years have weathered Brij Gopal's face too. He watches his sister distributing alms to the poor. One of the new ones is curious.

BEGGAR: *(curious)*
Is there a festival today?

BEGGAR: *(curious)*
कौन परब–त्यौहार का दिन है आज भाई ?...

OLD BEGGAR- GYAN SINGH:
I don't think so. And yet, every year for 27 years - she comes on this day to feed the poor.

OLD BEGGAR- GYAN SINGH:
सास्तरों का तो पता नहीं पर सत्ताइसों बरस हो गया – बिला नागा आतीं हैं आज का रोज...

NARRATOR: *(V/O)*
How could Bharati possibly forget! Those were momentous times.

NARRATOR: *(V/O)*
भला भूल भी कैसे सकती थी भारती – वो दौर ही कुछ ऐसा था...

EXT. RALLY GROUND – DAY

A) Close shots of crowds getting down from buses, tractors and bullock carts.

B) Shot of a group singing the Party song.

SINGING GROUP:
Long Live Praja Party
Long Live Praja Party

SINGING GROUP:
प्रजा पार्टी प्रजा पार्टी ... जिन्दाबाद...
प्रजा पार्टी प्रजा पार्टी ... जिन्दाबाद...

C) Flags unfurling/Banners unfolding.

D) Closer candid shots (Tele).

Something strange happens as the ground fills up. Making their way through the thousands of Prajatantrik Party supporters, the red flag bearing people – young men and women, peasants and workers – of the Liberation Front, led by Bhaskar Sanyal, march towards the stage. Three to four hundred followers join them.

Fifty five year old Bhaskar Sanyal, his hair white but eyes shining with determination, the bright sun of the people's movement, calmly leads the fearless group.

The I.G. Police who has been on the stage so far, instructs his men to get to their positions when he notices the first few red flags appearing at the eastern side of the ground.

Suddenly a helicopter appears and the crowd responds.

NARRATOR: *(V/O)*
Her father Ramnath Rai was the state's Chief Minister for 14 years... but her generation's heady romance with leftism had turned Bharati into a rebel.
Together with her charismatic mentor - the idealistic Bhaskar Sanyal, she stormed her father's public rally.

NARRATOR: *(V/O)*
पिता रामनाथ राय चौदह वर्षों से प्रांत के मुख्यमंत्री रहे थे... लेकिन अपनी युवापीढ़ी के समाजवादी रोमांस ने भारती को बग़ावत के रास्ते पर डाल दिया था –
आदर्शवादी वामपंथी विचारधारा के करिश्माई लीडर भास्कर सन्याल से आकर्षित हो कर उसने अपने पिता के ख़िलाफ़ ही झंडा उठा लिया था...

Nervously the I.G. barks into the walkie-talkie.

We see the cops looking at the charging red brigade.

NARRATOR: *(V/O)*
Indian politics was going through historic churning but Ramnath Rai was blissfully complacent. Only his astute political advisor and Bharati's foster brother, Brij Gopal had sensed the turning winds.

NARRATOR: *(V/O)*
वैसे भी देश का राजनीतिक इतिहास एक नया मोड़ ले रहा था – रामनाथ राय भले ही अपनी सत्ता को लेकर निश्चिंत थे – लेकिन उनके राजनीतिक सलाहकार और भारती के मुँह बोले भइया, ब्रिज गोपाल तो हवा का रुख पहचान ही रहे थे –

As Rai Saheb gets off the jeep his eyes meet his daughter's. She looks calm as she stands next to Bhaskar Sanyal. He looks disgusted as he manages a wry smile. Bharati does not react. Climbing the steps of the stage.

BRIJ GOPAL:
Comrade Bhaskar will try to draw you into an argument. Do not fall into his trap.

BRIJ GOPAL:
Comrade भास्कर आपको बहस में खींचने का प्रयास करेगा – उसके जाल में फँसना मत...

RAI SAHEB: *(patronisingly)*
I've been a politician for 20 years, Brij Gopal. I'm not a fool.

RAI SAHEB: *(patronizingly)*
बीस साल से राजनीति कर रहा हूँ ब्रिज गोपाल – घास नहीं काट रहा...

While several of the party leaders on the stage jump to their leaders' defense, there is some laughter and murmur amongst the audience. Bhaskar Sanyal walks closer to the stage as the guards watch nervously.

BHASKAR SANYAL:
Mr. Rai, we have no intention of disturbing your rally. But, if you permit me, I'd like to ask you a few questions on behalf of the people.

BHASKAR SANYAL:
राय साब, आपकी महारैली को *Disturb* करने का हमारा कोई इरादा नहीं है... लेकिन, अगर आपकी इजाज़त हो तो जनता की तरफ़ से मैं कुछ सवाल आपसे पूछना चाहता हूँ –

RAI SAHEB'S SUPPORTERS:
Hey! Stop him. Stop him. Hey! Stop him. Stop him.

RAI SAHEB'S SUPPORTERS:
अरे! रोको उसको! रोको!

RAI SAHEB:
Let him come.

RAI SAHEB:
आने दो... आने दो – उसे –

Rai Saheb takes the bait and signals the security to let Bhaskar Sanyal come on to the stage and speak.

RAI SAHEB:
The public on whose behalf, he wants to raise questions already knows the answers to them. And those who have been enticed by his red flag should also be aware of Ramnath Rai's political sacrifices.

RAI SAHEB:
जिस जनता के नाम पर ये सवाल उठा रहे हैं उनका उत्तर जनता अच्छी तरह से जानती है – और जिन्होंने इनके बहकावे में आके लाल झण्डे उठा लिये हैं वो भी रामनाथ राय की राजनीतिक तपस्या से अच्छी तरह से वाकिफ़ हैं...

His ministers and MLAs charge at Bhaskar Sanyal who by now, is on the stage. They roar their slogans.

BHASKAR SANYAL:
The issue isn't about the colour of the flag, Mr. Rai. Poverty, hunger and unemployment do not discriminate on the basis of colour. These people are besieged by their own empty stomachs, Mr. Rai. Offer them two slices of bread... make a couple of sweet promises... and they will pick up a flag of any colour!

BHASKAR SANYAL:
सवाल झण्डे के रंग का नहीं है राय साहेब... क्योंकि ग़रीबी... भुखमरी... बेकारी ये सब रंग पूछ के वार नहीं करती... ये पेट की मारी जनता है राय साहब... एक रोटी का आसरा दे दीजिए – दो मीठे वादे कर दीजिए... किसी भी रंग का झण्डा उठा लेगी...

BHASKAR SANYAL:
What kind of poverty is this, friends, which, in spite of their schemes funded by millions, billions of rupees just refuses to go away!

BHASKAR SANYAL:
अरे ये कैसी ग़रीबी है भाइयों जो इनकी सैकड़ों योजनाओं करोड़ों–अरबों–खरबों रुपये फूँक देने के बाद भी जाने का नाम नहीं लेती...

Brij Gopal signals the I.G. to prepare for C.M.'s exit. The I.G. orders the helicopter to get ready.

BRIJ GOPAL:
Sir will leave now.

BRIJ GOPAL:
सा'ब निकलेंगे –

BHASKAR SANYAL:
So as of this moment, we absolve you of any worry about our poverty. Enough is enough.

BHASKAR SANYAL:
तो आज हम आपको हमारी ग़रीबी दूर करने की जिम्मेदारी से आज़ाद करते हैं – बस कीजिए, बस कीजिए, बहुत हो गया...

BRIJ GOPAL:
Come on, uncle.

BRIJ GOPAL:
आइये, आइये मामा जी –

People clap again. Prajatantrik followers begin sloganeering. Rai Saheb is literally being whisked away by Brij Gopal.

People roar with approval. As Brij Gopal leaves the stage, he instructs.

BRIJ GOPAL: *(instructs)*
Switch the mikes off.

BRIJ GOPAL: *(instructs)*
Mike बन्द करो –

BHASKAR SANYAL:
As soon as the ballot is cast, you throttle democracy.

BHASKAR SANYAL:
Vote पेटी में डलते ही लोकतंत्र का गला घोंट देते हैं आप लोग –

The mikes are switched off.

BHASKAR SANYAL:
Don't be under the illusion that....

BHASKAR SANYAL:
इस भुलावे में मत रहिए...

The sound goes dead.

INT. RAI SAHEB'S PALATIAL BUNGALOW - LATE AFTERNOON

In his majestic drawing hall, Rai Saheb has been boiling with rage. Bharati enters the hall and begins to go towards her room ignoring her father.

RAI SAHEB: *(furious)*
Have you no shame at all! Conspiring against your own father!

RAI SAHEB: *(furious)*
शर्म नहीं आई आपको अपने ही बाप के ख़िलाफ़ इतना बड़ा षड़यंत्र करते...

Bharati turns to face him. Rai Saheb lashes at her.

RAI SAHEB:
Do you know that your revered leader is not worth even a penny.

RAI SAHEB:
आप जिसे भगवान मान बैठी हैं – वो दो टके का आदमी भी नहीं है...

BHARATI:
What I know is that for you people's worth is measured only with money.

BHARATI:
जानती हूँ बाबूजी... आपकी नज़र में तो बस टके वालों की ही कीमत होती है...

RAI SAHEB: *(screams)*
Shut up!

RAI SAHEB: *(screams)*
Shut up!

It is at this moment that the telephone rings and Rai Saheb picks it. The caller obviously asks for Bharati .

RAI SAHEB:
What? There is no Comrade Bharati here. Don't ever call here again!

RAI SAHEB:
क्या है?... यहाँ कोई *comrade* भारती नहीं है – दुबारा इस *number* पे *phone* मत करना।

He slams the phone down.

INT. BHASKAR SANYAL HOUSE - EVENING

Bharati quickly crosses the outer courtyard and enters the house. It's a simple house with a tiled roof. She crosses the outer room into the inner courtyard and is surprised to spot Bhaskar Sanyal cooking on the stove in a makeshift kitchen in the verandah.

BHARATI:
Sir! What are you doing?

BHARATI:
Sir! क्या कर रहे हैं आप ?

Bhaskar Sanyal seems to have just had a bath. His white hair still wet and body bare with a white 'lungi' *wrapped around his waist, he looks like an expert cook. He too, looks surprised to see her.*

BHASKAR SANYAL:
Cooking *khichdi*.... Will you have some?

BHASKAR SANYAL:
खिचड़ी पका रहा हूँ... खाओगी ?

She crosses the courtyard and picks up the spatula.

BHARATI:
Here, allow me..

BHARATI:
दीजिए मैं बना देती हूँ...

Bhaskar Sanyal tries to stop her –

BHASKAR SANYAL:
If you cook this...

BHASKAR SANYAL:
अरे तुम पकाने लगीं तो बन चुकी खिचड़ी...

BHARATI:
Oh, come on... just let me....

BHARATI:
अरे रुकिए ना... सुनिए तो सही –

There is a playful tussle between the two of them as Bhaskar Sanyal tries to take the spatula back from her. She laughs and pushes him away. Her youthful vivaciousness is infectious.

Suddenly the first showers come through the inner courtyard which is open to the sky and Bhaskar Sanyal becomes conscious. He turns around to put on a short-sleeved kurta hanging on the wall.

BHASKAR SANYAL:
It's going to rain. Let me drop you home.

BHASKAR SANYAL:
बारिश होने वाली है – मैं... तुम्हें छोड़ आता हूँ –

He turns back to see Bharati standing in the middle of the courtyard, spatula in hand, blissfully enjoying the rain.

BHASKAR SANYAL:
Are you crazy?

BHASKAR SANYAL:
अरे, अरे, पागल हो गई हो क्या – ?!

THE UMBRELLA THAT GOT WET

Given Jha's close attention to detail and authenticity, the art department had quite an experience sourcing properties. For the scene in Bhaskar Sanyal's house, they needed an umbrella that looked really old. After scouring scores of shops, they finally bought a very used one off a cobbler. The old, broken thing would open and shut with a lot of coaxing and would refuse to dry once it got wet! So before every retake, an assistant would have to go at the umbrella with a hair dryer! ■

BHARATI:
It's the first rain, Sir. I love the rain. Why don't you join me?

BHARATI:
पहली बारिश है *Sir!... I love the rain* – आप भी आइए ना !

Bhaskar Sanyal looks for the umbrella. She has turned her face to the sky and is savouring the drops. She drops the spatula and begins to twirl. Bhaskar Sanyal looks mesmerised as he steps in with the umbrella. Just as he opens it and reaches out to hold her extended arm, a strong wind blows his umbrella away. Bharati laughingly pulls him into the middle of the courtyard. She is in no mood to listen to him.

BHASKAR SANYAL:
Don't be childish... you'll catch a cold. Come on now...

BHASKAR SANYAL:
चलो–चलो, बेवकूफी मत करो – सर्दी लग जाएगी – अरे चलो अंदर चलो... चलो –

BHASKAR SANYAL: *(contd)*
Listen..listen..to me..you are crazy! You will catch a cold...

BHASKAR SANYAL (contd):
सुनो – अरे, अरे... सुनो... अरे, पागल हो गई हो क्या... सर्दी लग जाएगी –

She looks at him. Into his eyes....

BHARATI:
Nothing will happen to me....

BHARATI:
कुछ नहीं होगा हमें –

He seems to understand what she means and continues to look at her, his face shielding her eyes from the rain. Calmly she holds his head and kisses him. He trembles for a moment but is unable to withdraw. He is completely caught up in the moment. He takes her in his embrace. The storm begins to build.

INT. BHASKAR SANYALS BEDROOM - DAWN

The sun softly breaks through the dawn and in through the split of the window. After all the turbulence of the rainy stormy night, it is very quiet. Bharati sleeps blissfully in Bhaskar Sanyal's bed. He sits fully dressed, looking at Bharati. His eyes hold a defeated sadness as he looks at Bharati's calm face. He reaches out to touch her but decides against it. He slips a letter under Bharati's pillow.

BHASKAR SANYAL: *(V/O)*
Bharati...
I take full responsibility for what happened. You devoted yourself completely to me. But, I turned out to be weak... and ended up betraying your trust. What is done is done. But, I will never be free of this guilt. I'm going... leaving everything... and everyone....

BHASKAR SANYAL: *(V/O)*
भारती,
जो कुछ भी हुआ उसकी पूरी जिम्मेवारी मैं लेता हूँ। तुमने तो निश्च्छल आस्था से अपने आप तक को मुझे समर्पित कर दिया... मैं ही कमजोर निकला और उस विश्वास को रख नहीं पाया – दोष तो हो गया है भारती और कभी अपने आपको मैं दोषमुक्त नहीं कर पाउँगा – मैं जा रहा हूँ – सबको और सब कुछ छोड़ कर...

EXT. PATIO – DAWN

Bharati is sitting outside and reading Bhaskar Sanyal's letter and crying profusely.

BHASKAR SANYAL: *(V/O)*
I have obviously failed. My penance awaits me... Bhaskar.

BHASKAR SANYAL: *(V/O)*
शायद, तपस्या अधूरी रह गई थी – उसे पूरा करूँगा... – भास्कर।

INT. BRIJ GOPALS BENARAS HOUSE - NIGHT

Another stormy night. In his haveli, next to the Ganges in Benaras Brij Gopal waits anxiously.

Bharati shrieks with pain and the maid rushes, inside. The crying of a child rents the air. Through the flapping shutter Brij Gopal can see the midwife holding the baby.

He appears at the shutter. The midwife looks at Bharati who is barely conscious.

BRIJ GOPAL:
Get it here. Hurry up.

BRIJ GOPAL:
ले आओ जल्दी –

Brij Gopal takes the baby from the midwife and wraps him in his silk scarf.

BHARATI:
Where's my baby?

BHARATI:
कहाँ है... कहाँ है वो?

MIDWIFE:
Mr. Brij Gopal took him away.

MIDWIFE:
ब्रिज बाउजी ले गए –

BHARATI: *(crying)*
I just wanted to see him once....

BHARATI: *(crying)*
देख तो लेने देते एक बार...

Bharati is inconsolable.

EXT. RIVER BANK - DAWN

It is still dark. Some where down the stream next to the dhobi ghat the sky is just turning red when we see a boat hitting the ground. Brij Gopal places the baby on the boat. Slowly the sun begins to rise.

EXT. RIVER BANK - DUSK

Bharati sits alone at the Ghat as the sun sets. Brij Gopal watches her from a distance.

NARRATOR: *(V/O)*
Brij Gopal convinced the grieving Bharati into a marriage with Chandra Pratap.

NARRATOR: *(V/O)*
ब्रिज गोपाल ने बड़े जतन से समझा बुझा कर भारती को प्रांत में तेजी से उभर रही –

EXT. A RALLY – DAY

Chandra Pratap on the stage addressing a crowd.

NARRATOR: *(V/O)*
Of course it helped that he was the younger brother of Bhanu Pratap, the aggressive leader of the fast-rising Rashtrawadi Party.

NARRATOR: *(V/O)*
राष्ट्रवादी पार्टी के आक्रामक नेता भानु प्रताप के छोटे भाई चंद्र प्रताप से विवाह के लिए राजी कर लिया –

INT. RAI SAHEB'S HOUSE - NIGHT

It's a grand baraat *that comes to Rai Saheb's house. We see a beautifully bedecked Bharati being brought to the wedding platform.*

NARRATOR: *(V/O)*
No one realised that Brij Gopal had killed three birds with one stone. Besides securing Bharati's future, he also got Ramnath Rai's doddering party a strong alliance. And of course, Bhanu Pratap's Rashtrawadi Party harvested a windfall of much-needed election funds.

NARRATOR: *(V/O)*
किसी को अंदाज़ भी नहीं हुआ कि एक ही तीर से वो तीन शिकार कर रहे थे – उन्होंने भारती का भविष्य तो सुरक्षित किया ही साथ ही साथ एक तरफ रामनाथ राय की डूबती राजनीतिक नइया को मज़बूत गठबंधन का सहारा दिलाया – वहीं भानु प्रताप के राष्ट्रवादी को आने वाले चुनाव की *Funding* के लिए मोटा आसामी भी –

The open car of Chandra Pratap at the baraat *was being driven by Ramcharittar who was now his personal driver.*

EXT. GANGES RIVER BANK - DAWN (END OF FLASHBACK)

Bharati reaches Brij Gopal. Like always, he holds the silver tray with flowers and a lamp. He has been with her through the best and the worst.

She picks up the lamp with the flowers and the sun rises just as she prays with the lamp. She lets it float on the water. Tears well up in her eyes.

BRIJ GOPAL:
Wherever he is, he must be okay. Just send him your blessings.

BRIJ GOPAL:
ठीक ही होगा जहाँ भी है... बस आशिर्वाद दे दो उसको –

BHARATI:
O holy mother Ganga, please look after my son, wherever he may be.

BHARATI:
माँ गंगे... रक्षा करना मेरे बेटे की – जहाँ भी हो –

EXT. AZAD NAGAR KABBADI GROUNDS - DAY

A basti outside the Capital. The kabaddi *match is in progress. The home team cheers excitedly.*

SOORAJ:
Kabaddi…kabaddi…kabaddi…

SOORAJ:
कबड्डी..................... कबड्डी.........................कबड्डी..

CROWD CHANTING:
Sooraj! Sooraj!

CROWD CHANTING:
सूरज... सूरज...

The one survivor of the home team stands in the centre, ready to begin his charge. He bends down to pick up some mud and smears his forehead. The entire team of opponents are angling to catch him. People wait with bated breath as Sooraj teases his opponents but they keep backing out to get him deeper in. He knows he will have to act fast and he lunges, attacking the players. And suddenly as if they were waiting for this moment, they quickly circle him. Sooraj jumps the ring, touching a couple more of them but is caught as soon as he lands and the next moment the entire team is on him. Sooraj keeps his breath and begins to inch towards the line. Despite six of the opposite team holding on to him he moves inch by inch for the final touch. The whole arena explodes. Single handedly Sooraj has won the day for Azad Nagar.

EXT. AZAD NAGAR STREETS – DAY

While the centre of Azad Nagar is rocking with celebrations of the game's victory, Ramcharittar negotiates the narrow lanes in his master's Mercedes and stops it at his house. He is in a rush as he tells his wife…

RAMCHARITTAR:
Where are you going?

RAMCHARITTAR:
कहाँ जा रही हो ?

RAMCHARITTAR'S WIFE:
Sooraj is playing a *kabaddi* match.

RAMCHARITTAR'S WIFE:
अरे, कबड्डी चल रहा है सूरज का...

RAMCHARITTAR:
First give me something to eat. I have to go to the airport.

RAMCHARITTAR:
पहले दुई रोटी लगा दो सूरज की माँ... *एयरपोर्ट* जाना है –

She hands him a jug of water to wash his hands.

RAMCHARITTAR'S WIFE:
Who's coming?

RAMCHARITTAR'S WIFE:
अब कौन आ रहा है ?

RAMCHARITTAR: *(smiles)*
The boss' younger son, Samar.

RAMCHARITTAR: *(smiles)*
हमरे छोटे साहब समर...

RAMCHARITTAR'S WIFE:
Is it?

RAMCHARITTAR'S WIFE:
अच्छा –

RAMCHARITTAR:
He is coming from the US, for the big boss' birthday.

RAMCHARITTAR:
अमरिका से आ रहे हैं बड़े साहब के जनम दिन पर...

EXT. AZAD NAGAR GROUNDS - DAY

SOORAJ:
Kabaddi...kabaddi...kabaddi...

SOORAJ:
कबड्डी.................... कबड्डी........................कबड्डी.......

Sooraj wins the game for his team. Dalit M.L.A. embraces Sooraj and leads him to the pedestal.

DALIT M.L.A.- BALDEO PRAJAPATI:
Sooraj is like the sun! The new beacon of hope for dalits and the lower castes. We need bright and strong young leaders like him, who will take us forward.

DALIT M.L.A.- BALDEO PRAJAPATI:
सूरज सिर्फ नाम का ही सूरज नहीं – पिछड़े और दलित समाज का ऊगता सूरज है – आज हमको जरूरत है ऐसे ही मजबूत नौजवान लीडरों की – जो हमें विजयी बना सकें...

The youngsters begin to shout.

CROWD CHEERING:
Victory to Sooraj!

CROWD CHEERING:
सूरज भैया... जिन्दाबाद!

EXT. AZAD NAGAR STREETS - DAY

Sooraj is led all the way to his house in a procession, hoisted on the shoulders of his teammates. He jumps off their shoulders as he sees the Mercedes. Finding the car keys in the ignition, he jumps in, starts the car and zooms off. He's drives like a maniac in the narrow streets of Azad Nagar, his friends screaming and running behind.

EXT. RAMCHARITTAR'S HOUSE - DAY

Ramcharittar comes out of the house to find the car missing.

RAMCHARITTAR:
Huh? Where's the car?

RAMCHARITTAR:
अरे...गाड़ी कहाँ गया... अँ, अरे...

Just then Sooraj brings the car back, his friends and scores of children running behind it. Ramcharittar is livid as Sooraj gets out of the car.

RAMCHARITTAR:
Hey! Get away! Move! Have you lost it or what? What if something happened to the car?

RAMCHARITTAR:
अरे, हट, हट, हट, हट – पागल हो गया है का तू – कुछ हो गया गाड़ी को तो का जवाब देंगे हम–

One of Sooraj's constant companions Kisna boasts.

KISNA:
He's our racing champion... faster than the wind!

KISHNA:
अरे *racing champion* हैं अपने सूरज भइया – हवा भी ना छू सके गाड़ी को...

RAMCHARITTAR:
Champion, my foot! The car's a mess! Clean it now! It's time for the flight. Samar is returning from the US today.

RAMCHARITTAR:
अरे खाक *चैम्पियन* – सब कचरा लगा दिया गाड़ी पर – अब साफ कर – अरे, *फ्लाइट* का *टाइम* हो गया, समर बाबू *अमरीका* से आ रहे हैं...

Sooraj has always been defiant.

SOORAJ:
I don't wash rich people's cars.

SOORAJ:
हम नहीं धोते अमीरों की गाड़ी –

RAMCHARITTAR:
They are our masters, son. Our livelihood depends on them.

RAMCHARITTAR:
अरे बेटा मालिक हैं हमारे – रोटी चलती है हमारी उनसे –

SOORAJ:
I am my own master, father. And the truth is, their livelihood depends on us.

SOORAJ:
हमारे मालिक हम खुद हैं बापू – रोटी हमारी नहीं... उनकी चलती है हमसे –

RAMCHARITTAR:
It's impossible to argue with you!

RAMCHARITTAR:
तुमसे तो मुँह लगाना ही पागलपन है –

His wife intervenes as she comes out with a bucket of water and a duster.

RAMCHARITTAR'S WIFE:
Stop arguing with my son, will you? I'll clean it.

RAMCHARITTAR'S WIFE:
अरे अब बस भी कीजिए... जाने का का बोल दिया हमारे मुन्ना को... हम कर देते हैं, हटिए...

SOORAJ:
Give it to me, mother.

SOORAJ:
ला, माँ।

Sooraj takes the bucket from his mother and tossing the duster to Kisna. He swings the bucket and throws the water on the car with a violent force, the splash covers everyone around.

INT./EXT. MERCEDES - DAY

The black Mercedes is speeding on the highway. Samar is sitting in the passenger seat next to Ramcharittar. He pulls out a watch from his pocket.

SAMAR:
This is for you. It's time you got a new watch.

SAMAR:
ये तुम्हारे लिए काका, आपकी घड़ी बहुत पुरानी हो गई है ना –

Ramcharittar is touched.

RAMCHARITTAR:
You never forget, young master.

RAMCHARITTAR:
कभी नहीं भूलते तुम छोटे बाबू...

SAMAR: *(smiles)*
Just because I live far away, how can I forget you people!

SAMAR: *(smiles)*
अब इतनी दूर चले गये हैं, हमें सबकी याद तो आती रहती है –

RAMCHARITTAR:
We miss you, too. It's wonderful that you've come in time for the Diwali festival.

RAMCHARITTAR:
हमको भी तुम बहुत याद आते हो... अच्छा आये हो इस बार – कुछ ही दिनों में त्यौहार है...

SAMAR:
Nothing like that. I'm here only for Uncle Bhanu's birthday. My thesis is due next week.

SAMAR:
अरे काका, नहीं – मैं तो बस ताया जी के *birthday* पर आया हूँ – और अगले हफ्ते *papers* भी जमा करने हैं –

RAMCHARITTAR:
This year too... you won't be here for Diwali.

RAMCHARITTAR:
तो फिर इस साल भी त्यौहार पर नहीं रहोगे तुम –

Samar is distracted by the constant honking of a car behind them. He looks to find a red sports car trying to take over the other cars and causing a commotion. Ramcharittar too has been viewing in the mirror.

SAMAR:
Who's that driving like a maniac?

SAMAR:
ये कौन पागलों के जैसे चला रहा है गाड़ी...

RAMCHARITTAR:
Appears to be Indu....

RAMCHARITTAR:
लगता है इन्दु बिटिया है।

Before Samar can react the sports car overtakes the Mercedes and blocks the path with a screech. Indu jumps out of the car and screams at Ramcharittar.

INDU:
Couldn't you have waited for me?

INDU:
रुक नहीं सकते थे एक *minute* हमारे लिए...

Ramcharittar looks bewildered. Samar has stepped out of the car and reasons with her.

SAMAR:
And how was I to know that you were...

SAMAR:
मगर हमें कैसे पता चलता कि तुम...

Indu does not let him complete the sentence. She takes Samar in her arms and kisses him on the cheek.

INDU:
You should know! Understood?

INDU:
पता रहना चाहिए... समझे...

Samar smiles at this incorrigible girl. He tries to pull himself away but she won't let him.

INDU:
D'you know... I was driving at 200 kmph to reach you!

INDU:
पता है – दो सौ की *speed* से आ रही हूँ मैं –

SAMAR:
Who on earth gave you a license?

SAMAR:
तुम्हें *license* किसने दिया है –

INDU:
License to... drive or... to kiss you?

INDU:
किसका ? गाड़ी चलाने का या तुम्हें *kiss* करने का –

She looks at him mischievously. Samar is aware of the location. They are being stared at... But he also knows this girl couldn't care two bits...

SAMAR:
You're insane! You're mad.

SAMAR:
पागल हो तुम... *You're mad.*

INDU:
So I am. Mad about you!

INDU:
वो तो हूँ – *Mad about you.*

She hugs him again. He responds warmly and yet, is a bit reserved.

INDU:
I missed you.

INDU:
I missed you.

INT. SAMAR'S HOUSE - DAY

Indu's car with Samar in it, followed by the Mercedes enter the Bungalow.

Bharati comes out to hug her son. Indu has already done the customary hug.

BHARATI:
There you are!

BHARATI:
आ गए बेटा ! अरे...

INDU:
Hello aunty....

INDU:
नमस्ते *Aunti-*

BHARATI:
Hello...

BHARATI:
खुश रहो बेटा –

INDU:
Here's your parcel - safe and sound.

INDU:
Parcel सही सलामत *deliver* कर रही हूँ...

She gives Bharati a peck and runs back into her car.

INDU:
I'm off to the salon. See you in the evening at Uncle Bhanu's party.

INDU:
मुझे *parlour* जाना है... शाम को मिलते हैं, ताया जी के *birthday* पर –

She zooms off.

BHARATI:
This girl is a tornado!

BHARATI:
तूफ़ान है ये लड़की !

EXT/INT BHANU PRATAP'S BUNGALOW - DAY

The lawns outside the majestic house of the leader of the biggest political party – the Rashtrawadi Party, are being decorated for the grand event of the evening. Several cars are coming in and Babulal, a secretary to the leader is seen receiving the political guests. Hundreds of bouquets of flowers are lined up on the verandah. Inside, the large hall is full with several party M.L.A.'s and functionaries huddled in groups. Babulal brings in the new arrivals to Chandra Pratap who stands at the bottom of the stairs waiting for his elder brother and Party President Bhanu Pratap to come down. He has been talking to Bharati.

NARRATOR: *(V/O)*
In the last 30 years Bhanu and Chandra Pratap's Rashtrawadi Party had captured power thrice in the state. Bhanu Pratap's public charisma and Chandra Pratap's astute tactical skills had served them well indeed.

NARRATOR: *(V/O)*
तीस वर्षों में भानु प्रताप और चन्द्र प्रताप की राष्ट्रवादी पार्टी ने तीन बार प्रांत की गद्दी पर कब्ज़ा किया – बड़े भाई का करिश्मा और छोटे का राजनीतिक *management* ख़ूब तरक्की की –

NARRATOR: *(V/O)*
When their party could not win the last election, they installed Ramnath Rai's party in the government by supporting it from outside. Now when they asked him to, Ramnath Rai was reluctant to resign. Bhanu Pratap's son Virendra knew exactly how to handle such problems.

NARRATOR: *(V/O)*
पिछले चुनाव में जब बहुमत नहीं मिला तो बुढ़ऊ रामनाथ राय को बाहर से समर्थन देकर *rubber-stamp* वाली सरकार बनवा दिया ... अब वो इस्तीफ़ा नहीं दे रहे थे... ऐसे मामलों को सुलझाने का तरीका भानु प्रताप के बेटे वीरेन्द्र को अच्छी तरह मालुम था –

By now others in the hall have noticed the big boss and have begun to converge. Bhanu Pratap responds to greetings.

They are distracted by a cavalcade of screeching cars. Virendra Pratap, son of Bhanu Pratap jumps off his Land Rover and directs Babulal.

VIRENDRA PRATAP:
All the dozen legislators of his party are in the bus.

VIRENDRA PRATAP:
पूरा दर्जन प्रजातांत्रिक *MLA* लोग बैठे हैं *minibus* में –

BABULAL:
Okay.

BABULAL:
जी –

VIRENDRA PRATAP:
Take them to the guesthouse and feed them.

VIRENDRA PRATAP:
Direct guesthouse में उतारिए – ... नाष्ता करवाइए...

BABULAL:
Yes.

BABULAL:
जी।

He approaches the SUV parked right behind his own car. Bhanu Pratap and Chandra Pratap are seen emerging from the house as Virendra opens the SUV door.

VIRENDRA PRATAP:
Welcome, grandpa!

VIRENDRA PRATAP:
पधारिए नाना जी –

Aged beyond 75 years, but still looking majestic, Rai Saheb refuses to acknowledge Virendra's request and continues to look straight ahead. By now Bhanu Pratap and Chandra Pratap have also arrived and greet the old man. He continues to sit with stoic silence. Virendra has no patience.

VIRENDRA PRATAP:
Grandpa, I've hijacked your entire party. You're a general without an army! What's the use of tilting at windmills now?

VIRENDRA PRATAP:
नाना जी, पूरा *party hijack* कर के ले आये हैं हम – अब बिना सेना के सेनापति कहाँ हवा में तलवार भाँज रहे हैं ? – चलिए...

Bhanu Pratap feels his son is going too far.

BHANU PRATAP:
Virendra, show some respect.

BHANU PRATAP:
वीरेन्द्र... बुजुर्ग हैं हमारे –

Virendra leaves the door and moves away.

VIRENDRA PRATAP:
Well... let him respectfully retire then!

VIRENDRA PRATAP:
हाँ तो कहिए बुढ़ापे का धरम निभावें और कुर्सी छोड़ें –

Chandra Pratap comes up to Rai Saheb.

CHANDRA PRATAP:
Father-in-law, come. Please... Let's go inside and talk.

CHANDRA PRATAP:
बाबू जी, आइए, अन्दर चलके बात करते हैं – आइए –

Rai Saheb knows he has little option. Chandra Pratap helps him come down.

RAI SAHEB:
It's an outrage the way you are trying to topple my government!

RAI SAHEB:
ये कोई तरीका है घर बुलाने का... सरकार गिराने का ?

BHANU PRATAP:
Only with your blessings, of course.

BHANU PRATAP:
आपसे विचार कर के ही होगा सब कुछ –

Rai Saheb begins to walk.

RAI SAHEB:
Look here... This time my party bosses will insist on 100 seats.

RAI SAHEB:
देखो, इस बार सौ से कम सीटों में नहीं मानने वाली *high comand* –

VIRENDRA PRATAP: *(laughs)*
You can't score even 10 seats... aiming for a century! Keep your national party in Delhi. Here we...

VIRENDRA PRATAP: *(laughs)*
दस *seat* का ठिकाना नहीं है – चले हैं *century* मारने... *national party* होगा दिल्ली में... यहाँ पर...

Chandra Pratap stops him.

CHANDRA PRATAP:
Veeru, enough. Come, father-in-law.

CHANDRA PRATAP:
वीरू ... बस करो यार – आइए बाबूजी...

BHANU PRATAP:
Come....

BHANU PRATAP:
चलिए।

INT. CHANDRA PRATAP HOUSE - DAY

Sitting in the kitchen Samar is savouring the parathas cooked by Bharati.

BHARATI:
You never call me! It's only through your Uncle Brij that I get news of you.

BHARATI:
तू तो मुझे *phone* करता नहीं – बस, तेरे ब्रिज मामा से तेरी ख़बर मिलती रहती है–

SAMAR:
Mother, it's the time difference between here and America. Uncle Brij is a nocturnal bird.

SAMAR:
Time का फ़र्क है न माँ ... *America* में दिन होता है तो यहाँ रात... और ब्रिज मामा तो निशाचर हैं...

BHARATI:
Ok.

BHARATI:
चलो –

SAMAR:
It's easier to talk with him.

SAMAR:
बात हो जाती है उनसे –

Prithvi arrives.

PRITHVI:
Hey...!

PRITHVI:
ए....!

SAMAR:
Brother!

SAMAR:
भइया –

PRITHVI:
Already pouncing on Mom's parathas! You've become thin! Hasn't he, mom?

PRITHVI:
ओए... ... आते ही पराठों पे टूट पड़ा, हाँ... एकदम सूख गया है, है ना माँ ?

BHARATI:
Let him be... come, eat.

BHARATI:
अब छोड़ इसे और तू भी... बैठ –

She begins to put a plate for him.

PRITHVI:
No, I've to go to the party headquarters. I just came to see him.

PRITHVI:
नहीं माँ, मुझे तो *party headquarters* जाना है, बस... इससे मिलने आ गया।

INT. PARTY HEADQUARTERS - DAY

NARRATOR: *(V/O)*
While Virendra believed himself to be the heir to the political throne, Prithvi was jockeying for the same position. Hence, it was imperative that his supporters get nominated for these elections.

NARRATOR: *(V/O)*
वीरेन्द्र भले ही अपने आप को गद्दी का उत्तराधिकारी समझे – पृथ्वी अपने आप को ही उस कुर्सी में देखता था – इस बार चुनाव में अपने समर्थकों को *ticket* दिलाना ज़रूरी था...

At the party headquarters Prithvi and his cronies are huddled together to strategise.

PRITHVI:
First select the candidate, and then the hullabaloo. Create so much publicity that the party is forced to nominate them.

PRITHVI:
अरे भई पहले *candidate select* करो फिर हंगामा – एतना *publicity* करो उसका कि *party ticket* मिलना ही चाहिए...

YOUTH LEADER #1:
We'll fight to get that. We will create chaos in the party high command. We'll show them your power, Prithvi.

YOUTH LEADER #1:
लड़ के लेंगे *बॉस – पार्टी हाइ कमान्ड* को गनगना देंगे इस बार... पता चल जायेगा, पृथ्वी भइया का *पावर...*

PRITHVI:
Great!

PRITHVI:
शाबाश !

Suddenly they are distracted by a young woman party worker (Beena Kumari) who forces herself into the meeting room. She is quite a pretty thing and they all know her.

BEENA KUMARI:
Let me go! They're trying to stop me! I told them I had to talk to you.

BEENA KUMARI:
अरे आप समझ क्यों नहीं रहे हैं...देखिए ना, रोक रहे हैं हमें बाहर – हम कह रहे हैं *Sir* से ज़रूरी बात करनी है –

PRITHVI:
We're in a meeting. Please wait.

PRITHVI:
खास *meeting* चल रही है, आप बैठिए एक *minute...*

The woman gives the most seductive smile and disappears into the adjoining room. Prithvi looks at his watch.

PRITHVI:
So... that's it then.

PRITHVI:
समझ गए तुम लोग...

YOUTH LEADER #1:
Yes, sir.

YOUTH LEADER #1:
Yes, sir.

PRITHVI:
Move then.

PRITHVI:
तो चलो...

YOUTH LEADER #1:
Ok.

YOUTH LEADER #1:
Ok.

PRITHVI:
It's time for the party.

PRITHVI:
Party का भी *time* हो गया है – चलो...

YOUTH LEADER #1:
Ok Sir.

YOUTH LEADER #1:
Ok, sir.

PRITHVI:
Jagat... call for my car, too.

PRITHVI:
ए जगत, हमारा गाड़ी भी लगाने को बोलो...

JAGAT:
Ok Sir.

JAGAT:
Ok, sir.

They leave and Prithvi enters the adjoining room. The moment he enters the room the floozie is all over him.

BEENA KUMARI:
You seem to have forgotten me, sir.

BEENA KUMARI:
भूल गये आप हमको *sir...*

Her Sari cover slips down revealing her breast, Prithvi is instantly aroused. He has been with this woman before. She comes close to him invitingly. He grabs her. The woman smiles as she surrenders.

BEENA KUMARI:
There's going to be a fresh election, I hear.

Prithvi is at work and doesn't bother to answer.

BEENA KUMARI:
Election का हल्ला सुन रहे हैं *sir...*

BEENA KUMARI:
Won't you let a woman volunteer contest?

BEENA KUMARI:
महिला *party worker* को *chance* नहीं देंगे *Sir...*

Standing right there Prithvi turns her around and gets on with the job. She keeps up with doing the act very well but continues to talk.

BEENA KUMARI:
I can win, sir. Just let... let me contest from Sitapur. I'll definitely win. I grew up there. I was the students' union president.

BEENA KUMARI:
जीत सकते हैं हम, बस एक बार... एक बार हमें सीतापुर का *ticket...* दिला दीजिए....पक्का जीत कर आएँगे – घर है हमारा सीतापुर... वहाँ, *College* के *President* थे हम...

Prithvi finishes. Like an animal. Exhilarated and rejuvenated. He has this tremendous appetite for sex- fast and furious. He hurries to straighten his clothes. She too goes through the routine. As he begins to leave, she reminds him ever so enticingly.

BEENA KUMARI:
Sir, please don't forget me this time. The Sitapur ticket...

He is not amused

BEENA KUMARI:
Sir, इस बार भूलिएगा मत... सीतापुर का *ticket –*

PRITHVI:
That's the bloody problem with politics. Everyone treats it like public transport. Just flag it down and mount it!

PRITHVI:
यही तो स्साला *problem* है – सब लोग राजनीति को *public transport* का बस समझ लेते हैं – जहाँ देखो हाथ दिखा के रोक लिया और चढ़ गये...

If she is humiliated she doesn't show it and reminds him again as he steps out of the room.

BEENA KUMARI:
I've worked very hard, sir. And will continue to do so.

He has left.

BEENA KUMARI:
हम बहुत मेहनत किए हैं *sir...*और आगे भी करते रहेंगे।

INT. BHANU PRATAP'S DRESSING ROOM - DAY

In Bhanu Pratap's dressing room Virendra Pratap takes his father's coat from his mother and helps his father put it on.

VIRENDRA PRATAP:
Let me.

VIRENDRA PRATAP:
दे दीजिए –

BHANU PRATAP:
You handled grandpa Rai like a seasoned politician.

BHANU PRATAP:
बहुत अच्छा से *handle* किए तुम राय साहेब को...

MOTHER:
Then, why don't you reward your son?

MOTHER:
तो इनाम दीजिए न अपने बेटा को –

BHANU PRATAP:
Everything belongs to him anyway.

BHANU PRATAP:
सब कुछ इसी का तो है...

VIRENDRA PRATAP:
Father, let me select the election candidates.

VIRENDRA PRATAP:
इस बार *election* में *candidate* का *selection* हमको करने दीजिए ना बाबू जी...

BHANU PRATAP:
That's your uncle's prerogative.

BHANU PRATAP:
बेटा, वो तो तुम्हारे चाचा जी का जिम्मेवारी है –

VIRENDRA PRATAP:
That's why Prithvi... but I won't let it go on like this.

VIRENDRA PRATAP:
इसीलिए तो पृथ्वी वहाँ... मगर इस बार हम चलने नहीं देंगे बाबू जी।

Bhanu Pratap looks at his ambitious son.

INT. BHANU PRATAP'S HOUSE - DAY

Samar who has just arrived with his mother touches Bhanu Pratap's feet as he descends the stairs. Bhanu Pratap hugs his favourite child.

BHANU PRATAP:
So glad you're here.

BHANU PRATAP:
अच्छा हुआ तू आ गया –

SAMAR:
It's your birthday, Uncle. I wouldn't miss it for the world.

SAMAR:
आपका *birthday* है तायाजी – *I wouldn't miss it for the world.*

Bhanu Pratap hugs him very warmly, with deep feeling. One can see the special bond between the two.

Indu enters with her father, Rajkumar Sakseria and quickly goes on to greet Bhanu Pratap and claim Samar.

Rajkumar Sakseria is appropriately greeted by Chandra Pratap who presents him to his brother.

RAJKUMAR SAKSERIA:
Hello...hello...

RAJKUMAR SAKSERIA:
नमस्ते – नमस्कार –

CHANDRA PRATAP:
Mr. Sakseria...

CHANDRA PRATAP:
आइये सक्सेरिया साब –

INDU:
Hello, uncle.

INDU:
नमस्ते *uncle*...

BHANU PRATAP:
Bless you.

BHANU PRATAP:
खुश रहो बेटा –

RAJKUMAR SAKSERIA:
Hello.

RAJKUMAR SAKSERIA:
नमस्कार –

CHANDRA PRATAP:
Just got his tax problems sorted out by the Chief Minister.

CHANDRA PRATAP:
इनका *excise* और *sales tax* वाला तीनों *file* आज सबेरे ही *clear* करवा दिए हैं मुख्यमंत्री से...

Rajkumar's P.S. produces a beautifully carved box. He opens it up to show a diamond-studded pen.

BHANU PRATAP:
You never forget, Rajkumar....

BHANU PRATAP:
भूलते नहीं हो राजकुमार तुम कभी – हाँ...

Indu drags away Samar.

Rajkumar Sakseria joins up.

BHANU PRATAP:
And now you'll say...

BHANU PRATAP:
अब कहोगे...

CHANDRA PRATAP:
Happy Birthday to you !!

CHANDRA PRATAP:
Happy Birthday to you!!

RAJKUMAR SAKSERIA:
Happy birthday to you sir!!

RAJKUMAR SAKSERIA:
Happy Birthday to you, sir!!

They laugh.

CHANDRA PRATAP:
Just saying happy birthday won't do.

CHANDRA PRATAP:
मगर अब खाली *Happy birthday* से काम नहीं चलेगा...

RAJKUMAR SAKSERIA:
Always at your service. Have I ever disappointed you?

RAJKUMAR SAKSERIA:
हर वक़्त हाजिर हैं *sir* – कभी निराश किया है आपको।

EXT. OUTSIDE THE HOUSE NIGHT

Outside, the party is at its peak. There is a scramble amongst the political bigwigs to greet Bhanu Pratap as he steps out. Prithvi's young brigade are shouting slogans.

The band in attendance begins to play. Walking along with his younger brother in the shadow, son Virendra Pratap and Prithvi on the two sides and a few senior leaders of the party, Bhanu Pratap looks majestic. The atmosphere is charged. The entire media is there and the event is being telecast live. Just as he gets on to the stage a fantastic display of fireworks takes place in the background. A massive portrait of his adorns the backdrop on the stage, decorated with orange and green party colours. With great persuasion Bhanu Pratap gets the audience to calm down and begins speaking.

BHANU PRATAP:
Please be seated... quiet....

(contd)
After winning three elections, when the electorate rejected us, in the last election, we accepted their decision with humility. And we helped Mr. Ramnath Rai form a coalition government - supporting it from outside. But, as you know, in the last 18

BHANU PRATAP:
शांत रहिए, शांत रहिए, कृपया बैठ जाइये...शांत रहो – शांत रहो – बैठो, कृपया बैठ जाइये...

(contd)
तीन–तीन चुनावों में विजयी बनाने के बाद जब पिछले चुनाव में जनता ने हमें बहुमत से दूर रहने का आदेश दिया तो उसे सर आँखों पर रख कर हमने बगैर सत्ता के लोभ लालच के पूज्यनीय रामनाथ राय जी की गठबंधन सरकार को बाहर रहकर समर्थन देने का निर्णय किया – ... मगर जैसा कि

months... this government has revealed it's true face. Corruption has reached its zenith and the people are in agony. We can't bear to see the common man's pain any longer. So, we have decided to withdraw our support for Mr. Rai's coalition government.

आप सब जानते हैं कि पिछले अट्ठारह महीने में कैसे–कैसे नंगे राजनीतिक तांडव किए गये हैं – भ्रष्टाचार अपनी पराकाष्ठा पार कर चुका है और जनता त्राहिमाम कर चुकी है – ... अब हमसे आम आदमी का दर्द देखा नहीं जाता... इसलिए हमने इस निकम्मी सरकार से अपना समर्थन वापस लेने का निर्णय लिया है... शांत रहिए – बैठ जाइए...

SLOGAN:
Long live Rashtrawadi!

SLOGAN:
राष्ट्रवादी – ज़िन्दाबाद !!!

There is an uproar. Bhanu Pratap has been speaking haltingly. He seems to gasp for breath but continues valiantly.

The uproar increases. Chandra Pratap notices his brother's discomfort; he is now holding the mike for support and perspiring profusely. He moves towards his brother.

BHANU PRATAP:
The people know... that we aren't responsible... for this political turmoil.

BHANU PRATAP:
जनता जानती है... कि हम इस परिस्थिति के लिए कतई जिम्मेवार नहीं हैं –

And suddenly Bhanu Pratap collapses. He falls on his knees first, bringing the microphone down with him. There is stunned silence. Even Chandra Pratap looks bewildered and helpless. Virendra Pratap is the first one to run up the stage. He jolts his father.

VIRENDRA PRATAP:
Father...

VIRENDRA PRATAP:
बाबू जी! – बाबू जी!

CHANDRA PRATAP:
Brother...

CHANDRA PRATAP:
भइया...

BHANU PRATAP'S WIFE:
What happened?

BHANU PRATAP'S WIFE:
क्या हुआ ?

LEADER:
Mr. Bhanu?

LEADER:
भानु जी –

CHANDRA PRATAP: *(to Babulal)*
Call the hospital! Emergency...

CHANDRA PRATAP: *(to Babulal)*
भइया, भइया – *hospital phone* करो...

VIRENDRA PRATAP:
Father...

VIRENDRA PRATAP:
बाबू जी!

PRITHVI:
Get the car!

PRITHVI:
ए गाड़ी लाओ –

VIRENDRA PRATAP:
Father...

VIRENDRA PRATAP:
बाबू जी!

BABULAL:
Hello – K N Hospital -

BABULAL:
Hello – K N Hospital -

CHANDRA PRATAP:
Brother...

CHANDRA PRATAP:
भइया...

They begin to lift him. Stunned faces of the assembled people.

EXT. OUTSIDE THE HOSPITAL - NIGHT

The exterior is flooded with flashing lights of the ambulances, police and government vehicles. The media is trying to get any possible information on the situation.

Rai Saheb arrives and meets Chandra Pratap and Sakseria.

LEADER #1:
Hello

LEADER #1:
नमस्कार –

LEADER #2:
Hello.

LEADER #2:
प्रणाम –

LEADER #3:
Hello

LEADER #3:
नमस्ते –

RAI SAHEB:
Just as I handed in the resignation, I heard. Atleast, if I hadn't resigned...

RAI SAHEB:
इस्तीफ़ा देकर निकला तो पता चला– सरकार भी हाथ से गई और...

CHANDRA PRATAP:
Father-in-law... please!

CHANDRA PRATAP:
बाबूजी, आप भी–अभी...

INT. ICU – NIGHT

Bhanu Pratap is prostate while the doctors are trying their best to revive him. Doctors instruct.

EXT./INT. HOSPITAL - NIGHT

Brij Gopal arrives and is immediately ushered in as the media rushes in to get his byte.

Brij Gopal notices Rai Saheb and then Samar standing with Indu at the I.C.U. door and moves towards him. Samar too notices him and is happy to see him. Prithvi touches Brij Gopal's feet. Samar begins to touch his uncle's feet but Brij embraces him. Indu too touches his feet. Brij Gopal holds her too.

PRITHVI:
Uncle...

PRITHVI:
मामा जी...

BRIJ GOPAL:
I came from Benaras only to see you, and here I hear about this crisis.

BRIJ GOPAL:
मैं तो तुम्हें ही मिलने आया था बनारस से – यहाँ उतरा तो पता चला हादसे का –

SAMAR:
It's serious, uncle...

SAMAR:
Attack काफी *serious* है मामा जी –

BRIJ GOPAL:
I'll see.

BRIJ GOPAL:
हाँ, देखते हैं...

Brij Gopal moves towards Chandra Pratap and Rajkumar Sakseria who are talking to the doctors.

EXT. HOSPITAL – NIGHT

It is chaotic with the crowd and media. The hospital spokesperson steps forward.

DOCTOR:
While the heart has been revived, there's no movement in the body.

DOCTOR:
Heart revive हो गया है – लेकिन अंगों में कोई *movement* नहीं है।

JOURNALIST:
So, is he paralysed?

JOURNALIST:
तो क्या उनको लकवा मार दिया है ?

DOCTOR:
We'll have to wait for the ECG reports for that.

DOCTOR:
E.C.G. की *report* के बाद ही हम कुछ कह पाएँगे –

The TV reporter begins to sum up the information.

REPORTER:
The government has fallen and fresh elections are certain. But the leader of the state's largest political party is fighting for his life. Without party president Bhanu Pratap, what does the future hold for the Rashtrawadi Party? K. N. Hospital. Aditi Priya. Star News.

REPORTER:
सरकार गिर चुकी है – चुनाव निश्चित है लेकिन राज्य की सबसे बड़ी *party* के नेता इस समय जीवन–मृत्यु से संघर्ष कर रहे हैं – राष्ट्रवादी पार्टी के *president* श्री भानु प्रताप के बिना इस *party* का क्या होगा... – *K. N. Hospital, Aditi Priya, Star News.*

INT. HOSPITAL NIGHT

Tense faces outside the ICU. From his father in the ICU, a nervous Virendra Pratap looks at the bunch of youth leaders surrounding Prithvi. They appear to be having a discussion. Virendra Pratap's mind is racing. He begins to walk down the corridor. Brij Gopal notices him talking on the phone. As Virendra Pratap is walking down the corridor some of the senior party leaders join him.

VIRENDRA PRATAP: *(to Babulal)*
Go ahead.

VIRENDRA PRATAP: *(to Babulal)*
आप आगे बढ़िये –

BABULAL:
Ok.

BABULAL:
जी –

VIRENDRA PRATAP:
Before they try to pull a fast one, we should take control of the party.

VIRENDRA PRATAP:
देखिए, इसके पहले कि ये लोग होशियारी दिखायें – *control* अपने हाथ में लेना होगा– क्या कहते हैं आप लोग ?

SHUKLA:
We support you.

SHUKLA:
हम हमेशा आपके साथ हैं...

VIRENDRA PRATAP:
I'll see you all at the party office.
(on the phone)
Yes, Mr. Babulal

VIRENDRA PRATAP:
आप लोग *party office* पहुँचिए...
(on the phone)
हाँ, बाबूलाल जी...

On the other end of I.C.U. ward Prithvi has been talking on the phone.

PRITHVI: *(on the phone)*
Hello? What? Under no circumstances should that meeting happen. Book the entire Intercontinental Hotel. Got it?
(to his men)
Listen... round up party members and take them to the hotel.

PRITHVI: *(on the phone)*
Hello, क्या... किसी हालत में मत होने दो ये *meeting – Inter Continental Hotel* में सारा कमरा – *suites* जो भी हो *book* करो... समझे... और हाँ...
(to his men)
जो जहाँ भी मिले उन्हें गाड़ियों में इकट्ठा करो और सबको पहुँचाओ वहाँ पे –

PRITHVI'S MAN:
Ok.

PRITHVI'S MAN:
जी –

Brij Gopal watches with a concerned expression as they all move away.

INT. HOSPITAL ICU - NIGHT

Brij Gopal sitting next to Bhanu Pratap's bed. He whispers in his ears.

BRIJ GOPAL:
These impatient youngsters will destroy everything. Now, more than ever, the party needs your guidance.

BRIJ GOPAL:
सब कुछ खतम कर देंगे ये बेलगाम नौजवान लोग – भानु प्रताप... इस कठिन समय में तुम्हारे निर्देश की बहुत ज़रूरत है।

There is suddenly some movement on Bhanu Pratap's forehead. And then eyes. He almost heaves a sigh. The doctor looks surprised.

EXT./ INT. ON THE STREET/ IN THE CAR - NIGHT

Virendra Pratap and his cavalcade of cars have been racing towards the party headquarters when his phone rings. He takes the call and listens.

VIRENDRA PRATAP: *(tells the Driver)*
Turn around. Father has regained consciousness.

VIRENDRA PRATAP: *(tells the Driver)*
अरे ए, गाड़ी घुमाओ – होश आ गया बाबू जी को।

The cars take a screeching U turn.

INT. HOSPITAL ICU - NIGHT

Inside Brij Gopal is propping Bhanu Pratap up as a nurse stacks a few pillows. His face is expressionless but there is no mistaking the bright sharpness of his eyes as he looks at everyone gathered. The family is all there. A couple of party stalwarts too are there. His eyes flicker as Virendra Pratap enters with Bramhanand Tiwari.

BRIJ GOPAL:
As soon as he became conscious, he called for everybody.

BRIJ GOPAL:
होश में आते ही कहा... सबको बुला लो –

Bhanu Pratap clearly is labouring over his words as he begins to speak.

BHANU PRATAP:
Chandru....

BHANU PRATAP:
चन्द्रू ...

CHANDRA PRATAP:
Yes brother..

CHANDRA PRATAP:
जी, भैया –

Hearing his name Chandra Pratap steps forward.

BHANU PRATAP:
In these circumstances, the party...

BHANU PRATAP:
अब इस हाल में... *party...*

He is clearly labouring to speak. Chandra Pratap responds.

CHANDRA PRATAP:
Brother, please, we'll talk later....

CHANDRA PRATAP:
भैया *please...* हम बाद में बात कर लेंगे...

BRIJ GOPAL:
What?

BRIJ GOPAL:
क्या –

BHANU PRATAP:
Take charge of... the party... as it's working president.

BHANU PRATAP:
फिलहाल *party* सँभालो... *working president* तुम रहोगे...

No one really reacts except Prithvi whose eyes brighten up and Virendra Pratap who looks devastated.

VIRENDRA PRATAP:
What's the need for this, father? You...

VIRENDRA PRATAP:
इसकी क्या ज़रूरत है... बाबू जी आप –

Bhanu Pratap cuts him.

BHANU PRATAP:
And Prithvi... will both be general secretaries.

BHANU PRATAP:
तुम और पृथ्वी दोनों *general secretary -*

PRITHVI:
Uncle!

PRITHVI:
ताऊ जी...

Bhanu Pratap looks out of breath. The doctors begin to put the oxygen mask on him. Brij Gopal begins to herd everyone out. Prithvi Raj Pratap steps forward to touch Bhanu Pratap's feet. He looks jubilant and begins to express his gratitude.

Brij Gopal hushes him away.

BRIJ GOPAL: *(murmurs)*
Come on....

BRIJ GOPAL: *(murmurs)*
चलो... चलो –

Virendra Pratap looks shocked. As everyone is leaving a completely crestfallen Virendra Pratap comes upto Bhanu Pratap.

VIRENDRA PRATAP:
What have you done, father! Take it back! Please....

VIRENDRA PRATAP:
ये क्या कर दिया बाबू जी...बाबू जी... वापस लीजिए इसको... *please* बाबू जी, हम...

He is almost in tears. Brij Gopal helps the nurse take the propping pillows out. Bhanu Pratap's eyes look pained.

Virendra holds his father's hand.

VIRENDRA PRATAP:
This is a humiliation for me.... At least, make me the joint working president....

VIRENDRA PRATAP:
हमारा कद एकदम काट दिए बाबूजी आप... एँ... कम से कम हमको *joint working president -*

Bhanu Pratap shuts his eyes. Brij Gopal puts his arm around Virendra Pratap and leads him out as doctors and nurses begin to work on Bhanu Pratap.

BRIJ GOPAL:
Virendra... you're family! You should look beyond such things.

BRIJ GOPAL:
वीरेन्द्र तुम परिवार हो – पदवी–कद के बारे में तुम्हें नहीं सोचना चाहिए...

VIRENDRA PRATAP: *(murmurs)*
Uncle Brij, let me talk to father... everything will finish then. Father... Father!

VIRENDRA PRATAP: *(murmurs)*
मामा जी, बात कर रहा हूँ ना .... *please.* बाबूजी, सब खतम हो जाएगा – बाबू जी – बाबू जी –

BRIJ GOPAL:
Come on, come on...

BRIJ GOPAL:
आओ – चलो, चलो – चलो...

VIRENDRA PRATAP:
Father....

VIRENDRA PRATAP:
बाबू जी...

BRIJ GOPAL:
Come.

BRIJ GOPAL:
चलो।

Brij Gopal leads Virendra out. Samar steps forward from his place in the back of the room.

Out in the corridor Virendra sees the party bigwigs – even Bramhanand Tiwari congratulating Prithvi. His eyes meet Prithvi's and the hatred is there for all to see. Virendra Pratap doesn't even stop to meet Tiwari who has begun to approach him.

Inside the I.C.U. Samar sits next to Bhanu Pratap who is now breathing stably. Samar just holds his hand and wipes the spit dropping from his mouth.

BHANU PRATAP:
Go back.... back to America...

BHANU PRATAP:
जा, वापस जा तू।

Prithvi's supporters shout slogans outside.

SUPPORTERS:
Long live Prithvi! Long live the General Secretary! (4)

SUPPORTERS:
पृथ्वी भइया – ज़िन्दाबाद... महासचिव – ज़िन्दाबाद... (4)

INT./EXT. CAR - NIGHT

As Samar is driving back home he gets a call. It's Sarah.

SAMAR:
Hey.

SAMAR:
Hey.

SARAH:
Hi, I just saw on the Net! How's your uncle now?

SARAH:
Hi. मैंने अभी–अभी internet पर देखा – तुम्हारे चाचा की तबियत कैसी है?

SAMAR:
Looks bad Sarah. It's happened at such a critical time.

SAMAR:
उनकी हालत गंभीर है, सारा... और ये बहुत ही कठिन समय पर हुआ है...

SARAH:
I'm sure he'll get better soon. Listen, I am coming to New York to meet you at the airport.

SARAH:
वे जल्द ही ठीक हो जाएँगे – मैं New York आ रही हूँ – तुम्हें हवाई अड्डे पर मिलूँगी...

SAMAR:
You don't have to do that....

SAMAR:
तुम्हें आने की ज़रूरत नहीं है...

SARAH:
I want to... This weekend I want you just to myself before you get consumed by your presentation!

SARAH:
मैं आना चाहती हूँ... यह weekend मुझे तुम्हारे साथ बिताना है – इससे पहले की तुम अपने काम में व्यस्त हो जाओ –

Samar smiles.

SAMAR:
Love you...

SAMAR:
Love you.

SARAH:
Come soon, miss you...

SARAH:
जल्दी आना।

INT. PARTY HEADQUARTERS - DAY

The core committee meeting chaired by Chandra Pratap is on.

CHANDRA PRATAP:
I want us to discuss each candidate thoroughly.

CHANDRA PRATAP:
मैं चाहता हूँ जितने भी प्रस्तावित नाम हैं... सबों पर खुल कर विचार किया जाये...

Virendra Pratap enters along with his cronies. Babulal looks completely neutral. Virendra Pratap puts the list on the table.

VIRENDRA PRATAP:
I have already made the list. Just approve it!

VIRENDRA PRATAP:
List बना चुके हैं हम... आप लोग इसको *O.K.* कीजिए –

CHANDRA PRATAP:
Virendra, our party follows a democratic process. Each and every recommendation is discussed.

CHANDRA PRATAP:
वीरेन्द्र, *party* की एक लोकतांत्रिक प्रक्रिया है – सभी प्रस्तावित नामों पर विचार होगा

VIRENDRA PRATAP:
Will you be kind enough to tell us, which democratic process was followed to make you the working president?

VIRENDRA PRATAP:
कृपया बताने का कष्ट करेंगे कि आपका कार्यकारी अध्यक्ष पद पर चुनाव किस लोकतांत्रिक प्रक्रिया से हुआ था...

Everyone is stunned. There's tension in the air.

VIRENDRA PRATAP:
Uncle.... The very president by whose grace you're adorning that chair has seen this list.

VIRENDRA PRATAP:
हाँ – चाचा जी, जिस अध्यक्ष महोदय की कृपा से आप उस कुर्सी पर विराजमान हैं – उनको दिखा चुके हैं हम ये *list...*

Chandra Pratap, who has been calmly looking at the list.

CHANDRA PRATAP:
Then, surely you have his approval in writing.

CHANDRA PRATAP:
तो उनका आदेश पत्र भी होगा आपके पास...

Virendra Pratap is hugely disappointed. He comes close to his uncle.

VIRENDRA PRATAP:
This list will prevail! Discuss all you want.

VIRENDRA PRATAP:
List तो यही रहेगा... जितना विचार करना है कर लीजिए –

One of the senior members speaks.

SR. MEMBER:
How come you've put your name against Madhopur?

SR. MEMBER:
Top में माधोपुर *seat* पर आपने अपना नाम कैसे लिख दिया ?

BABULAL:
Mr. Bhanu Pratap has always contested from Madhopur.

BABULAL:
माधोपुर की *seat* से तो हमेशा बड़े साहब ही लड़ते रहे हैं –

VIRENDRA PRATAP:
And in father's absence, the seat is rightfully....

VIRENDRA PRATAP:
और पिताजी की अनुपस्थिति में उस पर पहला हक हमारा...

CHANDRA PRATAP:
No claim for Madhopur will be entertained. It is reserved for the party president.

CHANDRA PRATAP:
माधोपुर *seat* पर किसी दावे की ज़रूरत नहीं है... वो *seat party* अध्यक्ष के लिए सुरक्षित है –

SR. MEMBER:
And currently, that is Chandra Pratap. There is unanimity amongst the members.

SR. MEMBER:
और वर्तमान में वो चन्द्र प्रताप जी हैं –

SR. MEMBER:
Only the party president should contest from Madhopur.

SR. MEMBER:
माधोपुर से तो अध्यक्ष को ही लड़ना चाहिए –

Virendra Pratap comes closer to Chandra Pratap and says coldly.

VIRENDRA PRATAP:
Have you even fought a municipal election, that you're staking your claim to Madhopur?! I will never let your dream come true... honorable working president!

VIRENDRA PRATAP:
नगर पालिका का *election* तो लड़े नहीं आप आज तक – अब अचानक माधोपुर! ... हम आपका ये सपना कभी पूरा नहीं होने देंगे, कार्यकारी अध्यक्ष महोदय –

EXT. COMMUNITY STREETS - DAY

The political rally reaches the basti. Tremendous excitement is in the air as curious basti people join sloganeering. The basti has always supported Bhanu Pratap's party.

PRITHVI'S MAN:
He's here! The leader is here! He has come to Azad Nagar. We welcome him here. The people of Azad Nagar whole-heartedly welcome the leader. Long Live Prithvi! Long Live Prithvi! Long Live Prithvi! Victory to Prithvi!

PRITHVI'S MAN:
आ गये – आ गये... भाइयों और बहनों... महासचिव महोदय, आज़ाद नगर में पधार चुके हैं – स्वागत है – स्वागत है महासचिव जी का... आज़ाद नगर की धरती पर महासचिव पृथ्वी प्रताप जी का हार्दिक स्वागत है... पृथ्वी भइया ... जिन्दाबाद.... युवा शक्ति... जिन्दाबाद... राष्ट्रवादी पार्टी... जिन्दाबाद – पृथ्वी भइया... जिन्दाबाद – युवा शक्ति... जिन्दाबाद... पृथ्वी भइया... जिन्दाबाद –

Prithvi gets on the stage as several elderly backward leaders welcome him with garlands.

PRITHVI:
Everyone knows that 30 years ago our party reclaimed this land from the government and their agents and established Azad Nagar!

PRITHVI:
दुनिया जानती है कि तीस साल पहले सरकार और उसके ठेकेदारों से छीन कर इस ज़मीन पर हमारी *party* ने आज़ाद नगर बसाया था...

SLOGANS: *(chanted by crowd)*
Long Live Prithvi! Victory to Prithvi!

SLOGANS: *(chanted by crowd)*
पृथ्वी भैया – ज़िन्दाबाद... ... राष्ट्रवादी – ज़िन्दाबाद... ...

PRITHVI:
My heart beats for the poor and the lower castes.

PRITHVI:
हमारे दिल में ख़ास जगह है, यहाँ के ग़रीब और पिछड़ी जात के लोगों के लिए –

Suddenly amidst drumbeats and slogan shouting youngsters, Sooraj arrives.

As Prithvi looks on, a bunch of youngsters hoist Sooraj on their shoulders and dance around. Prithvi enquires from Babulal.

PRITHVI:
Who is this?

PRITHVI:
कौन है ये ?

BABULAL:
Our driver's son - Sooraj.

BABULAL:
अपने *driver* रामचरित्तर के बेटे हैं, सूरज...

The local area leader - Parshad (enthusiastically).

PARSHAD:
Also a *kabaddi* champion.

PARSHAD:
कबड्डी *champion* भी हैं सर !

PRITHVI:
This isn't a dance party. Tell them to stop.

PRITHVI:
बस हो गया – बन्द कराओ ये *dance party* दिन भर का *time* नहीं है हमारे पास –

Babulal quickly moves to get some order as Prithvi gets his OBC friend/candidate on to the stage.

PRITHVI:
I want that the candidate for Azad Nagar should be educated, able and from amongst you.

PRITHVI:
चुनाव आ गये हैं – आपका *leader* सही हो – पढ़ा–लिखा... जो आपका नेतृत्व कर सके... आपके बीच का हो...

Sooraj's man Kisna and others begin sloganeering.

KISNA AND CROWD:
Sooraj is our leader! Sooraj is our leader!

KISNA AND CROWD:
सूरज भइया – सूरज भइया... ... हमारा नेता – सूरज भइया... ...

Prithvi looks irritated as Sooraj calmly stands his ground. Prithvi signals to the local leader Parshad and Babulal.

PRITHVI:
Yeah. Okay.... Okay.... The Rashtrawadi Party candidate for Azad Nagar will be... Jeevan Kumar.

PRITHVI:
हाँ–हाँ ठीक है... ठीक है, ठीक है... और इस बार विधान सभा में आज़ाद नगर से राष्ट्रवादी *candidate* होंगे... जीवन कुमार –

He puts his hand on Jeevan Kumar's back. There is a hushed reaction. Babulal tries to instigate some claps.

SOORAJ:
Jeevan Kumar may belong to our caste, but that doesn't necessarily make him one of us.

SOORAJ:
जीवन कुमार हमारी जात के भले हों... हमारे बीच के कैसे हो गये ?

Prithvi is not used to being questioned in public. Sooraj further irritates him by asking.

SOORAJ:
He knows nothing about Azad Nagar. He's never set foot in our dirty lanes, and nor will he, once the elections are over.

SOORAJ:
इनको तो ये भी नहीं मालूम, कि आज़ाद नगर की आबादी कितनी है – ना ही कभी यहाँ की गन्दी गलियों में इन्होंने पैर रखा है, और न ही चुनाव के बाद इनके दर्शन होंगे...

PRITHVI:
Excuse me?

PRITHVI:
तुम्हारा मतलब ?

SOORAJ:
Mr. General Secretary, our candidate will be one of us! Not an outsider.

SOORAJ:
मतलब साफ़ है महासचिव जी – हमारा नेता हमारे बीच का ही होगा – *imported* नहीं चलेगा –

PRITHVI:
This isn't a *kabaddi* match. I am speaking of the Legislative Assembly election. And the Rashtrawadi candidate will definitely be Jeevan Kumar.

PRITHVI:
ये कोई कबड्डी *match* नहीं हो रहा – हम विधान सभा चुनाव के बारे में बात कर रहे हैं – और इस बार राष्ट्रवादी पार्टी के उम्मीदवार, जीवन कुमार ही होंगे।

There is a mild jubilation from the die hard party supporters in the crowd but Sooraj walks away taking most of the crowd with him.

SLOGANS: *(Sooraj's men)*
We protest! We don't want outsiders! Long live Sooraj !

SLOGANS: *(Sooraj's men)*
नहीं चलेगा – नहीं चलेगा... *imported* माल नहीं चलेगा – ज़िन्दाबाद – ज़िन्दाबाद... सूरज भैया ज़िन्दाबाद...

SLOGANS: *(Prithvi's men)*
Long Live Prithvi!

SLOGANS: *(Prithvi's men)*
पृथ्वी भैया – ज़िन्दाबाद... पृथ्वी भैया – ज़िन्दाबाद... पृथ्वी भैया – ज़िन्दाबाद...

EXT./INT. SOORAJ'S HOUSE - NIGHT

In Azad Nagar there is tension that night. They have all assembled at Sooraj's house. The elders quietly pass the hukkas around.

RAMCHARITTAR:
Try to understand. You're not aware that Jeevan Kumar's grandfather was a minister in the Central government.

RAMCHARITTAR:
अरे समझने का कोशिश करो... तुम लोग को मालूम नहीं है – मंत्री थे जीवन कुमार के दादा जी केन्द्र के सरकार में –

SOORAJ:
So? That makes it his birthright, does it? What does he know about us?! Educated abroad, owns mansions. He owns four Mercedes cars of the kind that you chauffeur, Dad! He wouldn't last a day here! How is he one of us!

SOORAJ:
तो ? बाप दादा मंत्री थे तो बेटे का हक़ हो गया ?... समझ क्या है उसको पिछड़ों के बारे में ?... अँग्रेजी *स्कूल* में पढ़ा है, विलायत की *degree* है उसके पास... आलीशान बँगले का मालिक... तुम जिस *mercedes* की ड्राइवरी करते हो वैसी चार–चार हैं उसके पास – एक दिन बस्ती में रहेगा तो तेल निकल जायेगा उसका – वो हमारे बीच का कैसे हो गया...

KISNA:
Enough is enough! It's do or die this time.

An elder interrupts him.

KISNA:
बस हो गया, इस बार आर या पार...

ELDER #1:
What is it that you people want? Whose job is it to select the candidate - yours or the Party's?

ELDER #1:
अरे भइया चाहते क्या हो तुम लोग – *कंडीडेट पार्टी सेलेक्ट* करेगी कि तुम लोग...

SOORAJ:
We'll choose our own candidate!

There is a moment's silence.

SOORAJ:
अपना *candidate* हम खुद खड़ा करेंगे –

RAMCHARITTAR:
What? You'll rebel against the Party?

RAMCHARITTAR:
बौरा गया है का बेटा... बग़ावत करोगे ?

ELDER #2:
Without the Party, you won't garner five votes. Instead, you'll end up dividing the lower caste votes.

ELDER #2:
पाँच *भोट* नहीं मिलेगा *party* से बाहर जाओगे तो... उल्टा *भोट* बाँट कर पिछड़ा को कमजोर करोगे...

SOORAJ:
So what do you suggest? That we continue to suck up to these politicians, while they plant their leaders on us?

SOORAJ:
तो क्या करें – सालों एड़ियाँ घिसते रहें ?... चापलूसी करते रहें उनकी?... और वो नेता उपर से टपकाते रहें...

RAMCHARITTAR:
It isn't like that, son. The Party cares for us. They treat us like equals. Look, Samar came just for a day, but he got me a new watch.

RAMCHARITTAR:
अरे बेटा जैसा तू सोचता है वइसा नहीं है सब, खयाल रखा है हम सबका *party* ने – अपने जैसा मानते हैं सबको – देखो चार दिन के लिए समर भइया आए मगर हमारे लिए घड़ी लाना नहीं भूले –

Sooraj knows he will not get support from the oldies. He gets up telling his father.

SOORAJ:
A watch?

SOORAJ:
घड़ी दिया है...

RAMCHARITTAR:
Yes

RAMCHARITTAR:
हाँ...

SOORAJ:
Yes. So that you report to work on time.

SOORAJ:
कि *time* से *duty* पे पहुँचो –

Father looks hurt.

ELDER #1:
That's the problem with you guys. You've barely learnt to walk, but want to fly!

ELDER #1:
यही तो साला *problem* है तुम लोग का, अण्डा फोड़ के निकला नहीं कि उड़ के सीधा माथा पर बैठने का ख़्वाब देखने लगते हो –

SOORAJ:
You guys are history! We generate the power. Then why should we hand them the switch?

SOORAJ:
अरे चाचा आप जैसों का *time* गया – *power* पैदा करें हम लोग, और *button* दे दें उन लोगों के हाथ में !

The elderly man can take it no more. He turns and leaves. The crowd is attentive to Sooraj .

SOORAJ:
From now on, no outside candidates allowed in Azad Nagar!

SOORAJ:
आज से आज़ाद नगर में विदेशी *candidate* का *entry* बंद !

Some of his supporters shout.

SOORAJ'S SUPPORTERS:
Who is our leader? Sooraj, Sooraj. Victory to Sooraj! Long live Sooraj!

SOORAJ'S SUPPORTERS:
हमारा नेता कैसा हो... सूरज भइया जैसा हो... सूरज भइया... जिन्दाबाद... सूरज भइया... जिन्दाबाद...

As Sooraj and his gang cross the street, Babulal steps out of his car.

BABULAL:
Do you know me?

BABULAL:
पहचानते हो हमको ?

SOORAJ: *(smiles)*
You're a big man. How is a nobody like me supposed to know you, Mr. Babulal?

SOORAJ: *(smiles)*
ऊँचे लोग हैं आपलोग – हमारी पहुँच इतनी उपर कहाँ बाबूलाल जी –

BABULAL: *(laughs)*
I like your attitude. But, these speeches and stunts will get you nowhere. Even if you win the election as an independent... big deal! Instead the party will punish Azad Nagar for its defeat. If you really want to change anything, join the party and fight as its candidate.

BABULAL: *(laughs)*
ताव में कोई कमी नहीं है तुम्हारे – लेकिन ऐसे भाषणबाज़ी, स्टंटबाज़ी करते रहोगे तो हाथ कुछ नहीं लगेगा... अकेले लड़ के जीत भी गये तो क्या कर लोगे... उल्टा *party* हार का बदला लेगी आज़ाद नगर से... हाँ, सचमुच कुछ बदलना चाहते हो तो *party* के भीतर लड़ो – *ticket* ले के।

Sooraj looks at him with intent.

INT. HOTEL/RESTAURANT DAY

Indu's car comes to a screeching halt at the hotel's portico. Samar is sitting next to her. He looks at her.

INDU:
Come on! Get down.

INDU:
चलो... उतरो –

He looks like he's protesting but she is already out of the car and walking down the corridor.

INDU:
Y'know, I'm going to contest the elections this time.

INDU:
पता है, *election* लड़ने वाली हूँ मैं इस बार –

Samar feigns surprise.

INDU:
And you'll see, I'll become the youngest woman minister ever.

INDU:
तुम देख लेना – मैं जीतूँगी और *youngest* महिला मंत्री बनूँगी –

SAMAR: *(amused)*
Really?

SAMAR: *(amused)*
अच्छा!

INDU:
Of course! And when you come the next time, I'll come to receive you in a car with a flashing red light.

INDU:
अहाँ, और अगली बार तुम आओगे ना – तो लालबत्ती मे आउँगी *airport.*

Samar realizes there is an occasion. The central table at the restaurant has been laid out. There are stewards, waiters, and a champagne bottle - the works. She has planned this lunch.

SAMAR:
Wow! Such a grand lunch for one measly vote of mine?

SAMAR:
Wow! एक मेरे *vote* के लिए इतना बड़ा *lunch!*

INDU:
For your vote?! Can't you be a little romantic?

INDU:
मैंने तुम्हारे *vote* के लिए ये *lunch organize* किया है!... तुम थोड़े *romantic* नहीं हो सकते ?

Samar looks at her with complete innocence as he asks.

SAMAR:
With you?

SAMAR:
तुम्हारे साथ ?

She is offended.

INDU:
No... With this waiter! Look here, don't ruin my mood. I want to have a serious chat.

INDU:
नहीं, इस *waiter* के साथ ! देखो, *mood* मत ख़राब करो – आज मैं बहुत *serious* बात करने वाली हूँ तुमसे –

SAMAR:
That's really serious...

SAMAR:
That's really serious...

Samar too wants to clear some misconceptions. The waiters produce the champagne bottle. She pops it. As the bubbles burst out she looks happy. Samar looks at her. Her happiness and energy is contagious. She pours the champagne and Samar begins to pick one of the glasses.

INDU:
Stop, Stop!

INDU:
Stop – stop...

Samar looks at her amused.

INDU:
Not just like that. First propose.

INDU:
ऐसे ही? पहले *propose* करो !

She smiles at him meaningfully.

SAMAR:
Okay, let's drink to your flashing red light.

SAMAR:
Ok, let's drink to your लालबत्ती!

INDU: *(shocked)*
Red light?

INDU: *(shocked)*
लालबत्ती ?

SAMAR:
Yes. When you become a minister, you will have a car with a flashing red light, won't you?

SAMAR:
हाँ, मेरा मतलब जब तुम *election* जीतोगी और मंत्री बनोगी तो लालबत्ती वाली गाड़ियाँ होंगी ना तुम्हारे आगे पीछे...

INDU:
Samar! When are we getting married? Why do you look so shocked?

INDU:
समर... हम शादी कब कर रहे हैं? *Why do you look so shocked?*

SAMAR:
Marriage... I... I didn't quite understand.

SAMAR:
शादी ? हम ? समझ में नहीं आया मेरे –

Indu thinks he is kidding again.

INDU:
You'll understand alright when the priest recites the vows, and I make you take 17 rounds of the sacred fire...

INDU:
सब आ जायेगा समझ में – जब पंडित मंतर पढ़ेगा... और मैं सत्रह फेरे लगवाउँगी –

SAMAR:
Stop. Stop!

SAMAR:
Stop – stop...

His tone startles her.

SAMAR:
Indu… I know how you feel about me.

She looks at him expectantly.

SAMAR:
But my feelings aren't the same for you, Indu. I mean, you're an amazing girl. So beautiful, full of life, honest... just lovely, but...

Indu interrupts before he can complete his sentence.

INDU:
You can't love me! Do you know this is the first time you've complimented me? Beautiful, amazing, full of life. You can say all this but... you can't utter three words... "I love you."

She sounds very hurt.

INDU:
And here I am...madly in love with you since childhood.

SAMAR:
इन्दु... *I know how you feel about me.*

SAMAR:
But my feelings are not the same for you Indu. I mean you're an amazing girl... So beautiful, full of life, honest, just lovely – लेकिन ...

INDU:
प्यार नहीं कर सकते मुझे... जानते हो आज पहली बार तुमने मेरी तारीफ़ की है – *beautiful, amazing, full of life...* इतना सब कहा... मगर, 'प्यार करते हो' – ये तीन लफ़्ज़ नहीं बोल सकते हो –

INDU:
और मैं, पागल की तरह बचपन से तुम्हें दिल में बिठाये बैठी हूँ –

It is beginning to get difficult for Samar. The tears in her eyes make him weak. He leans forward and holds her hand.

SAMAR:
I'm sorry. I won't be able to forgive myself.

SAMAR:
I'm sorry... मैं अपने आप को माफ़ नहीं कर पाउँगा –

Indu makes a gesture asking him to stop. Takes a pause, fighting hard to hold back her tears and doesn't succeed.

INDU:
Have you never loved me?

SAMAR:
We're just too different, Indu.

INDU:
तो तुमने कभी मुझसे प्यार नहीं किया ?

SAMAR:
हम दोनों बहुत अलग हैं इन्दु।

She can't take it any more. She pulls her hand away and gets up suddenly. He tries to protest but she leaves. In the process spilling the two champagne glasses. The glasses fall onto the floor. Samar sees her walking away. The staff at the restaurant pretend as if they have seen or heard nothing.

EXT. PARTY HEADQUARTERS - DAY

There is a massive chaotic scene outside the Party Headquarters. Several groups of people have gathered to support their candidates. There are slogans, speeches, and lobbying. Sooraj, too arrives with his friends and looks a bit daunted - not knowing who to approach. Brij Gopal's car arrives.

SOORAJ'S MEN: *(chanting)*
Victory to Sooraj! Hail Sooraj!

PARTY SUPPORTERS: *(chanting)*
Long live Rashtrawadi!

SOORAJ'S MEN: *(chanting)*
सूरज भइया... जिन्दाबाद... सूरज भइया... जिन्दाबाद...

PARTY SUPPORTERS: *(chanting)*
राष्ट्रवादी – ज़िन्दाबाद...

INT. PARTY HEADQUARTERS - DAY

As Brij Gopal enters the Committee Hall, Virendra Pratap and Prithvi are engaged in a verbal duel. Chandra Pratap looks hassled. Brij Gopal quietly takes his seat at the back.

VIRENDRA PRATAP:
I have a simple question for the working president: On what basis were the candidates' chosen?

VIRENDRA PRATAP:
कार्यकारी अध्यक्ष से मेरा सीधा प्रश्न ये है कि *party* के *ticket* दिए किस आधार पर...

PRITHVI:
Answer this first: On what basis did you announce your name from the Madhopur seat?

PRITHVI:
आप पहले ये बताइये कि माधोपुर से अपना नाम आपने कैसे *announce* कर दिया ?

Chandra Pratap tries to stop them.

CHANDRA PRATAP:
Prithvi Pratap! Virendra, you're well aware that the core committee discusses every candidature before taking any decision.

CHANDRA PRATAP:
पृथ्वी प्रताप...! वीरेन्द्र, तुम अच्छी तरह जानते हो कि हर *ticket* के लिए *core committee* पूरी तरह विचार करेगी – उसके बाद ही कोई निर्णय लिया जाएगा –

Sooraj appears at the entrance and stands there trying to draw attention to him. Some of the members notice as the security begins to question him.

SOORAJ:
I want to say something.

SOORAJ:
बात करना है हमको –

As others are distracted, Prithvi turns to look at the entrance and spots Sooraj .

PRITHVI:
You? What the hell are you doing here?

PRITHVI:
तुम?... तू यहाँ क्या कर रहा है ?

SOORAJ:
My name is Sooraj. I'm from Azad Nagar.

SOORAJ:
सूरज नाम है हमारा – आज़ाद नगर से –

PRITHVI:
Yeah... yeah...The *kabaddi* champ! But, what are you doing here?

PRITHVI:
हाँ–हाँ कबड्डी *champion.* कहिए क्या कर सकते हैं आपके लिए ?

Sooraj ignores the humiliation.

SOORAJ:
I want a ticket to contest the election.

SOORAJ:
Party का *ticket* लेने आये हैं...

PRITHVI:
Really now! We're running a charity fete here! You want a ticket, do you? Didn't you hear me when you were busy dancing around? Our party's candidate for Azad Nagar is Jeevan Kumar. Got that? Get out now! Security!

PRITHVI:
अच्छा! ख़ैरात बँट रहा है यहाँ... *party* का *ticket* चाहिए... सुना नहीं था तूने उस दिन – जब तू नौटंकी दिखा रहा था अपने *band* वालों के साथ... आज़ाद नगर से राष्ट्रवादी पार्टी के उम्मीदवार जीवन कुमार होंगे – जीवन कुमार... अब चलो यहाँ से... *marshal!*

The security marshals attempt to take Sooraj away. He just looks at them without moving. They look nervous.

Sooraj steps closer to the round table, facing Prithvi.

SOORAJ:
I had heard you. But perhaps, you could neither hear nor see that the people of Azad Nagar rejected your candidate instantly. I'm

SOORAJ:
हमने सुना था – लेकिन आपने शायद न सुना, ना देखा, कि आज़ाद नगर के लोगों ने आपके *candidate* को *reject* कर दिया है – ऐलान

the leader of the lower castes and they will support only me.

के साथ ही... हम *leader* हैं दलित और पिछड़ों के ... और लोग हमीं को *support* करेंगे –

One of the backward leaders Bhola Shankar from the Core Committee jumps up.

BHOLA SHANKAR: *(OBC Leader)*
What did you say! Who made you our leader?

BHOLA SHANKAR: *(OBC Leader)*
का बोला रे तू ! तू कब से हमारा *leader* बन गया है...

Another one gets charged. This is Nageena Nath.

NAGEENA NATH:
We sweated blood for the party but suddenly you become the leader, is it?

NAGEENA NATH:
अरे ख़ून पसीना दिया *party* को हमलोग – और *leader* बन जायेगा तू ?

SOORAJ:
Everyone knows where the fruits of your sweat are hidden. We'll make you account for that too one day! For now, I only want a ticket to contest from Azad Nagar.

SOORAJ:
सबको मालूम है नेता जी – आपके ख़ून पसीने की कमाई कहाँ गड़ी है... उसका हिसाब भी होगा एक दिन... अभी तो हम बस आज़ाद नगर से *party* का *ticket* लेने आये हैं –

Bhola Shankar and Nageena Nath are furious. They pounce on him.

BHOLA SHANKAR:
You'll take us to task, will you? I'll show you.

BHOLA SHANKAR:
तू हिसाब करेगा ?... हमरा ? सारी लीडरी झाड़ देंगे...

Ramcharittar enters.

RAMCHARITTAR:
Son, what are you doing! Is this the way to speak here?

RAMCHARITTAR:
अरे बेटा... ये क्या कर रहा है तू – ऐसी बातें करते हैं...

RAMCHARITTAR: *(to the Committee)*
Please, sirs... I apologise on his behalf. Come....

RAMCHARITTAR: *(to the Committee)*
हम माफ़ी माँगते हैं इसका तरफ से बाबू लोग ... चल बेटा –

Sooraj feels embarrassed.

SOORAJ:
Father, please....

SOORAJ:
बाबू जी आप चलिए...

RAMCHARITTAR:
Keep quiet now. Enough!

RAMCHARITTAR:
बस, चुप... चुप –

NAGEENA NATH:
Get him out of here! Throw him out!

NAGEENA NATH:
धक्का मार के निकालिए इसको...

PRITHVI:
Take him away. He thinks he can contest an election. Learn to drive instead of dreaming of leadership.

PRITHVI:
ले जाओ इसे – बड़ा आया है *party* का *ticket* लेने... *driver* बनाओ पहले – लीडरी करेगा –

Virendra Pratap has been keenly observing the scene. He looks at Babulal who nods. Chandra Pratap looks disturbed and irritated.

PRITHVI:
Security!

PRITHVI:
Marshal!

RAMCHARITTAR:
Come on..

RAMCHARITTAR:
चल बेटा...

Virendra Pratap signals the security to stop. Everyone stops.

VIRENDRA PRATAP:
He isn't going anywhere! He stays here.

VIRENDRA PRATAP:
कहीं नहीं जाने वाले ये... यहीं रहेंगे –

PRITHVI:
Here? Meaning?

PRITHVI:
यहीं रहेंगे !!... क्या मतलब है तुम्हारा ?

VIRENDRA PRATAP:
It's clear, Prithvi Raj. Sooraj happens to be a member of the core committee. No one can throw him out.

VIRENDRA PRATAP:
मतलब साफ़ है पृथ्वीराज... *party* की *core committee* के सदस्य हैं सूरज कुमार – कोई नहीं निकाल सकता इनको –

Everyone is surprised.

PRITHVI:
What is this nonsense! Who made him a member?

PRITHVI:
ये क्या बकवास है वीरेन्द्र ?... ये कैसे बन गया सदस्य ?

VIRENDRA PRATAP:
I did. The secretary of the backward and minority cell.

VIRENDRA PRATAP:
हमने बनाया है – *Backward and Minority Cell* के सचिव –

NAGEENA NATH:
But, Mr. Virendra...

NAGEENA NATH:
मगर वीरेन्द्र जी...

Virendra Pratap's look shuts Nageena up.

VIRENDRA PRATAP:
Please read the constitution. As general secretary, I have the right to nominate 3 members.

VIRENDRA PRATAP:
संविधान उठा के देख लीजिए – महासचिव होने के नाते हमको अधिकार है तीन सदस्य मनोनीत करने का –

He literally takes Sooraj by hand.

VIRENDRA PRATAP:
Excuse me. Come, Sooraj.
(pointing to Babulal)
Please place a chair for him beside mine.

VIRENDRA PRATAP:
Excuse me... आओ सूरज –
(pointing to Babulal)
इनकी कुर्सी हमारे बगल में रखवाइए...

BABULAL:
Ok.

BABULAL:
जी –

Prithvi is stunned. Chandra Pratap looks at Brij Gopal who has been watching the whole thing with great interest.

VIRENDRA PRATAP: *(to Sooraj)*
Please sit.

VIRENDRA PRATAP: *(to Sooraj)*
बैठो –

VIRENDRA PRATAP:
Respected Mr. Working President, please caution Mr. Prithvi Raj that without the approval of the core committee he shouldn't go

VIRENDRA PRATAP:
कार्यकारी अध्यक्ष महोदय – कृपया पृथ्वीराज को सचेत किया जाए कि *core committee* की सम्मति के बिना, कहीं भी *candidates* का ऐलान

around announcing candidates. And I propose that instead of Jeevan Kumar, the party candidate from Azad Nagar should be Sooraj Kumar.

ना करते फिरें हुँह... और मेरा प्रस्ताव है, कि आज़ाद नगर से *party* के उम्मीदवार के लिए जीवन कुमार का नाम हटा कर माननीय सूरज कुमार का नाम शामिल किया जाये –

Meanwhile Brij Gopal has walked up to Chandra Pratap and whispered an advise and left the committee hall.

BRIJ GOPAL:
Adjourn the meeting for now.

BRIJ GOPAL:
फ़िलहाल *meeting* स्थगित कर दो –

CHANDRA PRATAP:
The new proposals will have to be included in the agenda. Hence, this meeting is adjourned until further notice.

CHANDRA PRATAP:
समिति में हुए नये प्रस्तावों को एजेन्डे पर लाना होगा – इस आलोक में अगली सूचना तक *core committee* की बैठक स्थगित की जाती है।

INT. CHANDRA PRATAP'S HOUSE - NIGHT

Coffee is being served in the family lounge. Prithvi, joins Chandra Pratap and Brij Gopal, as Samar helps Bharati with the coffee tray.

BHARATI:
Take this.

BHARATI:
ले चलो –

CHANDRA PRATAP:
I'm feeling handicapped without Bhanu. It's becoming very hard to rein in Virendra. He staked his claim to Madhopur again today.

CHANDRA PRATAP:
भइया की कमी बहुत खल रही है... वीरेन्द्र को *control* करना मुश्किल हो रहा है – आज माधोपुर में सभा कर उसने अपनी उम्मीदवारी का ऐलान भी कर दिया –

BRIJ GOPAL:
So? Let him contest.

BRIJ GOPAL:
तो हर्ज़ क्या है, खड़ा होने दो उसको वहाँ से –

Chandra Pratap looks shocked.

PRITHVI:
C'mon, Uncle... you know that Madhopur is reserved for the party president. If he wins from there, he'll create havoc.

PRITHVI:
मामा जी आप भी जानते हैं, कि वो हमेशा *party president* की *seat* होती है – वहाँ से जीता तो कोहराम मचा देगा वो –

Samar pours the coffee.

SAMAR:
He can even lose.

SAMAR:
हार भी तो सकता है –

Chandra Pratap looks surprised. Prithvi smiles at Samar's ignorance. However, Brij Gopal looks at Samar with interest. Samar returns the look.

PRITHVI:
He can even lose. Are you aware that it is our safest seat? Even if we nominate a dog from there, it will win.

PRITHVI:
तू नहीं जानता छोटे – वो हमारा सबसे *safe seat* है... वहाँ से हमारी *party* का कुत्ता भी नहीं हार सकता...

SAMAR:
Brother, if the party can make you win the election, it can also make sure you lose.

SAMAR:
भैया *party election* जितवा सकती है – तो हरा भी तो सकती है –

Prithvi is now listening.

PRITHVI:
Sure. But losing Madhopur isn't good for the party.

PRITHVI:
सकती है, लेकिन माधोपुर का *seat* हारना *party* के लिए ठीक नहीं...

BRIJ GOPAL:
Precisely! If he loses from there, it'll finish his political career. Moreover, you'll get sympathy for giving up the seat.

BRIJ GOPAL:
इसीलिए तो... ऐसी *seat* से हारेगा तो *political career* खत्म हो जायेगा उसका – और *seat* छोड़ने के लिए *party* में आपको सहानुभूति मिलेगी वो अलग –

Brij and Chandra Pratap exchange looks. Prithvi too smiles at Samar.

CHANDRA PRATAP:
That makes sense.

CHANDRA PRATAP:
सो तो है –

Chandra Pratap is thoughtful. Bharati joins them with the coffee tray. Brij Gopal continues.

BRIJ GOPAL:
But your problem isn't Virendra. It is Sooraj!

BRIJ GOPAL:
तुम्हारी समस्या वीरेन्द्र नहीं – सूरज है –

Both Chandra Pratap and Bharati are alarmed.

Brij Gopal seems deeply disturbed. Chandra Pratap nods agreeing with Brij Gopal as he says.

CHANDRA PRATAP:
He has created a serious situation. If we give him Azad Nagar, it boosts Virendra's position. But, if we don't, we antagonise the lower castes. I don't know what to do.

CHANDRA PRATAP:
हूँ... परिस्थिति गंभीर कर दी है उसने – आज़ाद नगर से अगर सूरज को *ticket* देते हैं तो वीरेन्द्र का पलड़ा भारी होता है – नहीं देते हैं, पिछड़ों की ख़िलाफ़त मोल लेते हैं... कुछ समझ नहीं आ रहा है – क्या करें...

Brij Gopal is thinking.

EXT. SOORAJ'S HOUSE - NIGHT

Sooraj addresses the people of the basti.

SOORAJ:
We will talk in one voice.

SOORAJ:
...हम एक आवाज़ में बात करें।

Brij Gopal's car enters the basti.

People are surprised to find him there. As he walks towards Sooraj's house several people join in. Someone runs to inform Sooraj's house. There is obviously tremendous respect for Brij Gopal.

BHUPESH:
Sooraj, Mr. Brij Gopal is here.

BHUPESH:
भइया, ब्रिज गोपाल जी आये हैं –

SOORAJ:
Brij Gopal?

SOORAJ:
ब्रिज गोपाल जी...

BRIJ GOPAL:
How are you all... Hello...ok...

BRIJ GOPAL:
कैसे हो सब... प्रणाम – अरे...

RAMCHARITTAR:
Sir...

RAMCHARITTAR:
ब्रिज मालिक.... मालिक –

They lay out a cot for Brij Gopal. Sooraj's father Ramcharittar looks flustered.

BRIJ GOPAL:
Been a while since I had a cup of your tea.

BRIJ GOPAL:
बहुत दिन से चाय नहीं पिया ना तुम्हरी...

Sooraj appears. Brij Gopal looks surprised to find other OBC leaders from across the state present.

BRIJ GOPAL:
How nice! Mr. Batukeshwar, you too? Looks like all the Dalits are here! Looks like a massive convention.

BRIJ GOPAL:
अरे गोपाल – सुखदेव... आप भी हैं बटुकेश्वर जी... पूरे क्षेत्र का दलित समाज आ गया है यहाँ तो... लगता है कोई महासम्मेलन हो रहा है –

BATUKESHWAR:
Since elections are upon us we need to look at all possibilities.

BATUKESHWAR:
नहीं बृजगोपाल जी – अब चुनाव का *time* आ गया है ना... तो आचार–विचार समझना पड़ता है –

Brij Gopal looks at Sooraj.

BRIJ GOPAL:
Of course, of course. After all, this is the age of the youth.

BRIJ GOPAL:
हाँ–हाँ... नौजवानों का *time* है उनका तो विचार लेना ही पड़ेगा – बैठो–बैठो... बैठो –

RAMCHARITTAR:
Please sit...no matter what, we will never leave the party.

RAMCHARITTAR:
विचार कुछ भी हो – हम लोग *party* से कभी अलग नहीं सोच सकते –

BRIJ GOPAL:
The party is yours anyway.

BRIJ GOPAL:
अरे *party* भी तो आप ही लोगों की है–

Sooraj speaks up.

SOORAJ:
As far as elections go, you're right. But, what about after that?

SOORAJ:
हाँ, जहाँ तक *vote* का सवाल है आप की बात सही है... मगर उसके बाद ?

BRIJ GOPAL:
I know that you people are upset about the selection of your candidate.

BRIJ GOPAL:
पता है कुछ नाराज़गी है तुमलोगों के बीच – *Candidate* के फ़ैसले को लेकर –

SOORAJ:
We have decided that not just for Azad Nagar, but every local caste area, we only want local candidates.

SOORAJ:
हमारे बीच फ़ैसला हो चुका है, सिर्फ़ आज़ाद नगर ही नहीं... हर दलित इलाक़े के *local* उम्मीदवार को ही *ticket* देना होगा –

BRIJ GOPAL:
That is upto the party. Now that you're in the core committee, raise this issue there. For now, the Party president has sent me to inform you that the candidate for Azad Nagar will be from among you.

BRIJ GOPAL:
ये तो *party* का फ़ैसला होगा, अब तुम भी तो *central committee* पे आ चुके हो, वहीं पे इस मुद्दे को उठा लो... फ़िलहाल तो *party president* ने हमें यहाँ भेजा है कि आज़ाद नगर का उम्मीदवार आप ही के बीच का हो –

Everyone seems taken aback by Brij Gopal's declaration. Batukeshwar sounds overwhelmed.

BATUKESHWAR:
God bless you, Mr. Brij Gopal. As long as you are in the party, there will be no injustice.

BATUKESHWAR:
धन्यवाद बृज गोपाल जी – जब तक *party* में आप जैसा लोगों का स्तम्भ है अन्याय नहीं हो सकता –

RAMCHARITTAR:
Bless you, sir, for encouraging a poor man's son. Sooraj will not disappoint you.

RAMCHARITTAR:
बड़ा पुन्य होगा बृज मालिक – गरीब के बेटा को *party* में स्थान दिये... सूरज आपको निराश नहीं करेगा...

Everyone is nearly congratulating Sooraj – when Brij Gopal stuns everyone.

Sooraj's men sloganing.

BHUPESH:
Sooraj,

BHUPESH:
सूरज भइया...

SUPPORTERS: *(join in)*
Victory to Sooraj! Victory to Sooraj!

SUPPORTERS: *(join in)*
जिन्दाबाद – सूरज भइया... जिन्दाबाद – सूरज भइया... जिन्दाबाद –

BRIJ GOPAL:
The Party has decided that the candidate from Azad Nagar will be the party's loyal supporter, and your beloved – Ramcharittar.

BRIJ GOPAL:
इस बार, इस बार *party* ने निर्णय लिया है कि आज़ाद नगर से उम्मीदवार *party* के पुराने वफ़ादार और आप सबों के प्रिय... रामचरित्तर होंगे –

Stunned silence.

BRIJ GOPAL:
Democracy is alive and well in our party.

BRIJ GOPAL:
आज भी हमारी *party* का लोकतंत्र जीवित है...

Sooraj and his friends can't believe what they are hearing. His father is in disbelief. He rushes to Brij Gopal.

RAMCHARITTAR:
Sir, this is a mistake. The candidate is not me. It's my son, Sooraj.

RAMCHARITTAR:
मगर बृज मालिक – कोई ग़लती हो गया है – उम्मीदवार हम नहीं, हमारा बेटा सूरज है...

BRIJ GOPAL:
Ramcharittar, every father wants his son to move ahead. But he is still inexperienced. And is there anyone here who is more honest and hardworking than you? Does anyone have an objection, friends?

BRIJ GOPAL:
रामचरित्तर, ये तो हर बाप चाहता है कि उसका बेटा आगे बढ़े... लेकिन अभी उसे अनुभव की ज़रूरत है – और तुम्हारे जैसा ईमानदार, कर्मठ और सच्चा व्यक्ति कौन है इस बस्ती में... बोलो भाइयो, किसी को आपत्ति है इनके नाम पर...

No one responds. Brij Gopal looks at Sooraj.

BRIJ GOPAL:
Tell me, Sooraj ... do you object to your father's candidature?

BRIJ GOPAL:
बोलो सूरज – तुम्हें कोई आपत्ति है अपने पिताजी की उम्मीदवारी पर –

Sooraj knows he has been caught and fooled. He keeps his calm. He walks away and the meeting begins to disperse. Sooraj's father is protesting.

RAMCHARITTAR:
Why don't you people say something? Why don't you people say something? Sir... how can I be a candidate? I'm a mere servant of your family.

RAMCHARITTAR:
अरे, आप लोग कुछ बोलते क्यों नहीं– हाँ, मालिक, हम *candidate* कैसे हो सकते हैं... हम तो आपके परिवार के सेवक हैं –

BRIJ GOPAL:
Now, you are a servant of the people.

BRIJ GOPAL:
अब तुम जनता के सेवक हो –

No one seems to be looking at him. The other backward leaders too have realised the game but no one dares to protest.

RAMCHARITTAR:
Sir...

RAMCHARITTAR:
मालिक!

Brij Gopal has already walked away. Everyone is too shocked to walk Brij Gopal to the car. Suddenly Sooraj appears to open the door for him.

SOORAJ:
The decision to nominate my father was the right one.

SOORAJ:
बापू को *candidate* बनाने का फ़ैसला सही लिया आपने...

Brij Gopal takes a long pause.

BRIJ GOPAL:
In politics, there are no right or wrong decisions. Their purpose is merely to achieve a desired result. Whatever that might be.

BRIJ GOPAL:
राजनीति में फ़ैसले सही या ग़लत नहीं होते बेटा... उनका मोल तो बस मक़सद पूरा करने के लिए होता है – चाहे जैसे भी हो...

Sooraj takes it in.

SOORAJ:
I shall remember that.

SOORAJ:
याद रखेंगे –

BRIJ GOPAL: *(to driver)*
Let's go.

BRIJ GOPAL: *(to Driver)*
चल बाबा, चल।

INT. SOORAJ HOUSE - DAY

Sooraj steps out of his room. His mother comes with a pooja thali *and puts a* tikka *on his forehead.*

SOORAJ'S MOTHER:
I'm going to the Beesanpur temple to pray for your nomination.

SOORAJ'S MOTHER:
बिसुनपुर माता के मंदिर में चादर चढ़ाना है, मन्नत का – तेरे *election* की *ticket* के लिए –

Father steps in.

RAMCHARITTAR:
But why only today?

RAMCHARITTAR:
मगर आज ही जाना जरूरी है का ?

SOORAJ'S MOTHER:
Because it's your day off.

SOORAJ'S MOTHER:
अब आज तो आपकी छुट्टी है, फिर फ़ुर्सत कब मिलेगा –

Sooraj looks at his father.

SOORAJ:
Father's on a long vacation now. He will no longer be a chauffer.

SOORAJ:
अब बाबूजी की लम्बी छुट्टी – *driver* की नौकरी बन्द उस घर में –

RAMCHARITTAR: *(protests)*
What?!

RAMCHARITTAR: *(protests)*
इ का बोल रहा है सूरज –

SOORAJ:
I have decided. You're not going to serve that family. Take the car to Beesanpur.

SOORAJ:
बस, अब कुछ नहीं सुनना... नहीं करेंगे आप नौकरी वहाँ – गाड़ी छोड़ के जा रहा हूँ माँ

SOORAJ'S MOTHER:
We'll take the bus, son.

SOORAJ'S MOTHER:
हम चले जाएँगे बेटा, बस में।

Sooraj is already getting into a friend's open jeep.

INT. VIRENDRA PRATAP'S HOUSE - DAY

As Virendra Pratap steps out, guards run to take position in their waiting vehicles. Babulal catches up with him.

BABULAL:
The first list of candidates.

BABULAL:
पहला *list out* हो गया है...

A LEADER:
Hello, brother.

A LEADER:
नमस्ते भइया –

As Virendra looks at the list. Babulal adds.

BABULAL:
You proposed 55 names. Of those, he cleared only 12!

BABULAL:
पचपन में से खाली बारह नाम *clear* किये हैं –

Virendra looks angry. He throws the list back at Babulal as he gets into the vehicle.

VIRENDRA PRATAP:
And my request for funds?

VIRENDRA PRATAP:
Funds का क्या हुआ ?

Babulal looks scared as he reveals.

BABULAL:
He refused to clear them.

BABULAL:
Cheque sign नहीं किए अभी तक –

Disgust is written large on Virendra's face.

VIRENDRA PRATAP:
He will pay for this!

VIRENDRA PRATAP:
बहुत भारी पड़ेगा चचाजान...

BABULAL:
Bad times are here....

BABULAL:
Time ख़राब है।

INT. PARTY HEADQUARTERS - DAY

Sooraj has been waiting outside as Virendra Pratap arrives at the Party Headquarters where a presentation of the new posters and media designs are in process.

Chandra Pratap, Prithvi and other functionaries are all watching.

Brij Gopal is quietly sitting in the background. By some design the poster now has Chandra Pratap's face more prominently displayed than that of Bhanu Pratap.

PRITHVI:
We conducted a survey in every district. Seventy eight percent of the voters connect with Chandra Pratap. He is the face of our party.

PRITHVI:
सभी विधानसभा क्षेत्रों में हमने *survey* करवाया है और *seventy eight percent* मतदाता कहते हैं कि वो चन्द्रप्रताप जी से *connect* करते हैं – *He is the face of our party.*

Virendra Pratap begins to clap as the slide is projected.

VIRENDRA PRATAP: *(taunts)*
Chief minister designate!

VIRENDRA PRATAP: *(taunts)*
मुख्यमंत्री पद के दावेदार –

Chandra Pratap begins to get defensive but Prithvi is aggressive.

PRITHVI:
Why not?

PRITHVI:
Why not?

Sooraj protests.

SOORAJ:
The Party will decide that. Not you!

SOORAJ:
ये निर्णय आपका नहीं, *party* का होगा –

Prithvi pounces on him.

PRITHVI:
You shut up!

PRITHVI:
You – shutup !

SOORAJ:
No, you be quiet! This is the party office, not your home. Respect the decorum of this office.

SOORAJ:
चुप, आप रहेंगे – ये *party* का दफ़्तर है आपके घर की जागीर नहीं... यहाँ की मर्यादा का ख़याल रहे –

PRITHVI:
So, you'll teach me decorum, will you? Mr. Backward... minority cell secretary. The party has decided....

PRITHVI:
तो आप पढ़ाएँगे हमको मर्यादा का पाठ – *Mr. Backward* और *minority cell* सचिव... *party* फ़ैसला कर चुकी है – मुख्यमंत्री यही बनेंगे...

PRITHVI: *(contd) (He points to the screen)*
He will be the Chief Minister. If you have a problem with that....

PRITHVI: *(contd) (He points to the screen)*
अगर आपको ये चेहरा पसन्द नहीं है तो...

He shrugs his shoulders indicating they are welcome to leave.

VIRENDRA PRATAP:
The public recognises only one face, only one voice - that of Bhanu Pratap.

VIRENDRA PRATAP:
जनता सिर्फ़ एक चेहरे को जानती है – सिर्फ़ एक आवाज़ पहचानती है – और वो हैं भानु प्रताप –

Sooraj steps forward.

SOORAJ:
And you all know who his rightful successor is.

SOORAJ:
और उसके बाद उस स्थान का सही उत्तराधिकारी कौन है – आप लोग अच्छी तरह से जानते हैं –

He looks at Virendra Pratap.

SOORAJ:
The Party should not fail to recognise that.

SOORAJ:
Party उसे पहचानने में कोई भूल नहीं करेगी –

This is a chilling endorsement. Everyone is stunned. Virendra Pratap is delighted.

Brij Gopal who has been silently watching all that has been going on steps forward.

BRIJ GOPAL:
Virendra, your father has himself approved of this decision.

BRIJ GOPAL:
वीरेन्द्र, ये फ़ैसला उनकी सहमति के बाद ही लिया गया है –

He hands over a two line letter from Bhanu Pratap. Virendra is stunned to see this letter. He knows who has manipulated this.

VIRENDRA PRATAP:
When did father decide this?

CHANDRA PRATAP:
This morning.

BRIJ GOPAL:
Every decision of this Party is democratic. You know that!

Virendra knows he has been stumped.

VIRENDRA PRATAP:
Of course! I know who is behind all this. How only 12 of my 55 candidates are approved. How all my demands for funds are consistently denied.

SOORAJ:
Mr. Working President. This decision is not good for the party. The people will reject it!

Chandra Pratap steps forward.

CHANDRA PRATAP:
Young man, now I call the shots here. Learn to accept that fact. Better fall in line or fall by the wayside.

VIRENDRA PRATAP: *(scoffs)*
Fall in line! Wow, Mr. Working President!

CHANDRA PRATAP:
Enough Virendra Pratap! Final warning. The same Constitution that gives you the right to appoint him as a member...
(points at Sooraj)
...also grants me the right to suspend you from the party.

Virendra Pratap looks around as Chandra Pratap is lashing out at him and Tiwari tries to speak.

TIWARI:
Sir, Virendra is the general secretary of the party. How can you...

CHANDRA PRATAP:
So now, you'll interfere, will you?
(looks around)
I've been watching the kind of games that some people are playing. Looks like players will have to be rested during this election tournament.

VIRENDRA PRATAP:
कब लिया बाबूजी ने ये फ़ैसला !?

CHANDRA PRATAP:
आज सुबह ही कार्यकारिणी के सदस्य मिले थे उनसे –

BRIJ GOPAL:
हमारी *party* के सारे फ़ैसले लोकतांत्रिक होते हैं... तुम तो जानते ही हो...

VIRENDRA PRATAP:
हाँ, हम जानते हैं... कि कौन है इसके पीछे... कैसे हमारी पचपन की *list* में से सिर्फ़ बारह नाम *pass* होते हैं ... कैसे *fund* के नाम पर हमारे हर *demand* को नकार दिया जाता है –

SOORAJ:
कार्यकारी अध्यक्ष महोदय, ये रवैया *party* के हित में नहीं है –जनता इस फ़ैसले को नहीं मानेगी –

CHANDRA PRATAP:
बर्ख़ुरदार, अब यहाँ फ़ैसले मैं किया करता हूँ – और बेहतर होगा कि आप उनका पालन करें – *Better fall in line or fall by the wayside.*

VIRENDRA PRATAP: *(scoffs)*
Fall in line! वाह! कार्यकारी अध्यक्ष महोदय –

CHANDRA PRATAP:
बस, वीरेन्द्र प्रताप – आख़िरी चेतावनी... जो संविधान तुम्हें इसको
(points at Sooraj)
सदस्य बनाने का अधिकार देता है, वहीं संविधान मुझे भी तुमको *party* से *suspend* करने का अधिकार देता है...

TIWARI:
Sir, party के *general secretary* हैं वीरू जी, आप उन्हें इस तरह से *suspend...*

CHANDRA PRATAP:
आप बताएँगे हमें !
(looks around)
देख रहे हैं हम – काफ़ी लोग यहाँ *twenty-twenty* खेलने में लगे हैं – लगता है कुछ खिलाड़ियों को *rest* देना पड़ेगा इस चुनाव के *match* से !

EXT. STREET - NIGHT

A grim faced Sooraj drives through the street plastered with posters projecting Chandra Pratap as the Chief Minister.

INT. VIRENDRA'S HOUSE OFFICE - NIGHT

Whisky glass dangling in his hand, Virendra walks towards the life size poster standing in his living hall. He stares at it, a bitter smile breaks on his face.

VIRENDRA PRATAP:
Fall in line! Now I have to stand in line, eh? All my life, I doled out alms, and now I have to stand in line and beg?! My father built this party...and he is trying to kick me out of it?

VIRENDRA PRATAP:
Fall in line... तो हमें *line* में खड़ा होना पड़ेगा – एँ... सारा ज़िन्दगी देते रहे हम बाँट–बाँट के... अब *line* में खड़ा होके भीख माँगें इससे... हमरे बाबू जी का बनाया हुआ *party* में, हमें ही दबा रहा है, स्साला!

Virendra smashes his whisky glass at the poster. In his anger, he loses his balance. Sooraj steps forward just in time to hold and help him on the sofa.

VIRENDRA PRATAP:
I'll break it! I will break this party and form a new one.

VIRENDRA PRATAP:
तोड़ देंगे... साला इस *party* को ही तोड़ देंगे... एक नया *party* बनाएँगे ...

SOORAJ:
Do not make that mistake. That is what they want. This party is yours. They must leave, not you.

SOORAJ:
ऐसी ग़लती नहीं करेंगे आप... यही तो वो लोग चाहते हैं – ये *party* आपकी है – और इसमें से निकलेंगे वो लोग... आप नही...

Virendra would love this to happen.

VIRENDRA PRATAP:
How will you throw them out? How? See this poster? This man will become the Chief Minister!

VIRENDRA PRATAP:
कैसे निकालेगा ?... कैसे निकालेगा तू ?... देख रहा है ये *poster* – मुख्यमंत्री बनेगा ये...

SOORAJ:
I'll change the poster.

SOORAJ:
बदल देंगे इस *poster* को।

INT./EXT. CHANDRA PRATAP'S HOUSE -

Chandra Pratap arrives home. Several people including the media are waiting for him. He waves them off as they rush to him.

MAN:
Mr. Chandra Pratap is here.

MAN:
चन्द्र प्रताप जी आ गये –

Just then, Samar emerges with Bharati. A servant quickly rushes to grab his bag. Chandra Pratap is taken aback and guilty.

CHANDRA PRATAP:
You're off already, son?

CHANDRA PRATAP:
अरे बेटा, तुम्हारी *flight* का *time* हो गया –

SAMAR: *(smiles)*
Yeah, its OK Papa....

SAMAR: *(smiles)*
Yeah, its ok papa...

BHARATI:
Why are you so concerned? As if you've had any time for him!

BHARATI:
आपको क्या ? जब से आया है दो मुँह बात भी किया...

CHANDRA PRATAP:
You know how things have been...

CHANDRA PRATAP:
क्या करें अब... तुम देख ही रही हो...

Chandra Pratap looks at his watch.

CHANDRA PRATAP:
There's time still.
(to the servant)
Put Samar's luggage in my car. I'll drop him.

CHANDRA PRATAP:
Time है अभी...
(to the servant)
समर का सामान हमारी ही गाड़ी में रखवाओ – हम छोड़ के आएँगे *airport* पर...

Both Bharati and Samar are surprised.

BHARATI:
You?

BHARATI:
आप जाएँगे ?

SAMAR:
Papa – You don't have to do this.

SAMAR:
Papa – you don't have to do this.

CHANDRA PRATAP:
Come.

CHANDRA PRATAP:
Come.

INT./EXT. IN THE CAR - NIGHT

CHANDRA PRATAP:
This time I really didn't get to see you properly. Everything okay there? Your Ph.D.?

CHANDRA PRATAP:
इस बार सचमुच तुम्हें ठीक से देख भी नहीं पाया – सब ठीक तो है वहाँ – कैसा चल रहा है तुम्हारा *Ph.D.?*

SAMAR:
I'm done with the research. The presentation is next week.

SAMAR:
Research complete कर लिया है... बस, *submit* करना है अगले हफ़्ते...

Chandra Pratap looks shocked.

CHANDRA PRATAP:
Next week?

CHANDRA PRATAP:
अगले हफ़्ते ?

SAMAR: *(nods)*
Ya Papa, I'm done with my Ph.D.

SAMAR: *(nods)*
Ya papa, I'm done with my Ph.D.

CHANDRA PRATAP:
Fantastic! So, now we'll be calling you Dr. Samar Pratap!

CHANDRA PRATAP:
Fantastic! तो अब हम आपको डॉ. समर प्रताप कहकर बुलाएँगे !!

Samar smiles at his father. Chandra Pratap hugs him.

CHANDRA PRATAP: *(with an embarrassed smile)*
Tell me the title of your thesis again. I always seem to forget...

CHANDRA PRATAP: *(with an embarrassed smile)*
ज़रा फिर से बताना तुम्हारा *thesis* का *title* मैं, अक्सर भूल जाता हूँ...

SAMAR:*(with a kind smile)*
The subtextual emotional violence of 19th century Victorian poetry.

SAMAR:*(with a kind smile)*
The Subtextual emotional violence of 19th Century Victorian Poetry.

Chandra Pratap doesn't understand one bit but is surely impressed.

CHANDRA PRATAP:
Wonderful! Sounds so impressive.
(pause)
What's next?

CHANDRA PRATAP:
Wonderful! सुनकर बड़ा अच्छा लगता है...
(pause)
तो अब आगे क्या *plan* है ?

SAMAR:
There's an offer to teach.

SAMAR:
एक *teaching job* की *offer* है...

Chandra Pratap reacts.

CHANDRA PRATAP:
So you aren't coming back? Well... I suppose that's fine too. You'll be the first teacher in our family.

CHANDRA PRATAP:
मतलब तुम वहीं रहोगे? चलो, ये भी ठीक है... हमारे ख़ानदान में कोई *teacher* नहीं हुआ है आज तक –

Samar nods his head.

EXT. AIRPORT - NIGHT

At the airport the cavalcade of cars comes to a halt. Samar is embarrassed with all the security and attention.

SAMAR:
Papa, please... you should go now. This security thing is too much. I'll go.

SAMAR:
पापा आप, जल्दी जाईए... *All this security thing is too much* – मैं चला जाउँगा –

By now they have got the trolley and put his bag on it. Chandra Pratap steps forward.

CHANDRA PRATAP:
Let me see you in....

CHANDRA PRATAP:
मैं आता हूँ न तुमको अन्दर तक छोड़...

SAMAR:
No Papa. Please... You are blocking the traffic also.

SAMAR:
नहीं पापा *Please... you're blocking the traffic also -*

CHANDRA PRATAP:
Ok, son. Come, give me a hug. God knows when I'll see you again. These elections....

CHANDRA PRATAP:
Ok बेटा... अच्छा – *Come, give me a hug...* पता नहीं कब देख पाउँगा फिर तुमको... अब ये *election...*

His father has never sounded like this before. Touched, Samar hugs him.

SAMAR:
Bye Papa.

SAMAR:
Bye, papa...

CHANDRA PRATAP:
Love you, son.

CHANDRA PRATAP:
Love you बेटा।

Just as an emotional Chandra Pratap sits in the car, his phone rings.

CHANDRA PRATAP:
What is it, Babulal?

CHANDRA PRATAP:
क्या बात है बाबूलाल ?

BABULAL:
Mr. Bhanu's condition has suddenly worsened. We're going to the hospital.

BABULAL:
बड़े साहब की तबियत अचानक ख़राब हो गयी है – *hospital* से *phone* आया था, हम वहीं जा रहे हैं –

Chandra Pratap looks worried.

CHANDRA PRATAP:
Have the doctor call me.

CHANDRA PRATAP:
Doctor से बात कराओ हमारा पहुँचते ही–

BABULAL:
Okay.

BABULAL:
जी।

Chandra Pratap disconnects the phone. The car is moving now.

CHANDRA PRATAP: *(to the driver)*
Take me to the hospital!

CHANDRA PRATAP: *(to the driver)*
पहले *hospital* ले लो।

As his father's cavalcade moves away Samar heaves a sigh of relief. His phone rings. He smiles.

Samar turns to get in through the entrance at the airport, and is shocked to see Indu standing at the entrance, she is looking at him with honest, intense love. He walks up to her. She hugs him.

INDU:
What were you thinking? I'm not some tragedy queen. I'll abduct you from across the universe, if that's what it takes.

INDU:
क्या सोच के बैठे थे... हम कोई *tragedy queen* हैं – सात समन्दर पार से उठा लाएँगे तुमको...

Samar is amused.

SAMAR:
Really? New profession?

SAMAR:
अच्छा!... ये उठाने वाला धंधा कब शुरू किया ?

She hugs him again and whispers.

INDU:
I can't live without you... I love you.

INDU:
I can't live without you... I love you.

Samar knows she means it. For a moment he is moved but then begins to feel uncomfortable. He doesn't know how to respond. He disengages from her gently.

SAMAR:
Indu, I have to go...take care.

SAMAR:
Indu, I have to go... take care.

Turning around, he walks away into the concourse, as she stares at him, tears welling up in her eyes.

EXT. ROAD - NIGHT

There's a roadblock on the street.

CHANDRA PRATAP: *(instructs)*
Find out what's going on!

CHANDRA PRATAP: *(instructs)*
आगे *check* करवाइये ना –

CHANDRA PRATAP'S P.A.:
Security come in.
(To police cop)
Get them to move. Clear the road....

CHANDRA PRATAP'S P.A.:
Security come in.
(To police cop)
हटवाइए... अरे *clear* करवाइये जल्दी।

The police cop shoots Chandra Pratap and escapes on his motorbike.

INT. AIRPORT - NIGHT

Samar is in the queue for security check when he notices people gathering anxiously before a TV screen. Some non-political news is playing in the background and then suddenly he notices the Breaking News.

NEWS READER:
Another shocking setback to the state's most powerful family. According to initial reports, the working president of the Rashtrawadi Party... Mr. Chandra Pratap was fatally attacked in a shocking incident. Reports state that this attack took place on Ratanpur road on the way to the city from the airport. Mr. Chandra Pratap was in his car when the attack took place. It seems that he was shot. As a result of the incident traffic is blocked for miles. There is no information about his condition.

NEWS READER:
प्रदेश के सबसे ताकतवर राजनीतिक परिवार को एक और बड़ा झटका – अभी–अभी मिल रही ख़बरों के अनुसार एक दिल दहला देने वाली घटना में राष्ट्रवादी पार्टी के कार्यकारी अध्यक्ष श्री चन्द्र प्रताप पर जानलेवा हमला हुआ है। कहा जा रहा है कि यह हमला कुछ ही मिनटों पहले *airport* को शहर से जोड़ने वाली रतनपुर *road* पर हुआ... हमले के वक़्त श्री चन्द्र प्रताप अपनी गाड़ी में सवार थे। ये भी बताया जा रहा है कि उनको गोली मारी गई है। घटना के बाद से इस सड़क पर करीब पाँच *kilometre* लंबा *traffic* जाम लग गया है। उनकी हालत के बारे में अभी तक किसी भी तरह की जानकारी नहीं मिल सकी है।

His heart skips a beat as he sees his father's picture flashing on the screen. He walks out of the queue, his eyes dazed in disbelief. The newsreader begins to give a scratchy account.

It is at this moment that his phone begins to ring. He cannot take his eyes off the TV screen. He doesn't even realise his phone has been ringing. It's only when the airport manager comes running to him his spell gets broken.

AIRPORT MANAGER:
Mr. Brij Gopal for you...

AIRPORT MANAGER:
बृज गोपाल जी आपसे बात करना चाहते हैं...

Samar answers the phone.

SAMAR:
Uncle! How's papa?

SAMAR:
मामाजी, क्या हुआ ? *How is papa?*

EXT. CHANDRA PRATAP'S HOUSE - NIGHT

Brij Gopal is rushing out of the house. His car is waiting for him.

BRIJ GOPAL:
They've taken him to the hospital. I'll pick you up at the airport.

BRIJ GOPAL:
हाँ, *hospital* पहुँच गया है – तुम वहीं रुको *airport* पे – मैं आ रहा हूँ –

MAN:
Get the cars!

MAN:
गाड़ी निकालो जल्दी –

SAMAR:
That will take time. I'll come by cab.

SAMAR:
मामा जी देर हो जायेगी – मैं *taxi* ले लेता हूँ –

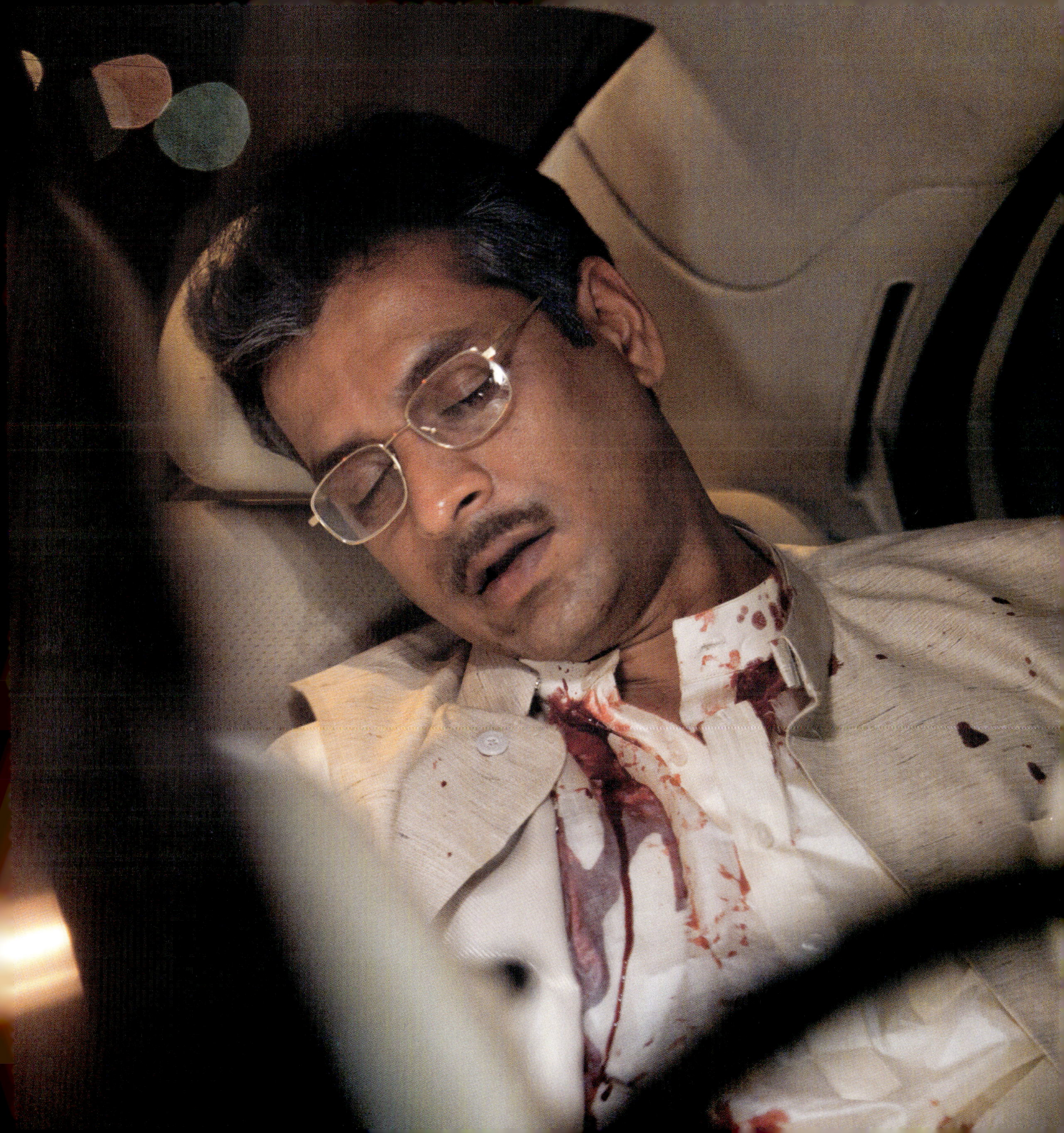

BRIJ GOPAL:
Just do as I say! Those who have done this, know that you're at the airport. You just stay there!

BRIJ GOPAL:
जो कहता हूँ वो सुनो – जिन्होंने भी ये किया उनको पता है तुम *airport* पर हो... *you just stay there.*

Samar notices that several airport security personnel have appeared around him. Brij Gopal has gotten into his car. He instructs the Security head.

BRIJ GOPAL:
Disconnect the cable TV...

BRIJ GOPAL:
घर के *TV* का *cable* बन्द कर दो –

SECURITY CHIEF:
Ok.

SECURITY CHIEF:
जी।

BRIJ GOPAL:
Security on red alert. My sister shouldn't know of this.

BRIJ GOPAL:
Security red alert पर... दीदी को पता नहीं लगना चाहिए...

SECURITY CHIEF:
Ok.

SECURITY CHIEF:
जी।

BRIJ GOPAL:
Stop all cars outside the gate!

BRIJ GOPAL:
चाहे किसी की भी हो, गाड़ी *gate* के बाहर...

SECURITY CHIEF:
Ok, Sir.

SECURITY CHIEF:
जी *sir.*

BRIJ GOPAL: *(to driver)*
Go! Go!

BRIJ GOPAL: *(to driver)*
चल, चल जल्दी *fast.*

EXT./INT. HOSPITAL - NIGHT

When Prithvi Raj's cavalcade of cars arrives at the hospital – some of his close party people are already there.

PRITHVI:
Where the hell was the security? What about the police?

PRITHVI:
*Where the f**k was the security?...* थे किधर पुलिसवाले ?

Prithvi runs down the corridor. At the ICU entrance he is met by the doctors.

DOCTOR:
It's a single bullet in the throat. He's very critical and has lost a lot of blood. We're trying to stop it.

DOCTOR:
There is a single bullet sir – गले में लगी है – *He is very critical. Blood loss* बहुत हो चुका है – *and we are trying to stop it.*

Prithvi looks worried as he doesn't find any security.

PRITHVI:
Where is the hospital security?

PRITHVI:
Hospital security कहाँ है ?

DOCTOR:
I have no idea, sir.

DOCTOR:
I have no idea, sir.

PRITHVI: *(to his men)*
Call the police chief!

PRITHVI: *(to his men)*
अरे ए... *D. G.* को *phone* लगा...

The nurse emerges from the door.

NURSE:
Doctor – Please...

NURSE:
Doctor, please...

The Doctor goes inside. Prithvi tells his people.

PRITHVI:
You guys, secure this area from all sides. Get more people. Move it!
(to the chap typing the number)
What happened?

PRITHVI:
और तुम लोग – आगे पीछे – चारों तरफ़ *position* ले लो – और आदमी सबको बुलाओ – चलो, *corridor* खाली कर...
(to the chap typing the number)
क्या हुआ रे ?

PRITHVI'S MAN:
He's not answering!

PRITHVI'S MAN:
Ring जा रहा है भैया जी, उठा नहीं रहे हैं...

PRITHVI:
Call his deputy then. Where the hell is papa's security!

PRITHVI:
I.G. देवदत्त को *फोन* लगाओ – साला बाबूजी का *security* गया कहाँ ?

It is at this point that a couple of police vehicles arrive at the hospital porch. Tall and heavy, Senior Superintendent of Police – B. Sharma gets off the vehicle and spots a group of Prithvi's armed men moving around the porch.

Prithvi spots B.Sharma in the corridor to the I.C.U. He is furious. He has never liked this debauched and corrupt officer.

PRITHVI: *(mutters to his men)*
Who sent this son of a bitch!

PRITHVI: *(mutters to his men)*
साले इस रंडीबाज को किसने भेजा ?

B.SHARMA: *(to his D.S.P.)*
Check their firearm licenses.

B.SHARMA: *(to his D.S.P.)*
License check करो सबका...

D.S.P.: *(to Cops)*
Check them.

D.S.P.: *(to Cops)*
ए, *side* में लेके *check* करो इसको –

Walks towards B. Sharma.

PRITHVI:
Back from the whorehouse, Sharma? Man the gates! We don't need cops here.

PRITHVI:
तो फ़ुर्सत मिल गई कोठा से *S.P.* साहेब... चलिए बाहर *gate* पर *duty* कीजिए... यहाँ ज़रूरत नहीं ख़ाकी वर्दी का –

S.P. B.Sharma is an old hand. He completely ignores Prithvi and continues to walk towards the I.C.U. and his half a dozen cops join him. The D.S.P. rounds up Prithvi's men as he checks their licenses.

Prithvi finds this behaviour audacious. He blocks the S.P.'s path – B.Sharma looks calm. Prithvi mocks.

PRITHVI:
You heard what I said? Out!

PRITHVI:
सुनाई नहीं पड़ा आपको ?... कहा ना बाहर निकलिए...

Tension grips the corridor.

B.SHARMA:
Let the police do its job, Mr. Prithvi Raj... or else...

B.SHARMA:
Police को अपनी *duty* करने दो *मिस्टर* पृथ्वीराज – वरना...

Prithvi reacts violently. He shoves the cop.

PRITHVI:
Or else? What will you do? Why have you come now anyway?

PRITHVI:
वरना... वरना, क्या कर लेगा तू – क्या कर लेगा तू... साला अभी आया है *duty* दिखाने...

B.Sharma loses his balance. His subordinates manage to support him. He has suddenly drawn his pistol out.

B.SHARMA:
Arrest the bastard!

B.SHARMA:
Arrest कर स्साले को...

He points the gun at Prithvi. For a moment the other cops freeze.

B. SHARMA: *(screams)*
Drag him away!

B. SHARMA: *(screams)*
Arrest him - खींच के ले जा इसको –

It is at this moment that Brij Gopal appears with Samar. Stunned at the scene, Samar runs towards them. By now the constables have held Prithvi who is vehemently strugglling. All the cops have their guns out and they hold Prithvi's men at bay. Prithvi continues to scream the choicest of abuses as he struggles and kicks the cops. But four of the cops together have him in control.

PRITHVI:
Arrest me, will you? You scoundrel! Get your hands off me! Let go! I'll chop you into pieces. You dare to arrest me, you beggar!

PRITHVI:
तू मेरे को *arrest* करेगा, तू मेरे को *arrest* करेगा साले भड़वे... हाँ, साले रंडीबाज़ – तू मेरे को *arrest* – ऐ छोड़, काट डालूँगा साले– तू मेरे को *arrest* करेगा... भिखारी साले... एँ...

SAMAR:
What are you doing?

SAMAR:
ये क्या कर रहे हैं आप लोग – ये क्या कर रहे हैं...

PRITHVI:
Now do you remember your duty.

PRITHVI:
रंडी के अँचरा में सोता है – अभी आया है *duty* दिखाने –

Samar nervously tries to help Prithvi.

PRITHVI: *(asking the cops)*
Come on... arrest me...

PRITHVI: *(asking the cops)*
Arrest कर... देखता हूँ मैं तेरे को... कैसे *arrest* करता है मेरे को –

SAMAR:
Sir, you can't do this! What are you doing?

SAMAR:
Sir, you cannot do this... ये क्या कर रहे हैं आप लोग – ये क्या कर रहे हैं...

Brij Gopal has rushed to the hospital staff who has gathered at the other end of the corridor.

DOCTOR:
B negative blood - we just don't have any!

DOCTOR:
B Negative – बिल्कुल नहीं है हमारे पास...

Brij Gopal looks at his two nephews. The cops have begun to drag Prithvi. Samar rushes to B.Sharma, still holding his gun.

SAMAR:
Leave him! Sir, you cannot do this!

SAMAR:
Sir, you can not do this... नहीं कर सकते आप –

B.Sharma suddenly slaps Samar with his hand still holding the gun. A shocked Samar reels on the floor. Brij Gopal goes on his knees to stop Samar's head from banging on the wall.

B.SHARMA:
Back off! I can do anything. Arrest him too!

B.SHARMA:
हट... *I can do anything... arrest* कर इसको भी –

PRITHVI: *(in background)*
You will pay for this!! You hit my brother! I will chop you into pieces. You're dead! I'll kill you. Hey you.

PRITHVI: *(in background)*
ए....ए..... काट डालूँगा साले... तूने छोटे को मारा, काट डालूँगा... ए... *S.P.* शर्मा, तू – तू देख, मैं तेरा क्या हाल करता हूँ... काट डालूँगा... ए बिकाउ साले... हट... छोड़ ए...

Brij Gopal realises the situation. He hasn't spoken a word. He waves the cops to stop as he helps Samar on his feet.

BRIJ GOPAL: *(calmly to Samar)*
Apologise to him.

BRIJ GOPAL: *(calmly to SAMAR)*
Say sorry - माफ़ी माँगो...

Samar is not able to open his mouth. Mutters through a clenched jaw. Even B.Sharma is surprised. B.Sharma looks at Samar whose face is still distorted with pain.

SAMAR:
Sorry.

SAMAR:
Sorry!

Brij Gopal rushes him down the corridor.

INT. OPERATING ROOM – NIGHT

The doctors are operating on Chandra Pratap as Brij Gopal and Samar look in from the gallery.

DOCTOR:
Detractors. Scissors, fast. Pass the forceps.

DOCTOR:
Detractors. Scissors, fast. Pass the forceps.

INT. HOSPITAL - NIGHT

Samar enters an adjoining room as the nurse readies Samar for blood extraction. Another nurse brings in an ice pack for his face which he rejects.

SAMAR:
Glass of water.

SAMAR:
Glass of water.

INT. OPERATING ROOM – NIGHT

DOCTOR:
Heart rate? Pass the mop... scissors.

DOCTOR:
Heart rate? Pass the mop... scissors.

There is the beeping sound of a flat line on the heart monitor. Chandra Pratap is no more.

INT. HOSPITAL - NIGHT

Brij Gopal turns and walk towards Samar. He gently places a hand on his shoulder. Samar wordlessly takes a sip from his glass. Blood spurts out from his mouth into the water.

INT. HOSPITAL ICU - NIGHT

Bhanu Pratap's mourns Chandra Paratap's death.

BHANU PRATAP:
Chandru...

BHANU PRATAP:
चन्द्रू...

Virendra Pratap enters the I.C.U.

VIRENDRA PRATAP:
I've asked for a CBI enquiry. The culprit won't get away! Given these circumstances, I'll have to take charge of the party. Father…I need your approval.

VIRENDRA PRATAP:
C. B. I. inquiry का माँग कर दिए हैं... बच नहीं सकता चाहे कोई भी हो... ऐसे में *party* का कमान हमको अपने हाथ में लेना होगा... बाबूजी, आज्ञा दीजिए...

He gives Bhanu some papers to sign. Bhanu turns his face away.

EXT. SADAR POLICE STATION - DAY

A huge crowd of Prithvi's supporters has gathered. The air is filled with tension.

PRITHVI'S SUPPORTERS:
Down with police autocracy! Down with police autocracy! Free Prithvi!

PRITHVI'S SUPPORTERS:
आज़ाद करो – आज़ाद करो... पृथ्वी को आज़ाद करो... नहीं चलेगी नहीं चलेगी – दादागिरी नहीं चलेगी... पृथ्वी तुम संघर्ष करो – हम तुम्हारे साथ हैं...

The police have a hard time containing the crowd that is now throwing stones and missiles. The police conduct a lathi charge and use tear gas to subdue the crowd.

INT. SADAR POLICE STATION – DAY

Brij Gopal is standing near the lock-up gate. Prithvi has been talking to him about his father.

PRITHVI:
If the killer isn't caught, we'll burn the city down!

PRITHVI:
आग लगा देंगे राजधानी को अगर चौबीस घंटे में पकड़ा नहीं गया तो–

BRIJ GOPAL:
Our people are on the job too.

BRIJ GOPAL:
हमारे लोग भी लगे हुए हैं पृथ्वी–

PRITHVI:
How is mom?

PRITHVI:
माँ कैसी है ?

BRIJ GOPAL:
She's putting up a brave front, but from within she...

BRIJ GOPAL:
उपर से तो हिम्मत दिखा रही है, लेकिन अन्दर से...

The lawyers who have been talking to the Sr. Police Inspector come up to Brij Gopal.

LAWYER:
SP Sharma himself filed the report. He's charged you under sections 353, 357 and 307. But you'll get bail.

LAWYER:
F.I.R.- S.P. शर्मा ने खुद लिखवायी थी – 353, 336 और 307 लगायी है... लेकिन *bail* मिल जायेगी –

SR. INSPECTOR RAM PRAVESH:
I've stated in my report. Mr. Prithvi had no weapons.

SR. INSPECTOR RAM PRAVESH:
हमने *search report* में लिख दिया है – आरोपी के *body* पर कोई भी *weapon* नहीं मिला है...

PRITHVI:
That's my only regret. If I had a gun I would've…

PRITHVI:
इसी बात का तो अफ़सोस रह गया साला – हाथ में *gun* होता तो हम उसे...

Brij Gopal calms Prithvi.

BRIJ GOPAL:
Prithvi!

BRIJ GOPAL:
पृथ्वी!

The Inspector nods. Brij Gopal begins to make a move.

PRITHVI:
Uncle. No one touches SP Sharma. I'll deal with him myself.

PRITHVI:
मामा जी, वो *S.P.* शर्मा को कोई दूसरा नहीं छूएगा – उसका हिसाब हम खुद करेंगे।

Brij Gopal nods as he realises the pain his nephew is going through.

INT. HOSPITAL – NIGHT

Samar, clearly in shock, is sitting in the corridor. They wheel in Chandra Pratap's body. Samar strokes his fathers face, battling mixed emotions of grief and anger, trying to control his tears.

INT. VIRENDRA PRATAPS HOUSE – DAY

Poster with a new design showing Virendra Pratap prominently, with pictures of Sooraj and Bhanu Pratap, is displayed. Virendra turns emotional as he hugs Sooraj.

VIRENDRA PRATAP:
You've made all my dreams come true, friend. You changed the poster!

VIRENDRA PRATAP:
सब अरमान पूरा कर दिए दोस्त... बदल डाला *poster* –

Sooraj smiles. The Superintendent of Police, Sharma is shitting bricks as he talks to Virendra Pratap.

S.P., SHARMA:
I'm screwed, Sir. Now, they believe I was involved even in your uncle's murder. If he gets bail...he'll kill me.

S.P., SHARMA:
हम तो बरबाद हो जायेंगे *sir...* अब वो लोग आपके *uncle* के *murder* में भी हम पर *doubt* कर रहा है... अगर *bail* मिल गया उसको, तो जिन्दा नहीं छोड़ेंगे हमको...

Sooraj comes in.

SOORAJ:
You didn't charge him appropriately. You should've used sections 376 and 341. He would've been in your custody.

SOORAJ:
आप *charge* सब ठीक से लगाये नहीं *sir* – 376 लगाना था – और उपर से 341 भी ठोक देते – सीधा आपकी *custody* में –

S.P., SHARMA:
Section 376? That's a rape charge.

S.P., SHARMA:
376? *rape* की दफ़ा है ये ...

SOORAJ:
Correct.

SOORAJ:
Correct.

We see the ticket aspirant political worker Beena Kumari emerging out of the shadows.

VIRENDRA PRATAP:
So tell me... where should we lodge the rape complaint?

VIRENDRA PRATAP:
बताइए किस *police station* में *F.I.R.* दर्ज करावें *S.P.* साहेब ?

S.P., Sharma looks unsure.

S.P., SHARMA:
Isn't she...

S.P., SHARMA:
मगर ये –

VIRENDRA PRATAP:
A totally genuine case, SP.

VIRENDRA PRATAP:
एकदम *genuine case* है *S.P.* साहेब –

SOORAJ:
Prithvi promised to make her a candidate and for three years he sexually exploited her.

SOORAJ:
Party ticket के नाम पर लगातार तीन साल तक पृथ्वीराज इनका यौन शोषण करता रहा –

S.P., SHARMA:
It's a serious charge. What if she backs out?

S.P., SHARMA:
Serious charge है – कहीं *Back out* तो नहीं करोगी –

BEENA KUMARI:
Sir, I've been through hell. Finally, I'm in safe hands now.
(she touches Virendra's feet)
I will get an election ticket here. There's no question of backing out.

BEENA KUMARI:
S.P. साहेब... बहुत *torture* से गुजरे हैं हम – अब जा के सही ठिकाना मिला है –
(she touches Virendra's feet)
यहाँ *ticket* ज़रूर मिलेगा – धोखा का तो सवाल ही पैदा नहीं होता।

EXT. COURT HOUSE - DAY

Thousands of party workers have gathered outside the district court. A stunned silence. Under heavy security Prithvi Raj Pratap is brought out of the court.

TV NEWS REPORTER:
There seems to be no end to the misery of the Rashtrawadi Party. In a sensational twist Prithvi Raj, who has already been charged for assaulting a police officer, has now been accused of raping a party worker. Denied bail, he's been remanded to police custody for 15 days.

TV NEWS REPORTER:
राष्ट्रवादी पार्टी की मुश्किलें कम होती नज़र नहीं आ रही हैं... एक सनसनीखेज़ खुलासे में पहले से ही *police officer* पर हमले के आरोपी पृथ्वीराज प्रताप को आज एक महिला *party worker* के *rape* के लिए *charge* किया गया। *Court* ने उनके जमानत की अर्जी को नामंजूर करते हुए पन्द्रह दिन *police custody* में रखने के आदेश दिये।

EXT. PARTY HEADQUARTERS - DAY

Outside the Party Headquarters several media vans are parked. Reporters rush towards Virendra Pratap and Sooraj as they are coming down the steps, followed by Senior Party Leaders and lawyers.

VIRENDRA PRATAP:
I deny every charge levied against Prithvi. We shall approach the High Court for his bail.

VIRENDRA PRATAP:
मैं, पृथ्वी पर उठ रहे सारे आरोपों को सिरे से ख़ारिज करता हूँ – हम उसकी जमानत के लिए *High Court* जायेंगे...

They all look at Sooraj.

SOORAJ:
Our supreme leader, Bhanu Pratap is still fighting for his life. First Chandra Pratap, now this. We are being attacked repeatedly. And on the pretext of investigating, the inept government is doing nothing. But the people demand answers. Victory to Rashtrawadi! Victory to Virendra Pratap! The party has called for a strike! Our party has declared a statewide closure tomorrow.

SOORAJ:
हमारे *supreme* नेता भानु प्रताप आज भी जीवन से संघर्ष कर रहे हैं... कल चन्द्र प्रताप, आज ये... हम पर लगातार आघात किये जा रहे हैं – और सरकार जाँच समितियों की आड़ में निकम्मी बनी हुई है... लेकिन जनता जवाब माँगती है– चक्का जाम – इन ज़्यादतियों के विरोध में हमारी *party* ने कल पूरे प्रदेश में बन्द का ऐलान किया है।

INT. SAMAR'S HOUSE - DAY

Samar is watching the proceedings on TV.

INT. POLICE STATION - DAY

Samar hands a piece of paper to Prithvi who erupts and chucks the paper back at Samar.

PRITHVI:
You want me to sign this? Have you lost it?

PRITHVI:
इसपे *sign* करें... पागल हो गया है तू ?

SAMAR:
You don't have a choice.

Prithvi is angry and exasperated.

SAMAR:
कोई *choice* नहीं है तुम्हारे पास –

PRITHVI:
Okay. Go home and take care of mom. I can deal with these people.

Samar is calm.

PRITHVI:
Ok. तू घर जा माँ का ख़याल रख ... हमको मालूम है कैसे *deal* करना है इन लोगों के साथ –

SAMAR:
But that's only if you get out.

Prithvi looks at Brij Gopal.

SAMAR:
मगर पहले यहाँ से निकलोगे तभी कुछ करोगे ना...

BRIJ GOPAL:
Your bail application was denied. Since it is a rape charge, women's organisations and the media are up in arms.

Prithvi tries to argue.

BRIJ GOPAL:
High Court ने तुम्हारा *bail reject* कर दिया है पृथ्वी... *rape* के मामले को लेकर *media* – और महिला आयोग काफ़ी तूल दे रहे हैं इसको –

PRITHVI:
But, how will signing this help?

PRITHVI:
हाँ... मगर इसपे *sign* करने से क्या फर्क़ पड़ने वाला है ?

SAMAR:
Leave that to me, brother. Trust me. I'll get you out of here.

SAMAR:
वो तुम मुझ पर छोड़ दो भैया – *Trust me,* मैं निकालूँगा। तुम्हें यहाँ से –

The two brothers look at each other. Samar's expression is unwavering and confident; Prithvi is not too sure of Samar. Samar extends the paper again to Prithvi. He looks at Brij Gopal. Brij Gopal nods. Prithvi takes the paper.

PRITHVI:
They'll pay for this heavily. Every one of them!

PRITHVI:
भारी कीमत चुकाएँगे... सब के सब।

EXT. VIRENDRA PRATAP'S HOUSE – DAY

Samar and Brij Gopal drive down to Virendra's house. They are both frisked by Sharma outside the house who doesn't forget to touch Brij Gopal's feet, but it is difficult to say if he is being obsequious or arrogant.

S.P., Sharma:
I've made a big mistake, Sir. Am appealing to your kindness. I am younger than you, so I deserve forgiveness.
(to Samar)
Sorry

S.P., Sharma:
बहुत बड़ा ग़लती हो गया बाउ जी हमसे... मगर आप ही का आसरा है... छोटे हैं हम, मगर माफ़ी का हक़ तो बनता ही है ना –
(to Samar)
Sorry!

If Brij Gopal is disgusted with this man, he doesn't show it. Keeps his cool and is very composed. As Sharma begins to frisk Samar he tries to touch Samar's chin patronisingly but Samar holds his hand and smiles coldly at him which sends a chill down Sharma's spine.

Virendra appears through the door.

VIRENDRA PRATAP: *(screams at S.P., Sharma)*
Hey Sharma! Have you gone mad? That's my brother, my uncle. Come, Uncle Brij.

VIRENDRA PRATAP: *(screams at S.P., Sharma)*
ए शर्मा, पागल हो गया है क्या ?... अरे ये हमारे भाई हैं... मामा हैं... आइए मामा जी...

INT. VIRENDRA PRATAP'S HOUSE – DAY

In the hall, Virendra Pratap does mock touching of Brij Gopal's feet and greets Samar expansively.

VIRENDRA PRATAP: *(O.S.)*
I don't know why this is happening.

VIRENDRA PRATAP: *(O.S.)*
पता नहीं क्यूँ हो रहा है ये सब...

VIRENDRA PRATAP: *(contd)*
Looks like someone cast an evil eye on us. I'm sorry that you're having to face this. But don't you worry. I will take care of everything. The party... as well as the family.

VIRENDRA PRATAP: *(contd)*
लगता है नज़र लग गई किसी की हम पर... तू भी कैसे *time* पर आया इस बार... लेकिन तू चिन्ता मत कर, सब संभाल लेंगे हम... *party* भी, और परिवार भी –

Samar's reaction is a cold silence. He notices Sooraj. Their eyes meet. Virendra notices and introduces them.

VIRENDRA PRATAP:
That's Sooraj... he's like family.

Sooraj and Samar exchange a cold look.

VIRENDRA PRATAP:
सूरज है... अपना ही है...

VIRENDRA PRATAP:
How is Aunt? Please sit.

Samar decides to come straight to the point.

VIRENDRA PRATAP:
चाची माँ कैसी हैं... बैठ ना – बैठ ?

SAMAR decides to come straight to the point.

SAMAR:
I'm taking Mom to New York.

Virendra is surprised, but only for a moment.

SAMAR:
माँ को मैं *New York* ले जा रहा हूँ –

VIRENDRA PRATAP:
The right decision. Absolutely! Don't worry about Prithvi. I'll move heaven and earth to get him bail. Without him this election....

VIRENDRA PRATAP:
सही *decision* है – बिल्कुल सही *decision* है... तू पृथ्वी की चिंता मत कर... हम ज़मीन आसमान एक कर के उसका *bail* कराएँगे – उसके बिना ये *election*... बिल्कुल नहीं –

SAMAR:
My brother won't contest the election. I'm taking him along too.

Virendra Pratap looks shocked. He looks at Sooraj .

SAMAR:
भैया *election* नहीं लड़ेगा... वो भी साथ जा रहा है हमारे –

SAMAR:
He's resigned from the party post.
(extends the letter)
He won't return from New York.

SAMAR:
भैया ने *party post* से *resign* कर दिया है –
(extends the letter)
वो अब *New York* से नहीं लौटेगा –

Virendra Pratap tries to keep his excitement in control.

VIRENDRA PRATAP:
You mean... he's never coming back?

VIRENDRA PRATAP:
हमेशा के लिए जा रहा है ?

SAMAR:
Never! The party is all yours.

SAMAR:
हमेशा के लिए... *party* पूरी तरह तुम्हारी रहेगी –

Virendra Pratap can't believe this. He passes the letter to Sooraj. Sooraj walks up to the window as he goes through its contents.

SAMAR:
Just one condition. All charges against him should be dropped.

SAMAR:
बस एक शर्त है – भैया पर लगे सारे *charges* खत्म हो जाने चाहिए–

They all look at Sharma.

VIRENDRA PRATAP: *(stutters)*
Uh...

VIRENDRA PRATAP: *(stutters)*
आ...

S.P., SHARMA:
Can be done. I'll manage the investigation report.

S.P., SHARMA:
हो सकता है। *Investigation report manage* करना पड़ेगा –

Samar walks up to Virendra and looks at Sooraj. He is speaking to Virendra, but clearly addressing Sooraj.

SAMAR:
One more thing. After three days is his court-hearing. Until then, if he... Or any member of my family is hurt in a mishap of any kind, I'll call this deal off.

SAMAR:
एक और बात, परसों भैया की *court* में पेशी है... इन तीन दिनों में *police custody* में उसको... या मेरे परिवार के किसी भी व्यक्ति को... किसी भी तरह की दुर्घटना में कोई भी आघात पहुँचता है तो मैं ये समझौता तोड़ दूँगा –

Virendra stares at Samar and then Brij Gopal who looks absolutely calm. Then Sooraj looks at Samar. Deadly calm. He nods.

SOORAJ:
Nothing of that sort will happen.

SOORAJ:
ऐसा कुछ नहीं होगा।

EXT. RASHTRAVADI PARTY HEADQUARTERS - DAY

A group of people crying. The imposing building has been decorated with massive flower wreaths. A huge portrait of Chandra Pratap adorns the exterior.

Massive crowd of men, women and party workers have gathered outside, forming long queues to pay their obeisance. Some of them are crying uncontrollably.

Police, security personnel and party workers guide the crowd as they go inside the party hall where Chandra Pratap's body has been kept on a flower bedecked platform.

Outside on a large raised platform under Chandra Pratap's portrait, a flame has been lit and a sarva dharma prarthana *is in progress.*

The spectacle is awesome. Virendra's car followed by Sooraj's arrives outside. Party workers and his supporters surge to get his attention. Sooraj looks tense but Virendra who is stunned by the massive response tries to play it cool. As Sooraj comes to his side –

VIRENDRA PRATAP:
Martyr's day, indeed! What a farce!

VIRENDRA PRATAP:
शहादत दिवस ! अच्छा नौटंकी है...

Sooraj doesn't say anything. They step inside.

INT. RASHTRAVADI PARTY HQ - DAY

As they step inside, Prithvi, Samar and Bharati stand together while Brij Gopal, Indu, Rajkumar Sakseria and other Senior Party functionaries are monitoring the VIPs.

The row of common people continues to move on. The walls of the hall are adorned by only Chandra Pratap's portraits interspersed with pictures of where he is seen along with Prithvi. There is no sign of Bhanu Pratap or Virendra Pratap anywhere. Sooraj stops at a distance after laying the wreath. He spots his father Ramcharittar, crying uncontrollably as he holds Chandra Pratap's feet.

RAMCHARITTAR:
Master... master... master... master..

RAMCHARITTAR:
बाबू जी... बाबूजी... बाबूजी... बाबूजी...

The sight disturbs him. Virendra Pratap steps forward. Brij Gopal escorts him up to Bharati. Across Virendra her eyes meet Sooraj's. She notices the coldness in his eyes. Virendra moves on to Prithvi and Samar, sarcasm written large on his face.

VIRENDRA PRATAP:
All this pomp... decorations... Huge photographs... What was the need for all this?

Prithvi joins him.

VIRENDRA PRATAP:
ये एतना तामझाम... फोटो–वोटो... का ज़रूरत था इस सबका –

PRITHVI:
Oh? Bothering you, is it? If you wish, we can put up yours too.

Virendra Pratap smiles at the loaded meaning.

PRITHVI:
क्यों, तकलीफ़ हो रही है, कहिए तो आपका भी लगवा दें –

VIRENDRA PRATAP:
Seems the cops didn't look after you well enough.

VIRENDRA PRATAP:
लगता है ख़ातिर हुआ नहीं ठीक से हवालात में...

Prithvi flares instantly but Samar holds his hand before he can charge.

SAMAR:
Brother, please... not now.

SAMAR:
भैया *please... not now.*

Virendra Pratap looks at Samar, his cold look sends chilling signals into Virendra's heart. But he returns the insinuation with equal fire. As he embraces Samar he whispers.

VIRENDRA PRATAP:
Enough of this circus, Samar.. .Your boat has capsised. Time to exit the scene now, for your own good.

VIRENDRA PRATAP:
नौटंकी बहुत हो गया समर... कमान कट चुका है – जितना जल्दी निकल जाओ अच्छा रहेगा–

Samar's face is expressionless as he looks at Virendra Pratap. He nods as he says,

SAMAR:
What is good for us, and what isn't will be our decision now, Veeru. And as soon as you step out, you'll know the public's decision too.

Virendra Pratap smiles at the confidence of this young cousin.

SAMAR:
हमारे अच्छे और बुरे का निर्णय अब तुम नहीं, हम करेंगे वीरू भइया... और जब तुम यहाँ से बाहर निकलोगे... जनता का भी जवाब मिल जायेगा तुम्हें –

BRIJ GOPAL: *(gestures to Virendra)*
Come on...

BRIJ GOPAL: *(gestures to Virendra)*
Come on...

EXT. RASHTRAVADI PARTY HEADQUARTERS - DAY

As Virendra and Sooraj step outside they see that the people who had been crying are now sloganeering.

CROWD CHANTING:
For all of eternity, we shall remember you... Chandra Pratap! You are immortal. Chandra Pratap! You are immortal. Chandra Pratap! Hail Chandra Pratap!

CROWD CHANTING:
जब तक सूरज चाँद रहेगा–चन्द्र प्रताप तेरा नाम रहेगा...
शहीद चन्द्र प्रताप– अमर रहे–अमर रहे...

Virendra Pratap feels dwarfed by the adulation given to his uncle. As he walks down the steps with Sooraj he says

VIRENDRA PRATAP:
Orchestrate as many slogans as you wish! After the funeral, a long and dark exile awaits you!

VIRENDRA PRATAP:
लगवा ले जितना नारा लगवाना है – किरिया–करम के बाद तो निकलना ही पड़ेगा, अज्ञात वनवास पर...

SOORAJ:
They aren't going anywhere. They never intended to.

SOORAJ:
कहीं नहीं जा रहे ये लोग... इनका कभी इरादा ही नहीं था देश छोड़ के जाने का –

Virendra Pratap looks baffled.

VIRENDRA PRATAP:
So Samar...?

VIRENDRA PRATAP:
तो क्या समर ?...

SOORAJ: *(nods)*
Trusting him was a big mistake.

SOORAJ: *(nods)*
भारी ग़लती किए भरोसा कर के।

INT. HOSPITAL - DAY

In the I.C.U. Bhanu Pratap waves Prithvi's resignation away.

BHANU PRATAP:
I can't accept this.

BHANU PRATAP:
हम इसे मंजूर नहीं कर सकते –

Virendra Pratap is stunned. He looks at Sooraj and then back at his father.

VIRENDRA PRATAP:
Father, you have to expel Prithvi from the party.

VIRENDRA PRATAP:
बाबूजी, आप... आपको पृथ्वी को *party* से निकालना ही होगा ! बस !

Bhanu Pratap looks unmoved.

SOORAJ:
He's a traitor. He'll destroy the party from within. Do this for your son.

SOORAJ:
गद्दार है वो बाबूजी... *party* में रहके *party* को बर्बाद कर देगा... *please* अपने बेटे के लिए उसे निकाल दीजिए...

BHANU PRATAP:
If I expel Prithvi it will trigger a wave of public sympathy for him.

BHANU PRATAP:
पृथ्वी को अगर निकाला... तो वो... *public* का *sympathy* ले जाएगा...

Virendra Pratap realises this. But is terribly upset that he will have to tolerate his enemy.

VIRENDRA PRATAP:
But father, tolerating him is just impossible for me! Both father and son treated me like dirt. I hate that man!

VIRENDRA PRATAP:
बाबूजी, उसको *tolerate* करना मेरे लिए ज़हर पीने के बराबर है! ... उस बाप–बेटे ने मुझे कुत्ते की तरह *treat* किया था।... *I hate that man!*

BHANU PRATAP:
Son... this is politics. Here, keep your enemies close to you.

BHANU PRATAP:
बेटा, ये राजनीति है – यहाँ दुश्मनों को अपने करीब रखो...

He chucks the resignation letter to the floor. Sooraj bends and picks it up.

SOORAJ:
The real enemy isn't Prithvi.
(looks directly at Bhanu Pratap)
It's Samar!

SOORAJ:
असली दुश्मन पृथ्वी नहीं –
(looks directly at Bhanu Pratap)
समर है।

Bhanu Pratap knows this and is pained by it. Virendra Pratap knows it too.

INT./EXT. SAMAR'S HOUSE - DAY

Samar and Brij Gopal step out of the house and walk towards the outhouse.

SAMAR:
This was expected.

SAMAR:
ये तो होना ही था –

BRIJ GOPAL:
Bhanu Pratap is a past master of this game. He knows that accepting the resignation would've made Prithvi a martyr.

BRIJ GOPAL:
हाँ बहुत पुराना खिलाड़ी है भानुप्रताप, जानता है कि इस्तीफ़ा मंजूर करता तो पृथ्वी शहीद बन जायेगा –

Samar takes a pamphlet out of his pocket. It's about the rally at Madhopur with Virendra Pratap's and Sooraj's photo on it.

SAMAR:
Have you seen this? Virendra has organised a mammoth rally in Madhopur. He'll announce his Chief Ministerial nomination.

SAMAR:
ये देखा आपने... माधोपुर में विराट *rally* बुला रहे हैं वो मुख्यमंत्री की उम्मीदवारी *announce* करेगा वो –

Brij Gopal smiles as he looks at the pamphlet and then at Samar.

BRIJ GOPAL:
The iron is hot.

BRIJ GOPAL:
लोहा गरम है।

Samar has a plan in mind.

EXT. MADHOPUR RALLEY GROUND - DAY

The crowd has gathered in full force. Just as a helicopter brings in Virendra Pratap and Sooraj, there is confusion and cheering as a cavalcade of cars arrive. Prithvi and Samar accompanied by Brij Gopal take the stage. Everyone on the stage looks a little confused but pay their respects to Brij Gopal.

STAR NEWS REPORTER MALTI JOSHI:
Here at the Rashtrawadi Party's rally where even as Virendra Pratap's helicopter landed, on the other side, Prithvi Pratap, Samar Pratap and Brij Gopal's convoy reached the stage. The crowd is confused even as the tableau on the stage becomes more dramatic. We will bring you a blow-by-blow account. From the Kothra ground, Madhopur, this is Malti Joshi, Star News.

STAR NEWS REPORTER MALTI JOSHI:
राष्ट्रवादी पार्टी की महारैली में जहाँ एक तरफ वीरेन्द्र प्रताप का *helicopter* उतरा वहीं दूसरी तरफ पृथ्वीराज प्रताप, उनके भाई समर प्रताप और बृज गोपाल जी की गाड़ियों का काफ़िला –... सभा में *confusion* की स्थिति बनी हुई है, और मंच पर एक ज़ोरदार *drama* चलने का अनुमान है। ... कोटरा *ground*... माधोपुर से ... *cameraman* अंजन दास के साथ मालती जोशी, *Star News.*

BRIJ GOPAL:
Please use the sofas down there.
(points to the ground)
Today, only family members on the stage. Please do cooperate...

BRIJ GOPAL:
आप सभी जाके –
(points to the ground)
नीचे *sofa* पर बैठिए – आज मंच पर सिर्फ़ परिवार वाले होंगे, *please...*

The security guards and Party workers begin to quickly take the chairs off.

As a baffled Virendra Pratap and Sooraj climb the stage, Prithvi leads Samar to the front stage. Brij Gopal, like a well orchestrated move, steps back into the rear of the stage to keep a check and hold on Virendra Pratap and Sooraj. Taking a cue and a bit of prodding from Brij Gopal the assembled Party members on the stage begin to clap. Samar takes the microphone and Prithvi too steps back to confront Virendra.

In the rear Virendra Pratap climbs the stage, furious.

VIRENDRA PRATAP:
This is too much. I will show them their status today.

VIRENDRA PRATAP:
इसकी तो... आज बता देंगे औकात इन स्सालों की –

Sooraj sees people clapping with enthusiasm. He stops Virendra Pratap.

CROWD CHANTING:
Long live Prithvi Pratap! Long live Veeru! Prithvi, please fight on... We are with you! Long live Brij Gopal!

CROWD CHANTING:
पृथ्वी भइया – ज़िन्दाबाद...

SOORAJ:
Veeru brother. Don't act in haste.

SOORAJ:
वीरू भाई *public* के सामने विवाद ठीक नहीं होगा–

But Virendra is raging as he gets on the stage.

VIRENDRA PRATAP:
But Sooraj, they...

VIRENDRA PRATAP:
सूरज ये लोग...

SOORAJ:
You know you can end their political career.

SOORAJ:
इनको राजनीतिक रसातल में पहुँचाने का उपाय तो है ही आपके पास –

BRIJ GOPAL: *(to Virendra's men)*
Please leave the stage.
(To Virendra & Sooraj)
You come this way...Come on...

BRIJ GOPAL: *(to Virendra's men)*
आप लोग नीचे चलिए...
(To Virendra & Sooraj)
आओ...

VIRENDRA PRATAP:
What's the meaning of this outrage, uncle?

VIRENDRA PRATAP:
ये क्या नौटंकी हो रहा है यहाँ पे मामा जी–

BRIJ GOPAL:
In politics, it's called hijack in broad daylight.

BRIJ GOPAL:
राजनीति में इसे कहते हैं दिन–दहाड़े सेंधमारी –

VIRENDRA PRATAP:
What do you mean?

VIRENDRA PRATAP:
क्या मतलब ?

BRIJ GOPAL:
Take care of yourself.

BRIJ GOPAL:
ये भी हम बतायें –

TWO-IN-ONE HELICOPTER

Like time, no money was wasted. They snipped the expenses they could without compromising the quality of the film. The script demanded there would be separate helicopters for various characters. This meant a considerable increase in the budget. So they decided to do some smart thinking. One helicopter was hired and some paint was bought. The helicopter was painted orange on one side so it was two colours on the two sides. It was shot from different angles in the respective scenes. So there! Two helicopters for the price of one!

CROWD CHANTING:
Long live Prithvi Pratap! Long live Rashtrawadi!

CROWD CHANTING:
पृथ्वी भइया... ज़िन्दाबाद... राष्ट्रवादी... ज़िन्दाबाद...

The audience looks on with anticipation. They are curious as Samar had seldom been seen in public.

SAMAR:
My name is Samar Pratap. I'm the youngest and I humbly greet you all.

SAMAR:
हमारा नाम... समर प्रताप है... सबसे छोटे हैं हम, और आप सब को प्रणाम करते हैं–

A group of young men begin to clap and then others join in. They have heard of the young Samar living and studying abroad. The reaction of the crowd is instantaneous.

At the rear matters have got heated up. Virendra flashes a paper:

VIRENDRA PRATAP:
You've resigned from the party, Prithvi! How will you fight now?

VIRENDRA PRATAP:
इस्तीफ़ा दे चुके हो तुम पृथ्वी प्रताप, किस हक़ से लड़ोगे ?

PRITHVI:
Throw it in the dustbin, Virendra. If you have the guts, throw me out in front of them.

PRITHVI:
उसे रद्दी की टोकरी में फेंक दो वीरेन्द्र – हमें जनता के सामने निकाल के दिखाओ ?

Samar continues to address the assembly.

SAMAR: *(O.S.):*
I've always been kept away from politics...

SAMAR: *(O.S.)*
हमारे पूज्य बड़े बाबूजी भानु प्रताप जी ने हमेशा मुझे राजनीति से दूर रखा –

SOORAJ:
Your wish will come true, Prithvi.

SOORAJ:
आपका ये अरमान भी पूरा हो जायेगा, पृथ्वी प्रताप जी...

Samar has been continuing with his speech.

SAMAR:
... and nor am I here to talk politics today. I only want to know one thing - My father, Chandra Pratap gave his life for you... at his elder brother's command. Does that martyrdom hold any value for you? Or not?

SAMAR:
और आज भी मैं यहाँ, राजनीति की बात करने नहीं आया हूँ... बस ये जानने आया हूँ आपसे, कि जिसने अपने बड़े भाई की आज्ञा पर... आपकी सेवा में अपनी जान दे दी– उस चन्द्र प्रताप का कोई मोल है कि नहीं आपकी आँखों में ?...

People go silent as Samar continues.

SAMAR:
I only want to know one thing - While his father lay dying, the police falsely accused Prithvi and physically dragged him away. Does his struggle mean nothing to you?

SAMAR:
और बताइए, कि अपने दम तोड़ते बाप के सामने, एक झूठे षड़यंत्र में पुलिस जिसे घसीट के लेकर गई... उस पृथ्वीराज प्रताप के संघर्ष का, कोई मोल है कि नहीं आपकी आँखों में ?...

It seems like the crowds have suddenly got the hint. People roar, and Prithvi's men are spread out in the audience.

CROWD CHANTING:
Prithvi, please fight on... We are with you!

CROWD CHANTING:
चन्द्र प्रताप–जिन्दाबाद... पृथ्वी तुम संघर्ष करो – हम तुम्हारे साथ हैं...

SAMAR:
There is no court higher than the people's court. And the people of Madhopur... have always done justice!

SAMAR:
जनता की अदालत से बढ़कर कोई भी अदालत नहीं है ... और माधोपुर की जनता ने, हमेशा इन्साफ़ किया है...

Prithvi's men who are spread out in the audience have been leading the slogan and the crowd follows them with enthusiasm.

CROWD CHANTING:
May Prithvi have justice!

CROWD CHANTING:
इंसाफ़ मिले–इंसाफ़ मिले... पृथ्वी को इंसाफ़ मिले...

SAMAR:
This is the hour of destiny, friends! In these trying times... the Rashtrawadi party needs a strong and able leader. Someone who cares about the poor, who fights for their dignity, and who will not hesitate to sacrifice his life for them! And you know very well who that is. And to strengthen his resolve, we have with us -our brother, Virendra Pratap, Dalit leader Sooraj Kumar, and our beloved, Brij Gopal. Elders, brothers, sisters, friends... that leader is your very own...

Samar pauses for effect. The public goes wild.

SAMAR:
फ़ैसले की घड़ी आ गई है... और आज इस कठिन घड़ी में राष्ट्रवादी पार्टी को मज़बूत कंधों की ज़रूरत है – उसकी ज़रूरत है जो गरीब का दर्द समझे, उसकी इज्ज़त के लिए लड़े और अगर ज़रूरत पड़े तो उसके लिए जान भी दे दे – आप सब जानते हैं कि वो कौन है... और आज, उसके इरादों को और भी पक्का करने हमारे साथ मौजूद हैं, भैया वीरेन्द्र प्रताप, दलित नेता सूरज कुमार और हम सब के पूज्य, ब्रिज गोपाल जी... बुज़ुर्गो, भाइयो, बहनो, दोस्तो... वो है आपका अपना...

CROWD CHANTING:
Prithvi Pratap! Victory to Prithvi Pratap! Long live Rashtrawadi Party!

CROWD CHANTING:
पृथ्वी प्रताप... पृथ्वी प्रताप... जिन्दाबाद... जिन्दाबाद... पृथ्वी प्रताप... जिन्दाबाद...

As he speaks he has walked to the rear of the stage and holds Virendra Pratap's hand, Prithvi holds the other hand and Brij Gopal holds Sooraj and walks to the front stage. They force all hands to be raised.

Prithvi waves at the audience. Sooraj and Virendra stand helplessly.

There is a very tense moment as they exchange looks.

INT. HOSPITAL I.C.U. - DAY

There are news cameras in Bhanu Pratap's I.C.U. Sooraj and Virendra are standing on ethier side of Bhanu Pratap.

BHANU PRATAP:
To preserve the integrity of the Party, I am pained to declare that Prithvi Pratap is hereby dismissed from the Rashtrawadi Party.

BHANU PRATAP:
Party की छवि को बचाने के लिए, बड़े दुःख के साथ हमने पृथ्वी प्रताप को राष्ट्रवादी पार्टी से निष्कासित करने का फ़ैसला किया है –

He raises his hand to indicate that the meeting was over and that he is tired.

INT. SAMAR'S HOUSE - LATER

Samar is helping his mother chop vegetables as Brij Gopal turns his attention away from Bhanu Pratap's press conference on the television. He smiles at Samar.

BRIJ GOPAL:
It went exactly the way you had planned.

BRIJ GOPAL:
जैसा चाहता था तू – वैसा ही हुआ।

Samar smiles.

EXT. IQBAL MAIDAN - DAY

Prithvi and his supporters make their way to the podium in an open jeep, followed by scores of people chanting slogans.

CROWD:
Long live Prithvi!

CROWD:
पृथ्वी भइया – ज़िन्दाबाद...

PRITHVI:
By dismissing me from my own party, they believe that... I have become homeless and orphaned. They're under a huge illusion. Even if they expel me from the party... how can they remove me from your hearts!

PRITHVI:
हमारी ही *party* से हमको निकाल कर वो लोग सोचते हैं – हमें बेघर और अनाथ कर देंगे... बहुत बड़ी ग़लतफ़हमी में हैं वो लोग... अरे भले ही हमें *party* से निकाल दें... हमारी जनता के दिल से कैसे निकालेंगे –

People roar. Prithvi puts a hand on his heart.

PRITHVI:
My home is in your hearts, and I'm not leaving that!

PRITHVI:
हम तो यहाँ घर बना कर बैठे हैं – कहीं नहीं जाने वाले।

People roar in support with slogans.

INT./EXT. SAMAR'S HOUSE - DAY

Brij Gopal and Samar are walking down to the outhouse which has become Samar's 'Operation Quarters'. Prithvi's cavalcade of cars is seen coming in. Prithvi is excited as he comes up to Samar and Brij Gopal.

PRITHVI:
It was as if the entire town had turned up for my meeting! The people are with us.

PRITHVI:
कमाल का *response* था छोटे... सारा शहर उलट पड़ा था इक़बाल मैदान में – *public* हमारे साथ है –

Samar smiles at his brother's enthusiasm.

INT. SAMAR'S OFFICE - LATE NIGHT / DAY

They enter the outhouse.. Samar has converted his outhouse into a massive strategy zone with computers and video screens. His boys have created a data bank on every candidate who contested elections in the last five years.

SAMAR:
The caste-wise combination of every constituency... the local issues, the candidates' election history, it's all here. The list of the top three candidates from every constituency.

SAMAR:
हर *constituency* के हर एक *booth* पर *caste wise* क्या *combination* है – वहाँ के *local* मुद्दे क्या हैं – किस *candidate* को क्या *votes* मिले – सारे *numbers* हैं हमारे पास – और ये रहे सभी सीटों पर *number* एक, दो और तीन *candidates* की *list.*

The screens are flashing. Prithvi looks impressed but worried.

PRITHVI:
Samar, we have only nine days to file nominations, and our party doesn't even have a name yet.

PRITHVI:
समर *nominations file* करने के लिए नौ दिन भी नहीं बचे हैं – और हमारी नई *party* का नाम भी *registered* नहीं है अभी –

SAMAR:
I know, brother. Remember, you had formed an organisation in college?
(calls out to a colleague)
Prabhu!

SAMAR:
I know भैया, आपने अपने *college* के ज़माने में एक मोर्चा *register* किया था –
(calls out to a colleague)
प्रभु...

A young man responds.

PRABHU:
Right away, sir!

PRABHU:
Right away, sir!

The large screen in the background brightens up with the name of his Party – Jan Shakti Party. Prithvi and gang look impressed.

SAMAR:
That's the name of you party. You're a youth symbol, and that will be your appeal.

SAMAR:
यही होगा आपकी नई *party* का नाम – *You are a youth symbol* भैया *and that will be your appeal!*

INT. SAMAR'S OUTHOUSE - DAY

Brij Gopal, Prithvi and Samar are in a meeting with a group of Muslim leaders. The Muslim leader speaks with respect.

MUSLIM LEADER- ARIF:
We respect you a lot. But you are well aware that our community has always suffered.

MUSLIM LEADER- ARIF:
बहुत मान है आपका हमारे बीच में... लेकिन आप तो जानते ही हैं कि हमेशा हमारी कौम ने धोख़ा ही खाया है...

BRIJ GOPAL:
I know that Arif. But times have changed. You can definitely trust us.

BRIJ GOPAL:
मानता हूँ, आरिफ़ भाई... लेकिन हालात वो नहीं रहे अब... आप भरोसा कर सकते हैं हम पर...

MUSLIM LEADER-1:
We do trust you, Brij sir, but you know that these political issues are very delicate.

MUSLIM LEADER-1:
भरोसा तो है, लेकिन ब्रिज भाई... आप भी मानते हैं कि सियासी हालात कितने नाज़ुक हैं...

MUSLIM LEADER-2:
We won't change our loyalty.

MUSLIM LEADER-2:
मुसलमान अभी मुट्ठी नहीं खोलेगा...

Brij Gopal gets up and embraces the leader.

BRIJ GOPAL:
I can understand.

BRIJ GOPAL:
समझता हूँ मैं।

Prithvi and Samar stand up respectfully. Arif does an adaab to Prithvi and Samar who return it. Arif turns to Prithvi.

PRITHVI:
Thank You.

PRITHVI:
जी शुक्रिया।

Brij Gopal sees him out of the room. Samar is looking worried.

SAMAR:
Uncle, their support is crucial... 33% of the voters in the 132 constituencies are Muslims.

SAMAR:
मामाजी, *support* इनका ज़रूरी है... हमारी एक सौ बत्तीस *constituency* में *thirty three percent voters* तो मुसलमान हैं –

PRITHVI:
They vote in a group and we can't bribe their vote.

PRITHVI:
एक मुश्त *vote* करते हैं ये... और इनका *vote* बिकाउ नहीं होता...

Brij Gopal nods.

BRIJ GOPAL:
Well then… we will need to strengthen our position. And as that happens, the Muslims will support us.

BRIJ GOPAL:
हाँ, तुम्हें अपनी ताकत बढ़ानी होगी – और जैसे–जैसे ताकत बढ़ेगी, मुसलमान तुम्हारी तरफ़ हो जाएँगे...

SAMAR:
Uncle, we also need to gain support of the small regional parties.

SAMAR:
पर मामाजी, जो बाकी दो–दो, चार–चार सीटों वाली *regional* पार्टियों को भी खींचना होगा –

Brij Gopal knows that it is important.

BRIJ GOPAL:
Talks are underway, but they are asking for a huge price.

BRIJ GOPAL:
बात कर रहे हैं हमारे लोग... लेकिन, कीमत बहुत उँची लगा रहे हैं।

INT. VIRENDRA PRATAP'S OFFICE - DAY

As Virendra climbs down the steps Babulal hands over sheets of printed papers to Sooraj .

BABULAL:
Here is the confirmation.

BABULAL:
सबका *confirmation* आ चुका है –

VIRENDRA PRATAP:
What's this?

VIRENDRA PRATAP:
क्या है ये?

Virendra Pratap looks at Sooraj who informs him.

SOORAJ:
We have removed Prithvi's name from every single bank account of the Party.

SOORAJ:
Party के जितने *bank accounts* हैं और दूसरे भी *funds* के खातों से पृथ्वी प्रताप का *signature cancel* करवा दिया गया है –

VIRENDRA PRATAP:
Great! Let him thrash about for every penny.

VIRENDRA PRATAP:
बस... पैसे–पैसे को तरस जाये साला...

SOORAJ:
Babulal, the businessmen?

SOORAJ:
बाबूलाल जी, वो *list* दिया था व्यापारियों का...

BABULAL:
I've instructed all of them.

BABULAL:
हाँ जी, सबको *phone* कर दिया है...

VIRENDRA PRATAP:
Let him fight the election as a beggar!

VIRENDRA PRATAP:
लड़ ले – भीख माँग के *election.*

INT./EXT. PRITHVI'S CAR – DAY

Prithvi is campaigning amidst crowds chanting slogans in his favour.

EXT. STREETS – DAY

Prithvi's man friday meets up the local dalit leader in the backyard and hands over a bundle of notes.

PRITHVI'S MAN AZAD:
We need a crowd of 300,000.

PRITHVI'S MAN AZAD:
तीन लाख का भीड़ *target* करना है – इस बार...

Dalit leader looks shocked.

DALIT LEADER - BALDEO:
You're asking for thousands, but offering peanuts for that.

DALIT LEADER - BALDEO:
लाखों का भीड़ और दे रहे हैं चिड़िया का खोराक...

PRITHVI'S MAN AZAD:
I'll... make sure you get the balance.

PRITHVI'S MAN AZAD:
अरे नाश्ता पानी करवाइए – बाकी भेजवाते हैं...

DALIT LEADER - BALDEO:
My dear sir, to organise crowds, one needs advance cash. Not credit. Don't waste my time.

DALIT LEADER - BALDEO:
नेता जी *public rally* में उधार नहीं *advance* चलता है – हाँ... खाली फोकट में *time* मत खराब कीजिए आपलोग –

PRITHVI'S MAN AZAD:
I'll... get it done.

PRITHVI'S MAN AZAD:
करवाते हैं – करवाते हैं।

Prithvi's man feels humiliated.

INT. OFFICE – DAY

Brij Gopal is meeting a group of businessmen. They are listening to him with rapt attention and great respect.

BRIJ GOPAL:
You've always supported us.

BRIJ GOPAL:
आप लोगों ने हमेशा हमारी मदद की है –

SETH #1:
We've already given to the party fund.

SETH #1:
Party को तो हम अपना चन्दा पहले ही भिजवा चुके हैं ब्रिज गोपाल जी...

BRIJ GOPAL:
That Party doesn't exist. I'm talking about Prithvi Pratap. After all, he will be your next Chief Minister.

BRIJ GOPAL:
अब वो *party* तो ख़त्म हो गई... मैं, पृथ्वी प्रताप की बात कर रहा हूँ... आपके अगले *C.M.* तो वही होंगे...

SETH #2:
May your words come true! We're always there for you. But times are tough.

SETH #2:
ईश्वर करे आपकी बाणी सही उतरे – हम लोग हमेशा आपकी सेवा में रहेंगे... लेकिन इस मंदी में *double* बोझा मत डालिए –

Seth folds his hand making Brij Gopal almost embarassed.

SETH #1:
Now that you've come personally please accept this offering.

SETH #1:
अब आप खुद ही आ गये हैं तो हमारे तरफ से ये आप रख लीजिए –

They hand over 5 cheques of Rs.1,00,000/- each. Brij Gopal looks at the cheques and smiles.

BRIJ GOPAL:
Looks like a couple of zeros have been missed out. I brought receipts for 50 million, while you are offering half a million.

BRIJ GOPAL:
लगता है कुछ एक *zero* कम पड़ गये हैं – हम रसीदें तो पाँच करोड़ की लाये थे – आप पाँच लाख का सहयोग देना चाहते हैं...

He leaves his chair and folds his hand.

BRIJ GOPAL:
I respect your status. Hence, I can't accept this. I'm leaving the receipts here, though.

BRIJ GOPAL:
आपकी प्रतिष्ठा का ख़याल है – ये नहीं ले जा सकते हम... लेकिन रसीदें छोड़े जा रहे हैं – अच्छा, नमस्ते –

ALL:
Thank you.

ALL:
नमस्ते।

INT. BRIJ GOPAL'S CAR/ SAMAR'S OFFICE – DAY

Brij Gopal is in his car talking to Samar who is in the outhouse office.

BRIJ GOPAL:
Looks like we've suddenly become political outcasts. I've spoken with Sakseria. I'm going to see him.

BRIJ GOPAL:
लगता है जैसे अचानक राजनीतिक अछूत बन गये हैं हमलोग... राजकुमार सक्सेरिया से बात किया है – उसी के पास जा रहा हूँ –

SAMAR:
I don't think in these conditions he'll bet on Prithvi.

SAMAR:
मामा जी, मुझे नहीं लगता इस हालात में, पृथ्वी भइया पर दाँव लगाएगा वो...

Brij Gopal knows this but hopes that he will anyway.

BRIJ GOPAL:
Your father had done a lot for him. Let's see.

BRIJ GOPAL:
तुम्हारे पिताजी ने उसके लिए बहुत कुछ किया है – देखते हैं...

Samar knows that but he also knows Sakseria's nature.

INT./EXT. SAKSERIA RESIDENCE - DAY

Brij Gopal's car enters Sakseria's mansion. Brij Gopal is met by the staff of Sakseria on the porch and taken to the hall. His arrival causes lot of attention. Brij Gopal just smiles as he waits. A little while later he turns as he hears Sakseria's boisterous laughter and he is surprised to see Sakseria escorting Virendra Pratap out.

SAKSERIA:
I'll visit your father today itself. Don't hesitate to call for absolutely anything.

SAKSERIA:
आज ही जायेंगे बड़े साहब के दर्शन के लिए... और बेहिचक *phone* कर दीजिए – कभी भी, कुछ भी हो –

VIRENDRA PRATAP:
For now, only what I've asked for.

VIRENDRA PRATAP:
बस *uncle* अभी तो जो कहा है वो करवा दीजिए...

Brij Gopal notices the bonhomie and smiles as Sakseria walks upto him.

SAKSERIA:
Of course! 500 million will reach you by this evening. Don't worry.

SAKSERIA:
हाँ–हाँ पचास करोड़ तो आज शाम तक ही भेजवा दूँगा – चिंता मत कीजिए –

VIRENDRA PRATAP:
I shall leave now.

VIRENDRA PRATAP:
ठीक है – चलता हूँ –

SAKSERIA: *(O.S)*
Mr. Brij Gopal! Hello. Please, come in.

SAKSERIA: *(O.S)*
अरे आप, नमस्ते ब्रिज गोपाल जी... कैसे हैं आप? चलिए न अंदर चलते हैं –

Brij Gopal smiles as he folds his hands.

BRIJ GOPAL:
No... just came to say hello.

BRIJ GOPAL:
नहीं, बस ऐसे ही आ गये थे हाल–चाल पूछने...

BRIJ GOPAL:
How is Indu?

BRIJ GOPAL:
इंदु बिटिया को नहीं देखा बहुत दिनों से – कैसी है वो?

SAKSERIA:
She's well... very well.

SAKSERIA:
ठीक है, बिलकुल ठीक है –

BRIJ GOPAL:
Okay then...

BRIJ GOPAL:
अच्छा चलता हूँ।

Sakseria looks a bit baffled but Brij Gopal puts his arm around him.

INT. SAMAR'S HOUSE/ NEW YORK - EVENING

Samar is on the phone. His face betrays the tension he feels.

Through the open door are visible several members of the core committee, obviously waiting for him to return to the meeting.

Sarah is at home. Her mother, in the background, is quietly doing her household chores, but listening to Sarah too.

SAMAR:
Why're you being so difficult Sarah?

SAMAR:
तुम ऐसे क्यों बात कर रही हो, सारा?

SARAH:
Am I being difficult?!
(shouting now)
You were supposed to return three weeks ago and...

SARAH:
मैं कैसी बात कर रही हूँ ? तुम तीन हफ़्ते पहले आने वाले थे और...

SAMAR: *(shouting back)*
My father was shot dead, remember?

SAMAR:
मेरे पिताजी की हत्या हुई है, भूल गयीं ?

On hearing his tone, M.K. who was waiting discreetly in the meeting room, quietly shuts the door to the meeting room.

SARAH:
Don't talk to me like that, Samar!

SARAH:
गुस्सा करने की ज़रूरत नहीं है, समर...

Samar gathers himself.

SAMAR: *(Conciliatory)*
Look, I'm sorry. It's just it's been -

SAMAR:
मुझे माफ़ कर दो – तुम्हें पता है कि यहाँ...

SARAH:
I check my phone fifty times a day seeing if you called. You never have. The only news I get is off the net.

SARAH:
मैं पचास बार phone देखती हूँ – कि कहीं तुमने call किया होगा– लेकिन नहीं... मुझे तो सारी ख़बर internet से मिलती है...

Samar doesn't want this conversation to go on further. Moreover, his Party workers are waiting for him.

SAMAR:
Listen, I can't talk right now... I'll be there as soon as I can, okay?

SAMAR:
देखो, मैं अभी बात नहीं कर सकता – मैं जल्द ही तुम्हारे पास आउँगा...

SARAH:
I'm coming there, Samar.

SARAH:
मैं वहाँ आ रही हूँ, समर...

He reacts swiftly.

SAMAR:
No, you're not!

SAMAR:
नहीं, ऐसा मत करो...

She's shocked at his tone. He gathers himself.

SAMAR: *(contd)*
Sarah, please listen, listen to me, Sarah. The time is not right. And I have some serious priorities out here.

SAMAR: *(contd)*
सारा, सुनो मेरी बात सुनो – इस वक़्त नहीं – और ज़्यादा ज़रूरी काम हैं...

Sarah wipes her tears and gets herself together. She speaks coldly now.

SARAH:
And obviously I don't figure in them...Thanks Samar..

SARAH:
हाँ, अब मेरी ज़रूरत नहीं है... शुक्रिया, समर!

SAMAR:
Sarah!

SAMAR:
सारा।

She disconnects the phone and slumps into her chair, breaking down. Her mother gives her a comforting hug.

Samar curses under his breath. He notices Indu's car arriving in the drive way. The attendants run to open the door for her.

ATTENDANT:
Mr. Samar is in the office. Should I inform him?

ATTENDANT:
समर भइया *office* में हैं – खबर करें ?

Indu looks in the direction of the outhouse. Samar is standing behind the glass door. Their eyes meet. She sees no expression on his face and turns towards the main door.

INDU:
I'm here to meet aunty.

INDU:
हम *aunty* से मिलने आये हैं।

Samar continues to look at her.

INT. KITCHEN, SAMAR'S HOUSE - DAY

Brij Gopal begins to pick up some cookies from the table. Samar looks calmly at Indu. Bharati notices them together and suddenly,

BHARATI:
Why don't you get married to Samar? Then you can be with me, always.

BHARATI:
शादी क्यों नहीं कर लेतीं तुम समर से – और फिर रह जाती हमेशा के लिए मेरे पास...

Indu is taken aback at the sudden proposal but recovers quickly.

INDU: *(tersely)*
I don't need to marry anyone for that.

INDU: *(tersely)*
आपके पास रहने के लिए हमें किसी से शादी नहीं करनी –

Bharati is well aware of the tiffs that Samar and Indu keep having but Indu sounds hurt. Bharati looks at Samar.

BHARATI:
Samar, have you fought with Indu?

BHARATI:
क्या कह दिया तूने इन्दु को ?

Samar looks at Indu.

INDU:
It's nothing. I'm fine.

INDU:
कुछ नहीं *aunty*... छोड़िए... हम ऐसे ही ठीक हैं...

Samar now walks up to face her.

SAMAR:
May I say something?

SAMAR:
क्या मैं कुछ कह सकता हूँ –

Indu looks a little alarmed.

INDU:
What?

INDU:
क्या !

Brij Gopal begins to get a little alarmed but Samar looks and says the words so easily.

SAMAR:
I have been a fool, Indu.

SAMAR:
I have been a fool, Indu.

Indu doesn't quite understand.

INDU:
What are you trying to say?

INDU:
तुम कहना क्या चाहते हो ?

SAMAR:
Just this... that not only does my mother, but even I like you.

SAMAR:
यही कि... तुम सिर्फ़ मेरी माँ को ही नहीं... मुझे भी अच्छी लगती हो –

Indu looks surprised and excited at the same time. Brij Gopal begins to look concerned.

INDU:
You're lying!

INDU:
झूठ बोल रहे हो तुम !

Samar looks at her with great intent.

SAMAR:
No! I didn't know then. I was confused.

SAMAR:
नहीं... तब मुझे पता नहीं था इन्दु – *confused* था...

Her breathing quickens as Samar holds her shoulders . He looks into her eye.

SAMAR:
I'm sorry.

SAMAR:
I am Sorry...

Indu's eyes are moist with tears. She can't believe her ears. Still looking at her, Samar tells his mother.

SAMAR:
Mom, I accept. Please speak with her dad.

SAMAR:
माँ मुझे मंजूर है... तुम इनके पिता जी से बात कर लो –

Indu's heart begins to jump with excitement.

INDU:
See... if this is a joke, I'll hammer you.

INDU:
देखो... बहुत मारूँगी अगर मज़ाक किया तो –

SAMAR:
Look at that! Threats of violence, already? Mom, do ask for an ambulance as dowry. Who knows when I'll have to go to the hospital.

SAMAR:
लो... अभी से मारपीट की बात... ए माँ, दहेज में एक *ambulance* मँगा लेना... पता नहीं कब *hospital* जाना पड़े।

Indu hugs him. He holds her calmly trying to comfort her excitement. His eyes meet Brij Gopal's. They know each other too well. For once Brij Gopal looks pained at the predicament and turns away.

INT. NIGHTCLUB – NIGHT

Samar and Indu are dancing at a club.

EXT./INT. SAKSERIA HOUSE – DAY

Bharati and Brij Gopal arrive at Sakseria's house. Sakseria leads them to the inner courtyard.

RAJKUMAR SAKSERIA:
Phenomenal response to Prithvi! His media management is excellent, fantastic.
(to Bharati)
Your younger son, Samar is a gem.

RAJKUMAR SAKSERIA:
कम्माल का *response* मिला है पृथ्वी जी को... और *media management is excellent, fantastic...*
(to Bharati)
भाभी जी, आपका जो दूसरा बेटा है न, समर – वो हीरा है हीरा...

BHARATI:
I'm here to ask something for him.

BHARATI:
उसी हीरे के लिए अँगूठी माँगने आई हूँ आपसे –

RAJKUMAR SAKSERIA:
Anything, anything, of course!
(To server who brings tea)
Thank you.

RAJKUMAR SAKSERIA:
क्यूँ शर्मिन्दा कर रही हैं ? सब कुछ तो आप ही का है –
(To server who brings tea)
Thank you.

BHARATI:
I'm very fond of Indu. And I'm sure, she'll keep Samar happy.

BHARATI:
इन्दु बहुत प्यारी है मुझे... हमारे समर को बहुत खुश रखेगी वो...

Brij Gopal has been a silent participant all this while. Rajkumar Sakseria gets a little emotional as he responds.

RAJKUMAR SAKSERIA:
I've been looking forward to this day. And you know what... Samar will make an excellent Chief Minister.

RAJKUMAR SAKSERIA:
बरसों से इसी बात का तो इंतज़ार था कि कब समर *India* वापस लौटे... वैसे एक बात कहूँ आपसे – समर में मुख्यमंत्री बनने की बहुत क़ाबिलियत है –

Bharati looks amused, even a bit surprised but Brij Gopal gets the import of Rajkumar Sakseria's dialogue.

BRIJ GOPAL:
No, it is Prithvi who'll be the CM. Samar is just helping him.

BRIJ GOPAL:
नहीं, मुख्यमंत्री तो पृथ्वी ही बनेगा... समर बस उसकी मदद कर रहा है –

Sakseria doesn't event flinch as he says,

RAJKUMAR SAKSERIA:
That's fine too. After all, Prithvi is the leader. Then, we should let Samar be. Let Indu marry Prithvi.

RAJKUMAR SAKSERIA:
चलिए, ये भी ठीक ही है – *leader* तो आख़िर पृथ्वी ही हैं – आप समर को आज़ाद ही रहने दें – मेरी बेटी का हाथ आप पृथ्वी प्रताप जी के हाथ में दे दीजिए...

Bharati goes blank. Brij Gopal had probably seen it coming and hides his emotions with a smile.

BHARATI:
How can you say that! That's impossible. Moreover, Indu loves Samar.

BHARATI:
कैसी बात कर रहे हैं आप भाईसाहब – असंभव है ये... और फिर इन्दु बेटी तो समर को ही पसन्द करती है –

Surprisingly. Sakseria shows no emotions.

RAJKUMAR SAKSERIA:
You don't worry about Indu. My choice will be her choice. See, if I am to finance a party, then obviously I will insist that my daughter should marry the CM designate. And in either case, she will come to your family.

RAJKUMAR SAKSERIA:
आप इंदु की चिंता ना करें – मेरी पसंद ही इंदु की पसन्द है – अब आप देखिए ना बहन जी... मैं अगर मुख्यमंत्री की *party* को *finance* करूँगा – तो ये भी तो चाहूँगा कि मुख्यमंत्री से मेरी बेटी की शादी हो... और फिर बिटिया आएगी तो आप ही के घर ना...

Brij Gopal just nods and smiles.

BRIJ GOPAL: *(to Bharati)*
Lets go...

BRIJ GOPAL: *(to Bharati)*
चलो।

INT. SAMAR'S HOUSE, KITCHEN - DAY

Brij Gopal, Bharati, and Prithvi all look stunned at what Samar has just said.

PRITHVI: *(protests)*
Have you gone mad? Stop talking nonsense. How can you even imagine that I'll marry Indu!

PRITHVI: *(protests)*
पागल हो गया है तू... अल्ल–बल्ल जो मुँह में आ गया बक दिया – सोच भी कैसे सकता है तू कि मैं इंदु से शादी करूँगा...

Samar knew Prithvi would react this way. He looks at Brij Gopal.

BRIJ GOPAL:
Samar is right, Prithvi. We don't have a choice.

BRIJ GOPAL:
समर ठीक कह रहा है पृथ्वी... हमारे पास कोई रास्ता नहीं बचा है –

Bharati's eyes are moist again. Prithvi's anger makes him more assertive.

PRITHVI:
Of course we do! I've decided. Samar will become the CM. So what if I don't get to sit on that chair? My brother will!

PRITHVI:
रास्ता है मामाजी – हमने सोच लिया बस... समर मुख्यमंत्री बनेगा... क्या हुआ जो हम गद्दी पर नहीं बैठे तो – हमारा भाई बैठेगा –

Samar protests.

SAMAR:
Ridiculous, brother.

SAMAR:
Ridiculous - भइया ...

Prithvi stops him.

PRITHVI:
Ridiculous? Wait a minute. You think only you can make sacrifices? And I can't? I don't care for a position that takes your happiness away.

PRITHVI:
एक *second* समर, तू सोचता है, तू ही मेरे लिए सब कुछ कर सकता है... मैं कुर्बानी नहीं दे सकता तेरे लिए... याद रख, परवाह नहीं ऐसी कुर्सी की जो तेरी खुशियाँ कुचल दे...

SAMAR:
Brother... my happiness lies only in making you the CM. And, you want to know the truth?

SAMAR:
भइया... मेरी खुशी बस इस बात में है कि तुम मुख्यमंत्री बनो – और सच जानना चाहते हो –

Samar looks at his mother. Brij Gopal knows what is coming, and holds Bharati's hand.

SAMAR:
Indu knows that I don't love her.

SAMAR:
इन्दु जानती है कि मैं उससे प्यार नहीं करता...

Bharati is hurt and Prithvi looks shocked.

PRITHVI:
Then why did you send the proposal?

PRITHVI:
तो तू रिश्ता क्यूँ ले गया वहाँ ?

SAMAR:
Because of you. Only Sakseria can fund your election.

SAMAR:
तुम्हारे लिए... सिर्फ़ सक्सेरिया अकेले तुम्हारा *election finance* कर सकता है।

Samar is silent.

PRITHVI:
To hell with his money! You're my younger brother. We'll do it on our own.

PRITHVI:
अरे भाड़ में जाये उसका पैसा – तू मेरा छोटू है रे... हम ऐसे ही लड़ लेंगे *election.*

Samar looks at his mother and Brij Gopal. Bharati has been crying.

BRIJ GOPAL:
That is no longer an option. If we don't accept his support, he'll offer it to Virendra. And marry Indu to him.

BRIJ GOPAL:
अब वो रास्ता भी नहीं बचा... अगर हम हाँ नहीं करते हैं, तो वो वीरेन्द्र को *support* कर देगा... और इंदु की शादी उससे करवा देगा –

Prithvi looks at Brij Gopal in disbelief. Samar walks up to Prithvi.

SAMAR:
Indu is a very nice girl. She'll learn to love you. And I know that you will look after her well.

SAMAR:
इंदु दिल की बहुत अच्छी है भइया... *she'll learn to love you..* और मैं जानता हूँ... तुम भी उसे बहुत खुश रखोगे।

INT. SAKSERIA'S GYM - DAY

Indu is livid and is finding it difficult to talk to her father who is walking the treadmill.

INDU:
How can you do this! Am I only a business proposal for you? Just another source of income??

INDU:
आप ऐसा सोच भी कैसे सकते हैं – मैं आपके लिए एक *business proposal* हूँ... कमाई का ज़रिया...

The treadmill comes to a sudden stop. Sakseria has hit the Stop button. He speaks very calmly.

RAJKUMAR SAKSERIA:
You're upset now. We'll talk later.

RAJKUMAR SAKSERIA:
तुम इस वक़्त बात करने की *condition* में नहीं हो बाद में बात करेंगे।

Sakseria looks at Indu steadily. She is shocked beyond belief at his coldness and runs out, devastated.

INT. SAMAR'S OFFICE - NIGHT

Later that night inside the outhouse they debate over the list. The room is full of young party workers and Brij Gopal is obviously the eldest. Samar pulls the print-out from the printer and hands a copy to Brij Gopal.

SAMAR:
Our list...

SAMAR:
हमारी *list* की इस –

Everyone is suddenly distracted because of Indu's entry. She looks devastated.

INDU:
Why are you doing this to me? Why?

INDU:
Why are you doing this to me? क्यूँ ?

BRIJ GOPAL:
Come... let's go to the other room.

BRIJ GOPAL:
आइए, बगल वाले कक्ष में बैठते हैं।

Brij Gopal immediately signals everyone to leave. If Samar is embarrassed, he doesn't show it as he looks at Prithvi.

SAMAR:
I'll handle this, brother.

Prithvi realises the delicacy of the situation.

He walks out leaving the space for Samar to deal with the issue.

SAMAR:
I'll handle this भैया...

INDU:
You say you don't love me... fine! Don't want to marry me... don't! But what right do you have to meddle in my life?

Samar stands rooted in a place and calmly looks at her.

INDU:
प्यार नहीं करते हो हमसे – मत करो... शादी नहीं कर सकते – मत करो.. लेकिन हमारी ज़िन्दगी से खेलने का क्या हक़ है तुमको!!

SAMAR:
You're forgetting that it was I who asked for your hand in marriage.

SAMAR:
तुम शायद भूल रही हो कि मेरे ही कहने से मेरी माँ ये रिश्ता लेकर गई थीं तुम्हारे घर...

INDU:
So what if my father spoke nonsense? I still love you! I have forsaken his house... his wealth... I'll go with you wherever you take me. I can't marry anyone else. I can't live without you.

Samar had expected this reaction from Indu.

INDU:
तो क्या हो गया जो मेरे बाप ने उलटी बात की – मैं तो प्यार करती हूँ तुमसे... उनका घर – दौलत सब कुछ छोड़ दिया मैंने... तुम जहाँ ले चलो – जैसे रखो मुझे परवाह नहीं है समर... *I can't marry anyone else... I cannot live without you!..*

SAMAR:
In these circumstances I can't marry you.

SAMAR:
इन हालातों में, मैं तुमसे शादी नहीं कर सकता –

INDU:
Please, Samar... Don't say that! Take back your decision.

INDU:
नहीं समर, *don't say that...* अपना फ़ैसला वापस ले लो...

SAMAR:
I can't take a chance with my brother's political career.

SAMAR:
अपने भाई के राजनीतिक भविष्य के साथ नहीं खेल सकता मैं इन्दु ...

INDU:
And my life? You have no problem destroying it!

Samar comes close to her.

INDU:
और मेरी ज़िन्दगी ? उसके साथ तुम जैसे चाहो खेलो –

SAMAR:
I am not destroying your life, Indu. I'm trying to protect it. You know that if we reject Prithvi's proposal... your father will marry you off to Virendra.

Indu is devastated and breaks down.

SAMAR:
मैं तुम्हारी ज़िन्दगी से खेल नहीं रहा इंदु – उसे बिखरने से बचा रहा हूँ – तुम अच्छी तरह जानती हो कि अगर तुमने भैया का *proposal reject* कर दिया... तो तुम्हारे *dad* तुम्हारी शादी वीरेन्द्र प्रताप से कर देंगे...

SAMAR:
Please try to understand, Indu. Whatever you may think of Prithvi... I know he will love you a lot. And then Mom's here too. You will be very happy here.

SAMAR:
समझने की कोशिश करो इंदु... तुम्हारी नज़र में पृथ्वी चाहे जैसा भी हो, तुम्हें बहुत प्यार करेगा... और फिर माँ है यहाँ... बहुत खुश रहोगी तुम इस घर में –

His cold and decisive manner leaves her helpless. It is at this moment that Bharati appears. Indu breaks down in her arms. Bharati is reminded of her own past as she tries to comfort Indu.

BHARATI:
This is how it's always been, child. We are the ones who're always expected to compromise.

BHARATI:
ये तो हमेशा होता रहा है बेटी – सारे समझौते बस... हमें ही करने पड़ते हैं।

INT. INDU'S ROOM – NIGHT

Indu is thinking about everything.

EXT./INT. WEDDING SCENE – NIGHT

Indu is marrying Prithvi and they take the seven rounds around the holy fire as the priest chants prayers. Brij Gopal and Bharati stand close to the ceremony while Sakseria has been welcoming the guests. Surprisingly, Virendra arrives.

VIRENDRA PRATAP:
Hello... hello...

VIRENDRA PRATAP:
नमस्कार ... नमस्ते, नमस्ते...

Sakseria greets him.

RAJKUMAR SAKSERIA:
We are indeed honoured by your presence. Come, sir...

RAJKUMAR SAKSERIA:
धन्य कर दिया आपने – अहोभाग्य हमारे जो आप पधारे... आइए वीरू जी।

Brij Gopal touches the feet of Ramnath Rai.

BRIJ GOPAL:
Hello.

BRIJ GOPAL:
प्रणाम –

RAMNATH RAI:
Hello... God bless you.

RAMNATH RAI:
जीते रहो –

Virendra Pratap watches the ceremony, his eyes also on the guests. There is suddenly commotion on one side. Someone taps Sakseria's shoulder.

BUSINESSMAN:
Mr. Sakseria, the super Chief Minister is here. Please do introduce me.

BUSINESSMAN:
सक्सेरिया साहब, *Super C.M.* आ रहे हैं – परिचय ना करवाइगा –

Virendra Pratap notices Samar hogging the attention. As he comes near Virendra Pratap takes a jewelery box from Babulal.

VIRENDRA PRATAP:
My father has sent this for the bride.

VIRENDRA PRATAP:
बाबूजी ने भेजा है – बहू के लिए...

SAMAR:
Thanks for coming...

SAMAR:
Thanks for coming...

Brij Gopal has joined them. Virendra Pratap ignores him and targets Samar smilingly.

VIRENDRA PRATAP:
Do you seriously believe that by selling your brother you can win the election?

VIRENDRA PRATAP:
तुम्हें क्या लगता है?... भाई को बेच के *election* जीत जाओगे –

Samar calmly smiles back at him.

SAMAR:
Looks like you're nervous.

SAMAR:
लगता है *nervous* हो गये हैं आप ?

Virendra Pratap laughs in response.

VIRENDRA PRATAP:
Let Sakseria stake as much loot as he wants. Your brother will still fall flat.

VIRENDRA PRATAP:
सक्सेरिया चाहे जितना भी माल लगा ले... तुम्हारा भाई मुँह की खायेगा इस *election* में...

Samar's smile sends a chill down Virendra's back.

SAMAR:
The fear of defeat is clearly visible on your face. Uncle, please look after him.

SAMAR:
हार का डर पूरी तरह झलक रहा है आपके चेहरे पर... मामा जी, सँभालिए वीरू भैया को...

SAMAR:
Enjoy the evening.

SAMAR:
Enjoy the evening.

Samar walks away..

VIRENDRA PRATAP: *(to Brij Gopal)*
Overconfident, eh?

VIRENDRA PRATAP: *(to Brij Gopal)*
Over confident... अँ !!

At the 'Marriage Bedi' Prithvi is tying the mangal sootra round Indu's neck. She turns to look at Samar. Their eyes meet.

INT. BEDROOM - NIGHT

It's Indu's and Prithvi's wedding night.. Prithvi comes to Indu but she moves away...

Prithvi takes a pillow and bed sheet and exits the room.

EXT. STREETS OF BACKWARD VILLAGES - DAY

The style of Sooraj's campaign is different. He is more personal and direct. He walks through the lanes of the dalit and backward villages. Some journalists interview him.

JOURNALIST #1:
Mr. Sooraj, an exclusive byte, please.

JOURNALIST #1:
सूरज जी एक *exclusive byte!*

Sooraj is always shy to talk about himself.

SOORAJ:
What can I say about myself? Speak to the people.

SOORAJ:
खुद के बारे में क्या बोलें ... आप, लोगों से बात कर लीजिए –

Journalists don't want to give up the opportunity to speak with him.

JOURALIST #2:
Some personal questions, please.

JOURALIST #2:
Sir कुछ *personal* सवाल पूछने थे आपसे –

SOORAJ:
You must be joking. There's nothing worth hiding in a poor person's life. My life is an open book. However, I can point you in an interesting direction.

SOORAJ:
मज़ाक कर रहीं हैं आप – हम ग़रीब–पिछड़े लोगों का क्या छुपा है. .. जो *personal* होगा... खुली किताब हैं... दरअसल आपको कहीं और होना चाहिए –

BhoPALS

Katrina, Ranbir and Arjun came together on the sets of Raajneeti and became friends. They would often be seen together playing cricket, digging into local delicacies or planning a prank. In the prank playing, they did not even spare each other! Once poor Katrina was tricked into gifting Arjun's old underwear to Nana Patekar! The trouble trio ensured there was always some action going on behind the scenes, and proudly called themselves the BhoPALS! ■

JOURNALIST #1:
What do you mean?

JOURNALIST #1:
आपका मतलब ?...

Sooraj signals them to come up to him. As he walks up to his car he talks to them. The villagers have begun to shout slogans in his support.

VILLAGERS:
Hail Sooraj!

VILLAGERS:
सूरज भैया... ज़िन्दाबाद...

As Sooraj sits in his car he waves at his folk. The journalists look excited.

JOURNALIST #2:
Thank you!

JOURNALIST #2:
Thank you!

EXT. HOTEL - DAY

At a hotel Prithvi Raj Pratap decides to have a press conference. The media is there in full swing. He takes his seat.

PRITHVI:
Hello... Please be seated.

PRITHVI:
नमस्ते... बैठिए – बैठिए...

FEMALE JOURNALIST #1:
Sir, how's your campaign doing?

FEMALE JOURNALIST #1:
Sir, कैसा चल रहा है आपका *campaign?*

PRITHVI:
Fantastic! In just 7 days, we've confirmed 200 plus candidates. And it's obvious that the people are with us.

PRITHVI:
Fantastic!... महज़ सात दिनों में दो सौ से अधिक सीटों पर उम्मीदवार खड़े कर दिए हैं – आप खुद देख सकते हैं जनता कैसे हमारे साथ जुड़ रही है–

The female journalist who was instigated by Sooraj intervenes.

FEMALE JOURNALIST #2:
It seems that your entire campaign is funded by Rajkumar Sakseria.

FEMALE JOURNALIST #2:
सुनने में आया है कि आपके *party* के *election* के लिए पूरा *cash* राजकुमार सक्सेरिया दे रहे हैं –

Prithvi covers his surprise with a smile.

PRITHVI:
See, ours in a new party. Whoever has wanted to help...

PRITHVI:
देखिए, हमारी तो नई *party* है – मदद करने वाले सभी को...

FEMALE JOURNALIST #3:
How much dowry did you collect from him?

FEMALE JOURNALIST #3:
अपनी बेटी इन्दु की शादी में कितना दहेज दिया उन्होंने ?

PRITHVI'S FRIEND: *(shouts)*
Hey!

PRITHVI'S FRIEND: *(shouts)*
ए....

Prithvi feels irritated and his friends get angry. He stops them by saying.

PRITHVI:
Look here... let's stick to election-related questions.

PRITHVI:
देखिए, अगर हम चुनाव संबंधी प्रश्न करें तो ठीक है –

Journalist #1 takes the cue.

समय

FEMALE JOURNALIST #1:
Well, this question is on everyone's lips. Even though Indu was openly seeing your brother... how come she got married to you?

FEMALE JOURNALIST #1:
यह सवाल तो सभी कर रहे हैं कि कैसे इन्दु के जब खुलेआम संबंध आपके छोटे भाई समर प्रताप से थे तो शादी आपसे...

Prithvi gets up and is now really angry.

PRITHVI:
This is my personal and family matter.

PRITHVI:
ए... ये मेरा *personal* और पारिवारिक मामला है –

FEMALE JOURNALIST #2:
Then, at least tell us about the compromises you've made in this marriage.

FEMALE JOURNALIST #2:
तो बस इतना बता दीजिए कि इस विवाह में किस तरह की *compromise* हुई है –

Prithvi feels humiliated and angry. His men shout and Prithvi gets up and turns away

FEMALE JOURNALIST #2:
Are you absolutely sure that while you are busy campaigning your wife isn't with your brother?

FEMALE JOURNALIST #2:
और क्या आप विश्वास से कह सकते हैं कि जब आप अपने *campaigning* के लिए सड़कों की धूल फाँक रहे हैं... तो आपकी पत्नि आपके छोटे भाई के साथ संबंध नहीं रख रही है...

Prithvi walks up to the journalist and gestures at her.

PRITHVI: *(red with anger)*
Hey - Shut up - Shut up ! You whore!
(gestures at all the cameras)
Stop this.

PRITHVI: *(red with anger)*
Hey - Shut up - Shut up ! You Whore!
(gestures at all the cameras)
बंद कर ये सब... बंद कर सब...

FEMALE JOURNALIST #2:
What's the meaning of this?

FEMALE JOURNALIST #2:
What's the meaning of this?

IRFAAN:
Stop this. Stop this at once!

IRFAAN:
क्या हो रहा है ये... बन्द करो... चुप रहिए आप लोग... बंद कर सब – हटिए...

FEMALE JOURNALIST #2:
What are you doing?

FEMALE JOURNALIST #2:
ये क्या कर रहे हैं –

Prithvi smashes the camera while the others continue to shoot. He threatens the journalist.

PRITHVI:
You asked a very filthy question. You will pay for this!

PRITHVI:
बहुत घटिया... बहुत घटिया सवाल किया है तूने है – इसका अंजाम तू भुगतेगी... ए, बंद कर ये सब...

FEMALE JOURNALIST #2:
Stop it!

FEMALE JOURNALIST #2:
Stop it!

PRITHVI:
Shut this. Shut this down!

PRITHVI:
हटाओ इन सबको – हटाओ इन सबको। ...

INT. INDU'S ROOM – DAY

The news about Prithvi's spat with journalists is all over the news. When he returns home Indu too has been watching the television.

VFiX IT!

A deal had been made with a leading television news channel and in the film, several 'journalists' carried microphones with the logo of that news channel. Somewhere along the way, due to some disagreements, the deal fell through and a new one was struck with Star News. But the entire film was full of shots with the logo of the previous channel prominently displayed. The VFX team was brought to the rescue and shot by shot, they slapped on the logo of Star News on the microphones. ■

NEWS ANCHOR:
Prithvi Pratap had already been charged with assaulting a police officer and of raping a woman party worker.

NEWS ANCHOR:
पृथ्वी प्रताप पर पहले ही पुलिस के एक आला अधिकारी से हाथापाई और यौन शोषण जैसे गम्भीर आरोप लग चुके हैं... हमने उनके इस व्यवहार के बारे में अन्य लोगों से प्रतिक्रिया ली...

On TV, Indu continues to watch as they broadcast, Sooraj gives his byte to a reporter. Sooraj notices the reporter and she says.

REPORTER - AKANKSHA:
Thank you so much, sir. Sir...one more thing, please.

REPORTER - AKANKSHA:
Sir, एक और *byte please* –

Sooraj looks reluctant at first but then smiles shrewdly.

REPORTER - AKANKSHA:
Mr. Sooraj... what do you have to say about Mr. Prithvi Pratap's recent outburst?

REPORTER - AKANKSHA:
सूरज जी, पृथ्वीप्रताप की इस हरकत पर आपका क्या कहना है ?

SOORAJ:
My sympathies are with him. His marriage itself was a huge compromise. Hence, it isn't surprising for him to lose his mental balance. And it's obvious that he can't cope with the stress of elections. He needs to rest.

SOORAJ:
हमें उनके साथ बहुत *sympathy* है... मजबूरी में शादी करनी पड़ी है... ऐसे में *mental balance* तो बिगड़ेगा ही – और लगता है *election* का दबाव वो झेल नहीं पा रहे – उन्हें आराम की ज़रूरत है।

Prithvi picks up the remote, switches the TV off and walks out of the bedroom.

INT. SAMAR'S HOUSE- DAY

It's early in the morning. Indu emerges from her bedroom to see Prithvi sleeping on the couch outside.

She spots Bharati setting up the tea tray for Samar who has been working all night in the outhouse office.

BHARATI: *(to server)*
This is for Samar.

BHARATI: *(to server)*
समर भइया के लिए –

Indu takes the tea tray from the server.

INDU:
I... I'll take this.

INDU:
हम... हम लेके जाएँगे –

Everyone looks alarmed as Indu steps out of the house walking to the outhouse.

EXT. SAMAR'S HOUSE - DAY

As Indu moves through the garden towards Samar's cottage, Brij Gopal's car arrives.

Along with Brij Gopal, Sarah too emerges from the car. Bharati and everyone else look curiously as Brij Gopal joins them with a smile.

BRIJ GOPAL:
Guess who this is!

BRIJ GOPAL:
पहचानो कौन ?

BHARATI:
Who?

BHARATI:
कौन?

Bharati looks curious and is then amused. Sarah seems to have guessed.

SARAH:
This must be Samar's Mom. Right?

SARAH:
ये समर की माँ होंगी...

Brij Gopal introduces her.

BRIJ GOPAL:
Absolutely! This is Samar's friend, Sarah.

BRIJ GOPAL:
Absolutely! - समर की दोस्त है – *सारा...*

Sarah smiles and folds her hands.

BHARATI:
Oh?

BHARATI:
अच्छा –

SARAH:
Namaste!

SARAH:
नमस्ते!

BHARATI:
Oh... yes, namaste.

BHARATI:
अरे, नमस्ते –

BRIJ GOPAL:
And this is...Samar's sister-in-law, Indu.

BRIJ GOPAL:
और ये समर की भाभी हैं...

SARAH:
Hi!

SARAH:
Hi.

Indu does a cold Namaste. She is not going to like this girl. However, Sarah is warm in her greeting with each one. Bharati comes to her.

BHARATI:
You didn't tell me she was coming!

BHARATI:
भइया आपने बताया नहीं कि ये आ रही है!

BRIJ GOPAL:
How could I? She called me at 3 a.m. from the airport.

BRIJ GOPAL:
अरे कैसे बताता ? सुबह तीन बजे *phone* आया इसका *airport* से –

Hearing the commotion, Samar emerges from his cottage. He stops short on seeing Sarah.

SAMAR:
Sarah!

SAMAR:
सारा!

They stare at each other a long moment. And then Samar rushes up to embrace her.

Bharati looks in surprise at Brij Gopal, who shrugs mischievously. Indu is bewildered.

EXT. SAMAR'S HOUSE GARDEN - DAY

Sarah and Samar are strolling in the garden, deep in conversation, From a distance, his security guards keep a watchful eye on the surroundings.

SAMAR:
Look Sarah, life here is different. I won't be able to explain everything. You'll just have to trust me.

SAMAR:
तुम्हें शायद यहाँ सब कुछ अजीब सा लगे... लेकिन समझना भी मुश्किल है... तुम शायद समझ ना सको...

She continues to look at him directly, for a long moment. As if making up her mind.

SARAH:
Do you still love me, Samar?

SARAH:
तुम मुझे प्यार तो करते हो ना, समर ?

SAMAR:
What kind of a question is this?

SAMAR:
किस तरह का सवाल है ये ?

SARAH:
Do you love me?

SARAH:
क्या तुम मुझसे प्यार करते हो ?

He looks at her.

SAMAR:
Of course Sarah, I love you very much.

SAMAR:
हाँ मैं तुमसे प्यार करता हूँ...

Sarah smiles finally.

SARAH:
Then you don't have to worry about me. I trust you completely.

SARAH:
तो फिर मेरी चिन्ता मत करो... मुझे तुम पर पूरा भरोसा है।

Despite all his tension, Samar is suffused with love for this good, strong, honest girl and taking her into his arms, he kisses her passionately. He notices someone watching them. It is Indu. She continues to look at him as he puts his arm around Sarah and walks away.

INT. OUTHOUSE – DAY

Samar walks through his outer office where computers are buzzing away, phones are ringing, and intense discussions are happening.

He enters his private office and stops in his tracks. Indu is standing at the other end facing him. He looks at her, a question in his eyes.

INDU:
The two of you look very nice together.

INDU:
अच्छा लगा तुम दोनों को साथ देखकर –

Samar is cautious as he doesn't know where this conversation is going.

INDU: *(contd)*
She obviously loves you a lot. But maybe she doesn't know...

INDU *(contd):*
बहुत प्यार करती है वो तुमसे... लेकिन शायद जानती नहीं...

Samar knows what is coming.

INDU: *(contd)*
That you can't love anyone.

INDU: *(contd)*
कि तुम किसी से प्यार नहीं कर सकते...

SAMAR:
Indu, please listen to me..

SAMAR:
इन्दु, *please listen to me...*

Her stance hardens - she is not going to let him maneuver her.

INDU:
No! You listen to me! You only know how to use people.
(snorts)
I don't even recognise this Samar.

INDU:
No! You listen to me! तुम बस इस्तेमाल करना जानते हो –
(snorts)
इस समर को तो हम पहचानते भी नहीं...

Samar hears her out in silence.

INDU *(contd):*
The darkness that I see in your heart, Samar...
(sighs)
I'm actually grateful to my father for rejecting your proposal. Because whatever your brother may be... he has a pure heart.

INDU *(contd):*
The darkness that I see in your heart, समर...
(sighs)
मैं अपने पापा का शुक्रिया करती हूँ... कि तुम्हारा *proposal reject* कर दिया. .. क्योंकि तुम्हारा भाई, जैसा भी है... उसका दिल सच्चा है –

There is a pause between them. This truth is deadly, but Samar is calm as he holds her gaze.

SAMAR:
You won't understand this, Indu.

SAMAR:
तुम कभी समझ नहीं पाओगी इन्दु...

INDU:
This much I do understand, Samar. That we don't exploit those who love us.

INDU:
इतना तो समझते हैं समर... कि जो हमसे प्यार करते हैं, उनका इस्तेमाल नहीं किया करते...

She walks to the door. As she nears him, she pauses.

INDU:
Sarah may not be able to bear it

INDU:
सारा शायद बर्दाश्त नहीं कर पाये...

She leaves. Samar is left to live with the truth of her words.

MONTAGE:

EXT. SOORAJ AND VIRENDRA PRATAP CAMPAIGNING- DAY

NEWS ANCHOR: *(V/O)*
The election campaign of Rashtrawadi Party has gone up. The campaigning was at full flow at the district Beerpur. There were huge rallies in several areas. The new president of the Party Virendra Pratap and the general secretary Sooraj Kumar delivered the speech too. If the presence of the voters is taken into consideration then this campaign has been thriving. Media has already made Sooraj Kumar, a hero of the backward class. The pace with which he has evolved in politics and with his gift of the gab he has already become a leader amongst the backward class and would be supported by them.

NEWS ANCHOR: *(V/O)*
राष्ट्रवादी पार्टी का प्रचार अभियान तेजी से ज़ोर पकड़ता जा रहा है... आज बीरपुर जिला राष्ट्रवादी पार्टी के चुनाव–प्रचार से सराबोर रहा... कई जगहों पर *party* की रैलियाँ हुईं... *party* के नए कार्यकारी अध्यक्ष वीरेन्द्र प्रताप और महासचिव सूरज कुमार ने *road show* भी किए... जनता की उपस्थिति को अगर पैमाना माना जाए तो ये प्रचार–अभियान बेहद सफ़ल हुआ है. .. *Media* पहले से ही सूरज कुमार को दलित सम्राट की उपाधि दे चुका है... जिस रफ्तार से उन्होंने सत्ता के गलियारों में अपने पैर जमाए हैं और साथ ही उनकी युवा और बेबाक् छवि की वजह से प्रदेश का पिछड़ा और दलित समाज अभी से उन्हें अपना नेता मान चुका है... राष्ट्रवादी पार्टी में उनके आने से दलित भोंटों का *support* तय माना जा रहा है।

EXT. VILLAGE STREETS – DAY

Sooraj walks through the lanes of the dalit and backward villages and his men walk with him. We see women bless him.

CROWD CHANTING:
Long live Sooraj! Victory to Sooraj! Long live Sooraj! Victory to Sooraj! Saviour of the poor...Sooraj!

CROWD CHANTING:
सूरज भैया जिन्दाबाद... सूरज भैया जिन्दाबाद...

As he comes out of the village an old man tells him.

SOORAJ:
Yes, uncle?

SOORAJ:
क्या चाचा –

OLD MAN:
There is no cause for worry here. Every single person is rooting for you.

OLD MAN:
यहाँ चिन्ता का कोय बात नहीं... बच्चा–बच्चा का जबान पर बस आपका ही नाम है।

Sooraj smiles.

INT. I.C.U. - DAY

A meeting is going on between Ramnath Rai, Bhanu Pratap, and Virendra when Sooraj walks in.

RAMNATH RAI:
On one hand you speak of our old alliance and yet, you are being secretive about seat-sharing. What I am supposed to tell the high-command.

RAMNATH RAI:
एक तरफ आप पुराने गठबंधन की बात कर रहे हैं – दूसरी तरफ सीटों का खुलासा भी नहीं करते... अब क्या जवाब दें हम हाईकमान को...

The three remain completely silent. Sooraj hands over a list of seats to Virendra Pratap who passes it on to Bhanu Pratap.

RAMNATH RAI: *(anxiously)*
Bhanu, I will have to declare the seats today.

RAMNATH RAI: *(anxiously)*
भानु – मुझे आज शाम तक सीटें *declare* करनी हैं –

Virendra steps in.

VIRENDRA PRATAP:
If you enjoy defeat, you can have more seats.

VIRENDRA PRATAP:
नाना जी, सीटें हारने के लिए चाहिए तो बोलिए...

RAMNATH RAI:
Virendra..dont forget that mine is a national party. Don't force me to take drastic decisions.

RAMNATH RAI:
वीरेन्द्र, प्रजातांत्रिक *national party* है कठोर फ़ैसले लेने पर मजबूर मत करो हमें –

VIRENDRA PRATAP: *(almost mocking)*
Give me a break grandpa. Don't forget that we have been lugging your national burden. The last time you had just 12 legislators and yet we made you the Chief Minister. So, this time don't expect even six. Now you decide.

VIRENDRA PRATAP: *(almost mocking)*
नाना जी, *please, please!...* आप मत भूलिए कि हम ढो रहे हैं आपकी राष्ट्रीय सवारी का बोझ – पिछली बार बारह *M.L.A.* थे आपके और मुख्यमंत्री बना दिया... ग़नीमत समझिए कि हम आज भी छः सीटें देने को तैयार हैं... फ़ैसला आपके हाथ में है –

Ramnath Rai is deeply disappointed. Bhanu intervenes.

BHANU PRATAP:
Veeru, make that 10.

BHANU PRATAP:
वीरेन्द्र, दस कर दो...

SOORAJ:
We will lose all of them. We can't take that chance.

SOORAJ:
सब हार जायेंगे बाबू जी – *chance* नहीं ले सकते –

Ramnath Rai walks up to Bhanu Pratap and whispers.

RAMNATH RAI:
Bhanu, the coalition will break. Ask him to release 20 seats. We will pay you a total of 400 million.

RAMNATH RAI:
भानु, गठबंधन टूट जायेगा – इससे कहो बीस सीटें दे दे – हर *seat* के दो–दो करोड़ पहुँचा दूँगा... पूरे चालिस करोड़...

Virendra almost smiles as he looks at Sooraj.

SOORAJ:
500 million.

SOORAJ:
पचास।

Ramnath knows he is cornered.

INT./EXT. RASHTRAVADI PARTY HQ. - DAY

Virendra Pratap arrives at the Party HQ. Babulal and Beena Kumari are already there. The crowd is chanting slogans to support the Party. The media is throwing a volley of questions.

MEDIA #1:
Sir, what are the terms of alliance with Prajatantrik Party?

MEDIA #1:
Sir, प्रजातांत्रिक पार्टी से गठबंधन किन शर्तों पर हुआ है ?

MEDIA #2:
Sir, who else is filing nominations along with you?

MEDIA #2:
वीरेन्द्र जी, आपके साथ और कितने लोगों की *nominations file* हुई हैं ?

MEDIA #3:
Sir, what's the terms and conditions of the tie up? How many seats are they contesting?

MEDIA #3:
Sir, सीटों के तालमेल का खुलासा कब होगा ?

MEDIA #4:
When can we expect the seat-sharing to be revealed?

MEDIA #4:
Sir, final का खुलासा कब होगा?

VIRENDRA PRATAP:
You will get to know it all very soon.

VIRENDRA PRATAP:
हाँ–हाँ सब पता चल जाएगा *time* आने पर...

BABULAL:
Patience... patience is always rewarded.

BABULAL:
सबर कीजिए, सबर का फल मीठा होता है...

INT. SAMAR'S OFFICE – DAY

Samar and Prithvi's men discussing.

MAN #1:
Everything is going in their favour.

MAN #1:
हर चीज उसके *favour* में हो रहा है समर भैया ...

MAN #2:
If you don't do something quick, we'll lose the plot.

MAN #2:
राष्ट्रवादी का भोटर नहीं टूटा ... तो बाजी निकल जायेगा हाथ से –

MAN #3:
Samar Sir, we need a masterstroke.

MAN #3:
समर भैया... कोई राम बाण चलाइए अब तो...

They look assured.

INT. BABULAL HOUSE – EVENING

When Brij Gopal calls up Babulal he is having a massage. His partner works on his body every night as he finishes his drink. Usually he would have jumped to answer the call from Brij Gopal but the situation in the past few days has changed dramatically, he picks up the phone at leisure.

BABULAL:
Yes, sir?

BABULAL:
हाँ बाबू जी...

BRIJ GOPAL:
I had asked you for a favour, Babulal.

BRIJ GOPAL:
कुछ काम बोला था तुमको बाबूलाल –

BABULAL: *(smiles)*
Your favour is not so easy to fulfill, sir. And it wouldn't be very ethical of me, would it?

BABULAL: *(smiles)*
आपका काम एतना आसान भी तो नहीं है न बाबूजी, आखिर इमान–धरम भी तो कोई चीज होता है –

BRIJ GOPAL: *(smiles)*
True. Sorry, I disturbed you.

BRIJ GOPAL: *(smiles)*
हाँ... *disturb* किया तुम्हारे आराम को... क्षमा करना –

Brij Gopal switches the phone off.

BABULAL:
He wasted my time.

BABULAL:
Time ख़राब है साला...

INT. SAMAR'S OFFICE - EVENING

Samar looks at Brij Gopal.

BRIJ GOPAL:
He is speaking of ethics. Imagine!
(laughs)
Now what are the ethics of a bandit? Tell me.

BRIJ GOPAL:
इमान–धर्म की बात कर रहा है...
(laughs)
अब डाकू का धरम क्या होगा... बोलो !

Samar smiles.

INT. BABULAL'S BEDROOM – DAY

Babulal wakes up with his paramour's throat slit open. He chokes with terror.

As he scrambles around in panic, desperately wondering how to erase the evidence, his cell phone is missing. He is dead scared now. Frantically looks for it when the landline rings. His face goes white with fear as he discovers a couple of photographs of him and the paramour under the telephone! It's Brij Gopal on the other end.

Brij Gopal has some more photos in his hand as he talks.

BABULAL:
Hello...Hello...

BABULAL:
Hello... Hello...

BRIJ GOPAL:
Babulal, yesterday you were giving me a lecture on ethics...

BRIJ GOPAL:
हाँ बाबूलाल, हम सोच रहे थे कल तुम कुछ धरम–इमान की बात कर रहे थे...

BABULAL:
I was... I was... I was completely out of line, sir...

BABULAL:
ग़लती हो गई बाबूजी... बहुत... बहुत बड़ी –

BRIJ GOPAL:
I can see that. Anyway, tell me where I should send these photos.

BRIJ GOPAL:
वो तो हम देख ही रहे हैं बाबूलाल – ख़ैर अब तुम ही बताओ कहाँ भिजवायें ये तस्वीरें हम...

BABULAL:
Please forgive me, sir...

BABULAL:
माफ़ कर दीजिए बाबूजी।

EXT. SAMAR'S HOUSE - DAY

Babulal's car arrives at Samar's outhouse office.

EXT. COURTYARD - DAY

Sarah comes out of the house in the external courtyard reading from a English-Hindi learner –

SARAH:
I – Main ...
(turns the pages)
Bahut...

SARAH:
I - Main...
(turns the pages)
Bahut...

EXT./INT. SAMAR'S OFFICE – DAY

Brij Gopal escorts a very obsequious Babulal who is sobbing with folded hands, to Samar's room.

Samar receives Babulal.

Babulal falls at Samar's feet, holding them and crying abjectly.

BABULAL:
I went astray... Please forgive me...

BABULAL:
भटक गये थे हम... समर भइया, माफ़ कर दीजिए एक बार माफ कीजिए –

Just then Sarah opens the door.

SARAH:
Main sakta..- I... can...

SARAH:
Main...

BABULAL:
I beg of you.... Please forgive me. Brother Samar the time is really bad.

BABULAL:
पता नहीं कैसे... *please* समर भइया, समर भइया *time* खराब आ गया है – सच, सच बता रहे हैं...

Sarah stops in her tracks, astonished at the scene in front of her. Brij Gopal comes to her and gently leads her out, shutting the door behind him.

BRIJ GOPAL:
The man needs some help... what's this?

BRIJ GOPAL:
The man needs some help... what's this?

Brij Gopal notices the Hindi-English book in Sarah's hand and laughs.

INT. SAMAR'S OUTHOUSE OFFICE - DAY

Samar hands over a sheet of paper to Babulal. He seems to know what is written.

BABULAL:
I was... helpless...

BABULAL:
एक बार...

SAMAR:
You already know this to be true. Now you only have to state it publicly.

SAMAR:
वही सब है जो आप अच्छी तरह जानते हैं – अब सारी दुनियाँ को बता दीजिए...

Babulal has gone white with fear.

BABULAL:
But... but...

BABULAL:
लेकिन...

SAMAR:
Never be afraid of the truth! I'm with you. Have no fear. No harm will come to you. Come.

SAMAR:
अरे साँच को आँच क्या बाबूलाल जी – हम हैं न – डरिए मत... कुछ होने नहीं देंगे आपको – आइए...

Babulal seems to have gone blank. Samar smiles as he fixes up Babulal's buttons.

SAMAR:
Don't you trust me?

SAMAR:
भरोसा नहीं है हम पर...

Tears in his eyes, Babulal nods his head. Samar looks up at M.K. who is standing at the door and nods. She turns around and goes inside. Samar puts his arm around Babulal and leads him out.

INT. MAIN OFFICE OF OUTHOUSE - DAY

TV camera crew have set up an interview.

CREW MEMBER #1:
This way…

CREW MEMBER #1:
इस तरफ...

CREW MEMBER #2:
Light-light...

CREW MEMBER #2:
Light-light...

CREW MEMBER #3:
And rolling...

CREW MEMBER #3:
and rolling...

CREW MEMBER #1:
Ok, ready. Silence please.

CREW MEMBER #1:
Ok, ready – silence please...

The female anchor begins.

ANCHOR:
Allegations and counter-allegations during elections are a common occurrence. But what we're about to reveal now will stun you. Today we have with us... a staunch loyalist of Rashtrawadi... Mr. Babulal.

ANCHOR:
प्रांत के राजनीतिक इतिहास में आरोप और प्रत्यारोप तो लगते ही रहे हैं लेकिन आज जो सनसनीखेज़ खुलासा हो रहा है वो देख कर आपके होश उड़ जाएँगे – आज इस वक़्त, हमारे साथ मौजूद हैं राष्ट्रवादी पार्टी के पुराने वफ़ादार श्री बाबूलाल जी...

BABULAL:
Having served the party faithfully for 25 years... it pains me to admit that the Rashtrawadi Party has become a den of corruption.

BABULAL:
पच्चीस वर्षों तक *party* की सेवा करने के बाद... आज मुझे बड़े दुःख से कहना पड़ता है... कि राष्ट्रवादी *party* भ्रष्टाचार का अड्डा बन चुकी है...

INT. VIRENDRA PRATAP'S HOUSE - DAY

Virendra Pratap is watching with stunned horror as Babulal continues. Sooraj joins him.

BABULAL: *(on TV)*
When Mr. Bhanu Pratap was in power, his son, Virendra Pratap took fixed kickbacks from every government contract.

BABULAL: *(on TV)*
जब भानु प्रताप जी की सरकार थी, तब उनके बेटे, वीरेन्द्र प्रताप जी का, हर सरकारी ठेके में हिस्सा *fix* था...

Through this speech a bunch of political workers and leaders watch the television in utter shock.

INT. AT MARKET – TV SHOWROOM - DAY

Public watching Babulal on television.

BABULAL *(On TV):*
He raked in billions. Even donations meant for the party fund were not spared.

BABULAL *(On TV):*
उन्होंने हज़ारों–करोड़ हिस्से में लिये... *party fund* में जो पैसा आया, वो भी पूरी तरह से उनके कब्ज़े में है–

INT. IN THE MAIN OFFICE – SAMAR'S OUTHOUSE - DAY

BABULAL:
Ever since Sooraj Kumar became general secretary this politics of cash has escalated.

BABULAL:
जब से सूरज कुमार *party* के महासचिव बने हैं ... तब से ये पैसों की राजनीति *party* के अन्दर और ज़ोर पकड़ रही है...

INT. VIRENDRA'S HOUSE - DAY

BABULAL *(On TV):*
In these elections...

BABULAL *(On TV):*
इस *election* में...

Virendra Pratap mutters in cold anger.

VIRENDRA PRATAP:
Get him here! Son of a bitch!

VIRENDRA PRATAP:
जहाँ कहीं भी है उठवाओ इसको – हरामी की औलाद...

Sooraj sounds cold as he says.

SOORAJ:
The men are on their way.

SOORAJ:
मैंने आदमियों को भिजवा दिया है –

VIRENDRA PRATAP:
I'm going to torture the bastard to death!

VIRENDRA PRATAP:
तड़पा–तड़पा के मारेंगे साले को –

SOORAJ:
Veeru, please calm down. This is Samar's ploy. It's imperative that Babulal publicly take back his own statement.

SOORAJ:
वीरू भाई जल्दबाज़ी ना करें... ये समर की चाल है – ज़रूरी है कि बाबूलाल अपने बयान से खुद पलटे...

INT. SAMAR'S OUTHOUSE OFFICE - DAY

Samar leads a shattered Babulal into his office.

SAMAR:
Don't worry at all, Babulal. Your safety is my responsibility now.

SAMAR:
ज़रा भी चिंता करने की ज़रूरत नहीं है बाबूलाल जी... बैठिए... आपकी *security* अब हमारी जिम्मेदारी है –

Babulal is still shivering. Samar puts his arm around him.

SAMAR:
Tell me... That night when you called my father at the airport...

SAMAR:
बस एक बात पूछनी थी आपसे – उस रात *airport* पर जब आपने बाबूजी को *phone* किया था...

A cold hand clutches Babulal's heart. He folds his hands and begins sobbing again.

SAMAR *(contd):*
Who asked you to make that call?

SAMAR *(contd):*
किसने कहा था आपसे *phone* करने को ?

BABULAL: *(Sobbing)*
Wh... what are you asking? I... don't understand...

BABULAL: *(Sobbing)*
ये... ये आप क्या पूछ रहे हैं – हमारी समझ में नहीं आ रहा है...

SAMAR:
Who asked you to call?

SAMAR:
किसने कहा था *phone* करने को ?

Babulal goes blank.

BABULAL:
Phone? I... I didn't call.

BABULAL:
Phone... हम नहीं किए थे *phone...*

Samar's eyes go cold. But, he smiles.

SAMAR:
Babulal... you are one of us. I respect you a lot. Please... don't insult me.

SAMAR:
बाबूलाल जी... आप हमारे अपने हैं – बहुत आदर–सम्मान है आपका हमारी आँखों में – *Please* हमारी *insult* मत कीजिए –

He stares at Babulal with piercing eyes. Babulal recovers, but looks down.

BABULAL:
S... s... sssir... I beg of you... Don't ask me this question.

BABULAL:
सरकार हम पैर पड़ते हैं आपके... ये सवाल आप हमसे मत पूछिए...

SAMAR:
Who asked you to call my father? Virendra Pratap... or Sooraj?

SAMAR:
किसने *phone* करवाया था हमारे बाबू जी को – वीरेन्द्र प्रताप... या सूरज ?

There's no avoiding Samar's direct gaze. Finally, Babulal looks down and whispers.

BABULAL:
Sooraj Kumar

BABULAL:
सूरज कुमार...

SAMAR:
Thank you. You have proved your loyalty. You're definitely one of us.

SAMAR:
Thank you. आपने साबित कर दिया कि आप कितने वफ़ादार हैं... बिलकुल अपने –

Babulal smiles with great difficulty. Samar escorts him to the door and outside.

SARAH:
Tu – mera ... Sisur hai.

SARAH:
Tu – mera... Sisur hai...

As Samar leads Babulal to his car, he sees Sarah outside. She's engaged with Brij Gopal.

Babulal suddenly takes Samar's hand and places it on his head.

BABULAL:
I just need your benediction.

BABULAL:
बस, आपका हाथ हमारे सर पर रहने दीजिए...

SAMAR:
Of course. You have my word.

SAMAR:
बिलकुल ... ज़बान दी है आपको –

Samar takes out Babulal's phone from his pocket and gives it to him.

SAMAR:
Here... your phone. I've entered my personal number into it.

SAMAR:
ये लीजिए, आपका *phone* - हमने अपना *Personal number register* कर दिया है इसमें...

Babulal takes his phone back eagerly.

BABULAL:
I'll always be in touch.

BABULAL:
हमेशा आपके *contact* में रहेंगे... *anytime!*

Samar smiles back at him.

SAMAR:
Anytime...

SAMAR:
Anytime.

Babulal has tears of gratefulness in his eyes as he holds Samar's hand to his head and departs.

As Babulal's car drives away Brij Gopal joins Samar. Samar speaks coldly.

SAMAR:
Sooraj. It was Sooraj.

SAMAR:
सूरज... सूरज था वो...

EXT. STREETS - DAY

As a relieved Babulal is driving home he receives a phone call. 'Samar calling'. He still has tears in his eyes. He smiles and whispers to himself.

BABULAL:
Anytime...

BABULAL:
Anytime.

As he presses the button to receive the call a bomb blasts and the car explodes!

Samar has heard the blast on his phone. If he is filled with any emotions about his father they do not show. Brij Gopal puts his arm around him to comfort him and takes the phone from Samar. Samar stares into space.

EXT. BABULAL CAR BLAST SPOT - DAY

The police, media and public have arrived at the spot and the media are taking photographs of the scene.

INT. OUTSIDE SAMAR'S HOUSE – EVENING

Samar goes for a run. Sarah watches him from the balcony.

INT. SAMAR'S HOUSE, SHOWER ROOM - LATER

As Samar stands under the shower, his eyes are closed and his face remains expressionless. It is only when he feels the touch on his back that it breaks into a smile. He knows the touch. It's been a long time. Sarah has joined him in the shower...

She whispers to him in Hindi-

SARAH:
Love you so much..

SARAH:
मैं प्यार... तुम... बहुत...

Samar breaks into a laugh at her Hindi.

SAMAR:
Who's been coaching you?

SAMAR:
तुम्हें हिन्दी कौन सिखा रहा है ?

SARAH:
Uncle Brij.

SARAH:
मामाजी...

Before she can complete the word, Samar kisses her urgently. They realise how much they have been missing each other.

INT. SAMAR'S BEDROOM - NIGHT

They make love. The TV is on, it's lights causing strange reflections on the bed.

As they finish, Samar rolls off her and lights a cigarette. He immediately sits up and begins gathering his clothes, Sarah props herself up.

Suddenly, her attention is drawn to the news on TV. Breaking news about Babulal! A picture of the destroyed car, with his photo in an inset.

TV NEWS ANCHOR:
The car attack was discovered at around 3 p.m. just off the Birpur by-pass. The blast is set to have occurred at around 2:50 p.m. Mr. Babulal and his driver died of severe burn injuries on the spot. There is no news of anyone else injured in the blast. Mr. Babulal was killed in a car blast on the Chatarpur road, while he was travelling. Both he and his driver died of severe burn injuries on the spot, their bodies charred beyond recognition. The cause of the blast is yet to be determined. However, initial evidence suggests...

TV NEWS ANCHOR:
हादसे की जानकारी लगभग तीन बजे शाम में मिली... blast लगभग दो बजकर पचास मिनट पर बीरपुर by-pass से कुछ दूरी पर हुआ... बाबूलाल और उनके driver की गम्भीर रूप से जलने की वजह से घटनास्थल पर ही मौत हो गई... blast में और किसी के हताहत होने की ख़बर नहीं है... छतरपुर रोड पर जा रहे बाबूलाल की मृत्यु car blast में हुई है... दोनों इतने ज़्यादा जल चुके थे कि उन्हें पहचानना मुश्किल हो रहा था... blast किस वजह से हुआ यह अभी तक पता नहीं चल सका है... हालाँकि घटनास्थल पर मौजूदा सबूत बतलाते हैं कि...

Sarah can't believe it!

SARAH:
Oh my God! That's him! That's the man I saw in your office this morning!

SARAH:
हे भगवान्! ये तो वही है! जिसे मैंने सुबह दफ़्तर में देखा...

Samar looks towards the TV casually.

SAMAR:
Yes, it's him – Babulal.

SAMAR:
हाँ, वो वही है – बाबूलाल...

Sarah is surprised at his coldness.

SARAH:
He is dead, Samar!!

SARAH:
वो मर गया, समर...

Samar has finished dressing up.

SAMAR:
Hmm, tragic! Must've got involved in something messy..

SAMAR:
हाँ, दुःख की बात है... ज़रूर किसी ग़लत काम में फँसा होगा...

Taking the remote, he clicks the TV off.

SAMAR:
Got to get some work done... Bye.

SAMAR:
कुछ ज़रूरी काम निपटाना है... Bye.

Samar kisses her and leaves. She stares after him, unable to reconcile his casual response to this horrible incident.

Something begins to gnaw at her from inside. Some terrible apprehension. She can't seem to get rid of Babulal's face from her memory.

INT. VIRENDRA PRATAP'S HOUSE - DAY

After Babulal's death Virendra Pratap is hounded by the media. As he walks in.

MEDIA #1:
Mr. Virendra Pratap, after Babulal's testimony on TV, didn't you threaten him?

MEDIA #1:
वीरेन्द्र प्रताप जी आज सुबह से ही बाबूलाल जी के बयान के बाद से उनको धमकी भरे *phone calls?*

VIRENDRA PRATAP:
Rubbish! He was a victim of a deadly conspiracy.

VIRENDRA PRATAP:
बकवास कर रहे हैं आप लोग... किसी भयंकर षड़यंत्र का शिकार बनाया गया है उनको...

MEDIA #2:
Who was behind this?

MEDIA #2:
कौन था इस षड़यंत्र के पीछे ?

MEDIA #3:
He openly accused you of corruption. So, did you...?

MEDIA #3:
आप पर सीधे–सीधे *corruption* के आरोप लगाये थे बाबूलाल जी ने – कहीं आपने –

VIRENDRA PRATAP:
Meaning? What the hell do you mean? That I got him killed?! He was like my family. One of the founders of this party.

VIRENDRA PRATAP:
क्या मतलब... क्या मतलब है आपका ?... हमने करवाया है ये ?... अरे परिवार थे, हमारे अपने थे बाबूलालजी... इस *party* की आत्मा से जुड़े थे।

Virendra Pratap leaves the room.

EXT. OUTSIDE RASHTRAWADI PARTY HEADQUARTERS - DAY

A prayer ceremony for Babulal has been kept in front of Party H.Q., Virendra Pratap offers flowers.

VIRENDRA PRATAP:
Babulal's murder will cost them dearly. Very dearly. They're scared, panic stricken! Their singular objective is to destroy our unity. But, brothers... Rashtrawadi's foundations aren't so weak as to be shaken by such incidents.

VIRENDRA PRATAP:
बाबूलाल जी की हत्या महँगी पड़ेगी उनको... बहोत महँगी... बौखला गये हैं वो – खलबली मच गई है – बदहवासी छाई है... *single point agenda* है कि कैसे हमारी एकता तोड़ें ... अरे भाइयों, राष्ट्रवादी की जड़ें इतनी कमज़ोर नहीं हैं कि इन हादसों से हिल जायें –

VIRENDRA PRATAP:
Baseless allegations. Imaginary scandals. They're scrambling around for dirt to throw at us! But, let them know, that if you spit at the sky... it will land back on your own face. The repercussions will be severe. The repercussions will be severe!

VIRENDRA PRATAP:
बेबुनियाद आरोप... मनगढ़ंत *scandals*... और खोद–खोद के कीचड़ उछाल रहे हैं हम पर – मगर आसमान में थूकने वाले को शायद ये पता नहीं है कि पलट के थूक उन्हीं के चेहरे पर गिरेगा... करारा जवाब मिलेगा – करारा जवाब मिलेगा।

EXT./INT. VIRENDRA PRATAP'S HOUSE - DAY

Sooraj arrives at Virendra's house. Inside, as several Senior lawyers pour over files Virendra greets him with renewed energy. He is talking on phone.

VIRENDRA PRATAP:
Inspector Sharma! Your vacation's over. Do something useful now.

He turns to Sooraj.

VIRENDRA PRATAP:
We're petitioning the court to reopen the rape investigation against Prithvi. Mark my words. We're also asking the election commission to disqualify him since he is a criminal.

SOORAJ:
That's fine, Veeru. But, for the election we only need people's support. Which we are assured of anyway. Why not let sleeping dogs lie?

VIRENDRA PRATAP:
Sooraj, in politics, you never let dogs sleep. You keep them awake so that when needed... they bark!

Virendra Pratap looks excited.

INT. PRITHVI'S CAR - DAY

Prithvi is driving with his cavalcade when his phone rings.

INSPECTOR BHOLA SINGH:
Make me talk to Prithvi…its urgent..

His aide gives him the phone.

PRITHVI'S MAN GAGAN:
It's Inspector Bhola Singh.

Prithvi looks at him.

PRITHVI'S MAN GAGAN:
Says it's urgent.

Prithvi takes the phone.

PRITHVI:
Hello?

INSPECTOR BHOLA SINGH:
Hello..sir.. The prey is here in the farmhouse of Mr. Virendra. The security is very tight.

PRITHVI:
Hmm...

VIRENDRA PRATAP:
अरे *S.P.* शर्मा साहेब छुट्टी पर से लौटो... और कुछ जलवा दिखाओ... बात होती है।

VIRENDRA PRATAP:
Court में कल *petition file* होगा और पृथ्वी के *rape* वाले मामले में *police investigation* दोबारा खुलेगा... देख लेना – *he will be behind bars... election commission* को भी *notice* दे रहे हैं कि ऐसे *criminal* आदमी को *disqualify* करो...

SOORAJ:
वो तो ठीक है वीरू भाई, लेकिन *election* तो हम जनता के समर्थन से ही जीतेंगे – और वो हमें मिल भी रहा है – गड़े मुर्दे उखाड़ने से कहीं ग़लत *message*...

VIRENDRA PRATAP:
सूरज... राजनीति में मुर्दे कभी गाड़े नहीं जाते उन्हें ज़िन्दा रखा जाता है – ताकि *time* आने पर वो बोलें...

INSPECTOR BHOLA SINGH:
पृथ्वी भइया से बात कराइये – *urgent* है...

PRITHVI'S MAN GAGAN:
Inspector भोला सिंह है *linc* पर –

PRITHVI'S MAN GAGAN:
बोलता है *urgent* है –

PRITHVI:
हूँ... *hello*...

INSPECTOR BHOLA SINGH:
जी प्रणाम *sir* – शिकार आया हुआ है छतरपुर में... वीरू भइया के *farmhouse* में... *security* में हमीं लोग हैं...

PRITHVI:
हाँ....

INSPECTOR BHOLA SINGH:
Tell me what to do.

INSPECTOR BHOLA SINGH:
बोलिए, क्या करना है –

PRITHVI:
Get your men out of there. I'm on my way.
(To driver)
Head to Chhattarpur farms.

PRITHVI:
अपने आदमियों को हटाओ वहाँ से... हम आते हैं...
(To driver)
छत्तरपुर *farms* लेना –

EXT./INT. FARMS - DAY

Near an isolated bungalow Prithvi's cavalcade stops a distance away. He gets off and walks with a couple of trusted men.

The police inspector orders the cops to go away.

INSPECTOR:
Come on..get going from here.

INSPECTOR:
ए चलो – चलो –

Inside, Sharma is watching news about Prithvi's campaign on the television, and drinking whiskey.

NEWS ANCHOR:
Party president Prithvi Singh did a road show in Madhavpur. There was a great amount of enthusiasm in people for this. Men, women, children and even senior citizens participated in it. First a rally at Ramna Maidan and now a road show at Madhavpur. With this new and youthful image Prithvi Singh is slowly gaining popularity among young voters.

NEWS ANCHOR:
जनशक्ति पार्टी अध्यक्ष पृथ्वी प्रताप ने आज माधोपुर में *road show* किया – इस *road show* का जनता में भारी उत्साह देखा गया ... पुरुष–महिलाएँ, बूढ़े, यहाँ तक कि बच्चों ने भी इस *road show* में इस हिस्सा लिया... पहले बड़ा रमना मैदान में विशाल रैली और अब माधोपुर में *road show...* क्या पृथ्वी प्रताप अपने शानदार *media management,* बेबाक भाषण शैली और अपनी युवा और दबंग छवि की वजह से जनता में तेजी से लोकप्रिय होते जा रहे हैं – आइये हम...

Suddenly Prithvi appears from the back door and Sharma instinctively looks back. On seeing a smiling Prithvi, Sharma goes white with fear. He realises his guards are missing and that he is surrounded by Prithvi's men.

PRITHVI:
When you play hide and seek with me, it creates magic in my heart...

PRITHVI:
अँखियाँ मिलाये कभी अँखियाँ चुराये – क्या तूने किया जादू...

Sharma trembles as Prithvi closes in on him.

PRITHVI:
Hey, Sharma! Where were you hiding, huh? That was one long vacation! I really missed you.

PRITHVI:
क्यूँ शर्मा जी, कहाँ छुप गये थे... बड़ी लम्बी छुट्टी लेकर – हमने तुमको बहुत *miss* किया –

SHARMA: *(mumbles)*
I... made a big mistake, sir.

SHARMA: *(mumbles)*
गलती हो गया...

PRITHVI:
Your slap packs a solid punch, pal. It does! Why don't you give me a sample?

PRITHVI:
यार...तू थप्पड़ बड़ा तगड़ा मारता है – सच्ची... एक *sample* दे ना...

Prithvi props his face towards Sharma. Sharma is trembling.

SHARMA:
It was a big mistake. I did apologise to...Brij Gopal

SHARMA:
भारी ग़लती हो गया – माफ़ी माँग लिया था हमने ब्रिज गोपाल जी से –

Prithvi's sudden slap sends him reeling on the floor.

PRITHVI:
So? Lovely, wasn't it?

PRITHVI:
बोल... कैसा लगा !... मज़ा आया न ?

Sharma holds Prithvi's feet.

SHARMA:
You did absolutely right. I deserved it! But now I'll be good. See, I'm the one who made that woman withdraw her complaint against you.

SHARMA:
बिलकुल सही किया बाउ जी आपने... हम इसी के लायक हैं – मगर आगे से ऐसा मौका नहीं देंगे... देखिए वो *ladies* वाला मामले में भी हम ही ने आपके... आपका *charge clear* करवाए थे...

PRITHVI:
Ah, that woman... Glad that you reminded me of her. I've to settle her account too.

PRITHVI:
हाँ!! वो *ladies* वाला मामला!! अच्छा याद दिलाया तूने, उसका भी हिसाब करना है।

As if Sharma finds a cue.

SHARMA:
I... I'll bring her to you, whenever you want.

SHARMA:
हम ले के आएँगे उसको आपके पास... जब आप बोलेंगे...

PRITHVI:
Good. Call her now.

PRITHVI:
अच्छा *idea* है... चल *phone* लगा उसको...

EXT. MARKET CENTRE – DAY

Beena Kumari gets a call from Sharma as she steps out of a market centre.

BEENA KUMARI:
Mr. Sharma! What's up?

BEENA KUMARI:
शर्मा जी, कैसे याद किया ! कहाँ हैं आजकल ?

SHARMA:
I'm here with the boss. He wants to meet you. Where are you?

SHARMA:
Boss को मिलने आया था... वो *meeting* में याद कर रहे है तुमको... कहाँ हो तुम ?

BEENA KUMARI:
Been shopping at the New Market

BEENA KUMARI:
बस... थोड़ा *shopping* कर रहे थे *New Market* में ...

SHARMA:
Huh? New Market?

SHARMA:
अँ, *New Market?*

Prithvi immediately signals his man, who is holding a baseball bat. He takes his bat and nods at his man.

PRITHVI: *(whispers)*
Call Nathu and Ballu. They should be there.

PRITHVI: *(whispers)*
ए, *phone* लगा... नाथू और बल्लू को उधर ही होंगे –

Sharma reacts as he sees Prithvi taking the bat and urges Beena on the phone.

SHARMA:
Wait right there. I'm sen... sending a car. Vee... Virendra's called you urgently.

SHARMA:
उधर ही रुकना तुम... गाड़ी भेजते हैं हम... *urgent* बुलाए हैं वीरू जी...

BEENA KUMARI:
Yeah, sure.

BEENA KUMARI:
जी, अच्छा...ठीक है!

The phone gets disconnected.

Bharati and Sarah are at the Sari shop in the same shopping centre.

INT./EXT. SARI SHOP – DAY

Sarah laughs as she tries to wrap the sari around her.

SARAH:
I love this one.

SARAH:
मुझे यह पसंद है...

BHARATI:
This is silk from Benaras.

BHARATI:
यह बनारसी silk है...

SHOPKEEPER:
Made by hand...

SHOPKEEPER:
सब हाथ का बना हुआ है...

BHARATI:
All hand crafted.

BHARATI:
पूरी हस्तशिल्प है...

Beena Kumari looks at her watch and dials a number. Suddenly a vehicle comes to halt near her and two men get off. A motorbike stops too and the pillion rider gets off. She recognises these men to be Prithvi's men. They close in on her, and she suddenly begins to shriek.

BEENA KUMARI:
Hey! Hey...hey...Let go! Let go of me.

BEENA KUMARI:
अरे !! छोड़ो हमें... कहाँ ले के जा रहे हो... कौन हो तुम लोग... छोड़ो... छोड़ो हमें...

PRITHVI'S MAN:
Come on sit in the car. Come on sit inside and don't shout...

PRITHVI'S MAN:
चुपचाप बैठो गाड़ी में... चिल्लाओ मत... बोल दिया न चलो चुपचाप...

BEENA KUMARI:
Let go of me! Help! Help! Save me!

BEENA KUMARI:
छोड़ो... छोड़ो... *help me please* - बचाओ – *help me please* - मेरी मदद करो – बचाओ...

The men don't look bothered. Beena tries to run but they hold her and begin to take her away. No one dares come close.

Sarah notices through the store window and stops wrapping the sari. She screams and rushes out as she sees the men dragging the woman to the vehicle. Scared shoppers run for cover while Sarah runs towards the woman.

SARAH:
Hey!

SARAH:
ए! ...

Two of the security guys run towards the spot while one keeps guard on Bharati. He seems to recognise the abductors and makes a call.

Samar answers the call.

SAMAR:
Tell me...

SAMAR:
हाँ – बोलो...

SECURITY:
Sir, our men are here.

SECURITY:
समर भइया, यहाँ अपने लोग सब आए हैं...

Sarah by now is struggling with the men who are pushing Beena Kumari in the car.

Samar is getting into his car.

SAMAR:
Who all?

SAMAR:
कौन लोग हैं ?

SECURITY:
I recognised Ballu. He moves with Prithvi.

SECURITY:
एक बल्लू को पहचाने *sir*...बड़े भइया के साथ रहते हैं –

Samar switches the phone off and the car zooms off. His security follows.

SAMAR:
Lets go to New Market..

SAMAR:
New Market चलो –

Sarah has got hold of one of Ballu's shirt and screams at him.

SARAH:
Let her go...

SARAH:
छोड़ो उसे...

By now they have taken Beena Kumari away in the vehicle and security has protectively covered Sarah who has become hysterical.

An alarmed Bharati rushes out.

BHARATI:
What are you doing?
(to the security)
Take care of this.

BHARATI:
अरे, क्या कर रही हो तुम ?
(to the security)
देखो तुम लोग !

SARAH:
Stop... someone help that poor woman – Help! Call the police.

SARAII:
बचाओ उसे... पुलिस को बुलाओ... ?

No one moves.

BHARATI:
Calm down Sarah – Sarah...

BHARATI:
शांत हो जाओ सारा, सारा...

INT. SAMAR'S CAR - DAY

Samar on his way to the New Market, he is driving like crazy and has been talking to Prithvi on phone.

PRITHVI:
Yes, Samar...

PRITHVI:
हाँ, छोटू बोल –

SAMAR:
Have you gone crazy, brother? Now that everything's going well, don't do anything stupid.

SAMAR:
Have you gone crazy भैया... अभी, जब सब कुछ ठीक चल रहा है... मत करो कोइ उल्टा–सीधा काम –

Prithvi smiles as he holds the phone in his bloody hand.

PRITHVI: It's done. Finished! You should've seen his face.	**PRITHVI:** काम तो हो गया है छोटू – *finish...* उसकी शकल देखने लायक थी...

It is at this point that Ballu drags Beena Kumari in.

Prithvi looks at her.

SAMAR: Brother, please listen to me.	**SAMAR:** भैया ... *please – just listen to me...*
BEENA KUMARI: Leave me... leave me!	**BEENA KUMARI:** जाने दो हमें... *please* - हमें जाने दो ... जाने दो हमें...

Samar tells him on phone.

PRITHVI: Just a sec... I've another favour to return. I'll call you later.	**PRITHVI:** एक मिनट छोटू – एक और *ticket* काटना है... तेरे को *phone* करता हूँ बाद में –
SAMAR: Please get out of there, fast! I am sending some guys to clean up....	**SAMAR:** आप निकलो वहाँ से भैया... जल्दी... *I am sending some guys to clean up...*

Beena Kumari begins to cry hysterically as she sees Sharma's dead body lying on the floor. The bloodied baseball bat in Prithvi's hand tells her the story.

Prithvi has switched the phone off and comes close to Beena Kumari and smiles as he bends over her.

BEENA KUMARI: Let me go....	**BEENA KUMARI:** जाने दो हमें... *please* - हमें जाने दो ... जाने दो हमें...
PRITHVI: Hey... how are you, sweetheart? Now, tell me... Where do you want to contest from? Huh? From Sitapur? Or from hell?	**PRITHVI:** ए... कैसी है रे तू ?... अब बोल ना... कहाँ का *ticket* दूँ ?... अँ सीतापुर का या जहन्नुम का ?...

Beena Kumari has gone white with fear.

EXT. NEW MARKET - DAY

A crowd has gathered and several media persons arrive in minutes. Along with his Security cover Samar too arrives.

The whole experience has shaken Sarah up. Samar holds her in an embrace.

SARAH: Somebody help her. They just.. they just took her away. Why doesn't anyone call the police!	**SARAH:** *बचाओ उसे... अभी–अभी उसे ले गये वो लोग... पुलिस को क्यों नहीं बुलाता कोई ?*
SAMAR: We'll do that, love... let's get you home first.	**SAMAR:** *उसे कुछ नहीं होगा, सारा... तुम घर चलो...*

PRACTISING PRAKASH

Shruti Seth had been spending sleepless nights getting more and more nervous about the intimate scene with Arjun Rampal. When she met Arjun, she realised he was even more nervous!!! On hearing this Jha offered to do a rehearsal with Arjun. With a straight face, he told Arjun he would happily act out Shruti's part with him! Shruti was eager to 'learn' by watching this rehearsal. While Arjun says he firmly declined Jha's offer, Jha claims they did do a rehearsal. Since the scene was shot in a locked set with just a couple of crew members, the truth remains elusive! ■

BHARATI:
Come, come. Let's go home.

BHARATI:
चलो, चलो – घर चलते हैं...

As he begins to take Sarah and his mother to the car, dozens of media persons surge in asking Sarah questions at the same time. She looks terrified.

Samar shields her from the cameras.

MEDIA MAN #2:
Ma'am one second please

MEDIA MAN #2:
Ma'am, one second, please...

MEDIA MAN #3:
Ma'am, did you see the kidnappers.

MEDIA MAN #3:
Ma'am, क्या आपने अपहरणकर्ताओं को देखा है ?

They are barking questions at them and Samar's security has a hard time getting them to the car.

MEDIA MAN #4:
...Mr. Samar Pratap...

MEDIA MAN #4:
समर प्रताप जी –

SECURITY:
Move back.

SECURITY:
पीछे हटिये आप लोग –

When suddenly a few irritated journalists confront him.

MEDIA MAN #2:
We are the media. She will have to talk. We have freedom of the press. She will have to talk.

MEDIA MAN #2:
देखिए आज़ादी है यहाँ *press* की – आपको बोलना पड़ेगा –

Samar faces the media and says.

SAMAR:
You're right. The media is free. But remember, your freedom cannot be used to terrorise us.

SAMAR:
ठीक कहा आपने – *Media* की आज़ादी है – लेकिन याद रखिए, आपकी आज़ादी हमारे लिए आतंक नहीं बन सकती।

INT. SARAH'S BEDROOM - LATER

Samar makes Sarah comfortable in bed and begins to pour a glass of water. She lays down, still looking a bit tense. And then suddenly springs up in bed, startling him.

SAMAR:
What happened, love?

SAMAR:
क्या हुआ, सारा ?

SARAH:
I've seen that man!

SARAH:
मैंने उस आदमी को देखा है...

SAMAR:
Who?

SAMAR:
किसे ?

SARAH:
The man.. The man who kidnapped that woman.. I've seen him around here somewhere..

SARAH:
वो आदमी... जिसने उस औरत का अपहरण किया... मैंने उसे यहीं कहीं देखा है...

Samar tenses but, gently pushes her back onto the bed.

SAMAR:
You're in a shock Sarah. You need some rest. The police will look into it. Come.

SAMAR:
तुम सदमे में हो, सारा... तुम्हें आराम की ज़रूरत है... पुलिस जाँच करेगी...

She lies back on the bed, still holding onto his hand. Samar gives her a pill and covers her in a blanket. He then kisses her on the forehead and leaves.

INT. VIRENDRA PRATAP'S HOUSE - NIGHT

Sooraj is talking on the phone with an inspector who was at the scene of crime – S.P., Sharma's murder.

INSPECTOR BHOLA SINGH:
Sir, this is Inspector Singh. SP Sharma was killed around 4 PM. We've found drugs on his body.

INSPECTOR BHOLA SINGH:
इं. सिंह बोल रहा हूँ– शर्मा जी का *murder* चार बजे के करीब हुआ है... *body* पर *drugs* का *packet* सब भी मिला है –

SOORAJ:
Clean it up.

SOORAJ:
साफ करवा दो सब...

INSPECTOR BHOLA SINGH:
Okay. I'll inform Veeru about this.

INSPECTOR BHOLA SINGH:
जी... वीरू भाई को *report* देने जा रहे हैं...

SOORAJ:
No! Don't bother. I'll tell him myself.

SOORAJ:
नहीं – तुम छोड़ दो – हम खुद बताएँगे –

INSPECTOR BHOLA SINGH:
Okay.

INSPECTOR BHOLA SINGH:
जी...

INT. SAMAR'S OFFICE – NIGHT

Samar is playing chess intently on his computer. He suddenly notices Sarah's presence in the room and is startled.

SAMAR:
Jeez, Sarah.. You gave me a start!

SAMAR:
अरे, सारा... तुमने तो मुझे चौंका दिया...

Seeing her intent look, he gets up concerned.

SAMAR:
What's up, honey?

SAMAR:
क्या बात है, सारा ?

SARAH:
That's what I've come to find out, Samar. What has happened to you?

SARAH:
यही तो मैं पता लगाने आयी हूँ... क्या हो गया है तुम्हें ?

SAMAR:
What d'you mean?

SAMAR:
क्या मतलब है तुम्हारा ?

SARAH:
You've changed, Samar.. Or maybe not. Maybe you were always like this.. And, it's just that I didn't see it.

SARAH:
तुम बदल गये हो, समर... या फिर शायद नहीं... शायद तुम पहले से ही ऐसे थे... लेकिन मैं पहचान नहीं सकी...

Samar doesn't want this to go further at all.

SAMAR:
What are you talking about Sarah?

SAMAR:
ये तुम क्या कह रही हो, सारा ?

Sarah's voice begins to get sharper.

SARAH:
I'm talking about what you do here in the name of family and politics!

SARAH:
परिवार और राजनीति के नाम पर जो कर रहे हो... उसकी बात कर रही हूँ...

Samar brushes it aside with a short laugh.

SAMAR:
C'mon, you can't believe what the media has to say.

SAMAR:
क्या बकवास है!... media का यक़ीन कैसे कर सकती हो...

SARAH: *(shouting)*
At least, don't insult me by lying to me, Samar! Those goons who kidnapped that woman, they were your brother's men. You knew that!
(pause)
And you killed Babulal!

SARAH: *(shouting)*
झूठ बोल कर मेरा अपमान तो मत करो, समर... जिन्होंने उस औरत का अपहरण किया, वो तुम्हारे भाई के गुंडे थे... तुम जानते थे...
(pause)
तुमने बाबूलाल की हत्या की...

Samar staggers internally. She knows! Of course she does.

SAMAR:
You stay out of this Sarah. This is politics.

SAMAR:
इसमें दख़ल मत दो, सारा... ये राजनीति है...

SARAH:
Right. And you have become a ruthless, conniving politician!

SARAH:
बिल्कुल! ... एक कठोर और चालाक नेता बन चुके हो तुम...

Samar brings down his hand hard on the door. She flinches.

SAMAR:
F**k! If this is what you believe, then I have nothing more to say to you.

SAMAR:
बहुत हुआ! ... भरोसा नहीं है मुझ पर – तो फिर मैं कुछ और नहीं बोलूँगा...

She smiles sadly.

SARAH:
You don't have to dismiss me, Samar. I have just come to tell you that I'm leaving.

SARAH:
मुझे निकालने की ज़रूरत नहीं है, समर... बस, यही कहने आयी थी – कि जा रही हूँ...

SAMAR:
Sarah...

SAMAR:
सारा...

SARAH:
I've seen enough politics and violence, Samar. You seem to forget that I grew up in Ireland. I saw my father and my brother killed when I was six years old. My child is not gonna to face that. Ever!

SARAH:
राजनीति और हिंसा बहुत देखी है, समर... शायद भूल रहे हो कि मैं आयरलैंड में पली–बढ़ी... छः साल की थी, जब अपने पिता और भाई की हत्या देखी... मेरा बच्चा ये सब नहीं सहेगा – कभी नहीं...

Samar is stunned. As she turns to go, he quickly reacts.

SAMAR:
Child?!! Wait a minute.. Are you saying that you're..?

SAMAR:
बच्चा ?!!... एक minute, क्या तुम...

SARAH:
Yes, I'm pregnant.

SARAH:
हाँ, मैं माँ बनने वाली हूँ...

He's delighted and comes to embrace her, but she doesn't let him.

SAMAR:
Wow! Sweetheart, that's terrific! I..

SAMAR:
कितनी ख़ुशी की बात है!

SARAH:
Please don't... don't... Please. I'm leaving....

SARAH:
नहीं... मत... बिल्कुल नहीं... मैं जा रही हूँ...

SAMAR:
I'll come with you!

SAMAR:
मैं तुम्हारे साथ आउँगा...

She turns around in complete surprise. He holds her by the shoulders and looks into her eyes seriously.

SAMAR:
I'll come away from all this.

SAMAR:
सब छोड़ कर आ जाउँगा...

She looks at him closely.

SAMAR:
Sarah...listen to me, I swear on our child! Just give me a few weeks. I need to finish this election, Sarah. They killed my father, Sarah. I must protect my brother now.

SAMAR:
सारा, मेरी बात सुनो... हमारे बच्चे की क़सम!... कुछ दिनों की मोहलत दो... चुनाव ख़त्म होने दो... उन्होंने मेरे पिताजी की हत्या की... मुझे अपने भाई को ज़िन्दा रखना है...

She breaks down and nods. He nods, embracing her.

SAMAR:
Everything will be okay, you'll see. I'll come to you very soon. Okay!

SAMAR:
सब कुछ ठीक हो जाएगा – यक़ीन करो... मैं जल्द ही तुम्हारे पास आउँगा...

INT. SAMAR'S HOUSE, HALL - NIGHT

Prithvi is sleeping on the couch. Indu comes and covers him with a shawl.

INT. INDU'S ROOM - NIGHT

Indu is sitting alone and thinking.

INT. VIRENDRA PRATAP'S OFFICE - DAY

The big TV screen has just been breaking the news. "Of the first phase 73 seats – 17 Rashtrawadi party candidates nomination papers rejected."

"Batukeshwar Tiwari and Brahmanand Shukla top the list."

A reporter is excitedly shrieking.

REPORTER:
Sensational Breaking News! It has never happened in the electoral history that so many nominations of the single party have been rejected... The Election Commission says that the nominations were filed wrongly... Many of the rejected candidates were Ministers in the last government... like Brahmanand Tiwari from Balrampur, Priyansh Shukla – Forbis Ganj, Shrikant Rajak – Janakpur... Shashi Singh – Wajidpur... Dr. Rajesh Raghuvanshi – Sariya.

TIWARI:
The papers were correctly filed, Veeru.

SHUKLA:
Yes, everything was in order.

Virendra explodes.

VIRENDRA PRATAP:
In order, my foot! Instead of originals, photocopies were submitted. Even the affidavits didn't have your signatures. We lost 17 seats without even contesting. Whose side are you on?

Sooraj walks in. His look is chilling.

SOORAJ:
I know whose side they're on. And who is behind this.

VIRENDRA PRATAP:
Why did you do this? Why?

Shukla breaks down.

SHUKLA:
Hang us if you wish, Veeru... We were compelled.

Virendra jumps at the distraught Shukla and holds him by the neck.

VIRENDRA PRATAP:
You don't even deserve to be hanged.

SOORAJ:
Shut up!

REPORTER:
सनसनीखेज़ ख़बर... देश के चुनावी इतिहास में ऐसा पहले कभी नहीं हुआ कि एक *party* के एक साथ इतने *nominations reject* किये गये हों – चुनाव आयोग का कहना है कि उम्मीदवारों ने अपने *nominations* ग़लत *file* किए थे... *reject* किए गए सत्तरह उम्मीदवारों में अधिकांश *party* के आला नेता हैं और उनमें से कुछ राष्ट्रवादी पार्टी की पिछली सरकारों में मंत्री रह चुके हैं। इनके नाम हैं – ब्रम्हानंद तिवारी, बलरामपुर। प्रियांश शुक्ला, फारबिसगंज। श्रीकांत रजक, जनकपुर। शशि सिंह, वाजिदपुर। डॉ राजेश रघुवंशी, सरिया।

TIWARI:
कागज तो सब सही जमा हुआ था वीरू जी...

SHUKLA:
जी... सब कुछ *order* में था –

VIRENDRA PRATAP:
घंटा *order* में था ! जहाँ *original* जमा करना था वहाँ *photo copy...* अरे *affidavit* तक में आपका दस्तख़त नहीं था... बिना लड़े ही सत्रह सीट गँवा बैठे !!... ऐ... किसकी *side* में हैं आपलोग ?

SOORAJ:
हम जानते हैं किसकी *side* में हैं ये लोग... और कौन करवा रहा है ये सब!

VIRENDRA PRATAP:
क्यूँ किया ऐसा ? क्यों ?

SHUKLA:
फाँसी पे चढ़ा दीजिए वीरू जी... मजबूर किया गया था हमको...

VIRENDRA PRATAP:
फाँसी पर चढ़ने के लायक बचेगा तब तो साला...

SOORAJ:
चुप!

Sooraj holds Virendra Pratap back and pushes the two away. They hastily rush out of there.

Virendra Pratap is completely devastated. Sooraj tries to comfort him.

INT. OUTHOUSE OFFICE - DAY

The interior of the outhouse office is buzzing with activity. Party candidates and workers are huddled congratulating Prithvi as Samar and Brij Gopal walk in. Some members are screaming slogans of support for Prithvi.

SLOGAN:
Victory to Prithvi Pratap! Victory to Prithvi Pratap!

SLOGAN:
पृथ्वी प्रताप... जिन्दाबाद... पृथ्वी प्रताप... जिन्दाबाद...

SAMAR:
There were 23, but only 17 were rejected. How?

SAMAR:
तेईस थे ना... तो फिर सत्तरह कैसे *reject* हुए!?

BRIJ GOPAL:
Six of Sooraj's men backed out.

BRIJ GOPAL:
सूरज के *group* वाले छः के छः *back out* हो गये हैं...

M.K. pulls out a sheet from the printer and walks upto Samar.

M.K.:
Opinion poll result for the first round. Of 73 seats, they're predicting 45-47 for us.

M.K.:
Opinion poll results – Sir... पहले *round* की *seventy three* सीटों में से चालिस से पैंतालिस हमें मिल रहे हैं –

PRITHVI:
That's nonsense!

PRITHVI:
बकवास कर रहे हैं सब –

They're all dismayed by her negative sounding reaction.

PRITHVI:
Out of 73, we shall take 52.

PRITHVI:
तेहत्तर में से बावन सीटें लेंगे – इस बार –

And a cheer of jubilation goes up. Supporters shout slogans.

SLOGAN:
Victory to Prithvi Pratap! Victory to Jan Shakti Party!

SLOGAN:
पृथ्वी भइया... जिन्दाबाद... जनशक्ति पार्टी... जिन्दाबाद...

Samar puts a garland around Prithvi and the brothers smile at each other.

INT. PRITHVI AND INDU'S ROOM - DAY

Prithvi comes to his room. He still has a light smile on his face. He goes to the bureau and removes his watch.

And then to his surprise, Indu wraps her arms around him from behind. She rests her head tightly against his back. Shocked, he doesn't know how to react.

INDU:
I'm sorry..

INDU:
I'm sorry ! ...

Prithvi is suddenly overcome with emotion.

INDU:
I failed to understand you.

INDU:
हम समझ नहीं पाये आपको ठीक से...

He takes her hands, drawing her closer to him. She whispers.

INDU:
I love you.

INDU:
I love you.

He turns around. Holding her tenderly, he makes his own confession.

PRITHVI:
Even I love you very much. Just didn't know how to show it.

PRITHVI:
प्यार तो हम भी बहुत करते हैं आपसे... बस बताना नहीं आया...

She squeezes into the garland, getting very close to him. They look into each other's eyes for a moment. The electricity is powerful. He kisses her neck and she squirms with pleasure. The urgency takes over. He brings her mouth to hers and they kiss. It's deep, it's passionate, it's hungry... and long. They make love.

EXT. VILLAGE - DAY

Prithvi is surrounded by men, women, and old men who surge to hold his hand. He embraces them. One old man steps forward.

OLD MAN #1:
You! You're the one I'll vote for. For 25 years, I voted for Rashtrawadi Party. But this time, I will vote for you!

OLD MAN #1:
देगा – तुमको ही *भोट* देगा – पच्चीस साल से राष्ट्रवादी पार्टी को *भोट* दिया है – लेकिन इस बार, तुमको ही *भोट* देगा...

OLD MAN #2:
No one can defeat you.

OLD MAN #2:
बेटा, कोई हरा नहीं सकता तुमको...

OLD MAN #3:
Bless you, son.

OLD MAN #3:
जीते रहो बेटा...

OLD MAN #1:
Victory to..

OLD MAN #1:
ज़िन्दाबाद... ज़िन्दाबाद...

CROWD CHEERING:
Victory to Prithvi Pratap! Victory to Prithvi Pratap!

CROWD CHEERING:
पृथ्वी प्रताप... जिन्दाबाद... पृथ्वी प्रताप... जिन्दाबाद...

Prithvi looks overwhelmed.

INT. VIRENDRA PRATAP'S HOUSE – DAY

Virendra is watching the news on TV that is covering Prithvi's campaign.

NEWS ANCHOR:
Samar Pratap seems to have boosted... his brother Prithvi Pratap's campaign tremendously. In villages, towns, big cities, in every corner of the state.

NEWS ANCHOR:
छोटे भाई समर प्रताप ने पृथ्वी प्रताप के *political campaigning* को नई ऊँचाइयाँ दी हैं... गाँव–शहर, गली–कूचे, बाज़ार–दुकान, पूरे प्रदेश के लोगों में युवा नेता पृथ्वी प्रताप की जनशक्ति पार्टी के प्रति जबरदस्त रुझान दिख रहा है।

Sooraj enters as the lawyers stay in the background. Virendra has been drinking.

SOORAJ:
The Election Commission rejected our petition against Prithvi. It's waiting for the court's decision.

SOORAJ:
Election Commission ने पृथ्वी वाले मामले में हमारा *petition reject* कर दिया – कहते हैं पहले *Court* फ़ैसला करे...

Virendra smashes a glass on the table. He is completely devastated.

VIRENDRA PRATAP:
What the hell is going on here! First Babulal… then Sharma… the nominations conspiracy! That little brat is now dictating our future?! And you, Sooraj? You can't do anything.

VIRENDRA PRATAP:
ये हो क्या रहा है – पहले बाबूलाल… फिर शर्मा… फिर *nomination* में गद्दारी… साला कल का छोकरा – बाप बन रहा है हमारा – और तुम सूरज, तुम कुछ कर भी नहीं पा रहे…

Sooraj understands Virendra's desperation, and feels sorry for him.

SOORAJ:
It will work out.

SOORAJ:
सब ठीक हो जायेगा…

VIRENDRA PRATAP:
Like hell it will! Just keep consoling me… since you can't offer me any confidence!

VIRENDRA PRATAP:
ख़ाक ठीक हो जायेगा… बस दिलासा ही देते रहना हमको… भरोसा तो नहीं दे सकते…

Virendra Pratap looks shaken and trips. Sooraj quickly gets hold of him. Virendra pushes Sooraj away and struggles to stand on his own .

VIRENDRA PRATAP:
Virendra Pratap doesn't need… anyone's support.

VIRENDRA PRATAP:
वीरेन्द्र प्रताप को किसी सहारे की ज़रूरत नहीं है…

EXT. SAMAR'S HOUSE – EVENING

The driver opens the boot and the servants begin loading the luggage.

Sarah emerges from the house and goes to Bharati. She bends down and touches Bharati's feet.

Sarah turns to Indu and goes up to her.

SARAH:
Indu. I know what you've been through.. But, I hope you can forgive Samar….

SARAH:
इन्दु, समझती हूँ तुम पर क्या गुज़री है… हो सके तो समर को माफ़ करना…

INDU:
It's okay, Sarah. I've found my happiness..

INDU:
कोई बात नहीं, सारा… अपनी ख़ुशी पा ली मैंने…

SARAH:
Prithvi is a wonderful person.

SARAH:
पृथ्वी बहुत अच्छा इन्सान है…

The two of them hug.

Prithvi enters the gate in his car and sees the driver leaving.

PRITHVI:
Daya?

PRITHVI:
ए दया –

DRIVER DAYA:
Yes, sir?

DRIVER DAYA:
जी साब –

PRITHVI:
Where are you off to?

PRITHVI:
कहाँ जा रहा है ?

The driver sheepishly shows his little finger.

DRIVER- DAYA:
To the restroom, sir.

DRIVER- DAYA:
एक *minute* में आता हूँ *sir* -

PRITHVI:
They've to leave for the airport. Hurry up.

PRITHVI:
जल्दी करो – *flight* का *time* हो रहा है –

Prithvi drives on ahead but sees in his rearview mirror that the driver gets onto a motorbike and drives away. He is puzzled for just a second and then realises the sinister implications of that. He races his car towards the porch.

Prithvi dives out of it and runs to Samar and Bharati who are approaching the car. He also sees Sarah leave Indu and go towards the car.

PRITHVI:
Samar! Samar! Wait! Don't go near the car. Step back!

PRITHVI:
Shit, समर, समर, समर... हटो – हटो – हटो... गाड़ी के पास मत जाना... हटो –

Prithvi pushes Samar out of the way.

BHARATI:
What happened Prithvi?

BHARATI:
अरे क्या हुआ पृथ्वी ?

PRITHVI:
Take care of mother.

PRITHVI:
माँ को सँभाल...

Samar falls towards Bharati and takes her down protectively with him, totally perplexed.

Prithvi rushes towards Sarah, who has already reached the car. She reaches for the handle of the rear door.

PRITHVI:
Sarah…

PRITHVI:
सारा!!!...

He jumps towards her, but she has already begun opening the door. He is in mid-air, when she opens the door.

The car explodes.

After the explosion, Samar staggers up. He is stunned by what he sees. Sarah has been flung far away. She lies still. On the other side of the wreckage is Prithvi. Samar stumbles towards Sarah. He goes to her and falls on his knees. He reaches out for her and holds her.

Indu has meanwhile also stood up and reached Prithvi's body. She sits next to it, holds his head, and begins to wail.

Samar comes to Prithvi's body –

SAMAR:
Brother..brother..

SAMAR:
भइया... भइया...

Brij Gopal comes running out on hearing the blast. A shocked Bharati tries to stand up but collapses again. Brij Gopal catches her just in time. His grief turns to intense anger.

INT. SOORAJ'S HOUSE – NIGHT

Sooraj is in bed with high fever and his mother is applying cool strips of cloth to bring it down.

SOORAJ'S MOTHER:
The fever isn't subsiding at all. He is still passed out.

SOORAJ'S MOTHER:
एक तनिक बुखार कम नहीं हो रहा है जी... बेहोश है एकदम –

BLOW UP THE MERCEDES?!

For the shoot, a Mercedes Benz was bought because it made more sense to buy than hire one. It soon became the love of a lot of assistants. And then it came about that it was to be blown up! Hearts broke. Blow up the Mercedes?! The Mercedes almost became a damsel and the assistants racked their brains to figure out a way to save her. But no one had to do anything in the end. Turns out there was never a plan to blow up the beauty.

After some amount of remodeling, (pssst...) another sedan was put in place of the Mercedes and that car was blown up! ■

RAMCHARITTAR:
Nothing seems to be going right. Everything will fall apart.

RAMCHARITTAR:
कुछ भी तो ठीक नहीं हो रहा सूरज की माँ... सब खतम हो जायेगा –

EXT./INT. BASTI SOORAJ'S HOUSE - NIGHT

In the middle of the night, Brij Gopal arrives at Azad Nagar, surprising everyone.

BHUPESH:
Brij Gopal, sir.

BHUPESH:
बृजगोपाल जी...

RAMCHARITTAR:
Sir?

RAMCHARITTAR:
अरे ब्रिज मालिक – आप ?

BRIJ GOPAL:
Where is Sooraj?

BRIJ GOPAL:
सूरज कहाँ है ?

RAMCHARITTAR: *(scared)*
What is the matter?

RAMCHARITTAR: *(scared)*
पर... बात क्या है मालिक !?...

BRIJ GOPAL:
Where is Sooraj?

BRIJ GOPAL:
कहाँ है सूरज ?

RAMCHARITTAR:
He is sleeping. He has a fever. Should I wake him up?

RAMCHARITTAR:
यहीं, सो रहा है – तेज बुखार है उसे, उठा दें ?

They are at Sooraj's door. Brij Gopal holds Ramcharittar's hand and says.

BRIJ GOPAL:
You won't be able to see this. It's better that you stay here.

BRIJ GOPAL:
ना, तुम देख नहीं पाओगे... अलग ही रहो तो ठीक है –

RAMCHARITTAR: *(scared)*
Sir... please say something. What are you doing, sir!

RAMCHARITTAR: *(scared)*
मालिक... बिरिज मालिक... आप कुछ तो बोलिए... ये, ये क्या कर रहे हैं मालिक ?

Brij Gopal holds his hand, pushes him out of the backdoor and locks it from inside.

BRIJ GOPAL:
The family that fed you... supported you... gave you a life. He wants to destroy that same family?

BRIJ GOPAL:
जिस परिवार ने तुमको रोटी दी, सहारा दिया... ज़िन्दगी दी, उसी को खतम करने पे तुला है –

Brij Gopal draws out his gun. Ramcharittar is stunned and begins to cry.

RAMCHARITTAR:
Sooraj would never do that.

RAMCHARITTAR:
ऐसा नहीं कर सकता हमारा सूरज...

BRIJ GOPAL:
He is doing it! You gave birth to a snake.

BRIJ GOPAL:
यही, यही करते आया है – साँप को जन्म दिया है तूने...

RAMCHARITTAR:
That can't be! If he were my own blood, I would have believed it. But he is a blessing from God. Everyone worships him.

RAMCHARITTAR:
ऐसा मत कहिए मालिक... खुद की जनी औलाद होती तो मान भी लेते... वो तो भगवान की देन है – पूरा समाज पूजता है उसको...

BRIJ GOPAL:
What did you just say?

BRIJ GOPAL:
क्या कहा तूने ?

RAMCHARITTAR:
We were childless. It was 30 years ago that... I found him in a boat at sunrise... near the Sukhamaniya ghats at Benaras.

RAMCHARITTAR:
हम तो निःसंतान थे – तीस साल हो गया... सूर्योदय के *time* में बनारस के सुखमनिया घाट पर एक नाव में मिला था हमको...

The wife comes in with the piece of cloth.

RAMCHARITTAR'S WIFE:
He was wrapped in this cloth, and had this jewellery.

RAMCHARITTAR'S WIFE:
इसी वस्त्र में था मालिक... और ये... ये गले में हार था...

RAMCHARITTAR:
No one knows about this. Sooraj himself doesn't know.

RAMCHARITTAR:
कोई नहीं जानता मालिक... हम उसको भी नहीं बताये आज तक।

Brij Gopal is stunned and memories flash like bolt. He looks at Sooraj sleeping like a child and walks away.

INT. SAMAR'S HOUSE - EVENING

On her proverbial rooftop, Bharati sits alone. Much like she did those many years ago when another cataclysm had thrown her life into a tragic upheaval. But, this time, while her eyes are moist, her expression is angry. There's a cold rage in her eyes against those who have done this to her.

Brij Gopal finds her there. Immediately, she rounds on him, demanding an answer.

BHARATI:
How can Sooraj do this to me when you are around?

BHARATI:
भैया, तुम्हारे होते हुए ऐसे कैसे कर सकता है सूरज हमारे साथ ?

Brij Gopal is finding it difficult to tell her the truth. She looks up questioningly. Brij Gopal is distraught.

BRIJ GOPAL:
I can't do anything to him.

BRIJ GOPAL:
मैं उसे कुछ नहीं कर सकता...

She is really surprised, and angrier now.

BHARATI:
Why not?

BHARATI:
मगर क्यों ?

BRIJ GOPAL:
Because he is... your son.

BRIJ GOPAL:
क्योंकि, क्योंकि वो, तुम्हारा बेटा है...

BHARATI:
What??

BHARATI:
हँ...क्या ?...

Bharati reels, totally disoriented.

BRIJ GOPAL:
Your first born... who I snatched from your womb.

BRIJ GOPAL:
तेरा पहला जना है – जिसे मैंने तेरी कोख से छीना था।

Lightning strikes Bharati's heart. The truth that she has tried to keep hidden within herself, now hits her like an avalanche.

She catches her breath, digesting this truth and then looks up at Brij Gopal. They both cry at their unfortunate situation.

EXT./INT. AZAD NAGAR - DAY

Brij Gopal brings the car to a halt. With him is Bharati.

In the distance is visible Sooraj, who sits with his back to them. As Brij Gopal gets off the car he sees that Sooraj's men are around them, their eyes fixed on him, guns pointed.

He helps Bharati out of the car.

BRIJ GOPAL:
From here on, you'll have to walk alone, sister.

BRIJ GOPAL:
यहाँ से आगे का रास्ता तुझे अकेले ही तय करना होगा भारती।

Bharati looks at Sooraj and slowly walks towards him.

As he hears Bharati approach him, Sooraj stands up and turns to face her but doesn't look at her, guilt still gnawing at him. Bharati looks at him as if seeing him for the first time. Tears begin to well up in her eyes. It is a tense moment as they stand awkwardly, unable to say anything. Finally, Sooraj speaks.

SOORAJ:
Please tell me... what I can do for you.

SOORAJ:
कहिए, क्या कर सकता हूँ मैं आपके लिए ?

Bharati tries hard to stop herself from crying. She wants to say a thousand things but is unable to speak a word.

BHARATI:
An unfortunate mother has come to ask forgiveness from her son.

BHARATI:
एक अभागिन माँ अपने बेटे से माफ़ी माँगने आई है....

Sooraj is totally thrown by this extraordinary statement. He lifts his eyes to look at her in amazement.

SOORAJ:
Your son? Who is your son here?

SOORAJ:
आपका बेटा!... यहाँ कौन है आपका बेटा?

BHARATI:
You, Sooraj. You are my son.

BHARATI:
तुम सूरज... मेरे बेटे हो तुम...

Sooraj's face clears now. He knows that this woman has been traumatised by her son's death and he thinks she has lost her mental balance.

SOORAJ:
Listen... I understand you're in shock... I am sorry for your loss.

SOORAJ:
देखिए, आप सदमे में हैं – मुझे दुःख है आपकी अवस्था पर –

Bharati interrupts him decisively now.

BHARATI:
No, Son... it is true! Ramcharittar isn't your father. Thirty years ago he found you at the riverside in Benaras.

BHARATI:
नहीं, बेटा!... ये सत्य है – रामचरित्तर तुम्हारे पिता नहीं हैं ... तीस साल पहले उन्हें तुम बनारस के एक घाट पर मिले थे –

Shock, surprise, anger. Sooraj feels all of this at once.

SOORAJ:
What kind of a joke is this!

SOORAJ:
किस तरह का मज़ाक है ये...

Bharati shakes her head sadly.

BHARATI:
Son, I gave birth to you. You are my first born. The elder brother of Prithvi and Samar.

BHARATI:
बेटा, मेरी ही कोख से जन्में मेरे ज्येष्ठ पुत्र हो तुम... पृथ्वी और समर के बड़े भाई...

Sooraj has had enough and he erupts.

SOORAJ:
You are lying! You want to protect your son.

SOORAJ:
झूठ बोल रही हैं आप – समर को बचाने का नाटक कर रही हैं आप...

Bharati breaks down, shaking her head. He looks at her. No woman could fake such tears. With great effort, she manages to speak.

BHARATI:
Your father was Bhaskar Sanyal. I worshipped him. One day, we got carried away in a storm of emotions. He blamed himself and forsook everything. I was an unmarried girl.

BHARATI:
तुम्हारे पिता भास्कर सान्याल थे... भगवान मानती थी मैं उनको... भावना की आँधी में एक दिन सब घट गया... किन्तु हमारे संयोग को अपनी भारी भूल मान कर उन्होंने सब कुछ त्याग दिया... मैं कुँआरी थी बेटा...

Sooraj can't contain his bitterness now.

BHARATI:
Please forgive me, son. I was bound by the limitations of my family's honour. I was helpless.

BHARATI:
मुझे माफ़ कर दो बेटा... मर्यादा की बेड़ियों में जकड़ी – लाचार थी मैं –

Sooraj stares at her, unable to respond to this plea. But, his anger is rising.

SOORAJ:
So, why're you telling me this now?

SOORAJ:
तो अब क्यों बताने आयी हैं यहाँ ?

BHARATI:
Come home. That is where you belong... Samar will happily accept you.

BHARATI:
घर लौट आ बेटा – वहीं जगह है तुम्हारी... समर भी खुशी–खुशी मान देगा तुम्हें...

He was curiously listening to her but now turns his face away. She feels desperate and continues urgently.

BHARATI:
The party will also get a boost. More over, you are the eldest. You should be the leader.

BHARATI:
और भी बल मिलेगा *party* को तुम्हारे आने से... बड़े हो बेटा... गद्दी भी तो तुम्हीं सँभालोगे...

Sooraj looks stunned by the proposal but soon anger takes over.

SOORAJ:
Beg your pardon? Leader?! Wow! In one breath you make me your son and in the next you play politics with me!

SOORAJ:
क्या कहा आपने? गद्दी? वाह! एक ही साँस में बेटा बनाया और राजनीति भी खेल गईं...

Bharati realises her mistake.

BHARATI:
That's not true. I was...

BHARATI:
नहीं बेटा... मैं तो –

Sooraj snaps at her.

SOORAJ:

Do you really believe that by dangling the promise of power you can twist my integrity? You have given birth to me but I am the son of Ramcharittar Kumar and Shanti Devi. My soul is that of a Dalit. Mrs. Bharati Pratap..I wont make the same mistakes that you did. When no one supported me and left me alone… Virendra Pratap was the only one who lent me his support. Offered me his friendship, gave me respect and an identity. Only he has the right to my loyalty. Until my last breath I will stand by him.

SOORAJ:

क्या सोचती हैं आप... गद्दी का लालच दे कर मेरा इमान बदल देंगी – आपकी कोख से भले ही मेरा जन्म हुआ होगा, मगर रामचरित्तर कुमार और शांति देवी का बेटा हूँ मैं... मेरी हर साँस में एक दलित की आत्मा बसती है – और भारती जी, जो ग़लती आपने की मैं नहीं करूँगा – बड़े कठिन समय में वीरेन्द्र प्रताप ने मुझे सहारा दिया, मान दिया, पहचान दी... मेरी निष्ठा पर सिर्फ़ उनका हक़ बनता है... मरते दम तक उनका साथ दूँगा।

She looks at him defeated. There is to be no relief, no reassurance for her.

Sooraj watches her crying and turns away. There are no easy answers in this situation.

He doesn't look at her as he folds his hands, hiding his own tears. He walks away leaving her even more distraught than before.

As he leaves the ghat he stops at Brij Gopal who is waiting near the car. A difficult moment for Brij Gopal as Sooraj looks at him.

INT. SOORAJ'S CAR – DAY

Sooraj is sitting by the window overwhelmed by what he has just heard.

EXT. DRIVEWAY, CHANDRA PRATAP'S BUNGALOW - DAY

A car arrives. From it alights Samar. He helps Sarah's Mother out. Bharati and Brij Gopal are waiting for them.

It is a painfully sad moment when Bharati and Sarah's mother's eyes meet. Then Bharati walks towards her and embraces her. They silently weep on each other's shoulders, as Brij Gopal and Samar watch sadly.

SARAH'S MOM:

Bharati…

SARAH'S MOM:

भारती...

Bharati escorts her inside.

INT. STATE ENCLOSURE – DAY

Sarah and Prithvi's bodies are lying in state in the enclosure. They have dressed Sarah in the same Benarasi *sari she had liked at the shop. Behind them several pandits perform rituals and chant the Gayatri mantra softly.*

Sarah's mom looks at her daughter and caresses Sarah's face. She then notices Indu sitting next to Prithvi and walks upto her.

EXT. HILL MAIDAN - DAY

Samar holds the flame of the burning torch as he approaches their laid-out bodies.

Thousands of people have assembled for the funeral. As Samar lights the pyres, they all stand up.

As the pyres burn high, Samar goes to Sarah's mother, and puts his arm around her shoulder in support. Brij Gopal is standing next to Bharati who has her arm around Indu who has not yet cried. She just looks at the flames.

INT. BHANU PRATAP'S ROOM – LATER

Bhanu Pratap is shocked on the news of Prithvi's death, and is staring blankly. Virendra Pratap is sitting next to him. Virendra puts his hand on his shoulder to give support and says.

VIRENDRA PRATAP:
Don't you trust me, father? I will never let the Rashtrawadi Party go down. The final victory will be ours.

VIRENDRA PRATAP:
भरोसा नहीं है हम पर बाबूजी ?... राष्ट्रवादी पार्टी के नाम पर हम बट्टा नहीं लगने देंगे – अंतिम जीत हमारी ही होगी...

INT. SAMAR'S HOUSE - EVENING

Indu cries inconsolably. Samar's heart hurts seeing her like this. He tries to stop his own tears as he puts his hand on her shoulder.

SAMAR:
God, it appears, is testing us severely. But you will not break. Please Indu...

SAMAR:
शायद वो बहुत कठिन परीक्षा ले रहा है... मगर तुम टूटोगी नहीं इन्दु...

Indu looks more anguished than comforted.

SAMAR:
You will have to be strong. I know you will be strong.

SAMAR:
Please इन्दु... तुम्हें मज़बूत होना ही पड़ेगा – *I know you will be strong.*

His calmness surprises her as he reaches out to comfort her.

INT. HALL, CHANDRA PRATAP'S BUNGALOW - DAY

The Party supporters see Samar and crowd around him. Brij Gopal disappears inside.

PARTY LEADER #1:
Everything is over.

PARTY LEADER #1:
सब कुछ खतम हो गया –

PARTY LEADER #2:
We are orphaned. Samar... Now you are our only hope.

PARTY LEADER #2:
अनाथ हो गये हम लोग, समर भैया– अब तो आप ही का सहारा है –

Before their distress can get out of hand, Samar raises his hands to quieten them.

SAMAR:
It is true that we have suffered a very tragic blow. But don't forget that… the resolve that our leader Prithvi had undertaken is alive even today. Brothers, nothing is over and nor are we orphans.

SAMAR:
ये सच है... कि वक़्त ने हम पर बड़ा गहरा आघात किया है... लेकिन ये मत भूलिये कि हमारे नेता पृथ्वी प्रताप ने जो संकल्प लिया था, वो आज भी ज़िन्दा है... भाइयो, कुछ भी खतम नहीं हुआ है... और ना ही हम अनाथ हैं –

Just then Brij Gopal escorts Indu out to face them.

BRIJ GOPAL:
Come on.

BRIJ GOPAL:
चलो बेटा –

She does a namaste to the crowd. They look at her in awe, but are still a tad uncertain about what is to come.

SAMAR:
This is Mrs. Indu Prithvi Pratap. Jan Shakti party's new leader. Under her leadership, we'll contest the elections... and be victorious!

SAMAR:
आप हैं श्रीमती इंदु पृथ्वी प्रताप – जनशक्ति पार्टी की नयी *Leader!* इनकी *leadership* में हम चुनाव लड़ेंगे, और जीतेंगे...

BRIJ GOPAL:
I, Brij Gopal, as the mentor of the Jan Shakti Party nominate Mrs. Indu Prithvi Pratap as Jan Shakti Party's new president.

BRIJ GOPAL:
मैं, बृज गोपाल, जनशक्ति पार्टी के संरक्षक की हैसियत से विधिवत् श्रीमती इंदु पृथ्वी प्रताप का नाम जनशक्ति पार्टी के अध्यक्ष पद के लिए प्रस्तावित करता हूँ।

The party leaders in the front row catch the drift and immediately second the proposition.

PARTY LEADER #4:
We support this nomination.

PARTY LEADER #4:
हम इस प्रस्ताव का समर्थन करते हैं...

And immediately the rest of the crowd shouts their support.

PARTY LEADERS:
You have our support!

PARTY LEADERS:
समर्थन है ! समर्थन है !

As if on cue, Brij Gopal takes the ceremonious thaali with the diya from his man standing behind and offers it to Indu.

She puts her palm over the diya and begins to take the oath, background music rises and begins to dissolve into campaign sounds of cheering crowds.

INDU:
I, Indu Prithvi Pratap, take this vow, in the presence of God. I will be a member of the Jan Shakti Party for life, and follow every rule, and command of the party. Long live Jan Shakti! Long live India!

INDU:
मैं, इन्दु पृथ्वी प्रताप... ईश्वर को साक्षी मान कर शपथ लेती हूँ कि आजीवन जनशक्ति मोर्चा का सदस्य रहते हुए... *party* के नियमों एवं अनुदेशों का पालन करूँगी। जय जनशक्ति – जय भारत ।।

EXT. VILLAGE GROWNDS - DAY

As Indu begins to campaign the dice turns She generates tremendous sympathy and connects immediately with the people. She emotionally delivers her speech.

INDU:
My tears haven't dried up yet. And I won't allow them to dry up. Until I get an answer from you! Tell me... How can you tolerate these unending attacks on me? My father-in-law was brutally murdered. But, you remained silent. His own son was humiliated and driven out of his party. But, you remained silent. The *henna* applied on my hands for my wedding hadn't even faded and they mercilessly made me a widow. But, even now, you remain silent! Why? Answer me! Are you going to vote my family's killers into power? (No!) Is this your sense of justice? (No!) Does my sacrifice count for nothing? (It does! It does!) Answer me! (It does! It does!) People roar their disapproval.

INDU:
हमारे आँसू... सूखे नहीं हैं अब तक..... और इन्हें सूखने देंगे भी नहीं हम, जब तक हमें आपका जवाब नहीं मिल जाता– बताइए..... कैसे बर्दाश्त कर रहे हैं आप लोग हम पर हो रहे सारे अत्याचारों को? हमारे पिता से बढ़कर ससुर की हत्या कर दी गई और आप चुप रहे... उनके खून पसीने से खड़ी की गई *party* से उनके ही बेटे को बेइज़्ज़त करके निकाल दिया... और आप चुप रहे.... अभी हमारे हाथों की मेंहदी का रंग भी नहीं उतरा था... और हमारा सुहाग बेरहमी से उजाड़ दिया –... और आप सब !! अभी भी चुप्प हैं!!! क्यूँ ??... जवाब दीजिए हमें कि कैसे हमारे परिवार के हत्यारों को *vote* दे कर सत्ता की कुर्सी पर बिठाएँगे आप लोग ?... क्या आपका न्याय यही बोलता है ?... हमारे बलिदान का कोई मोल नहीं ?... जवाब दीजिए हमें –

CROWD CHANTING:
Victory to Indu Pratap!

CROWD CHANTING:
इंकलाब........ जिंदाबाद इन्दु प्रताप संघर्ष करो – हम तुम्हारे साथ हैं इंकलाब........ जिंदाबाद......

INT. VIRENDRA'S BUNGALOW - EVENING

Virendra is sitting and getting drunk in frustration. The news on the television:

NEWS ANCHOR:
All initial reports seem to point towards a majority for Indu Pratap. After the history of conflict with the Rashtrawadi Party... violence was anticipated but... barring one or two incidents,

NEWS ANCHOR:
सभी रुझान इंदुप्रताप की जनशक्ति पार्टी को बढ़त दे रहे हैं – राष्ट्रवादी पार्टी के साथ हुए पारिवारिक कलह और भयंकर चुनावी जंग में खून–खराबे की आशंका की जा रही थी... लेकिन इक्का–दुक्का वारदातों को छोड़कर

elections were peaceful. There were a few complaints against the EVMs. From Bada Bazaar, in Balrampur with cameraman Ram Narayan, this is Mukta Tiwari for Star News.

चुनाव लगभग शांतिपूर्ण रहे – हालाँकि कई जगहों से *EVM* को लेकर शिकायतें आयीं... – बड़ा बाजार, बलरामपुर, *cameraman* रामनारायण के साथ मैं, मुग्धा तिवारी, *Star News.*

EXT. TEA STALL - DAY

In a tea stall near the election booth.

ONE MAN:
Muslims, Hindus, all seem to be in one line.

ONE MAN:
क्या दाढ़ी वाले – क्या टीका वाले... सब एक्के *line* में लगे हैं –

BISHAMBHAR:
It's entirely a one-sided contest. The widow is going to sweep it all away.

BISHAMBHAR:
Total one sided मामला है भाई – ले जायेगी बिटिया सब समेट के...

EXT. VILLAGE SLUMS – DAY

Sooraj reaches a village's slum area. His people gather around him.

MAN:
Hello sir..

MAN:
नमस्ते सर... प्रणाम सूरज भइया –

SOORAJ:
How're things?

SOORAJ:
कैसा चल रहा है यहाँ ?

MAN:
Here we had no problems but... reports from other areas aren't too encouraging.

MAN:
यहाँ तो सब ठीक हो गया है – मगर बाहर का खबर ठीक नहीं है –

Sooraj seems to knows this already.

INT. VIRENDRA PRATAP'S HOUSE – LATER

On the TV we see the following reports.

NEWS ANCHOR:
Most exit polls predict 120-130 seats for the Jan Shakti Party led by Indu Pratap. If the result goes this way then in the 207-member legislative assembly, Jan Shakti will hold a clear majority. The party workers of Jan Shakti are already celebrating. On the other side, the Rashtrawadi party office is a picture of gloom.

NEWS ANCHOR:
लगभग सभी *exit polls* इंदु प्रताप की नेतृत्व वाली जनशक्ति पार्टी को डेढ़ सौ से उपर सीटें दे रहे हैं। यदि ऐसा होता है तो दो सौ सात सीटों वाली प्रदेश की विधान सभा में ये स्पष्ट बहुमत की स्थिति होगी। जनशक्ति पार्टी के कार्यकर्ताओं में अभी से ही जश्न का माहौल है। वहीं राष्ट्रवादी पार्टी के खेमें में मायूसी छाई है।

VIRENDRA PRATAP: *(on the phone)*
What is the report?

VIRENDRA PRATAP: *(on the phone)*
हाँ *report* बताओ सब जगह का –

News continues on the television.

NEWS ANCHOR:
There seem to have been some stray complaints about the malfunctioning of Electronic Voting Machines.

NEWS ANCHOR:
हिंसात्मक वारदात की ख़बर नहीं है.... *EVM* को लेकर शिकायतों पर चुनाव आयोग की प्रतिक्रिया अभी तक नहीं आयी है –

A shot of an agitated middle-aged man complaining.

MIDDLE-AGED VOTER:
The machine in our booth just wasn't working. No matter which button we pressed, the vote registered elsewhere.

MIDDLE-AGED VOTER:
हमरे *बूथ* का *मशीन* एकदम बिगड़ा हुआ था, जौनसा भी *बटन* दबाया, *भोट* कहीं और ही जाता था...

NEWS ANCHOR: *(contd)*
From three other places, similar complaints were...

NEWS ANCHOR: *(contd)*
सारंगढ, मणीगाछी और लोरमी से भी *EVM* में ख़राबी की शिकायतें आईं जिस वजह से मतदान देर से शुरू हुआ....

Virendra Pratap reacts to this news with concern.

VIRENDRA PRATAP:
He has rigged the machines. I am dead sure!

VIRENDRA PRATAP:
साला सब *Machine* का *setting* गड़बड़ कर दिया – *hundred percent!*

INT. SAMAR'S OFFICE – NIGHT

Samar is smoking a cigarette and thinking.

INT. VIRENDRA'S HOUSE – EARLY MORNING

One of the regular party workers arrives and asks the house staff.

PARTY WORKER:
Where is the boss?

PARTY WORKER:
कहाँ हैं भैया जी –

HOUSE STAFF:
He's been up all night watching TV reports.

HOUSE STAFF:
रात भर से बैठे बस *TV* देख रहे हैं...

PARTY WORKER:
It's urgent.

PARTY WORKER:
Urgent बात है...

Once inside, he dials a number on his own mobile phone and approaches Virendra Pratap as he talks on the phone.

PARTY WORKER:
I'll just put him on.

PARTY WORKER:
हाँ, अभी बात कराते हैं।

In the background, the TV is playing.

NEWS ANCHOR:
So Raghav, tell me are the EVM's actually tampered with...

NEWS ANCHOR:
नमस्कार राघव, तो क्या सचमुच *EVM* से किसी तरह की छेड़छाड़ संभव है –

NEWS REPORTER RAGHAV:
Listen, hacking an EVM is no big deal – If a hacker gets access to the machine for just 10 minutes between the time polling ends and the counting begins, he could alter the result using a simple software.

NEWS REPORTER RAGHAV:
देखिए *EVM* को *hack* करना कोई बहुत कठिन काम नहीं है... *polling* खतम होने के बाद और *counting* शुरू होने से पहले यदि किसी *hacker* को दस मिनिट के लिए भी *machine* का *physical access* मिल जाए तो बड़ी ही आसानी से एक छोटे से *software* की मदद से किसी भी तरह का फेरबदल किया जा सकता है –

VIRENDRA'S PARTY WORKER:
Sir, its Moti. Some suspicious activity at Bankepur.

VIRENDRA'S PARTY WORKER:
भैया जी, मोती भाई का *phone* है... बता रहे हैं कि बाँकीपुर *factory area* में कुछ *disturbance* देखे हैं ।

Virendra Pratap takes the phone quickly.

VIRENDRA PRATAP:
Tell me....

VIRENDRA PRATAP:
हूँ... हाँ, बोल मोती...

MOTI: *(on phone)*
Sir, Samar and his men are here since last night with computers, antennae and other stuff. I heard they're tampering with the voting machines by remote.

MOTI: *(on phone)*
भइया, सात–आठ गाड़ी में समर भइया और उनके लोग कल रात से यहाँ आये हैं – *Computer, antenna* और ना जाने क्या–क्या ले कर... सुन रहे हैं कि *remote* से सारा बक्सा का भोट बदल रहे हैं...

Virendra's face goes into contortions of rage. He explodes with anger.

VIRENDRA PRATAP:
What the...! Keep an eye on them. I'm on my way.

VIRENDRA PRATAP:
इसकी माँ का – तू नज़र रख... मैं आ रहा हूँ...

He rushes out of there immediately telling his party worker.

VIRENDRA PRATAP:
Follow me to the Bankepur area.

VIRENDRA PRATAP:
पहुँचो तुमलोग बाँकीपुर *factory area* में.

VIRENDRA'S MAN:
Okay.

VIRENDRA'S MAN:
जी।

Virendra gets into his car and zooms off before his security realises what's going on. The party worker who was with him looks baffled. Security scramble to catch up.

SECURITY:
Come on. Hurry up!

SECURITY:
ए जल्दी करो साहब निकल गये...

VIRENDRA'S MAN:
Hurry up! Hurry up!

VIRENDRA'S MAN:
ए गाड़ी निकालो जल्दी...

Security questions the party worker as to Virendra Pratap's whereabouts.

SECURITY:
Where did he go?

SECURITY:
कहाँ गये साहब –

PARTY WORKER:
I have no idea. He just drove off.

PARTY WORKER:
कुछ बोले नहीं – गाड़ी उठाये और चले गये...

INT./EXT. VILLAGE HOUSE - DAY

A minute later Sooraj rushes out of the village house while talking on the phone with Virendra's security.

SOORAJ:
What do you mean? Where was the security? He must've said something.

SOORAJ:
ऐसे कैसे हो सकता है... *security* कहाँ थी – अरे कुछ तो बोला होगा...

SECURITY:
Nothing at all. He isn't answering his phone.

SECURITY:
Sir कुछ बताया नहीं... *phone* भी नहीं उठा रहे...

He realises that this could be a trap for Virendra. He gets into his car and begins calling up Virendra but doesn't get any response.

EXT. FACTORY AREA – DAY

Virendra races to the factory area and realises his phone is ringing only when he stops outside the shut down factory at Bankipur. He answers the phone.

VIRENDRA PRATAP:
Yes, Sooraj.

VIRENDRA PRATAP:
हाँ बोलो सूरज –

SOORAJ:
Veeru... where are you?

SOORAJ:
वीरू भाई, कहाँ हैं आप अभी –

VIRENDRA PRATAP:
Near the defunct Bankepur cable factory.

VIRENDRA PRATAP:
बाँकीपुर *cable factory* जो बन्द पड़ी है उसी के बाहर...

SOORAJ:
I'm on my way. Don't get out of the car.

SOORAJ:
मैं पहुँच रहा हूँ – आप गाड़ी से नहीं निकलना *please...*

Virendra who has spotted the several cars with equipments and antennas parked outside is already slowly moving into the factory gate.

VIRENDRA PRATAP:
By then that Samar would've changed all the bloody votes.

VIRENDRA PRATAP:
तब तक तो ये साला समर सब *vote* बदल देगा *machine* का –

SOORAJ:
Come on... that's impossible!

SOORAJ:
कैसी बात कर रहे हैं – *impossible* है ये सब करना –

Virendra almost laughs, his face contorting with bitterness.

VIRENDRA PRATAP:
What is impossible now is to trust anyone, Sooraj. Using some fancy hi-tech tricks, he is snatching our votes from under our noses and you say...

VIRENDRA PRATAP:
Impossible तो है अब किसी पर भरोसा करना सूरज – यहाँ *internet* और *(Beep)* से *connection* भिड़ा के हमारे ही सामने सब *vote* बदल रहा है साला और तुम बोलते हो...

Sooraj knows Virendra's state of mind. He urges.

SOORAJ:
Just don't get out of the car! I'm on my way.

SOORAJ:
बस आप गाड़ी से नहीं निकलेंगे – मैं पहुँच रहा हूँ...

Virendra is already getting inside the factory.

Moti who had called up Virendra watches as Virendra's vehicle drives in. He has been hiding outside.

MOTI:
He's here. Alone.

MOTI:
आ गये हैं... अकेले हैं।

INT. WAREHOUSE - DAY

As Virendra enters the warehouse, there's no one there, only a sinister silence.

As he drives around the rusty machines we find him followed by several hidden guns. As he comes to stop in the middle we spot Samar's eyes with Brij Gopal right behind him. Samar whispers to his men –

SAMAR:
Nobody shoots. His car is bullet-proof.

SAMAR:
गोली मत चलाना कोई भी – उसकी गाड़ी *bullet proof* है –

Virendra at his wheel looks around for any activity. He is within Samar's shooting range. His car's engine is still running. Everyone waits with bated breath...

It is at this point that Sooraj enters through another gate. One of Samar's sharp shooters notices him and immediately informs him.

SAMAR'S MAN:
Sooraj Kumar is here too, sir.

SAMAR'S MAN:
सूरज कुमार का गाड़ी अन्दर आ गया है *sir* –

SAMAR:
Don't shoot.

SAMAR:
Don't shoot.

Brij Gopal turns to spot Sooraj. Sooraj spots Virendra's car and calls him.

SOORAJ:
Yes? Veeru... nothing is happening here. It's better we leave.

SOORAJ:
वीरू भाई, यहाँ वैसी कोई कार्रवाई नहीं चल रही – निकल जाना ही ठीक रहेगा...

VIRENDRA PRATAP:
Didn't you notice outside?

VIRENDRA PRATAP:
तुमने बाहर देखा नहीं ?

SOORAJ:
There is no one outside...

SOORAJ:
बाहर तो कोई भी नहीं दिखा...

Brij Gopal has spotted Sooraj. He tells Samar.

BRIJ GOPAL:
They're talking on the phone. We can't wait for long.

BRIJ GOPAL:
दोनों *phone* पर बात कर रहे हैं... ज़्यादा देर इन्तज़ार नहीं कर सकते –

Samar knows this and is thinking of a move. Virendra from inside his car.

VIRENDRA PRATAP:
They are hiding somewhere. I'll take a look.

VIRENDRA PRATAP:
कहीं तो छुप के बैठे हैं यहीं – मैं उतर के देखता हूँ –

SOORAJ:
No! Don't step out. I'll have a look.

SOORAJ:
नहीं !!! आप नहीं उतरेंगे – मैं देखता हूँ –

He clicks the phone off, opens his door softly and steps out. He knows that there will be several guns pointed at him. He quietly moves towards the central point of machines. Brij Gopal and the others lose sight of him. Samar has his eyes fixed on Virendra Pratap.

SAMAR:
No one shoots... until Veeru steps out.

SAMAR:
No one shoots - जब तक ये गाड़ी से नहीं निकलता –

There is tension in the air. Brij Gopal frantically tries to spot Sooraj and continues to cover for Samar.

Just then, Sooraj stealthily arrives behind them. Virendra Pratap sees him, though Samar and the others can't. Samar is in Sooraj's line of fire. But, he doesn't shoot.

Brij Gopal sees Virendra's line of vision and turns around. He sees Sooraj and Virendra Pratap shouts.

VIRENDRA PRATAP:
Shoot, Sooraj! Shoot him, Sooraj!

VIRENDRA PRATAP:
सूरज गोली मार ! – गोली मार सूरज... गोली मार सूरज...

But, Sooraj doesn't shoot. Virendra is confused for an instant, but immediately draws his own gun and steps out of his car. And, Samar shoots him in the chest.

And then, Sooraj begins to fire. Brij Gopal pulls Samar down.

BRIJ GOPAL:
Samar!

BRIJ GOPAL:
समर...

In the ensuing shootout, Sooraj manages to bring down a couple of Samar's men but is unable to reach Virendra's car which has come under heavy fire.

Virendra is gasping with the bullet wounds. Sooraj runs to his car as Samar chases him. Sooraj dives into his car and races for the spot where Virendra has fallen.

SOORAJ:
Veeru... fast...

SOORAJ:
वीरू भाई जल्दी...

Taking shelter of the door he pulls Virendra off the ground and takes the wheel. In the process he loses his phone.

Even as the shots continue, Sooraj manages to drive out of there like a bat out of hell.

INT. VIRENDRA'S CAR - DAY

In the car, Sooraj is driving fast, shaking Virendra to stop him from going into a stupor.

SOORAJ:
Veeru... Veeru...

SOORAJ:
वीरू भाई... वीरू भाई...

VIRENDRA PRATAP:
Huh...

VIRENDRA PRATAP:
हुँ....

SOORAJ:
Don't close your eyes!

SOORAJ:
वीरू भाई...वीरू भाई, जागते रहिए *please*... आँख बन्द मत करना ...

VIRENDRA PRATAP:
Ok-ok.

VIRENDRA PRATAP:
Ok – ok.

EXT. HIGHWAY BRIDGE - DAY

Sooraj is nearing a bridge. He speeds up. Just as he is about to drive onto the bridge, he sees that cars from the other side have got onto it, leaving him no place to pass. He stops for a moment, and looks back. Samar's car is moving in.

SAMAR'S MAN:
Get the car out... out... stop.

SAMAR'S MAN:
ए... गाड़ी निकाल... निकाल गाड़ी – ए रुक जा –

It's too late to turn back now. So, Sooraj speeds up. They brace for the impact, shocked.

Sooraj tries to drive through them, but his right wheels go over one car and his car overturns above the ground and landing on its hood, skids off the bridge onto the mud, on the ground below the road.

Son of a gun

This was the first film in which Ranbir Kapoor held a gun. Nana Patekar and Ajay Devgan gave him tips on how to hold it, and how to shoot without blinking. Convinced about Samar taking up a gun, Ranbir worked hard to look convincing himself. By the end of it, he was so excited he carried the gun in his pocket the whole day! He did not want to part with it! "It gives you a sense of power, a sense of madness, which is dangerously addictive," he says with a grin. ■

After a second, he springs back into action. Sooraj pulls himself out of the car and tries to extricate Virendra out.

SOORAJ:
Veeru. Veeru…

SOORAJ:
वीरू भाई…

Meanwhile, Brij Gopal brings his car to a stop at the side of the bridge. Samar emerges.

As Sooraj has got Virendra Pratap halfway out of the window, he looks up and encounters Samar's cold eyes. Samar has a gun in his hand. Sooraj throws his gun down.

SOORAJ:
Let's finish this war right here, Samar. Just allow me to take Veeru to the hospital. Then I'll come wherever you want me to. My life is in your hands. I am bound by my commitment to protect my friend. Come on, Veeru...

SOORAJ:
इस युद्ध को यहीं खत्म करते हैं समर... बस... वीरू भाई को *hospital* पहुँचाने दो हमें – फिर जहाँ कहोगे आ जाएँगे – गिरवी है हमारी जान तुम्हारे पास... वचन दिया है हमने... अपने दोस्त की जान बचाने का – चलो वीरू भाई –

Samar hesitates. Sooraj begins to drag Virendra towards another car.

Brij Gopal knows that if Samar lets him go now, he will never be able to finish the job.

BRIJ GOPAL:
What are you waiting for, Samar?

BRIJ GOPAL:
देख क्या रहे हो समर...

SAMAR:
He is unarmed.

SAMAR:
निहत्थे हैं ये मामा जी...

BRIJ GOPAL:
So? Did they kill your father and brother on the battlefield? Don't get trapped in questions of justice and ethics. This is the time! Don't lose sight of the goal for which you entered this fight. Remember, in politics victory is all that matters. And, your victory will remain incomplete as long as he is alive. Come on. Finish him!

BRIJ GOPAL:
तो ?... तेरे भाई और बाप को क्या खुली जंग में ललकार कर मारा था इन्होंने ?... न्याय और नियम के पचड़े में कमज़ोर मत बनो समर – नीति को समझो... जिस संकल्प को लेकर इस संग्राम में उतरे हो उसे पूरा करो... याद रखो राजनीति में हमेशा... जीत को मान मिलता है... और तुम्हारी जीत तब तक पूरी नहीं होगी जब तक ये जीवित है – *Come on finish him.*

Just then, Sooraj notices that Virendra Pratap is dead with his eyes open. He slumps in defeat and Samar calls out.

SAMAR:
Sooraj!

SAMAR:
सूरज !

Sooraj looks up at Samar and Samar shoots him.

EXT. STREETS - DAY

Lok Jan Shakti Party wins by a landslide. The party workers and supporters are jubilant on the streets.

INT. PARLIAMENT - DAY

Indu is being sworn in as the Chief Minister.

INDU PRATAP:
I, Indu Pratap, swear in the name of God that I will uphold the Indian Constitution with dedication, honesty and respect. I shall

INDU PRATAP:
मैं, इन्दु प्रताप, ईश्वर की शपथ लेती हूँ कि मैं, विधि द्वारा स्थापित भारत के संविधान के प्रति सच्ची श्रद्धा और निष्ठा रखूँगी। मैं, भारत की प्रभुता और

always seek to preserve the unity and diversity of India. As the Chief Minister of the State I promise to perform my duties with dedication and a clear conscience. Without any fear or partiality, without love or hate, I will be just towards all people according to the Constitution..

अखंडता अक्षुण्ण रखूँगी। मैं, प्रदेश के मुख्यमंत्री के रूप में अपने कर्त्तव्यों का श्रद्धापूर्वक और शुद्ध अंतःकरण से निर्वहन करूँगी तथा मैं भय या पक्षपात, अनुराग या द्वेष के बिना, सभी प्रकार के लोगों के प्रति संविधान और विधि के अनुसार न्याय करूँगी।

INT. BHANU PRATAP'S GARDEN - DAY

Bhanu Pratap sits on his wheelchair impassive. He's looking ahead and not at Samar who is kneeling in front of him holding his hand, and touching his forehead to it. In this position, Samar speaks.

SAMAR:
I never wanted to do, any of the things that I did.

SAMAR:
जो कुछ भी किया, वो मैं कभी नहीं चाहता था...

Samar looks up now, a plea in his eyes. Their eyes meet.

SAMAR:
You, of all people, know this, uncle.

SAMAR:
एक आप ही हैं ताउजी जो यह जानते हैं!

Then he lowers his head onto Bhanu Pratap's hands again.

SAMAR:
Please forgive me.

SAMAR:
मुझे माफ़ कर दो...

Bhanu Pratap doesn't reply. But, quietly takes his hand away from Samar's grasp.

Samar looks up. Bhanu Pratap is looking away. They both know, there is to be no forgiveness.

Samar gets up with a heavy heart. Bhanu Pratap is still looking away. A thin spittle drools down the side of his mouth.

Samar wipes it off gently with his handkerchief and walks away.

INT. HALL, SAMAR'S HOUSE – DAY

Samar enters. It is evident from his body language that he is disheartened and he notices Indu is in the hall. The file is lying on the table, while she stands facing the window, looking outside. She hears Samar approach but doesn't turn around.

SAMAR:
I am sorry, Indu. I am sorry that I hurt you so much. I know that you may never be able to forgive me.

SAMAR:
I'm sorry Indu. Sorry for hurting you so much. शायद तुम फिर कभी मुझे माफ़ नहीं कर पाओ –

She turns around. Samar finds it difficult to meet her eyes.

INDU:
Do you really have to go?

INDU:
जाना ज़रूरी है क्या?

It hurts him to look at this woman who has lost so much but he nods, gently.

SAMAR:
I always wanted to stay away from politics. I feared the demons that it brings out. But, that is exactly what happened. I couldn't escape my circumstances... and ended up losing everything. But,

SAMAR:
तुम जानती हो मैं हमेशा राजनीति से दूर रहना चाहता था – इस खेल में जो अंदर का शैतान निकलकर आता है, उससे डरता था... मगर वही हुआ आख़िर... हालातों से बच नहीं पाया और... उस खेल में मैंने सब

I know... I know that you're not like that. Your heart is pure. You'll be okay. My world was very different, Indu... in which I only had Sarah. Now, I must look after her mother.

कुछ खो दिया... लेकिन मैं जानता हूँ कि तुम... लेकिन मैं जानता हूँ कि तुम वैसी नहीं हो... दिल की सच्ची हो... सँभाल लोगी अपने आपको... मेरी दुनिया अलग है इन्दु... उसमें बस एक *Sarah* थी... *Now, I must look after her mother.*

They look at each other. And then Indu smiles, unexpectedly.

INDU:
But, you'll have to return soon.

INDU:
लेकिन तुम्हें जल्द ही वापस आना पड़ेगा...

He looks at her with a question in his eyes.

INDU:
There's something of your brother with me. I am going to be the mother of his child.

INDU:
तुम्हारे भैया अपना अंश छोड़ गये हैं हमारे पास... माँ बनेंगे हम –

She touches her stomach lightly.

Samar's face breaks into a slow broad smile. He is genuinely happy.

SAMAR:
Wow, Indu! Wow... I mean that's... It's been a long while since this family received some good news. Congratulations!

SAMAR:
Wow Indu... wow, I mean that's... अरसे के बाद इस *family* में कोई खुशख़बरी मिली है... *congratulations!*

INDU:
Come back soon.

INDU:
जल्दी आना!

Samar comes to her, and stops.

SAMAR:
Of course, I will. But on one condition.

SAMAR:
ज़रूर आउँगा – लेकिन एक शर्त है...

She looks puzzled.

SAMAR *(contd):*
You have to come to receive me in a car with the flashing red light.

SAMAR *(contd):*
अगली बार लालबत्ती वाली गाड़ी में लेने आना मुझे !

Indu laughs and they hug each other, a mix of laughter and tears. They are friends again.

SAMAR:
Bye.

SAMAR:
Bye.

EXT. DRIVEWAY, SAMAR'S HOUSE - DAY

As Samar steps out with Sarah's mother, Bharati and Indu, he goes ahead to the car. From behind the car emerges Ramcharittar. He is not in his driver's uniform.

SAMAR:
Uncle, you?

SAMAR:
काका तुम !

STICK BOSTON STICK!

In a particular scene, Ranbir was supposed to wear a sweatshirt with BOSTON written on it. Costume Designer Priyanka Mundada looked all over Mumbai but did not find one she liked. A day before the scene was to be shot, there was still no Boston sweatshirt, and a DIY quickfix was the only option. So Priyanka got 'BOSTON' printed on metallic paper, had it cut out and minutes before the shot, stuck it on a plain sweatshirt with Fevicol! She instructed Ranbir to be very careful lest the appliqué fall off! The entire morning, Ranbir was spotted patting his chest every few minutes! ■

Samar's words are loaded with guilt. Brij Gopal sees the situation and comes towards them.

BRIJ GOPAL:
Ramcharittar is part of the family. Where can he go?

BRIJ GOPAL:
परिवार है रामचरित्तर... आख़िर कहाँ जायेगा...

Ramcharittar suddenly chokes up with emotion.

RAMCHARITTAR:
I am the one who has always driven you to and from the airport. As a child, you played in my lap...

RAMCHARITTAR:
हमही तो आपको लाते – ले जाते रहे आज तक *airport*... बचपन से गोद...

Ramcharittar breaks down as he is reminded of Sooraj. Samar stands looking at Ramcharittar for a moment.

He understands his pain.

SAMAR:
Please forgive me.

SAMAR:
माफ़ कर देना मुझे...

And then bends down and touches his feet. Ramcharittar hesitates for a moment. Even Brij Gopal watches. And then Ramcharittar touches Samar's head. It is a forgiving touch. He then fold his hands to salute Samar.

SAMAR:
No, Uncle.

SAMAR:
नहीं काका।

EXT. RUNWAY – DAY

The flight takes off.

CLOSING CREDITS